Fairy Tale

Book 1: Winter's Bite

ALICIA J. BRITTON

STABLEGATE PUBLISHERS
Clifton Park, NY

For Greg, Andy, Jacob,
and Emily Rose

CONTENTS

This day's black fate on more days doth depend:
This but begins the woe others must end.

WILLIAM SHAKESPEARE, *Romeo and Juliet*

PROLOGUE

Much farther north than most humans would dare settle, December unleashed its relentless fury. Animals from field mice to black bears buried themselves in their shelters, though if the winter stayed as cold as it was, their shelters would be their tombs.

The plant kingdom was not faring much better. The black spruce trees scattered across the ridge were vulnerable to the wind. Each gust tested the elasticity of branches already laden with snow. Many limbs tore away from the trunks and tumbled down the rocky embankment.

And hidden beneath those rocks were the caves that sheltered the fairy city of Pyxis. Survival was not guaranteed for the fairies either, but that had less to do with the wind and snow than with the presence of evil among them. The Sauvageau family had for many years been bringing to life the meaning of their name . . . *savage*. . . .

CHAPTER 1
Unworthy

The only chill Queen Andromeda Sauvageau ever felt was in her heart. On this particular night, she was alone in her lavatory and in a foul mood. Her bath when she had entered it had been as scorching hot as her fair skin could tolerate, yet she was indifferent to the clamminess that had crept in amid the softening bubbles and fine oils. No matter how long she had been soaking, she could not wash from her mind the wingless abomination she considered the King of the Unworthy. When she lifted a delicate mirror to her face, it was as if his reflection were there alongside hers . . . *laughing, laughing, laughing. . . .*

When she was unable to tolerate the reflection any longer, she flung the mirror across the room. It shattered into thousands of pieces, some as fine as ice crystals. Her unmatched beauty would never return. And only his death would restore her dignity.

A light tapping suspended her revenge fantasy.

Lyra, one of her chambermaids, opened the door. She flew inside and landed next to the trickling cascade beside the queen's head. "Your Excellency, I'm sorry to interrupt, but . . ."

Andromeda watched the sweet young servant bite her lip and wring her hands around the rag she was holding. She loved making others uncomfortable with just her stare, and Lyra was among the most susceptible.

Lyra finally lifted her chin and found her tongue. "General Gustave said there is an urgent matter to discuss. He wishes to see you immediately."

With Andromeda's nod, Lyra left the room.

Andromeda assumed this unscheduled meeting would be a waste of her time, an encroachment on her much-desired solitude. Nevertheless, she stepped out of her bath and summoned her servants, who swarmed to her. Lyra returned with her gown and threw it around her shoulders while two other servants swept up the broken splinters of the mirror and two more fussed with her shadow-colored wings.

Once dressed, the queen dismissed her servants with a single backhanded wave and sat down at her vanity table. She ran a comb through her dark hair and couldn't prevent herself from staring at the web of black scars on the left side of her face. She slammed her comb down and took a deep breath. When she was calm enough to move, she went to find her general.

***

General Cygnus Gustave was pacing the floor and practicing aloud what he would say to the queen. He hoped she would consider his news valuable even if the King of the Unworthy lived on, undiscovered.

Before he had chosen the right words, Andromeda blasted through the room's double doors and, with a fluid motion, pushed them backward as she propelled herself forward. "How dare you disturb me at this time of night, Cygnus!"

The general waited for the doors to slam shut from the momentum before he spoke. He braced himself for the crash; even so, he twitched in response.

"Your Excellency, there is a new development. . . ."

She hovered to the ground and sat on her throne at the head of the table. "Has *he* been found?"

"No, not exactly, but—"

"Then by no means do I find word of any new development pertinent."

"Please, let me finish!" Cygnus roared, though immediately he regretted raising his voice and shrank before her. "There is relevancy, I promise," he continued. "We think we have found one of Prince Rigel's—"

"I hardly think Rigel is still *worthy* of that title," the queen interrupted again.

"Well, the King of the Unworthy, if that should please you more!" Cygnus waited for her reaction, expecting praise or a sign of appreciation.

11

Other than a slight raise of one eyebrow, her expression remained unchanged. "But as I started to say, we think we have found one of his sons. And one son may have led us to another."

Andromeda sighed and lifted her curled fingers into view. The shiny black polish on her nails shimmered in the firelight like volcanic glass. "Why is it you 'think' you have found a son? Why don't you know for certain? I want facts, not more baseless speculation."

"We've been listening to the whispers among the witches in Salem. Their idle talk of fairy magic led us nowhere for ages. But finally we came across a man who bears the mark of a Modifier."

"That doesn't tell us anything!" Andromeda's curled fingers now formed a fist, which she slammed on the table. "There are numerous Bottom-Dwellers who have assimilated into the human world."

"Surely there are, but with the diamond mark? And fair-haired? Strong in body, but weak of mind? I had to go down south to see for myself. My Lady, the resemblance is striking and I confirmed the mark is genuine."

"I need more than your word. Show me proof."

"I will get some. . . . I will do better. I—"

A firm knock on the door silenced the general. He knew the queen did not handle interruptions lightly.

"Expecting visitors, Cygnus?" she hissed. "More incompetence, I would imagine . . ."

"No, Your Excellency." He forced a smile as he hovered backward. "I'm not sure who is there." Cygnus pulled one of the doors open. His second in command, Crux Chevalier, flew into the room with the confidence one would expect from a fairy with such a surname. The Chevalier family was one of the wealthiest in Pyxis. Its young male scions typically began their careers in high-ranking positions in the Pyxis Royal Air Brigade and then assumed noteworthy positions in the regime. The role of chief counselor to the queen, for example, had been held by Crux's father, Malus Chevalier, until his death of natural causes a few years prior, and few others in the queen's regard ever experienced such a mundane passing. The position remained unfilled, though in Cygnus's expert opinion Crux was unlikely to receive the promotion. The young fairy was not destined for politics. His questionable tactics had earned him the nickname "the Brute," and his skills were better suited for military operations. Crux was, however, the most likely contender for general once Cygnus was granted the honor of retirement.

"Lieutenant Chevalier, this isn't a good time," Cygnus whispered through clenched teeth.

"I assure you, General Gustave, this is the perfect time," Crux boasted, and then he gave the queen a respectful bow. "Hello, Your Majesty. I am honored to bring you these."

The queen's nod beckoned Crux forward, and he presented an armful of thick papers as if each one were solid gold. He was abnormally tall and brawny for a winged fairy, but the first piece of paper unfolded to a rectangle seven inches long and was thus taller than he was, though not by much.

The paper was a photograph plucked from the Modern World, hundreds of miles south, and exhibited a face Cygnus recognized.

"*This* one," Crux said derisively, "is called Christopher MacRae. The picture was taken by the U.S. Army."

Andromeda studied the picture carefully; when she looked away, a wicked half smile curled onto her face.

Crux dropped the first photograph to the floor and opened the second one. There were three people huddled together and smiling. "This is Joseph MacRae at his academic institution's commencement ceremony. On his left, a woman he knew as his mother, Skylar MacRae, now deceased. And on his right is his father. Joseph's father may call himself Scott MacRae, but he is not capable of fooling you, My Queen."

This time Andromeda shot from her chair. "So where is he, then? Bring him to me!"

"Your Majesty, please try to understand," Cygnus replied. "The gutless imposter remains at large. As far as we are aware, he has not made contact with his family in years."

"Get the brigade into their homes immediately and search everything. If you cannot determine *his* whereabouts, bring his children to me."

"There are two grandchildren as well. Shall I bring—"

"Yes. The grandchildren will ensure their cooperation. And, General, kill anyone else who gets in the way."

"Of course, My Lady. Anything you wish."

At the queen's nod, the two officers bowed and turned to leave. When their backs were facing the queen, Cygnus spotted Crux's unique forked tongue slick over his teeth. The general's protégé was eager to earn his star, and the hungry, untamed predator inside of him was ready for the hunt of a lifetime.

CHAPTER 2
Sleepless

Christopher MacRae woke up with a jolt, sweating and out of breath. He sat up in bed and peered into the darkness all around until he had assured himself that he was in a safe place. The glow of his alarm clock illuminated nothing out of the ordinary. But, as always, the numbers angered him. He had used them to count the minutes—*hours*—of wasted time far too often.

He shivered and felt the hairs lift on his arms. A howling wind outside merely seeped in at the edges of his bedroom window, and the security of the room convinced him to lie back down. He pulled the covers over his head and hoped to find enough inner calm to go back to sleep.

Alana, his wife, rolled over and tucked her arms around him. "You okay?"

"It's nothing."

"Then why are you shaking?"

"It's cold in here, that's all," he lied. "Let's go back to sleep."

"Sure?"

"Yup."

They both closed their eyes and he began stroking her silky hair. Deep down, he did want to tell her about his recurring nightmares. She would offer sympathy and support even if she could never truly understand. Then again, he didn't want to scare her or make her worry more than usual. He had already begun to feel discouraged by the way she looked at him, her eyes filled more with pity than with anything else.

14

Chris fell into a state of light sleep, but the battle in his mind raged on.

He was a soldier again, wandering around war-torn Baghdad. The sun was a fiery sliver on the distant horizon. He tried to focus on specific objects and faces, but it was as if he were looking through eyeglasses with the wrong prescription. His senses needed to be sharp and clear, yet they provided him only with haze and distortion.

A hooded figure emerged from behind the twisted remains of a car. Chris reached for his gun, but his holster was empty. Dropping to his knees, he scrambled to find some object he could use as a weapon. Accompanying the sound of sand swooshing though his fingers was the slow and unmistakable sound of boots approaching. When Chris lifted his head, he caught a glimpse of the hooded man's eyes—molten red and possessed. Then Chris was looking down the barrel of his own gun.

Bang!

Chris jolted awake once again. Believing sleep a lost cause, he rolled his legs to the side of the bed and grabbed for his sweatshirt on the floor. He sorted front from back, in from out, and threw the sweatshirt over his head. Just as his head popped through the neck hole, he heard something whiz by his ear. "What the . . . ?" He struggled to free his hands through the arms of the garment.

"What's wrong now?" Alana groaned.

"Did you hear that?"

"Hear what?"

"Never mind."

"You were probably dreaming again."

"This time I *know* I was already awake," Chris replied, slightly agitated.

Then he heard another sound, a vibration followed by a familiar ping. Alana reached across the bed and picked up his cell phone from the nightstand.

"You must have heard your phone. There's a text." She used her thumb to bring it up. "It's from Joe." She leaned over and held out the phone for him.

Chris wasn't convinced that the first noise he'd heard had been his phone. The timing was off, and the high-pitched buzz had been like a bullet in motion, but without the initial bang. He scanned the room hesitantly. Then he took the phone out of his wife's hand.

Merry Xmas, bro! Hope the kids liked the package.

The message was uniquely Joe for two reasons. First, the odd timing. It was four in the morning here in Massachusetts, three hours earlier in Joe's time zone—and Christmas had been the day before. Second, the disconnect. Chris and Alana's two children—twins, a boy and a girl, four years old—had received no package from their uncle.

Chris rubbed his eyes. "Yeah, Merry Christmas . . . ," he mumbled. The text wasn't an ideal holiday greeting, but Chris did give his brother a little credit for trying. Maybe by next Christmas, Joe would call or perhaps Chris would be ready to call him.

He set the phone down and toyed with his wedding ring. He took one more look around and, with a sigh, decided to give sleep one last chance. Still in his sweatshirt, he rolled back into bed.

"What did he want?" Alana asked.

"Nothing that can't wait till it's light out."

"Okay. Love you."

He wrapped himself around her and kissed her underneath her ear. "You too."

***

"Excuse me!" Joseph MacRae shouted for the third time.

Once again, his voice didn't pierce the noise. The shirtless monstrosity with muscles the size of barrels still stood before him and didn't budge from the doorway.

Joe looked around for an alternate route. There was another passage behind the bar, but the bar was next to the DJ, and the promise of free drinks and music had attracted a sea of bouncing bodies. With five cocktails in hand, Joe decided to press onward rather than backtrack.

He elbowed past the people who had seeped into the cracks of free space during his moment of hesitation. When the man in his way swayed to the side with deep, hyena-like laughter, Joe capitalized on the opportunity to sneak by. But just then the man swayed back into his original position and crashed into Joe's drinks.

Joe fumbled to hold on to the glasses while the cosmopolitan, the Midori sour, the rum and Coke, and the Bloody Mary sloshed onto the man's white silk boxers. Then his clear gin and tonic shifted forward and splashed too. It mixed all the colors into a mire of brown, red, and green.

Joe's eyes had a long way to travel before they reached the man's face. Despite the pom-pom of a Santa hat bouncing against his temple, he did not look cheerful.

"Watch it, Four-Eyes."

Joe hadn't heard an insult that pathetic since elementary school. A few snarky comebacks came to mind, as always, but he didn't have a death wish. He kept even his smirk internal. "Uh, sorry." Joe averted his face and tried to edge through the doorway.

When the man put his arm down, it made for an impressive barrier. "Where do you think you're going?"

The room was warm and the situation made it seem warmer. Joe could feel his glasses sliding off the bump of his nose. With his hands still full, he couldn't even correct their position. And perhaps it didn't matter; they would probably be broken in a few seconds anyway. He saw the sloppy swing rising for his face in double—one image hazy, one crisp and clear. He ducked, turned, and watched in awe as the punch hit the girl behind him. While her hands lifted to her nose, the man next to her sent another swing floating through space.

Joe may have seen the start of the fight, but he wasn't going to stick around and wait for its conclusion. He scurried off before the brawlers could realize the drink-spiller was gone. And he couldn't help but wonder how his life had come to this.

He had come to L.A. to write screenplays. Unfortunately, he hadn't been writing much lately, not anything he wanted to write. He had a few touch-ups to complete on the horror movie script he'd co-written, but otherwise he had become the errand boy for the project. And since the project had run out of money, he was essentially working for free—something he could not afford to do much longer.

So money was the reason the film crew was mixing business with pleasure at Walter Burbank's Christmas party. Walt was a notorious Hollywood socialite who, while his parents were Christmassing at their Italian villa, had decided to throw the party of the year. Eddie, the horror movie's charming, eye-catching male lead, had secured the invitation, and Annie, their production manager, saw Walt's party as a business endeavor. She'd insisted that some essential members of the cast and crew attend to stir up enthusiasm while she secured a future meeting with Walt's people.

It was a good thing Annie was capable of taking the reins on the business end of things, because everyone else just wanted to have a good time. Working on Christmas resulted in a feeling of distaste, even among those whose dysfunctional families left them free of holiday commitments. Joe included himself in this group; his mother was dead, his father apparently vanished off the face of the earth, and he and his only brother were not on speaking terms.

Joe returned to the couch where his crew had been and set what remained of the drinks on the art-deco coffee table. Ten minutes before, everyone had been thirsty, but Eddie had disappeared to God only knew where, Annie must have been tracking down important people, and the rest of the group had scattered to the wind.

And Joe did not feel particularly jolly when left to his own devices. He was outgoing enough to make friends easily, a trait he inherited from his mother, but he closed himself off before those friends could scratch the surface. Because of his New England upbringing, some Californians might have said he had too much snow and not enough sunshine in his blood.

Joe needed a break from the party anyway, so he sat down and took out his phone. There were no new messages. *That's easy enough to remedy,* he thought. *Everyone I know is just expecting to hear from me first. I may as well get my brother over with. . . .*

About a dozen text messages later, the lights in a connecting room flickered for a second. The disturbance drew his attention to a baby grand piano, and his mood brightened.

He looked over his final message.

To: Rebecca

I miss you. Call me if you're ever in town.

"This will probably be my biggest regret in the morning," Joe mumbled. Then he gulped down the last of his weak gin and tonic. "Eh, screw it."

He hit send and went into the ballroom. The lights had a dimmer switch; he increased the brightness and sat down on the piano bench. It was the most spectacular piano he had ever seen. The black keys were so polished that he could see his reflection. Even though it had been a while since he'd played, he had an excellent memory for some of his favorites and enough knowledge of music theory to make anything sound good. He played some jazzy Christmas carols, and within a few minutes he'd drawn in a small crowd.

His eyes briefly lifted to a girl with candy-cane stockings and too many facial piercings. She pranced like an elf toward another girl, who was leaning against the far end of the piano. The second girl looked like a naughty Mrs.

Claus. Her outfit didn't leave much to the imagination. She was attractive, so Joe didn't mind, but it made him wonder when Christmas had become an excuse to wear little more than lingerie in public. This was no turtleneck-and-trousers New England Christmas party. But for the time of night and location on the globe, Joe didn't see anything out of place.

Except for the man against the far wall whose gray pants and matching lace-up vest made him look like a member of the North Pole Secret Police. Joe may have accepted the man's strange attire as just another costume, but there was something odd about his stance. He kept himself alone in a room full of clusters, stood stone-faced silent while others were mingling, and was staring at Joe as if Joe mattered, something no one ever did.

Joe's left pinkie slipped past his octave spread. He quickly corrected his mistake and carried on as if he hadn't noticed his observer. But Joe couldn't remain calm. His chords became louder and more dissonant, the tempo faster. Empowered by his music, he looked back up. He was tired of being pushed around, so he stared back, hard.

The room's low-hanging light fixture flickered again, and then the bulb burst. Everyone gasped. By the time Joe's eyes adjusted to the dimness, the strange man was gone, but he left behind a thick unease.

Joe resolved the phrase he was playing and then slipped back out of the room. It took him a second to figure out where he was in relation to the mansion's front entrance. He turned down a hallway and recognized the gigantic portrait of Audrey Hepburn. When he rounded the corner at the end of the hall, he caught a glimpse of a man in gray. Joe turned around and found the stairs.

The second floor was a maze of ostentatious halls and places he wanted to avoid, like the bar and the dance floor. He took a few unfamiliar turns and saw another stairway at the end of a long hall. Doors were closed, lights were dim. Moans of pleasure and the smell of an illegal substance were an unnerving presence along the way.

He sped down the stairs and almost lost his footing in the process. At the bottom, he followed the reassuring sound of voices. He entered the well-lit kitchen and headed toward a door leading outside.

"Where do you think you're off to, Joey Mac?"

Joe turned around. He would know that husky female voice in his sleep. It was Annie, his production manager.

He released an anxious breath. For the first time ever, he found her presence comforting. And she had a sarcastic half smile on her typically humorless face, so her meeting with Walt Burbank must have been a success. Plus she'd called him Joey Mac, which was always a good sign. She gave him all sorts of nicknames depending on her whims and frame of mind—Joey, Mac, Joey Mac, Brainiac, Blue Eyes, Dimples. The list went on and on. And if something had her riled up it would be "MacRae, Goddammit!"

Joe crossed his arms and casually glanced over his shoulder. "Just getting some air." His voice cracked when he spoke. He shifted his weight and fiddled with his glasses, hoping she wouldn't detect his anxiety, or the lie. He was getting the hell out of there no matter what she said.

"Am I safe to assume you'll be rejoining us momentarily?"

"Without a doubt," he said, winking at her. Joe had been on good terms with her lately. She seemed to like his quick wit and his way of deflecting her wrath through obedience and fear. He also had more common sense and intelligence than most of the celebutants and D-listers she dealt with on a regular basis.

"I'm just messing with you, Joey Mac. For our purposes, this party's over."

"I'll probably take off, then."

He gave her a Hollywood-style hug and kiss goodnight, and turned to go.

"Get that script cleaned up," she called after him.

He waved once but didn't turn back. "Yep. I'm on it."

Outside, he made his way past the crowd by the pool. From a distance, he recognized the crew's new special effects nerd accepting his car keys from the valet. Joe didn't have his own car, so he didn't hesitate to flag down a potential ride.

The young man agreed to take Joe to Venice, even though it was a few neighborhoods out of his way. Joe couldn't even remember his name, but he listened to the crewman babble on about tech stuff. As they drove, Joe shielded his face with his hand and checked the side view mirror. He wasn't even sure why he was worried—the man in gray had done nothing, really—but that feeling of unease he'd had wouldn't subside.

His coworker lingered in the right lane for most of the ride and rarely broke the speed limit in his energy-efficient car. Joe watched all the Porsches and Ferraris zoom by; he was grateful for the ride but even more grateful he wasn't being chased.

The kid eventually dropped Joe off in front of his building, a turn-of-the-century hotel converted into hundreds of cramped, poorly maintained studio apartments that housed struggling artists, street performers, jaded musicians, and theater junkies, most of whom seemed to be littering the sidewalk with their tattooed bodies and clouds of smoke. That number of people at this late hour on Christmas night would have been odd anywhere else but was just life as usual in Joe's neighborhood.

The entrance hall was just as packed. It was a challenge to stay on guard—there was no way he could notice everything and everyone—but Joe did his best.

Elevator or stairs? he wondered. The old-fashioned elevator seemed too enclosed, but it was busy going up and down with people, none of them overtly suspicious. He then craned his neck to see the end of the hall. The eerie glow of the exit sign by the stairwell helped him make his choice: the elevator.

He was first in line and squeezed in the back corner while a festive crowd loaded in. Most of the others exited on the third floor, two left on the fourth, and by the time Joe reached his floor, the sixth, he was the only one remaining.

His hall was empty, his door a long way away. Only one flickering fluorescent light in a caged shell guided his steps.

He reached his door, out of breath, and then he felt ridiculous for being so paranoid. He couldn't think of a good reason why anyone would be stalking him.

When he opened the door, everything appeared to be in its normal state of disarray. After fastening the deadbolt and the chain, Joe turned on his bedside lamp and emptied his pockets onto his nightstand. He stripped to his boxers and T-shirt, set his glasses down, and got into bed. Then he checked his phone one last time. There were still no messages. He put the phone back down and turned off the light.

He eased his eyes shut. Sleep wasn't far. He'd had a long night, and all of life's stresses, real or imaginary, had sapped him of energy.

His mind soon raced with pre-dream thoughts. But then he forced himself to full consciousness. He felt empty for some reason, like something was missing. It *was* the first Christmas he'd ever spent alone, he decided after a few moments of reflection. He tossed to his side, convinced he had found the reason for his temporary insanity. He was about to close his eyes again when a light from the building next door reflected off something by his bathroom. The shine disappeared before his foggy vision could narrow in on the source.

A creak in the floor had him bolting upright and reaching for his lamp. He switched it on and strained both his ears and eyes. But all was silent and still, so he soon convinced himself that the reflection he'd seen must have been from his bathroom mirror and that the creak was just a creak.

Joe was about to shut off the light and bury his head under his pillow when he realized what he'd been missing. There should have been a framed picture on his nightstand, one that he liked. He looked uncharacteristically photogenic in it and, more important, he was with both his parents. It was the last time the three of them had been together, on film anyway.

His alarm clock, his books and magazines, and the usual coat of dust were all in place. But not the picture.

Joe got out of bed, crouched, and felt around. He soon came across shattered glass underneath the nightstand. And on the floor by the wall he spotted the back of the wooden frame. He pulled it out and flipped it over, ready to see his mother's smiling face. But the frame shook out of his hands when he saw the jagged remains of glass, black cardboard, and nothing else.

He tried to get his feet underneath him while grabbing for his pants and his essentials—keys, phone, wallet, glasses. Then the lamplight glinted off a long, shiny blade emerging waist-high from the bathroom. He abandoned his struggle to get his pants on and stumbled to the door.

Joe regretted locking up so tightly now that he was on the inside trying to get out. Just as he felt a presence sneaking up from behind, the door flew open and he fled.

Mid-sprint down the hall, he tripped to a stop. A man in gray with a spiked gladiator helmet blocked his only route of escape. Joe took a hesitant step backward and crashed against something as hard as a brick wall. A hand flew over his mouth before he could fill his lungs with enough air to make even a pitiful squeal.

The hand covering his mouth and nose was replaced by a vial of liquid. Joe panicked for life and breath, and had to swallow. As the liquid scorched his insides on the way down, the only working fluorescent light in the hall flickered and then popped.

Joe watched the red glow of the exit sign at the end of the hall fade to black as his eyelids fell. He never had any hope of making it there.

***

I will go, and I will go alone. . . .

Cassie's own words echoed in her head as she packed. They had ended the hours of planning and bickering at the emergency midnight Forum for Freedom. It was the right thing to say, or so she'd felt at the time. Now, of course, she doubted her ability to take on such a difficult task by herself. She knew the caves and crevices of Pyxis better than most other fairies, but she was no more threatening than a fairy child, and wingless on top of that.

She couldn't dwell on her decision. There was no time. Every thought wasted on the past was a thought not properly invested. She redirected her mind to packing her sack and anticipating all possible scenarios. One missing item could make the difference between life and death.

She jumped when she heard a knock.

"Cassiopeia?" The tip of a cute nose popped through the crack in the door. "It's me. May I come in?"

"Yes, you may."

Carina zoomed into the room with her arms full. "I brought the robes you asked for. And the shoes." She lifted them for demonstration while still hovering in the air. She had grown so tall over the last year and was not yet adept at judging heights in tight spaces, but she flew everywhere anyway. Her light gray wings flapped against the ceiling until she settled on the floor and let them go limp down her back.

Cassie nodded and gestured toward the free spot on the bed.

Carina cradled the robes against her chest and sat down with a bounce next to the half-packed sack. "I can't believe it's true! Out of all the fairies in attendance, they picked you!"

"I volunteered," Cassie admitted halfheartedly as she darted to her bureau. She rummaged through her things until she located her stash of matches. She returned to the bed and added the pouch to a side compartment of her sack. Then she knelt down and dug under her bed for the weapons that had been donated to the cause a couple of weeks earlier.

She lifted them one at a time to the candlelight. Most of the weapons were chipped or caked with rust. There were a few decent swords, though too large for her sack and too cumbersome to carry. She selected a knife that looked to be in the best condition and ran her finger lightly along its edge. Then she pressed harder and did not draw blood. She added it reluctantly to her sack and hoped she would not need it for self-defense.

"I do wish I could come with you," Carina said. "Vela wouldn't even let me go to the forum."

"She's just looking out for you. And I agree with her. You're better off staying here if you would like to live to see your sixteenth birthday."

"I know." Carina sighed, but her disappointment didn't seem to last. She looked dreamy again in no time. "Do you think they're handsome?"

Cassie was shoulder-deep under her bed again and had her ear pressed against the floor. "The MacRae brothers?" She paused and lifted one eyebrow. Then she slipped into the crack between the bed and the wood planks of the floor. She crawled back out with a wad of rope in hand. "Honestly, I haven't thought about it," she said with a shrug as she plucked the light coating of dust from her dark hair.

"You haven't? Not even once? Wouldn't it be incredibly romantic if—"

"Carina, they're practically family."

"Not by blood. And if they truly were like family to you, you'd be better off letting them die. Love, or the possibility of it, seems like a much better reason to risk one's life."

"What about duty and honor, or justice? And how about freedom? I would die for any one of those reasons!" Cassie was standing now, one hand clasped over a tight fist, the rope dangling from her wrist.

"I still say love," Carina blurted.

Cassie's resolve lifted and she emitted a *humph* that blew a strand of hair from her eye. "Call it intuition or destiny. Call it what you may. I'm supposed to meet them, yet I don't know why. As far as I am aware, it is only to help them. My dreams have never alluded to anything more." She added the rope and the clothing to her sack and pulled the drawstring closed. Then she ushered Carina toward the door and blew out her candles. "And besides, they are fairy-males, even if they are unaware of it. As always, I will keep my expectations low. That way I will not be disappointed."

Though they both giggled, Cassie's chest also tightened. In her heart she knew falling in love was too dangerous. She intended never again to put someone she cared for in peril. Since it was impossible for her to survive outside of Pyxis by herself, she lived a humble life, a *secret* life as far from the Aerial Palace as possible in terms of both distance and ideology. Yet sometimes she had a feeling her mother's eyes were near and that they would surely take more interest in her life if she were happy.

Cassie met Carina in the doorway; they entered the hall and stood together. Before Cassie could come up with the right good-bye, Carina trapped her in a tearful hug. "Please be back by evening. Do not even consider the alternative."

Cassie nodded because she couldn't say what she was really thinking—that she would, in all likelihood, never return.

"Are you certain you will be all right by yourself?" Carina's emerald-colored eyes sparkled down at her with sincerity. "I'm fast and clever, and I do not fear them."

Cassie covered her head with the hood of her cloak and threw her sack over her shoulder. "Your family needs you and would never forgive me if something were to happen to you. You must stay here, though I admire your courage. Go to sleep. There are only a few hours left until breakfast. You have to admit there would be mutiny downstairs without your berry tartlets."

Carina gave her a sad, compliant smile and as she headed toward her own room across the hall, Cassie locked her door and then took the first few steps of her daunting quest.

Halfway down the long hall of rented rooms, Cassie turned for a last look. Carina was still clinging to her doorknob.

Cassie shooed her inside with more conviction. Once Carina entered her room, Cassie left the building.

She didn't think she feared Andromeda's Gray Coats either. But she had not yet left the safety of the Aurora Borealis, the only place she had ever considered home.

***

Chris cracked his eyes open enough to see the early morning light through the curtains. The wind was still rattling the loose windowpanes and puffing up the curtains, but when the gusts subsided, he thought he heard faint whispers.

He was facing his wife's side of the bed with one arm wrapped around her, the other tucked under his pillow. He made his best effort to seem asleep while he listened, alternately thinking of what he could do to ready himself for a confrontation and trying to convince himself that the voices were in his head.

Soon he heard footsteps, more than one set. He lowered his left arm around the side of the bed and grasped for a plastic toy or a hardcover book, something useful, but then his fingers closed on something even better. Just as they did, though, there was a quick, painful tug on his leg and then Chris was falling. His back and head hit the wooden floor. He was disoriented, but

25

he saw a gray blur of intruders—too many to count—closing in on him in his vulnerable position.

When Chris heard his wife's scream, both of his hands clutched his lucky baseball bat. He sat up and swung at the figure closest to him with home-run intensity.

The bat struck his attacker's thigh. The man's leg buckled and his knee hit the floor. Chris exploited the momentary victory by pushing to his feet. He swung again and hit the incapacitated one on the neck just below his spiked helmet. The man toppled over. His sword clattered to the floor and spun out of reach.

As another figure moved in, Chris dropped the bat and dived for the sword. On his stomach and elbows, he fumbled for control of it. Then there was a sharp stomp between his shoulder blades and a debilitating weight driving Chris into the floor. But Chris whipped to his back and grabbed the man's leg. While his attacker was off balance, Chris jolted upright and drove the sword into his abdomen.

He yanked the sword away with one swift motion. The second enemy collapsed to the ground. Chris stumbled away and, with the bloody sword in one hand, picked up the baseball bat with the other.

The remaining intruders backed Chris into the corner of the room. His eyes darted to Alana and then to the enemies still standing. One, two, three, four, five. *Five left!* And one of them had a sword propped against Alana's neck.

Chris attempted to clear the terror-induced lump out of his throat. He needed to sound scary, not scared. "Who are you? What do you want? I'll do whatever you ask. Just let her go!"

"Put your weapons down!"

The closest intruder lunged for the sword. Chris lunged back and the intruder retreated.

"Kill her!"

"Wait!" Chris crouched down, one vertebra at a time. "Look . . . I'm putting both weapons down—"

"Don't do it, Chris!" Alana wailed.

Chris's eyes darted over to her again. She was usually the levelheaded one, always calm in any crisis. He then thought of their children, asleep in their rooms down the hall, and hoped they wouldn't awake and stumble into danger. He didn't know what his next move should be, but if Alana said hold on to the weapons, that seemed as good a plan as any. He stood back up and resumed his defensive position.

"We were going to leave her alone because she is meaningless to us, but . . ." The apparent leader of the intruding gang took a few moments to turn over the maimed bodies of his fellows with his foot. "You did kill two of my Gray Coats. That makes her expendable."

The arms of Alana's captor seemed to swallow her whole as he drew her closer. When the leader nodded, the brute pressed his sword deeper into her neck. He adjusted his grip with a set of fat, tattooed knuckles. Each tattoo was an asymmetrical black star with a white ring in the center.

Even in the low light of dawn, and with shock and dread flooding his mind, Chris committed the strange symbol to memory. Since the intruders had helmets covering their eyes and half of their faces, the star, which he'd also noticed on the necks of two others, might be their only defining feature.

Then Chris saw blood trickling down Alana's throat. "Don't!" he pleaded. "Kill me instead!"

Chris dropped the bat and the sword and lowered to his knees. He put his hands behind his head, pinched his eyes shut, and hoped the deathblow would be clean and quick.

His eyes eased back open when the leader emitted a cruel chuckle.

"You are in no position to give orders. Besides, the queen wants you alive. Now drink this so we can be on our way."

Chris suddenly had hands all over him—hitting, clutching, scratching, binding, pulling. Then he had a vial of liquid pressed to his lips. When he didn't react, the intruders pried his mouth open and splashed the liquid inside.

He spat and thrashed around until a hard metallic blow to the side of his head forced him into submission. Then more of the foul-tasting liquid was poured into his mouth and there were hands making sure he couldn't breathe unless he swallowed it.

Through the chaos, Chris heard the slash of a sword and a distant whimper. Drowsy and devastated, he felt a rumble of collapse throughout his body. His fate was entirely in the hands of these faceless monsters, whoever they were.

CHAPTER 3
Leverage

Chris's consciousness ebbed and flowed like the ocean, and he even thought he could hear the waves breaking on the sand and drifting back to a tranquil place. But every time the surf glided across the sand, it traveled farther than the time before and then retreated with less vigor, and each new wave brought in a crash of pain. His bones ached, his skin stung, and his head felt like it was drowning in cheap rum.

"Uncle Joe, my turn, my turn!"

Chris recognized the voice of his daughter, Morgan. His eyes fluttered open. He saw blotchy figures in the distance, but he couldn't make out her face. It was too dark. His hearing seemed to be sharper, at least. He heard movement, giggling, and heavy breathing. And there was a strange smell, musty and stagnant.

"You have to give your brother a turn first. You can't fool me that easily, princess."

The second voice made him believe he was dreaming. Chris struggled to lift his head. It fell back down with a clunk against whatever he was lying on—something cold, hard, and unforgiving.

"Looks like your dad is starting to wake up."

"Daddy! Daddy!"

Chris forced himself to his knees and took Morgan in his arms. Her twin brother, Ryan, slid down from his piggyback ride and launched himself at his father. Chris hugged them both, one in each arm, thankful they were all right. They were still in their Christmas pajamas and seemed cheerful. Chris hoped this meant they had been treated with some degree of humanity while he was unconscious.

"Daddy, we're in a cage, and Uncle Joe is here, and he says we're having an adventure!" Ryan piped.

Then Chris watched a white T-shirt approach. Chris knew it was his brother even before Joe's face came into view. It was the way Joe carried himself—confident and insecure at the same time. Some things never changed. Other things did change, however. Either Joe had lost weight or his exaggerated jawline was the seasoning that came with age and physical maturity. And without his glasses there to act as a shield, Joe's wariness was in plain sight. Perhaps it had nothing to do with the glasses and his fear would have spilled out regardless. Their situation just might be that dire. But then Joe smiled tentatively. It added a touch of relief and a hint of mischievous humor to his face, and conjured up some mixed emotions for Chris. As the charmer, the tireless bullshitter—sometimes funny, but more often than not outright annoying—Joe was practically his polar opposite. They didn't even look alike; Joe's hair was darker, his eyes lighter. And after their mother's funeral, they had parted on bad terms and hadn't spoken since.

"You look like you might need a hand, bro." Joe gently eased the children aside, helped Chris to his feet, and gave him a quick, awkward hug. "I know. Not exactly the family reunion I was anticipating either."

"Where the hell are we?" Chris whispered.

They were in some kind of cage, and there was an orange glow behind the bars, but Chris was more concerned with the darkness. The cage appeared to be set within a cave whose rocky, uneven sides curved toward a low overhang at the entrance. At the rear was a black so deep it had to be the birthplace of evil, a monster in its own right, and it was breathing frigid air at them. He was still wearing the sweatshirt he'd pulled on earlier, but aside from their shirts he and his brother were both clad only in their boxers.

"I have no earthly idea. I hoped you would know," Joe whispered back. "I'm still struggling with what day it is," Joe added with a shrug. "Or whether it's day at all or just one long, bad night. You were out at least eight hours longer than we were. Your kids were getting worried. They're charming, by the way, nothing at all like their father."

The jab barely registered because Chris's attention zoomed to the two men in gray sitting by a fire outside the bars. He immediately charged toward them. "Hey, you! Yeah, I'm talking to you! Why don't you pick up your sorry asses and let us out of here?"

The prison guards didn't even look away from the greasy bones they were sucking.

Chris hit the bars with his palms and began to prowl like a caged lion that just realized its roar was useless.

Then Joe stepped forward. "Yeah, um, hi. I'm Joe, and you've met my brother, Chris," he said, pointing over his shoulder. "And these are his kids, Morgan and Ryan. We don't know why we're here, but while we're waiting to find out, we're pretty much sitting around in our underwear. Do you think you could get us some blankets and maybe some food, and then we can discuss our circumstances like rational human beings?"

The guards grunted to each other in another language. *French maybe?* Chris thought.

Then one of them wiped his mouth with the sleeve of his uniform and walked away. He returned with a couple of dingy blankets.

"Food will come later," the guard snarled. "If you are lucky."

Joe slipped the blankets between the bars. "Thanks." When Joe turned around, Chris had a glare of awe and disgust waiting for him. "What?" Joe chucked him a blanket. "At least we won't freeze to death."

Chris squatted down and wrapped the blanket around his children. It smelled like it had been in a cave for a thousand years and had been peeled off a hundred corpses. And he wasn't sure if Joe was right—the blanket had almost as many holes as it had stitches, so they still might freeze to death.

"Dad, I'm thirsty," Ryan said.

"I'm sorry, kiddo. I am too. We'll have to wait a little while, though," Chris replied while smoothing out his son's dark hair. "Why don't you two try to rest?"

"Daddy, is Mommy coming soon?" Morgan asked this time.

"No, she's probably back at the house, but I'm sure she misses you very much." Chris didn't want to say anything to dampen their spirits. "Stay warm and stay here. Can you two do that for me?"

Ryan and Morgan nodded in unison. They then took the blanket, tented it over themselves on the ground, and began to peek out through the holes.

Chris took a seat next to his brother on the opposite side of the cage and watched his children play, envious that they needed only each other and a blanket fort to escape to a better place.

"Man, they really did a number on you." Joe lightly touched the side of Chris's head. "No wonder you were the last to wake up. They must have needed an elephant tranquilizer to get you down."

Chris shrugged, but he knew from the throbbing sting that there must be a decent-sized gash there. He had cuts and bruises all over his hands, wrists, and the portions of his arms not covered by his scrunched-up sweatshirt. Joe's scrutiny and a sudden whole-body shiver compelled Chris to pull his sleeves down over his battered fingers.

Joe then snapped open the second blanket and offered a portion. Chris declined with a wave. He would rather freeze.

Just as Chris closed his eyes to allow himself to focus, Joe asked, "What do you think this is all about anyway? Did some terrorists follow you home or something?"

"Terrorists with helmets and swords? I doubt it. Maybe they were following you. Did you piss off any sadistic theater freaks in the City of Angels?"

"All right, sorry. Bad time to joke," Joe conceded.

Chris sighed in an effort to calm his misdirected anger. "Forget it. We obviously need to be on the same team, even if it's the first time in our lives we ever worked together."

"Agreed. So how did Alana get out of all of this fun? Did she escape maybe?" After a long pause, he said, "Chris?" Then Joe didn't press further. "I'm sorry. I didn't realize. . . ."

Chris shrugged again. Without knowing for sure, he'd rather say nothing.

The rattle of keys interrupted the silence, and their heads turned toward the bars.

"You there." A fat guard pointed at Joe. "The queen wants to see you first."

The color left Joe's face. He looked to Chris with wide eyes and then started to get up. But Chris pulled him back down and stood in his place. "I'll go instead." His younger brother was good at many things, but withstanding intimidation and violence was not likely among his talents.

"The queen's orders are not to be contradicted," the fat guard countered.

"It's cool, Chris. I'll go," Joe murmured.

"No, it's not!" Chris blocked his brother's passage with his arm.

The guard paused and gave a signal. Footsteps came along the corridor toward the back of the cave, and when the lock clicked open, there were more guards streaming into their cell than Chris could take on. So he circled his arm around Joe's neck and backed away from the door to buy a few moments. His advice to Joe might be the only hope they had. "Stay calm," Chris urged. "Lie if you have to, and don't give them what they want or we're all dead!"

And that was all he could say before they were dragged apart. Chris caught one last glimpse of his brother being taken out of the cell by the scuff of his T-shirt.

Then, before he could reach toward his children, Chris felt his feet being taken out from under him. His cheek hit rock and his eyes saw only darkness. He wished it were due to unconsciousness, but unfortunately, a giant boot had his face pinned toward the black hole of the cave. Then his hands were bound at the wrist, his mouth gagged. Both of his ears were blocked as well, but he could still hear the screams of the two he was supposed to be able to protect.

***

Joe clenched his jaw so his teeth wouldn't chatter and wrapped his bound hands into fists so his fingers wouldn't tremble. He had been able to talk himself out of trouble before. He even considered himself good at it. But he wondered how he could persuade these people to show mercy. They seemed like seasoned killers who would do unthinkable things to extract what they wanted.

Down he marched, deeper into the torch-lit earth. When he slowed to watch his step, he received a push; when he fell, he was lifted back to his feet with a harsh grip. Without his hands for balance or shoes to enhance his traction on the slippery, uneven slabs of rock, he had no choice but to stumble. He also added a few falls on purpose to slow the pace. He wasn't exactly looking forward to whatever the destination might be.

At a fork in the path, the guards stayed to the right and brought Joe to the back of a dead-end corridor. They pushed him into a rusty chair with arm and leg shackles.

"Is the medieval torture contraption really necessary?"

They made no answer.

While they secured his limbs, Joe noticed a variety of sharp objects hanging from the wall. The sweat, labored breathing, and light-headedness began at once. He closed his eyes and prayed to whoever might be listening. His mother's face came to mind. If she was truly there for him in spirit, as she had promised to be, she would give him the strength he lacked.

Mom, I know I wasn't the best son in the world, but I need you to get me through this.

Joe opened his eyes and spiraled back to reality. He felt calmer than before, a necessity for clear thinking. If he knew what all this was about, he could mentally prepare some plausible inaccuracies. He and Chris had not been born to a life of luxury and privilege, and he had not ever earned much money. Nor did he have wealthy friends, not close ones anyway. So money wasn't what they were after. But what, then? Information? About what, though? The guards wore armor and held swords. No technology, no modern-day weapons. It was as if he and Chris and the children had been teleported to another time and place. *So what could I have that they would want?*

A faint buzzing sound crept into Joe's awareness. It continued to get louder until it was all he could hear. Then he saw something he did not anticipate, a creature that looked like a large black butterfly. It flew erratically but with purpose, moving quickly, hovering in new locations every few seconds. It landed on his forearm. Even without his glasses, Joe saw something that made his jaw drop.

"Let's get right to the point, shall we?" said the creature, a tiny woman with wings. Black was her motif from her slicked-back hair to her eyes—whose iris and pupil seemed to be one—to the spiderweb of scars that climbed down her face toward her queen-of-darkness dress. And even though she was only about three and a half inches tall, Joe didn't have any problem hearing her. Somehow, the low drone of her voice seemed to echo in his head.

"Yeah, um, sure."

"You tell me what I want to know, and then you and your family are free to go."

"What are you? A fairy or something?" Joe asked boldly, letting his curiosity outweigh his fear.

"I ask the questions! You supply adequate answers!" she hissed.

"Got it. I was just wondering."

"When was the last time you saw your father?"

"He abandoned us when my brother and I were kids. Very sad. Hard to cope. Mom always took it the hardest." Joe had always been good at making up stories on the spot.

"Don't lie to me! I saw the photograph. Care to try again?"

Joe looked away from the fairy and tried to piece together what he knew. The men in gray had obviously found the picture in his apartment. That much he had already guessed, but who were they? And where the hell *was* his father? Joe had never considered looking into the reason why Scott MacRae had left his family. His mother seemed crushed after her husband had vanished, but she was never bitter or resentful, and barely spoke a word about it, almost as if she were protecting him for some reason. Joe, however, had had less faith. He had always made the assumption that his father led a double life—another woman, other children, all younger, cuter, needier—and just decided one day to end the charade and choose between the two.

Suddenly, the fairy pulled a glittery dagger from her dress and stabbed him in the arm. Joe screamed. The puncture from the tiny weapon was not likely to be fatal, but the burning sensation was unbearable.

"I'm going to ask you one more time. Where is your father?"

"I don't know."

"When did you last see him?"

"I don't remember."

"Who are his friends?"

"Beats me."

The fairy whizzed up to his forehead and lifted her dagger above his right eye.

"Am I making myself perfectly clear?" She laid the blade against his eyelid and toyed with it.

"Yes, indeed," he said. "As much as I'd love to help, I haven't seen or heard from my father since the summer after I graduated from college. That was several years ago. I left for medical school on the West Coast that August. He left my mother sometime that winter, and no one has heard from him since. He didn't even show up for my mother's funeral this past March, so your guess is as good as mine. He could be dead for all I know."

"If only I were that lucky," the fairy said, still threatening his eye. "Where did he say he was going?"

"He never told anyone. One day he was just gone."

"Speculate."

"I have no idea! And apparently I didn't even know the guy that well. He never mentioned that *you* were tracking him down."

Joe figured he'd lose an eye for that outburst, and he blinked as if that would somehow stymie the little stinger of a blade. But no stab came; instead, the fairy queen's weight lifted off his forehead.

His eyes reopened when he felt two points of pressure on his arm. The black-winged fairy had been joined by a second fairy, this one clad in a red-and-blue uniform with a strange sigil on his breastplate—a distorted star that looked three-dimensional on his portly chest.

"Do you need more time with this one, My Queen?"

"No, General, we're finished here. Bring in the angry one. He might be of more use to us."

Joe produced a short, dry laugh. "Sadly, I believe you are mistaken."

"That may be so," the fairy queen uttered in a tone Joe would have expected from a storybook villain. Her words slithered right into his ears and gave his whole body a chill. "Nevertheless, there is a good chance he can be brought to his knees with the right leverage."

She gave a signal, and two of the human-sized guards in gray released Joe from the chair and escorted him out like a criminal. He felt some relief at this reprieve but feared what the word "leverage" might mean. There was only so much Chris could take in one day without buckling.

***

Chris saw the chair with the shackles and planted his feet into the ground. There were hands all over him in an instant, but he wasn't going to make their job easy. He turned himself into a squirming hellion. Despite his unruliness, the guards lowered him into the chair. Some then held him in place while others began to fasten the shackles.

One of the guards walked away and left Chris with more freedom to thrash. But the guard returned with a pitchfork and aligned the center tine with Chris's Adam's apple.

Chris put his hands up to declare his surrender. The guard lowered the pitchfork and with the others went to work holding, pinning, and then locking Chris's limbs into place. When the last lock clicked, a hideous winged creature landed on his arm.

"Christopher, you are here today because I am dying to know where your father is. Tell me what you know," said the creature, a tiny woman laced with black.

Chris looked right through her because the capacity in his heart for wonderment was infiltrated with barbs of hatred. He heard her command, but he would not, under any circumstances, provide her with what she wanted.

"Don't make me resort to violence," the black-winged fairy said.

Still, he said nothing.

"Suit yourself," she said, and then turned to the guards. "Now, my Gray Coats, bring in his children!"

"Wait!" Chris cried out.

She gestured for the guards to halt.

"I don't know who or *what* you are, or why you want to find my father, but . . . what harm could my children ever have caused to you?" Chris leaned forward as far as his constraints would allow. "They are just babies. If my father is the reason your people broke into my house, put a sword to my wife's neck, and are threatening my children, then I'll track him down myself and kill him with my bare hands!"

"As tempting an offer as that is, I prefer to do things my way, which means you tell me what you know."

Chris leaned back into his chair and looked away. "I don't have a clue where he is."

"I am certain you know more than you are letting on. Just think. I have been seeking vengeance for actions your father took long ago. I came close several years back, and as a result, he fled, abandoning your sick mother. He never told you the truth about his past, and now you are here and he is not. He will get what he deserves, no?"

Her pathetic attempt at manipulation caused Chris to let out an angry chuckle. Then he looked right at her and hoped his eyes were just as cruel and cold as hers were, though he knew that was impossible. "I see what you're trying to do, but it won't work. I could give you all the sad details, but you and I both know I'm a dead man either way. So why bother?"

"I like you, Christopher MacRae." She cocked her head to the side and sneered. "You're realistic. And right now you are fighting not only for your life but also for the lives of your children."

"You wouldn't dare!"

"Don't try me. In fact, my patience is waning. You have given me nothing, and I see only one reason to keep any of you alive—to lure your father—"

"And what makes you think he'll come?" Chris suddenly shouted. The jerk of his body launched the fairy into flight.

"The children will be the first to go," she continued, her voice even louder than the shrill sound of her wings. "And your brother will follow. Guards, bring them to me!" she commanded, and then she flew off.

"Don't listen to her! She's insane! She's delusional, evil. . . ." Chris's voice trailed off once the guards were gone and there was no one left to listen.

Chris's eyes darted around and then zoomed in on one of his wrist shackles. It had a loose screw. He twisted his wrist and hand so hard against the metal that he feared the rattling would draw the guards back in. He paused, and although his whole hand was red and raw, he refused to give up. The screw had moved about a centimeter. He had only about two centimeters left to go.

The struggle between the rusty screw and his nearly skinless wrist continued. Chris altered his approach a number of times, and with one last desperate attempt, the screw clanked on the stone below, sending an echo into the darkness.

Then hope slipped away when two guards returned. They unshackled him without noticing the missing screw and guided him back the way they'd come, but Chris could tell there was something bigger going on. There was urgency mixed with their brutality, and the fairy had sent only two escorts, not the six he'd had earlier. He didn't want to get ahead of himself, but maybe there was something left to hope for.

CHAPTER 4
Flight

Joe tried to stay upbeat for his niece and nephew. Before his interrogation, they had been receptive to his attempts to lighten the mood. But having seen their father subdued and carried off, they were no longer willing to play or laugh.

"Hey, do you two know any stories? What's your favorite?" Joe asked. "Ryan?"

His nephew shrugged.

"How about you, Morgan?"

"Mommy reads me 'Snow White.'"

"'Snow White,' huh?" *A fairy tale, an oddly relevant selection,* he thought, given that their own tale had taken a fairy turn. "How about 'The Tortoise and the Hare' instead?" *An inspirational underdog story!*

"I want 'Snow White.'"

Morgan's startling forcefulness reminded him of Chris. She even had his willful brown eyes.

"All right," he complied, unwilling to challenge even a small female MacRae. "A long time ago, in a galaxy—"

"That's not how it goes, Uncle Joe. It starts 'Once upon a time,'" she corrected, and Ryan nodded in agreement.

"Right, sorry, just kidding," Joe teased. "Once upon a time, a beautiful princess lived in a kingdom ruled by her evil stepmother. Jealous of Snow

White's beauty—" He broke off when he heard the rattle of keys and the creak of their cage door.

Some guards streamed into the cell. The first to enter had the scar-faced fairy on his shoulder. The children stared at the winged creature with wide eyes, and she in turn leveled her gaze on them. Joe then realized what she'd meant by the word "leverage."

"She's the evil stepmother!" he shouted to his niece and nephew. "Don't listen to her. Do whatever you can to get away!"

Joe rose to his feet and stood in front of the children. He curled his hands into fists and held his stance firm.

One push, however, was enough to knock him off balance. He hit the cage bars and then felt a suffocating forearm at his throat.

Morgan and Ryan put up the fight of their little lives with teeth, flailing arms, screams, and tears. Before long, though, the guards had them lifted over their shoulders.

With the twins in tow, the gray horde funneled toward the door. Ryan reached toward his sister with outstretched fingertips. Joe thought it was just a desperate gesture of protection, but then Ryan vanished. And while the guard who had been carrying the little boy tried to come to terms with the impossible, Morgan disappeared as well.

"Look, you fools, they're up there!" the fairy queen shouted. "You! Follow them on foot. You! Get the Royal Air Brigade. Don't let them escape!"

Just as Joe's consciousness began to wane, the pressure on his throat lifted abruptly. He collapsed to his knees and coughed air back into his lungs. Once he was alone and could breathe again, he had a good laugh.

Wings. Now, why didn't I think of that?

***

When the guards returned Chris to the cage, Morgan and Ryan were missing, just as he had feared they'd be. But his brother was there.

"The kids! It was—" Joe began.

"Where are they?"

Joe helped Chris untie his hands. "That I don't know. But it was incredible. The guards and that evil little fairy came to take them away, and they were pitching a fit. Then, out of nowhere, they shrank, sprouted wings, and flew away!"

39

"They just *flew* off?" Chris asked. "Are you sure you didn't get your head thrown into the ground one too many times?"

"Well, I was about to go unconscious a few minutes ago, but . . ."

Chris lifted an eyebrow.

"I didn't imagine it, though. I swear!" Joe pointed to something on the ground. "Look, those are their pajamas."

Chris wanted to believe his brother, but then he would have to believe in magic and accept not only that he had just seen a fairy but also that his children were fairies too. "Great, except they're four," he said, trying to keep his voice level. "How far away from danger could they get?"

Chris cradled his skinned wrist with his sweatshirt to slow the bleeding, and then he slid into a sitting position against the cage bars. With his elbows on his knees, he tried to massage the pain, stress, and misery from his face.

Joe tossed a small rock in the air and caught it. "Why are you sitting? This could be our only chance to make a break for it!"

"What do you have in mind? Busting the lock open with that little pebble you have?"

"There could be another way. Maybe they brought us to fairyland for a reason. Your kids just flew away, for God's sake! Maybe it's in our blood. If we could only figure out how to transform and quickly—"

"Hello. Over here!"

They turned toward the small voice. On the ground in front of Chris's feet, a hooded creature was waving for their attention.

Chris snapped forward onto his knees and snatched the fairy off the ground before it had a chance to run or fly away. "Give me one good reason I shouldn't crush you like a bug." He brought the palm-sized creature closer to his face for a better look. His grip loosened when she swept off the hood of her cloak. Her hair was as dark as her penetrating eyes, and her beauty seemed too pure to be real. But her appearance was not what held his attention. Her thoughts seemed beyond her, almost like fragments of images or words, but they were too complicated and numerous for him to interpret.

There was one thought, however, that she was transmitting with angelic clarity. *You don't want to kill me.*

Chris blinked away from the fairy's spellbinding stare.

With wide eyes and an open jaw, Joe crouched down and reached for her. He nearly touched her with his open hand, but then his fingers curled closed and his arm lowered. "Chris, put her down! Step away from the fairy princess!"

———

40

Chris didn't know what else to do. He eased her back on the ground.

"Thank you," the cloaked fairy said. "I can give you two reasons to let me live: I can help you escape, and I know where your children are. We don't have a lot of time, so listen carefully," she urged. "You are Modifiers, both of you. You can be one of two forms—small like me or human-sized. Switching from one form to another requires simple imagination or deep concentration, the latter more likely in your case, but find what works for you. Clear your head and think of nothing else except yourself as my size." Her tone was smooth and direct. "Here." She rummaged through the sack at her hip and handed them each a brown doll-size robe and a miniature pair of shoes. "Hold these tight in your hand. They should still be there once you've Modified."

Joe sat next to his brother and closed his eyes. Within a minute or two, he disappeared. His clothes fell to the ground, and after a bit of rustling he emerged wearing the full-length robe.

Chris looked at his miniature brother with a mix of shock and competitive disappointment. Chris then closed his own eyes and tried to focus but couldn't tame his unruly thoughts. He saw his wife's frightened eyes. He imagined her blood pooled on the floor of their bedroom and the fat beast with the tattoo wiping his blade. Then he heard the commanding voice of the vengeful fairy. Next, he heard actual footsteps, quick in pace. He opened his eyes and saw a guard pass by, glance in, and run off even faster than he'd approached.

"You must focus. He'll return soon, and more will follow," the cloaked fairy said.

"Try to picture yourself wearing the little robe," Joe added. "That's what worked for me."

Chris rubbed his temples and shut out, as best he could, the strange world around him. *Wearing the clothes . . . small man . . . large cavern. Small man. Small clothes. Fitting between the bars. Freedom!*

Certain he'd failed again, he opened his eyes. He could only see darkness and realized he was underneath his sweatshirt. Unlike in science fiction movies, where changing size or shape was often a drawn-out process accompanied by music or sound or lights, he had sensed nothing; the change had just happened from one instant to the next. His small hands were shaking, but he managed to get the robe over his head and his arms in the tight holes. Then, with some hopping, he slipped his shoes on and maneuvered himself out of the pile.

As soon as Chris emerged, the cloaked fairy waved him onward and began to run. Joe stumbled along beside her.

Chris noticed both of their backs as they ran—no wings. He sprinted to catch them and checked over his own shoulder while he ran. He didn't have any either. Without the wings he'd expected, he felt even more vulnerable than before. They might be able to slip out of their cage if they were quick about it and they could play a better game of hide and seek, but beyond that what could they do?

The cloaked fairy arrived at the bars first and paused there. She looked down the cave's corridor in both directions. "Follow me," she whispered. She crossed to the other side of the tunnel, leading the way through a maze of pebbles that to Chris were now the size of boulders, and the three of them ducked into a dark crevice. Chris was the last to get out of sight, and just in time. He glanced over his shoulder and saw guards the size of giants streaming past and a fleet of flying fairies overhead.

Their mysterious savior returned with a rope in hand. Chris followed the rope up the escarpment with his eyes until it was out of sight.

"Got a name, Princess?" Joe asked.

"Cassiopeia. Please, call me Cassie." She gave Joe a slight smile, but when she glanced at Chris her face returned to neutral.

"Do you think we can trust her?" Chris whispered to his brother.

He had a better view of the fairy now that he was her size. Or, actually, he wasn't precisely her size. She was petite, even by fairy standards it seemed, and small-boned, just as the black-winged fairy had been.

"I don't think we have a choice," Joe said, making his voice loud enough for Cassie to hear too. He winked at her when she glanced over.

Chris wanted to smack some sense into him. *A pretty girl shows up, and three minutes later Joe is flirting with her. Typical.* But at least she seemed to have some good sense; she was too busy rummaging through her sack to pay Joe's efforts much mind.

Cassie pulled out a knife, clasped the backside of the blade, and offered Chris the handle. "Here. The last one in line should cut the rope."

Chris took it from her and examined the blade. It was a little rusty but large enough to do some damage if necessary. And Chris was good with knives. It was his weapon of choice in close quarters.

He didn't have a pocket, and the belt along his waist was only made of fabric, so he went over to the pile of excess rope on the ground and cut himself a strip. "What difference does it make if some fairies have wings?"

Chris asked as he tied the knife to his lower leg. "Won't they be able to follow us?

"The ones with wings won't be able to fit through some of the cave's tight spaces. They'd have to climb behind us and the rope will be gone before that happens."

"But how come—" Joe began.

"I'm sure you have plenty of questions," Cassie said, "but now we must go. I promise I will answer them later."

She started climbing at a speed that seemed impossible and quickly disappeared behind a veil of darkness.

Joe wasn't nearly as nimble as she was, and Chris was stuck behind him. There was more stopping than going, and they didn't have much help from the smooth rock face.

At last, there was a foothold. Joe was the first to take advantage of it. Chris cut off the excess rope while he waited and watched it drop out of sight. Then a pebble hit the back of his head.

"Watch it, Joe!"

He looked back up and saw Joe sliding down the rope. And then they collided.

Chris put a quick loop of rope around his raw wrist. The pain was almost unbearable, but their sliding did slow to a stop. After waiting, though, for too long, Chris's strength started to wane and the pain became too much. He was dangling off the end of the rope and Joe's weight was not lifting from his hands. And he had nowhere left to slide.

"I can't hold you much longer!" Chris warned.

"My hands. They keep slipping."

Cassie then came sliding down with ease and control. "Here, try this." She smoothed a handful of grit on the rope above Joe's hands. "We're almost to the top," she added, "and then there will be more hiking and less climbing."

The grit helped tremendously and it wasn't long before Cassie was offering them both a hand over the cliff. She then sat down, crossed her legs, and dug through her sack. She took out a pouch of matches and the pieces of a lantern that she put together and soon had glowing.

"It looks like springing us wasn't exactly spontaneous," Joe said, sitting down beside her.

"No, not exactly." Cassie rose to her feet. "There have been rumors regarding your arrival for weeks. Are you two ready? We must hurry so I can lead you into Pyxis unnoticed."

Chris and Joe exchanged glances. "Pyxis?" Joe finally asked.

"It's our city, hidden from the human world. We should be there soon. As I promised, I'll explain everything when we get there."

"I'm already detecting a pattern. Pyxis? Cassiopeia? Aren't those both constellations?"

"And you've met another—Andromeda—though I suppose you were not formally introduced. She's the queen and, by blood, my mother," Cassie explained.

"You can't be serious!" Joe said. "I thought I was joking about the whole princess thing."

"Don't worry. Let's just say my mother and I are not close." Cassie threw her sack over her shoulder and started walking.

"But . . . wait up. . . ," Joe pleaded as he scrambled to his feet.

Instead of following his brother and the fairy right away, Chris walked back over to the escarpment they had just conquered. The surge of hope he'd felt earlier had subsided. Now he looked down and wondered if a successful escape was what he'd truly wanted.

He spread his fingers on his left hand. Even though he was a fraction of his original size, there was still an indentation, smoother and paler than the rest of his hand, where his wedding ring had been. With the ring on the floor of the cage and the finger likely to return to normal in a few days, any solid evidence that he had ever been married would vanish. No, that wasn't true— his and Alana's children were alive, and he now had to find them. Chris turned away from the ledge with a new sense of purpose.

He caught up to Joe and Cassie, and focused on the hike. Soon he spotted what had to be a fairy city—Pyxis—through a clearing between two boulders. It reminded him of a Dr. Seuss Christmas. Everything was curvy, pointy, or slanted. Not a single building seemed to include a right angle. Even more curious were the little doors and windows swirling around the cave's stalactites and stalagmites. They were a pearly, off-white color tinged with orange in the city's abundance of firelight.

At his new size Chris wasn't a good judge of dimension, but the city seemed to be in a crevice that was no more than a couple of feet high, though higher in a few places and lower in others. Its width and length, however, were much more expansive. From where he stood, he could not see the outer limits.

When he stepped forward, ready to move on, an ominous multistoried castle came into view. It was by far the most prominent structure in the city. Though it was built in the same unique style as the other dwellings, it didn't remind him of Christmas. It took his breath away, and not in a good sense.

"The Aerial Palace," Cassie told him. "That's the place we're trying to avoid."

Yeah, no kidding.

"Its beauty is legendary, but so are its dark secrets," she continued. "We'll be staying somewhere much more humble."

"And that humble place—that's where my kids are?" Chris asked.

"Yes, the inn where I live. They flew in with Carina, a friend of mine. By this time, they should have arrived."

She blew out her lantern and then led them through a narrow passageway that soon resembled a crooked fairy lane.

CHAPTER 5
Aurora Borealis

At the end of a street called Boreas Lane, they turned onto South Main Street, a wider cobblestone road lit with oil lamps on posts. Cassie paused in front of a three-story building. A wooden sign above the main entrance said AURORA BOREALIS in dull gold letters. Through the small square windowpanes, Chris caught a glimpse of ordinary life in Pyxis.

The first floor of the inn included a tavern. The solemn glow of the fireplace and the torches didn't seem to subdue the mood. The crowd was diverse and lively. The sounds of laughter, song, strong opinions, and movement reached him as a hum of indistinguishable noise.

Establishments like this existed across the globe in the human world. The patrons, however, were a new sight to him entirely. It wasn't so much their fairy clothing—layers of billowy fabric as well as vests, belts, scabbards, and pointed felt hats—as it was their wings that fascinated Chris. They varied from white to black and every shade of gray in between, and they also varied in size, shape, symmetry, and strength. Some fairies could barely hover off the ground, while others, such as the servers, could hold trays of refreshments and buzz across the room in the blink of an eye.

Other fairies remained on the ground, with their wings draped like shimmery fabric down their backs, and still others stayed grounded for lack of wings.

Since Morgan and Ryan had, according to Joe, sprouted wings—something he would have to see to believe—Chris couldn't help but wonder if and when he too would get wings.

Cassie peered in the inn's window and then tugged on the handle of the front door. For some reason, though, she let it drop and led them to an alley on the left side of the building. In near darkness, they stepped over rubbish and a sleeping fairy before they reached a side door. Cassie opened it with a simple key, and they followed her inside.

They climbed a rickety spiral staircase to a hallway on the third floor. She led them past a series of portraits on the walls. The candlelight eerily accentuated the solemn faces in the old paintings, and the uneven floorboards announced their presence by creaks and groans.

Doors kept clicking open and then clapping shut. Chris could feel multiple eyes following their movement. Even the eyes in the portraits appeared to follow in their direction. He was more than ready to get out of the hall when Cassie unlocked a door on the right labeled 13 SOUTHWEST.

The room contained a bed, a fireplace with embers glowing, and a crooked end table stacked neatly with books. A hand-carved bureau stood between the entry door and another doorway that led to an unlit room.

While Joe gazed around, Chris squatted beside the bed, where two small figures lay amid soft blankets. He recognized the sound of his children's breathing, but lowered the blankets from Ryan's and Morgan's faces to make sure they were unharmed. They were dressed in fairy clothing and curled around each other, and their newly sprouted wings didn't seem to be interfering. They looked healthy and peaceful.

"I'll give you a few moments to settle in," Cassie whispered. "There is a washroom over there and clean clothes for you piled on the chair. I'll be in the room directly across the hall for a few minutes. Then, if you feel so inclined, we can get something to eat downstairs." She grabbed some of her own clothes to change into and left the room.

"Can you believe this place? It feels like we might run into a fairy William Shakespeare!" Joe proclaimed. "Though it's not exactly the luxury you would expect a princess to live in."

Chris had to agree. The inn had an old-world feel to it, and Cassie's room was neat and organized but small and unornamented except for one seascape on the wall. Although he had probably seen similar paintings a thousand times in his life without ever giving them a thought, this one caught his eye, though for some flaw in it rather than for any beauty. The setting sun appeared too vibrant, and the ocean underneath it seemed too stagnant. It was as if the painter had never felt the warmth of the sun or experienced the power and magnificence of the ocean.

He checked the bottom right corner of the painting. The last four letters of the flowery script all looked like lowercase *e*'s, but he deciphered the name to be Labelle.

Chris then turned his gaze from the signature and grabbed the clothes off the chair. They unfolded in his hands as he lifted them. With all of its strings and pleats, the white shirt seemed more appropriate for a female fairy than for him, but at least it looked spacious enough. He couldn't say the same for the pants. He tried to swap the gray animal-hide trousers with the other pair on the chair, since Joe was shorter and smaller than he was, but they looked equally small. He shrugged, grabbed a candle, and headed to the washroom with the fairyland attire in his grip.

Inside, there was a primitive toilet and a basin full of icy water. He first washed the dirt and blood from his face and hands. The cold water jarred him initially but soon felt good on his cuts and bruises. He didn't need the chest-high mirror to confirm that his face was one swollen, amorphous mass. After the guards' beatings, he didn't even think he would recognize himself.

Joe was browsing through Cassie's pile of books when Chris came out of the washroom. He barely muffled his laugh. "Nice pants."

"Oh, yeah? Let's see how you look in them," Chris shot back as he tugged at the coarse fabric on the side of his neck. He then draped the heavy robe he no longer needed over the back of the chair.

Joe grabbed the other set of clothes and strolled to the washroom. "Well, they can't be a bigger fashion don't than the Jesus robes."

Just as Joe disappeared, Cassie tapped on the door and came back into the room. She carried with her a bottle of clear liquid and some gauzy white cloth. "I brought this for your wrist." She came over to him and reached for his hand.

Chris pulled his arm up and away. "It's fine."

"Don't be silly." She stood on her tiptoes and gently took his hand into hers. He didn't resist a second time.

She moistened one of the strips of cloth with the liquid in the bottle. "This is going to hurt."

Chris tried to hold still. It did sting, though, and he couldn't hold back a flinch.

"Sorry," she uttered with a grimace.

"Don't be. And since we're getting apologies out of the way, I'm sorry for the way I acted earlier."

She glanced up at him and gave him a tentative grin. "Don't be." Her eyes quickly dropped and she resumed her work.

"And thanks . . . for everything."

"You are very welcome. I would do it again in the flutter of a fairy's wing. There. All set."

She tied the last bow of his bandage and walked toward the end table. When she set the bottle down, her shaky hands almost knocked it over. She grabbed for it with both hands to stabilize it.

"Can I ask you something?" Chris said while she was fumbling around on her table.

Cassie spun back around and gave him her full, wide-eyed attention and an encouraging nod.

"How did you know I wouldn't kill you?" Chris asked. "It would have been easy, like snapping a twig with my human-sized thumb."

"Because I didn't feel afraid."

It was a strange answer, and judging by her behavior, he wasn't sure it was true. Her eyes lowered and narrowed, and her head shuddered as if she regretted her answer. The entire process made her seem like a skittish child. Because of her size and the layers of clothing that made her look like an orphan, he may have even believed she was a child, but her eyes suggested otherwise. They were innocent but intelligent and somehow darkly seasoned.

She turned her back and fiddled with the objects on her table again, but she shrugged in a way that suggested she knew he was watching her. He knew he was making her nervous, and why wouldn't she be? Even if she had forgiven him for threatening to kill her, he remained a hostile presence.

Chris looked to the washroom door, wondering why Joe was taking so long. Joe did have his uses. He knew how to puncture an oppressive silence and make it seem as if nothing was wrong in the first place.

When Joe finally strolled out, he took a spot by Chris's side. He made a ta-da gesture with his hands to model the new clothes. In a way the outfit worked for him, fashionable almost; he would blend right in. Chris, for his own part, felt like a jock in a ballerina costume.

"So you said there's food in this place?" Joe asked.

Cassie nodded. "Shall we?" she asked, and then headed toward the door.

Joe and Chris exchanged looks.

"You two go." Chris gazed at the bed. "I'm not comfortable leaving them alone."

"Carina was watching them before we arrived. If you want, I could get her or someone else I trust to stay with them," Cassie suggested.

Chris thought for a second. He would have preferred to stay with his sleeping children and relax in peace and quiet, but he also needed to know what was going on in this place called Pyxis. Sleep, regardless of his choice, was out of the question. "Would they stay right here?"

"That can be arranged, I think. I'll check." Cassie left the room and came back moments later with a blond, green-eyed fairy. "This is Carina. Her family owns this inn. She followed me to your cell against the wishes of her sister, Vela," Cassie added while tossing a scolding smile in her young friend's direction. "I hope Vela's not too upset with you . . . with us." Cassie looked back to Joe and Chris. "It was fortunate Carina did follow me. She flew in with the children while I was waiting for an opportunity to approach the two of you."

"It's so nice to finally meet you," Carina said. "And welcome. It's an honor to have you here."

Chris and Joe's glances crossed at the use of the word "honor," but they said nothing, thanked Carina for her assistance, and then followed Cassie downstairs.

The tavern was still bustling, and Cassie guided them to a table in a dark corner. Regardless of her efforts, their entry attracted attention. Fairies stopped talking to their neighbors. They rested their forks and full drinks on the table with loud, echoing clunks.

Chris selected a chair across from his brother, and they both slouched in their seats. Cassie was the only one who seemed at ease. She stood by the end of the table and waved to a redheaded fairy drying dishes at the bar. The fairy, when she noticed, zipped over and they embraced like old friends meeting by chance after a long separation.

"See, I told you I'd be back in no time," Cassie said to her. "Christopher, Joseph, this is Vela. She keeps me out of trouble."

"I try to anyway," Vela said. "I'm glad all of you made it here in one piece, especially you, Miss Cassiopeia." She leaned toward Chris and Joe. "She thinks she can take on our world's treachery singlehandedly."

"It wasn't singlehandedly," Cassie objected. "I followed a truly inspired plan put together by exemplary individuals, and everything fell into place."

"Inspired? You do realize, my dear, whom you sound like. You have obviously been spending too much time with Pierre," Vela said with her hands on her hips.

"Is that a bad thing?"

Vela contorted her lips to the side as her answer. She didn't seem the type to hold back, ever, but in this rare case she let the matter rest. "You must be famished," she said instead. "I'll get the boys in the back to whip you up something special. My treat."

"All right, Princess," Joe said as soon as Vela flew away. "I can't take it anymore. Why are we here? And, by the way, why is everyone in this establishment staring at us?"

"Well," Cassie said as she took a seat in the chair next to Chris, "those questions are related. People are staring at you because of who you are and what you represent."

"And what do we represent exactly?" Joe pressed.

"You represent the hope that Pyxis will be free from tyranny someday."

"That's a bit heady. And I'm guessing this has something to do with our father, since the angry queen bee wants to find him so badly."

"Precisely. Rigel challenged my family, the Sauvageaus, the rulers of Pyxis. Not only that, he crippled them, and unlike anyone else who ever posed a challenge to my family's sovereign rule, he made it out alive."

"Rigel?" Joe asked.

"Yes. You know your father, of course, as a human named Scott MacRae, but he is a Modifier, and among the fairies he is known by the star name Rigel," Cassie said, pausing for a moment to let her words sink in. "Both of you have four black dots at the back of your neck in the shape of a diamond. That is your fairy mark, and it signifies that you are of your father's kind."

Chris slumped down farther in his chair and crossed his arms. "Couldn't this Rigel character be someone else besides our father—a distant cousin or something?" he said, and then his eyes darted to the front door as it opened. Accompanied by the ring of a bell, two brash-looking redheaded male fairies entered.

Cassie glanced too but didn't seem concerned. "That is unlikely. Before he entered the human world and became your father, Rigel was his city's only survivor. He gave himself the human name MacRae as a sort of reminder; the name, from an old Scottish clan, means 'son of grace.' "

"So our father was, uh, involved with the queen a long time ago. Does that mean he's some kind of royalty too?" Joe asked.

"Yes, he was a prince of Polaris, a Modifier city that was too large and powerful for Pyxis to tolerate. But, to avoid a war, the two cities signed a treaty, and an arranged marriage completed the agreement. I am confident that by now you can guess who the bride and groom were."

"Andromeda and our father. Wow. But clearly it wasn't a match made in heaven." Joe leaned forward, put his elbows on the table, clearly intrigued.

Chris, however, remained silent. Although he'd been fascinated by the fairies and their manifold wings, he remained suspicious of this subterranean world. Moreover, he had long harbored anger at his father, and the revelation that his father's actions had been the catalyst for the upending of Chris's entire life in the space of less than a day was turning that anger into something closer to hate.

Chris stayed in this dark place even after Vela fluttered over with a tray of food and mugs of ale. Joe and Cassie devoured the meat with gravy, the sweet berry preserves, and the toasted bread while Chris merely picked. The anger inside him was occupying the space meant for nourishment.

After she'd had enough to eat, Cassie sipped her ale and dabbed her face with a cloth napkin. "Would you like to hear more?"

"Definitely," Joe replied. "This story was starting to get interesting. You left off at the part where our father married your mother."

"After their wedding, the stories say, the Pyxis princess Andromeda and the Polaris prince Rigel were fiercely yet fleetingly passionate. That passion, however, did not mature into fondness."

Joe laughed and simultaneously winced. "That's a diplomatic way of putting it."

After an awkward pause Cassie continued. "Before long, all that heat and fire turned deadly. Your father found out about a plan to eliminate Polaris from the fairy world, despite the treaty, and he confronted Andromeda about it. In the battle that ensued, he gave my mother the scars on her face and killed her beloved father, the king. He then fled the Aerial Palace, but he didn't leave empty-handed. He stole something, but only he and Andromeda know what it was. Was it a sacred or magical artifact? Something valuable or merely sentimental? I'm not certain. Finding both him and it, though, was an undertaking worthy of grand armies and large fortunes. Andromeda looked everywhere for many years, but your father had changed his size and his name and had assimilated into the human world, an advantage of your kind."

"Our kind?" Joe asked. "Are we different from your kind? How many kinds of fairies are there?"

"There are the Modifiers, like you. Many have settled in Pyxis, though most not by choice. Overall, they are not in the majority, but they are common in the southern part of the city, I'd say up to one in ten. Now, I am obviously bound to the ground too, so I mean no disrespect when I tell you that Modifiers are sometimes referred to as Bottom-Dwellers. It's not a phrase we fairies use in polite conversation, but I wanted to inform you, in case you hear it.

"As you can see around you, most fairies are Royals, meaning they have wings. They have the advantage of flight, but can never become the size of a human. Then there are the Constants—fairies like me. Though my mother is a Royal, I am not; I can neither fly nor change form.

"Finally, there are your children, Chris. They can do both. Before today, Royal Modifiers existed only in legend. They have been much sought after, though never found. The Royals may scoff at your size-changing capabilities, yet they are really quite envious. Any fairy capable of both flight and modification would be of particular interest to my mother. . . ."

Chris's chair ground across the stone floor as he stood. "If she plans on hunting down my children . . . No offense—this has been real fun and all— but we need to leave Pyxis and find a safer place."

Cassie stood too and clasped his arm. "Chris, I understand your concern. Unfortunately, there is no easy way out. This cave is neatly tucked away in the boreal forest in Nord-du-Québec, the northernmost section of Canada's Quebec province. The nearest road is, in human terms, nearly a kilometer away, and the nearest town much farther. This region is nearly uninhabited. And, I'm sure you are aware, it is December. You don't have the appropriate clothing or transportation—"

He cut her off by lifting his hand. "Canada? How did we even get here? Did those gray-coated bastards drag us through the snow for hundreds of miles? I doubt it. So if they got us in, there has to be a way out."

"Unfortunately, as I explained, I do not have the power of a Modifier, and I am not sure how my mother's Gray Coats were able to bring you here from such different parts of the human world. I do know that there has to be a way, but we will need time to find it."

"Chris, she's right," Joe said. "We need some rest and a feasible plan before we do anything rash. Please sit. We'll come up with something."

Chris collapsed back in his chair. Unconsciously needing some reassurance, he reached for his wedding ring. He became even more infuriated when reminded once again of its absence. "And by the way, about sixty shady characters are staring at us. How many minutes will it take before *they* swarm this place?"

"There will always be some danger," Cassie admitted as she eased back into her chair. "I hope I can assure you that Andromeda's Crown Champions and Gray Coats rarely fraternize in the South End. They consider it below their status."

Chris leaned back and crossed his arms. "Not convinced, but whatever."

He needed her to instill him with confidence. But the return of the childlike fear in her eyes had the opposite effect on him. They were still in danger and ill-prepared to deal with it.

Soon a lanky, wingless fairy with a five o'clock shadow interrupted their silence. "Cassiopeia, *mon petit ange*! It is so nice to see you again," he crooned with a melodic and flirtatious French accent.

Cassie rose from her seat to greet him. He gave her a kiss on each cheek, and his hand remained on her back a little longer than necessary. Even without an introduction, Chris had already guessed he was Pierre, the source of Vela's unspoken qualms.

"Can I join you for an ale?" the fairy asked, holding up the mug he already had in hand.

Cassie gestured to the empty chair next to Joe. "Certainly. Chris, Joe, this is Pierre Delacroix. He is originally from Quebec City and, like you, had a human childhood. Pierre, these are the brothers Christopher and Joseph MacRae."

"Of course, of course!" Pierre said with phony surprise. "I've heard so much about you! How does it feel to be the sons of the revolution?" He pulled the chair closer and slid into it with snake-like fluidity.

Joe squinted one eye and emitted a quick chuckle. "Are we?"

"Absolutely! Your presence here will inspire those who find tyranny inexcusable. My readers will be just as excited as I am."

"Pierre is the editor of *The Pyxis Discourse*," Cassie informed them. "It's a publication dedicated to bringing democracy to Pyxis."

"And this right here is our secret weapon." Pierre placed his hand on Cassie's back again. His sway and goofy smile made it clear that the ale he'd brought to the table was not his first of the evening. "She has given us vital information about the Aerial Palace's layout and routines. And now you two might be what we need to bring real change to Pyxis. Your father would be the last missing piece. He is a born leader and an inspiration to us all! If you want to bring Andromeda to justice, you may want to find him."

"We don't know where to look," Joe admitted.

"If I were you, I would retrace my steps," Pierre suggested. "A fairy of Rigel's status never goes anywhere without a purpose. Think of places you have been and people you have known."

"And, because of the children, Andromeda will also want to find other people related to you. They are all in danger," Cassie added.

"There are children? What am I missing? What's wrong with them?" Pierre asked.

Cassie and Joe exchanged wary looks. Then they both looked to Chris, as if seeking his permission.

"Well?" Pierre persisted.

Joe gave Chris an apologetic shrug. "They can fly."

"Why was I not immediately informed?" cried the fairy. "This is bigger than big!"

"Not big enough to be in your little newspaper. Right, Pierre?" Chris made sure to ask.

"No, no, certainly not!" Pierre puffed in defense. "I always do what is best for Pyxis, even if it means personal sacrifice!"

When Pierre looked away, Chris shot his eyes to heaven. Going by his first impression, Chris believed Pierre to be about as trustworthy as a leprechaun next to an unattended pot of gold. With his ridiculous green hat, he even looked like a leprechaun. Well, not really, but he certainly didn't look like Robin Hood.

"I wonder how they inherited the wings," Joe said with a twinkle in his eye. "Maybe our mother was a fairy too. Unfortunately, she died back in March, so we can't ask her about it. Chris, don't we have an aunt in Connecticut? Do you think she would know anything? But I wonder if wings are considered a dominant or a recessive trait—"

Chris kicked his brother under the table, a little too hard.

"Ow! What was that for?"

"Do I really need to tell you?"

"No worries. Your secrets are safe with me, my friends," Pierre assured the brothers, though unconvincingly. "Joe, you seem to know something about heredity. Did you have an opportunity to study the natural sciences?"

"Well, I was almost a medical doctor, but that didn't work out. I currently write screenplays for the movies. Or at least I did before I was beaten, drugged, and brought to this lovely place."

"You write for the American movies? I used to watch them as a boy. . . ."

The conversation turned trivial and Chris stopped listening. He zoned out further when the bell on the door rang again. A wingless fairy with a shaved head and shifty eyes entered the tavern. Their casual glances locked briefly, and though the fairy's eyes moved on, Chris detected a glimmer of recognition in his face.

"And Chris was in the military," Joe was saying. "Right, Chris?"

"What? Sorry, um, yeah. The army."

Something caught his eye just then and sent his blood coursing through his veins like hot lava, ready to burst through rock. The shifty-eyed fairy lifted his mug to his jowl with a set of fat, tattooed knuckles. Chris had seen those tattoos, back in the early dawn of that long day, gripping the sword being held to his wife's neck!

The fairy thumped his mug on the table and threw some money down. He gave Chris one last sly glance and then strutted out of his seat. The door slammed on his way out and the ringing bell set Chris in motion.

***

"Chris? Are you all right?"

Cassie's words were lost, unheard, wasted. Chris was out of his seat an instant later.

He snatched a sword out of an unsuspecting fairy's scabbard. The clang made everyone's spine tighten. There was an unavoidable wave of turning heads; all eyes followed him. Gasps and whispers accompanied each of his steps. After Chris nearly tore the door from its hinges, the eyes turned to the table where he had been sitting.

"Oh, God!" Joe was already out of his chair and edging his way around the table. "This has 'not good' written all over it!"

Cassie rose too and stumbled along at his heel. "What happened? He just exploded!"

"That's Chris," Joe said flatly. "Get used to it. My guess is he saw something he didn't like. We need to find him before he does something stupid."

Cassie and Joe wove their way out of the tavern and stopped in the middle of South Main Street. There were fairies strolling or fluttering by along the lamp-lit cobblestones and a few mouse-drawn carts moving past, but there was no sign of Chris.

Joe ambled to the nearest crossroad with Cassie close behind. When they paused to check both ways, Joe began explaining to Cassie what likely had happened during Chris's abduction. Pierre joined them and stepped into the lead with his torch. He was just in time to hear a plot-thickening twist to their already newsworthy story.

"He didn't elaborate, but apparently they may have killed his wife," Joe was saying.

"That's horrible!" Cassie said. "I wish I had known. I would have—"

"There's nothing you could have done differently."

"Perhaps," she said. "But you should know that when I came to the cage today, I expected to find only the MacRae brothers. The children were a surprise. And I did not stop to ask what might have happened to their mother. Out of respect for Chris's worry, I should have kept you all safe in my room this evening."

Assuming Chris was chasing one of his captors and was fortunate enough to survive, then Cassie would consider the episode a lesson learned. Andromeda's scouts were already in place. Also, and even more frightening, Andromeda's Gray Coats had cast a heavy footprint in the human world. This could only mean the queen's quest for revenge had overshadowed her standard protocol for secrecy. The implications were profound; Andromeda was capable of anything.

They continued to check down alleys and around street corners until they reached the outer edges of Pyxis. They approached the last streetlamp on South Main Street; the narrow path ahead was too dark and too slippery for safe travel.

Then, as they were considering how to proceed, a shadowy struggle in the rock-crevice alleyway to their left brought them to attention. It was a battle of strength. There was a hand on a throat and an immobilized sword shaking in the air. After a knee hit a groin, the sword broke free and its tip went in and through. There was a winner and a loser. The loser had a sword jutting through his neck, just below the chin, and slumped to the ground.

With little regard for her own safety, Cassie sprinted over and ignored the calls of caution from Pierre and Joe. Though relieved to find Chris the victor, she realized that he was near collapse. Shaking all over, he put his hands to his face. At that moment his opponent twitched, still dangling on the edge of life. Chris pulled himself out of his fit and lunged for him.

Joe arrived in time to restrain him. "Come on, Chris. Let it go. It's over."

Cassie knelt by the dying fairy and looked at the tattoo on his hand. "Chris was right. This fairy meant to do us harm. His hand carries the sigil from the Pyxis coat of arms, the Crown Star. He's a Gray Coat, a Modifier who serves as one of the queen's mercenaries."

Pierre knelt down and nodded in agreement. "Your brother is lucky to still be with us," he said looking up at Joe. "These killers are well trained and accordingly ruthless."

Chris finally stopped squirming and began to walk with Joe's guidance.

"We need to get him out of here," Joe said as they passed. "He's been through enough for one day."

Cassie nodded and handed him her key to the Aurora Borealis. "I'll be right behind you."

With Pierre, she witnessed the Gray Coat's last breath. She made sure his pulse had stopped before she removed his belongings, including his swords and vest. And then she stood and fought back tears.

Pierre cocked his head and gave her a pout, as if she were an injured child. "Do you need assistance, *mon petit ange?*"

"I need more than assistance."

She knew it was only a matter of time before the other Gray Coats realized what had happened. The queen's entire army would be in the area looking for them soon enough. And she didn't know where to go, what to do, whom to turn to.

Because of her thoughts, her fears, and regrets, she didn't see Pierre draw near until his hand brushed her cheek. Her flinch was too intrinsic to control, and it was costly. Once she recovered from her brief blip of terror, she watched his eyes go cold.

"Well, I would suggest you remain at the Aurora Borealis for now," he stated. "We will try to schedule an emergency meeting on the morrow to see what the committee has to say." Then he left her there alone and contemplating the meaning of his words. "You're on your own, my little angel."

While waiting longer than expected, Joe dozed off sitting against Cassie's bed. His sluggish eyes reopened when the door rattled. He was fighting an exhaustion he had never felt before and knew by the way Cassie entered the room that he would have to continue the fight.

A whirlwind of nerves, the fairy princess paced back and forth over the same creaky floorboard, electrifying the room with her tension. It was enough to make Joe's ears ring.

She suddenly stopped, glanced at Joe and the children, and calmed herself enough to speak in a voice that would not wake them. "Where is he?"

Joe bobbed his head toward the washroom.

Two fast paces later, her ear was against the door. "Chris?" She tapped the wood with just her fingernail and then listened again. "Why won't he answer?" she whispered to Joe.

"I'm not sure. I've never seen him like this before."

She had missed the worst of it too. After the lock had clicked, Chris's stumbling seemed to break everything in his wake, and he had proceeded to expel every drop of nourishment from his body. It was turning out to be a great night—or day or whatever it was. It was hard to tell the difference in Pyxis.

Cassie finally relaxed, just a touch, and settled in the chair by her bedside table. "Do you know that plan you mentioned before? Now is the time. We need to set something in motion before the Gray Coats report to the Royal Air Brigade."

Joe leaned his head back against the bed. "All right. What are we up against?"

Cassie took in a deep sigh and released it slowly. "They will hunt us down. We cannot stay in Pyxis; we must leave the city immediately. I know of only three passages that allow exit from Pyxis in the winter. You already know about one way—the way we entered, through the caves. We could try going back that way and exiting through the Gray Coat barracks, but they will be on high alert there, and I do not recommend it.

"Second is the main gate, for Royal fairies, but it is heavily guarded. Unfortunately, you need wings and proper identification to pass through without question. Anyone deemed Unworthy has been placed on the Extermination List and will not be allowed to exit."

Joe nearly choked on his own tongue. "Extermination List! This is no joke. If we get caught, we're done, aren't we?"

Averting her gaze to the floor couldn't hide the morbid truth that passed over her face like a shadow. She chose not to address Joe's question but instead picked up where she'd left off. "There is also one exit via the Aerial Palace. It is at the back of the dungeon. The gate is always locked, and is—"

"Let me guess . . . heavily guarded?"

Cassie didn't answer, but she didn't have to. Joe was catching on that her nonanswers were as good as confirmations.

"And another thing," Joe said, trying not to think about things that were heavily guarded, "once we do manage to exit this cave, what do we do then? Where in Canada did you say we were?"

"The closest human town is Chibougamau," she replied.

"I've never even heard of it."

"It has more than seven thousand inhabitants. But the average high temperature at this time of year is negative ten degrees Fahrenheit. With two small children, no clothing, no gear . . ."

"Are we at least near Quebec?"

"Quebec City is over five hundred kilometers south of us."

Joe closed his eyes and started rubbing them. His intent was to clear his vision, but when he removed his fingers, there was more grit and grime in his eyes than before.

"What are you thinking?" Cassie asked.

He dropped his hands and looked up at her. Only her eyes seemed to pierce through the blurry film shrouding his vision. "The words coming to mind are not appropriate for your presence. To paraphrase, we are . . . completely out of luck."

"At least we have these." She dangled a set of keys in her hand. "They have to be good for something."

Joe blinked a few times and restored his vision to that less-than-perfect place that was normal for him without his glasses. "What are those?"

"They're the Gray Coat's. I also took his weapons."

She rummaged through the sack at her feet. Joe peeked inside with her and nodded at the sight of the two short swords and the vest of smaller weapons—knives and daggers. Everything looked sharp and efficient. "Why didn't I think of that? Do you think all this will help us?"

"The keys could make the palace option more plausible. If we could get inside, we might be able to distract the guards, or sneak past them. The plan is almost too audacious for us to consider, but that's why it might work."

"Do you know your way around well enough to get in and out without being discovered?"

"I did live there for sixteen years. Now, what would be the best way to get in?" she asked herself aloud.

Joe let her think for a while. "What did you come up with?"

"I know there are some obsolete wooden conduits that used to deposit wastewater into the West River. I used to play near them as a child. As far as I'm aware, they haven't been blocked off yet."

"That doesn't sound particularly pleasant. Still, it's the best idea I've heard so far."

As the last of his words were said, the washroom door swung open. Chris walked out—no explanation, no apology—as if he had been simply using the washroom all along, and not having a mental and physical meltdown.

For Cassie, Chris's emergence seemed to signify the end of planning and the start of implementation. She darted to her bureau, giving Chris no opportunity to feel ill at ease. And like coconspirators, he held the sack for her as she packed, and neither of them made a single comment about what had happened in the alley.

Joe just stared at Chris and grew irritable when Chris neglected to acknowledge the stare. So Joe grabbed the nearest thing on Cassie's nightstand and chucked it at his brother.

The newspaper hit Chris in the back of his head. "Ow! Do you really need to throw things at me?" Chris whirled around while rubbing the tender spot on his head.

"What on earth were you thinking?" Joe said as patronizingly as possible. "You could have been killed! If you haven't noticed, you have two kids counting on you to . . . I don't know . . . stay alive! If you pull this kamikaze shit again, Chris, so help me God, I will—"

Joe cut himself off when he noticed the newspaper's title. "*The Pyxis Discourse*," he announced with false reverence as he picked it up off the floor.

He took a moment to study the cover image. A possessed-looking fairy had a black spider over her lips. Then he flipped the paper open. " 'Black Widow Whets Fangs on Rigel the Magnificent's Unsuspecting Sons,' page three, by Pierre Delacroix," Joe read to them. He turned the page to their story. "Your mother has a charming nickname," he said when Cassie glanced over.

"And it is well deserved," she said. "She has a knack for killing husbands."

Joe skimmed the article and chuckled. "Oh, this is rich. It gets even better. 'Citizens of Pyxis, the fate of the brave and the strong is in your hands. Will we do what we must to prevent the torture and torment of these innocent victims?' " Joe stood up and pretended to be giving an inspirational speech. " 'The time of complacency and self-preservation is over! If we fail to act, then democracy is as good as dead. . . .' A little over the top, don't you think? You can practically read it to the tune of 'La Marseillaise'—*dun dun dun DUN dun dun dun DUUUNN dun dun*," Joe sang with corresponding hand gestures that an orchestral conductor might use.

"Pierre means well," Cassie muttered with a shrug. "He's the reason you are here. Without that article, you would still be in the queen's hands."

"I'm sure your boyfriend does mean well, but. . ."

He paused and looked into her face to gauge her reaction and saw exactly what he had hoped for—indignation.

"I never said . . . He's not my . . . Oh!" she nearly shouted.

Joe raised his eyes and his hands to heaven and mouthed "Thank you." Then he gave her a wink. "Well, someone should tell him that. And then maybe he'll keep his greasy paws to himself. Wait. Did I just say that out loud?"

He was attempting to make her laugh to ease the moment, but she didn't even crack a smile. And while she stared at him, blankly, as if he were speaking gibberish, one of Chris's eyes fluttered, the classic expression of his annoyance.

"C'mon, Joe. Quit clowning around. Let's get some sleep. Then, in a few hours, we'll wake the kids and get the hell out of this death trap."

"You think this is a death trap? Wait until you hear our plan," Joe said lightly.

"Joe, I'll leave it to you to give Chris the details," Cassie said. She outlined sleeping arrangements and a plan for gathering more supplies, then excused herself from the room.

Joe summarized the escape plan for Chris and updated him on the other, less feasible options as well.

"So that's the best you've got?" Chris said with a scowl on his face. "We just walk right into the queen's palace and hope we go unnoticed?"

"Cassie seems to think it's our best option. Do you have a better idea?"

"I guess not." There was defeat already in his voice. "I'm not waiting till May. We'll get out of here, one way or another, as soon as possible."

Chris's words hung in the air. They would be free of Pyxis soon enough. Perhaps they would be walking out. More likely, they'd be running. And of course there was the chance they'd be flying—but in the worst way possible.

Joe tried to picture himself changing from a fairy into an angel, and winced. If there existed a pleasant afterlife, he wasn't sure he'd make the cut on such short notice.

CHAPTER 6
Expect the Unexpected

After a joyful reunion with the waking children and a hasty breakfast, the MacRaes stepped into the hall of the Aurora Borealis with their sacks and their weapons, and with Joe and Chris wearing their robes with fake wings attached. The children, of course, had wings—real wings!—of their own.

Despite the expected perilousness of the day ahead, Chris did not restrain his children's excitement and noisy chatter, because otherwise even Joe seemed stressed to silence. Perhaps along the cobbled streets of Pyxis, the children added the element of conventionality required to travel unnoticed. It took the pressure off Chris to act natural.

The safe segment of their journey ended when they approached Main Street in the North End. The dangerous part was about to begin.

While they waited for Cassie's signal, Chris watched fairies pass by the mouth of their alley. Some had pushcarts. Others had baskets of goods. A few had clothes or jewelry draped over their arms, and some merely existed, perhaps too hungry, sick, or weak to do more than slink by.

The alley brightened when a fairy on stilts paused at the opening. The torch he juggled set off a wave of dancing shadows.

Then Cassie gathered everyone together. "We should travel down Main Street alone or in small groups. The street ends in front of the palace. The main gate will be right in front of you. Bear left on Royal Way and keep walking until you get to the bridge. There is a steep slope on the right side of the bridge, yet it is possible to climb down. We will meet again underneath it. Shall I go first and continue on with Morgan?"

Chris considered the question for a moment. Since twins had a way of attracting attention, it was a good idea to keep them apart. And Morgan seemed to like Cassie. They were acting like long-lost sisters. His only misgiving was in terms of safety. What would happen to Morgan if a problem did arise?

Chris nodded once he mustered up some optimism.

And with that, Cassie gave them each a comforting touch on the arm. "See you at the bridge. Good luck." She offered her hand to Morgan, and they stepped into the busy street.

"Here's to crazy," Joe said with a hesitant smile and his fist in the air.

"More like suicidal," Chris replied.

"Thanks for darkening the moment."

"I'm here for ya. Be careful out there, Joe."

"Same to you."

Joe slapped and squeezed Chris's shoulder and then he left too.

"Ready, kiddo?" Chris squeezed Ryan's hand and Ryan looked up with the dark, almond-shaped eyes he'd inherited from his mother. The look might have been debilitating for someone else. For Chris it was motivating. What Alana would want most was the survival of her children.

When Ryan squeezed his hand back, Chris decided they were ready.

The eased their way onto Main Street, a more chaotic thoroughfare than what Chris had seen from the alley. He would never purposely subject himself or his children to a place like this—crowded and mucky. The street reminded him of his recurring nightmares, but Pyxis was even more bizarre and fantastical than his warped dreams.

There were fairies walking or hovering around, and vendors soliciting customers in multiple dimensions. The fire was the most eye-catching. Street performers juggled torches, streetlamps flickered, dancers twirled and leaped around bonfires, and braziers wafted scents of roasted nuts and crispy meat.

Chris squeezed his son's hand tighter due to his own uneasiness. He guided him to the center of the action even though his parental instincts told him to stay to the side.

"Would you like to buy a flower, sir?"

"No. No thanks," he answered with a polite wave.

"Save your applause until the end of the next death-defying stunt. . . ."

"Looking for a good time, handsome?"

A copper-haired fairy stepped in his way. Her aged face was clownish with lipstick and rouge. She looked ravenous too, not for lack of food, obviously, but in a way that suggested she took pleasure in her work and liked to cause trouble.

"No, thanks," Chris said, and he hoped that would be enough.

Chris moved around her, Ryan bouncing along at his heel, but then copper-haired fairy was in front of him again. Her wings had a chewed-up-and-spit-out appearance, so he was surprised she could fly so fast.

"My, my . . ." Her hand clasped the bandage around his wrist.

As Chris pulled his hand free, he felt naked before her wandering eyes.

"Looks like you had a rough night, soldier. I could always take your mind off it."

"I said no," he whispered to avoid drawing attention to himself, but with his tone and hard expression, he made sure she knew he meant it.

She smirked and then stepped aside. "Suit yourself."

Chris hurried along, but just when he thought the situation was under control, she shouted, "Nice wings!"

He scooped Ryan into his arms and pushed forward at an uncomfortable pace. If others were watching, he didn't want to know; the best solution was distance. And in his haste, his shoulder knocked into a fairy buzzing in the opposite direction. The bump wasn't hard enough to be painful or offensive, yet for some reason a fist grabbed the neck of his robe.

"Watch where you're going, fool!"

Chris's eyes latched on to the crooked star on the fairy's breastplate. With Ryan in his arms, though, he couldn't reach for the sword at his belt.

The fairy's mean black eyes flicked over Chris—a child in his arms, fake wings, blond hair, his father's eyes, nose, chin—but he carried himself as if he were too superior to waste his time focusing.

Chris was released just as quickly and unexpectedly as he'd been grabbed. Astounded by his luck, he moved on but felt the dread of next time. He'd already had two narrow escapes and he wasn't even halfway to his destination yet.

Before long, a fairy sprawled beneath a blanket on the ground blocked his path. While he was side-stepping over her, she shifted and muttered, "Rigel the Magnificent will come again."

"Magnificent indeed," Chris mumbled under his breath once he passed her.

"Whaja say, Dad?" Ryan asked.

"Nothing important."

A young male fairy with soot on his face then stepped in front of Chris. He looked side to side warily and then flipped open one side of his cloak. "Get your *Pyxis Discourse*. Christopher the Valiant seeks revenge. Only five greens!"

"No thanks," Chris grumbled, but if he'd had five greens, he would have considered buying one to see what had been printed about his family. Chris had been suspicions about Pierre's motives and ethics as soon as he'd slithered onto the scene. Still, he couldn't believe Pierre had had the nerve to promise secrecy but then, within hours, publish news of everything that had taken place the previous night.

Chris was thinking of all the "valiant" things he would like to do to Pierre's already crooked nose when he heard, "*Royalist Review*. Get your *Royalist Review*! Murderous Bottom-Dwellers on the loose!"

There were screams and a scuffle broke out. Then three fairies threw torches at a building marked by a *Royalist Review* sign. A few others tossed in glass bottles, and the building exploded with flames.

Chris forced Ryan's head into his shoulder and jogged to the other side of the street. He had to lower his own head when a swarm of uniforms flew past with weapons in hand. He didn't need his eyes to know what happened next. The sound of open slaughter told a gruesome story.

He walked as fast as he could without actually running. By the time he approached the intersection of Main Street and Royal Way, his calves were burning as if they too were on fire.

Before he turned the corner, Chris looked up at the monstrous Aerial Palace. It was eerie, perhaps all the more because in Pyxis there was no sky, no natural light, no weather. He imagined lightning, thunder, sheets of rain, and wind strong enough to slice roof tiles off the palace towers—but within the cave there was not even breeze enough to make a flag flutter, and the towers stood in a profound stillness.

He could not believe they would be inside the palace later in the day. Running away from it seemed to make more sense.

Out of the corner of his eye, Chris saw the castle's main gate open. More uniformed soldiers zipped onto Main Street. Before long, Chris heard more screams in the distance. For the sake of their escape plan, he hoped the disturbance at the newspaper office would become a full-blown riot, the bigger the better. A busy army was a distracted army.

He turned onto Royal Way and encountered a new kind of danger—privilege and power, and long expanses of quiet, free space. The residences were multistoried, well lit inside and out, and built out of light-colored stone. They also included glasswork that gave off an icicle appearance. Some of the fanciest and most expansive mansions even had gems and blocks of silver or gold sparkling among the elaborate stonework. Among these, the whites of lingering eyes seemed to glow from the windows. Judging by their wealth and proximity to the palace, these Royal fairies were likely friendly to the queen and wary of those who were not. They would know their neighbors—their styles, their schedules, their habits. To protect themselves and their prominent positions in society, they would no doubt alarm the authorities if Bottom-Dwellers were spotted out of place. And Chris was the third one with fake wings to pass by, wings that couldn't even fool a common whore.

"Daddy, I wanna go home!" Ryan suddenly wailed.

Chris buried his son's sobs in his shoulder and picked up the pace. "Me too, kiddo. Me too."

***

"I should have been the last to leave." Cassie peeked out from beneath the bridge for the third time. "The whole plot was outlandish. And the worst is yet to come."

"Yeah, perhaps, but we made it here in one piece," Joe whispered from his seated position, somewhere in the dense darkness. "He'll make it. Have some faith. And stop pacing so much. Someone might see you."

Cassie continued her restless motion, and when she couldn't stand to wait any longer, she revealed a sliver of herself into the open. There was still no sign of Chris or anyone else.

Morgan tugged on her cloak upon her return. "Do you see him—my dad?"

"No, not yet, my darling."

Cassie scooped Morgan's loose honey-brown hair into a bundle and gave her a reassuring smile, hoping it was enough to mask her dread.

Morgan nodded solemnly, but then her eyes sparkled. "Daddy!" she cried as she flew toward her father.

Chris set Ryan down and squatted to accommodate his daughter's height. She clung to him around the neck and did not let go. When he stood back up, she had settled into a place in his arm that seemed comfortable and natural.

Chris, however, looked uneasy. He checked out from underneath the bridge more than once, as if he expected unwelcome company.

His behavior inspired Cassie to hurry. She removed their fake wings and threw them into the West River, where they churned, tumbled, and drowned in the current. Then she gathered their supplies and initiated the journey onward.

For the most part, she felt confident the rocky slope on the right would hide them from view. But light, or a lack thereof, and the West River provided the next set of challenges. In near darkness—even the strike of a matchstick was a risk—they had to watch their step. The river's winding path and fierce current could easily drag them away and its steep decline culminated in a waterfall with no known bottom. Luckily she had each step committed to memory. It was the only reason she wasn't dwelling on the nightmarish alternative.

When Cassie turned around to check on her companions, Joe was a few paces behind and soon joined her side. They both watched Chris approach with the twins. Morgan was hovering above his head, and Ryan was twisting Chris's arm behind his back.

Chris didn't seem to mind playing their game of flying tug-of war and as long as the children were entertained, they didn't seem frightened.

"He seems to be doing better," Cassie whispered to Joe. "Do you think he'll be all right?"

"I don't think he has a choice."

Cassie and Joe laughed when the twins tangled Chris's arms into a knot.

"Children with wings," Chris said when he joined them. "It adds a whole new dimension to parenting. Sorry to keep you waiting."

"You're doing fine. We're almost there anyway," Cassie said, pointing ahead.

Her enthusiasm earned her a curious look from Chris, so she ducked her head, walked on, and made a mental note to tone down the encouragement. She continued leading the way and was the first to arrive at the conduits.

There were three conduits to climb over, and on top of the fourth, Cassie crouched down and struck the softened wood with the hilt of her sword. Once she produced a hole large enough for everyone to enter, Chris lowered her inside.

By the time everyone else entered, Cassie had three torches lit. "Just to warn you," she whispered as she handed off the torches, "what you see in this channel may not be pleasant."

"Why? What's down here—or do I even want to know?" Joe asked. Before she could answer, he picked up a piece of bone from underfoot. He showed it to Chris and then let go of it in a rush. "Nope. I don't want to know," he said, wiping his hand on his side.

After that, they moved on, but the bone had set the mood. The children, at Chris's instructions, flew quietly behind him, while the adults eased along the damp wood. They huddled close together, looked before they stepped, and listened before they completed turns.

At one such turn, Cassie gasped and pressed herself against the wall. Joe and Chris quickly drew their swords. Two gray rats scurried around the corner. A third rat twisted its head around and twitched its nose at them.

The rat's nose and whiskers continued to survey them. No one moved as the rat deliberated, moving its head from face to face. It was as if it was weighing its hunger against its chances of survival. Chris seemed the most appealing to the rat—it lingered over his face the longest—but as Chris raised his sword, the rat turned its eyes on Joe, blew air through its nostrils bitterly, and then disappeared into the darkness.

"You weren't kidding, Princess," Joe said once it was obvious the rat wasn't coming back. "I think I just saw my life flash before my eyes!"

Cassie shrugged. "They're not usually aggressive with us."

"That's reassuring. What else can we be expecting? Do the fairy rats ever grow wings?"

Cassie checked around the next turn and waved them forward. "Not today, hopefully."

"In this place, I'm not even sure you're kidding!" Joe replied as he followed.

After the turn, the steepness of the slope made walking a challenge. They often had to use their one free hand to avoid slipping backward. The twins stayed in the air. Once the wood began to level out again, the air grew heavier with a disturbing warmth.

"What's that smell?" Chris whispered to Joe.

Cassie overheard him. "It means we're nearly there."

"That's good news, right?" Joe asked.

This time she didn't answer. They would see for themselves soon enough. But she did pause to rummage through her sack. "I would put these on the children. And while they are wearing them, they should not fly."

She handed Chris two pieces of cloth. He looked puzzled at first, but then awareness came to his face. After a moment of persuasion, the children folded their wings and succumbed to the blindfolds. Then Chris and Joe lifted them up.

As they rounded the final curve, a mound of bones arose in front of them. Its chilling height and breadth were the culmination of years of unencumbered slaughter. And judging by the ruddy hue of fluids at the mound's peak, some of the corpses might even be warm to the touch.

The pile was nearly twice as imposing as Cassie remembered, but she kept her mind occupied on the only advantage—elevation. Reaching the trapdoor would be easy even for her. So she climbed to the top and wedged her torch in the skeletal fragments at her feet.

As usual, the trapdoor was locked and from the inside, but it rattled open to create enough space for the keys and her hand. She followed her hand along the chain keeping the door tethered to the ground and found the lock.

Key after key, she tried and failed, tried and failed. Finally, she pulled her hand back out to rest and reconsider.

Then Chris stepped forward as if to help, but he hesitated when his foot crushed through the bones. "Try the hinges," he suggested as he removed his foot.

She nodded and, moving toward the opposite end of the trapdoor, used her sword as a lever. Eventually the ancient wood began to splinter away from the metal hinges. And at last the door broke free, tumbled inward, and hung by the stubborn chain.

Cassie lifted her torch and climbed upward into the palace. Once she confirmed the chamber was clear of imminent danger, she stuck her head back into the pit. "Are you ready?" Chris and Joe exchanged hesitant glances and then trod onto the pile.

Joe and Ryan were nearing the top when the bones began shifting with a hollow tone. They paused and waited, but it became apparent that the entire pile was on the verge of collapsing. While Chris held back, sinking little by little, he ushered his brother forward.

Focusing on the race against time and gravity, Joe managed to lift Ryan inside the hole. Then Joe jumped for the ledge. He made it in up to his waist and squirmed to safety.

As Chris began to move again with Morgan at his hip, the hollow tinkling became a rumble. With each step, the bones ate away at his speed and progress. Then one of his steps collapsed through to his thigh and his torch bobbled out of hand. It rolled out of reach and settled near the base of the mound, where it lit some remnants of fabric littered among the debris.

The fire began to climb, devouring the foundation below his feet. Waist-deep and stuck despite his desperate effort, Chris knew he had only one choice. "Fly, Morgan!" he cried as he ripped the blindfold from his daughter's eyes.

Chris threw her into the air and her white wings flapped open. Cassie called to her from above, and the child fairy spiraled toward the hole overhead. Then, just underneath the opening, she twisted toward the flames and froze. Cassie had to pull her in by her waist and set her abruptly aside. There was no time to console her.

Cassie and Joe dived to their stomachs and dangled their arms just as Chris made a jump for them. In a fog of bone dust and smoke, they heaved Chris over the ledge. One elbow and then two, and once one of his knees was secure, Cassie let go and reached down for the broken trapdoor, pulled it upward, and covered the hole lengthwise as soon as Chris crawled inside.

They all stood, brushed off the filth of death, and oriented themselves to their new situation. They were in a dungeon alcove with an unoccupied cell at the back. A suit of armor and a pitchfork propped the cage door open. The shadows cast behind the bars suggested there were other defunct weapons and armor there as well. Otherwise, the room contained broken furniture, once elegant in its prime, and an old chandelier scattered about in ruin.

Cassie moved carefully around the broken glass and, from the room's archway, peeked into the hall. "The main corridor is to the right," she whispered, handing her torch to Joe. "I'm going to get a closer look."

She eased herself down the passage with her back to the wall and stopped just before her body met the angling torchlight. But she could see what she needed to see. The guard station was vacant, though the dungeon was not. Nearly every cell contained three or more prisoners withering away in the shadows.

Then she darted to the opposite wall so she could get a view of the escape route. The gate was closed, which meant it was also locked. Her hand went to her pocket, and she pulled out the Gray Coat's keys. She squeezed them together to keep them quiet and then signaled the others to come forward.

Chris extinguished the torches and everyone joined Cassie by the wall. After nods of readiness, Cassie darted out first. Joe and Chris were quick at her heel. At the gate, Cassie fumbled to find the right key. After a few failed attempts the lock clicked.

"There should be a tunnel on the right. It's the only opening along that hallway, and you'll feel the cold air coming from it. It's a steep climb, mostly of ice, but it leads to the forest," Cassie said. Then she turned to leave.

"Cassie, where are you going?" Joe hissed.

"Prop the gate open, but don't wait for me. There is something I must do."

***

Chris watched in awe as Cassie began to run from cell to cell, using the keys to free the prisoners, pointing to the other end of the hall, and simulating a couple of turns with her hand.

Some of the freed fairies gave her embraces with tears in their eyes. Singles, doubles, clusters then scurried away and disappeared into a passage on the left just before the guard station.

"She's crazier than you are!" Joe said as he relit their torches with the final torch on the wall. "It's a full-time job around here trying to rein in the crazy."

"I resent that." Chris kicked a loose stone from the wall and positioned it to keep the gate ajar. "She asked us to start along the tunnel; let's go."

Cassie was already heading back in their direction, when suddenly she stopped, her eyes wide. She whirled, drew her sword, and stood motionless.

"What is she doing?" Joe asked with stress and urgency ringing in his tone.

"I'll find out. Why don't you go on with the kids?"

"No, I'll get her." Joe blocked Chris's motion with his hand. "They're your kids!"

"Joe, just go!"

They glared, they tensed. Chris couldn't believe Joe was challenging him. Joe may have wanted to be the hero, but Chris doubted his brother had the skills to substantiate the gesture.

73

Joe's good sense must have kicked back in because he stepped aside and took Ryan's and Morgan's hands in his. "All right! Fine!"

As Joe left with the children in search of the tunnel, Chris jogged to Cassie and grabbed her arm. "Cassie, we have to go."

She kept her gaze straight ahead, and her body went rigid. A loud boom echoed above them. It shook loose rocks and debris from the ceiling. Chris crouched and lifted his arm above his head. When the dust settled, his eyes swept over the ceiling and then zoomed in on the guard station. Still empty.

"She's very angry," Cassie said in a haunting voice.

"I bet. C'mon!" Chris attempted to pull her away again.

"She knows and she's coming. . . ."

"How do you know she's—"

He saw Andromeda emerge at the end of the corridor, formidable and wild with fury, some kind of long stick in her hand. At first he wasn't sure what it was, but as she flew closer he could see it was a scepter. It had a glowing orb on top and jewels arrayed like stars around it.

She slammed the scepter on the ground, and a ball of light shot forth with an accompanying boom. Chris's and Cassie's weapons flew out of their hands.

"Chris, run! You'll never make it unless I stay and fight!"

"Cassie, look at me." He twisted her shoulders in his direction. Her terrified face was still fixed on Andromeda.

"Look at me!" he urged, and she finally did. "Now, either you're going to run with me or I'm going to die right here standing next to you."

But Cassie turned her gaze back to her mother. Andromeda hovered forward slowly and deliberately; her black wings made the air tremble.

"Please," Chris urged again. "C'mon!"

When Andromeda was almost close enough to touch them, Cassie finally spun toward Chris.

Together, as one, they began to run. They made it to the end of the corridor and slipped behind the gate. Chris slammed it shut and snatched the keys from Cassie's shaking hands.

"Go!" he yelled, to snap her out of her trance. She picked up the torch Joe had left for them and ran into the darkness.

Chris wrapped his hand around the bars and stuck a key in the gate's keyhole. He flinched when Andromeda landed in front of the gate, but he regained enough composure to glare into her black eyes with equal vehemence. Then he cocked his head defiantly as he snapped the key in two.

As Chris darted into the darkness, Andromeda rattled the jammed gate and slammed her fists against it. And then, in a voice that seemed to hiss inside his head, she said, "She'll unravel you and your brother, and lead you to your demise. You'll see. . . ."

Chris shuddered and hoped beyond hope that the wicked queen was wrong.

CHAPTER 7
Return to Normalcy

Chris found the tunnel and moved as fast he could manage in complete darkness and along a surface that had to be pure ice. He was using his hands almost as often as his feet. On a straightaway, he could see a torch bobbing in the distance. He could at least see the outline of his feet, so he began to run. When he caught up to Cassie, he took the torch from her and led the way at his pace.

"How . . . ?" she asked, stumbling to keep up. "How did you stop her?"

"Broke a key in the lock," he said between breaths. "It'll probably only buy us a few extra minutes."

"You"—she slowed down and then stopped—"saved my life."

He glanced back and swept his arm forward to urge her to hurry. "I guess that makes us even," he said, but it came out with a little too much bite. "I wouldn't worry," he added, softening. "I'm sure you'll get a chance to pull ahead."

He couldn't tell if Cassie smiled at that, but her presence seemed to become less dark and, since she knew the way through the tunnel, she took the lead. They trudged on for what felt like a very long time. They paused once more to rummage in the sack for an extra weapon, expecting the need for one within moments. Cassie explained that there were few who knew about this particular exit from Pyxis. The tunnel led to an inconspicuous rock crevice. But there was no way of knowing what they might encounter once they emerged into the night. Regardless, the best remaining fairy weapon in their possession, a knife, wouldn't do anyone much good once Chris Modified back to his human size.

At last, the tunnel melded into a bluish path that curved upward. Before long, he felt a breeze and then a full-fledged wind. It moaned on its way to greet them and stung his exposed skin. At last they saw trees, the bright moon, and the starriest sky he had ever seen. Chris felt he would never look at the night sky the same way again. And suddenly there was a burst of green—the Aurora Borealis, not the tavern, but the real thing, the Northern Lights. Its natural beauty had a valid, scientific explanation and was such a strange and timely contradiction to the unnatural turn his life had taken.

As they exited the mouth of the tunnel, a blast of wind nearly knocked over their tiny bodies, and Chris realized they had another enemy to contend with, one he couldn't outwit or overpower. Within moments, he felt as if he had been standing in the cold for hours. Aside from the small clearing where they stood, the snow was over their heads. Joe and the twins were nowhere in sight; a set of fairy-sized footprints ended at what was to Chris a sheer cliff of snow.

Chris knew that he had to Modify as quickly as he could, and that he would have to clear his mind to make the transformation work. But before he could even close his eyes, he saw two spots of yellow glinting in the moonlight and bearing down on the patch where he and Cassie stood. Behind those spots was the snowy white body of an owl, wings outstretched, plunging toward them.

Chris pushed Cassie behind him toward the entrance of the tunnel. The owl's talons snapped open, and Chris positioned the knife for a hopeless fight. But just then the whir of a machine startled the great bird, which changed course mid-dive. The owl soared out of sight as Chris saw the skis of a human-sized snowmobile crest the snowy embankment and slide to a halt.

The driver swung a leg off the machine and pulled off a helmet. It was Joe. He had somehow managed to Modify to his normal size, make his way through the frozen world, find clothes and transportation, and return to the mouth of the tunnel.

Chris just shook his head and placed the knife back in Cassie's sack. "We're gonna have company very soon."

"All right." Joe patted his pocket, then held a gloved hand down toward Cassie and Chris. "The children are safe in here. Plus, I have a plan, and car keys."

"Perfect," Chris said. "Good job."

Joe collected Chris into the same hand as Cassie. "See? I'm not as useless as you make me out to be."

"I never said you were—"

Before Chris could say more, Joe added him and Cassie to a pocket in the gray snowsuit he stole and secured the flap. Then Joe revved the engine and propelled the machine forward.

"Daddy? Are you there?" Morgan asked from within the dark folds of the pocket. "Ryan and me are going fast with Uncle Joe!"

"I'm here. Are you two holding on tight?"

"Yep."

"Yep."

Chris crawled over the linty fabric to find them. He and Cassie secured themselves next to the children and held on to their hands.

Chris's nerves calmed a bit until Joe's snowmobile suddenly banked a hard left and went airborne for a moment. They popped up and jumbled together when the machine landed. When they had settled back down, Chris counted heads, all luckily still present. Then there was a different kind of motion—a scramble, a twist, and then a rhythmic jarring. Joe had disembarked from the snowmobile and was running.

More twisting followed, and then a leap. A door slammed, and gunfire erupted, sounding to Chris's fairy ears like a thousand bombs. And then a different engine kicked to life. With squealing wheels, they were in motion once again.

Chris jumped, pulled the side of Joe's pocket down, and lifted an edge of the flap. Cold air rushed in, and so did some light from the vehicle's dashboard. They seemed to be gaining speed. Chris began to fight his way clear from the saggy, uncooperative fabric of the snowsuit pocket.

"Sorry," Joe said as Chris leaped from Joe's right leg to his left. "I didn't forget about you. I'm just preoccupied with the company we've got behind us."

Chris jumped to the armrest and climbed up to the door handle. Then he wedged his fingers between the window and its rubber trim. He pulled himself to a kneeling position so he could see the side-view mirror.

There were two snowmobiles chasing them, one on each side of the snowbound road, and there were headlights from what appeared to be another SUV closing in on them from behind.

"They're gaining on us!"

"You don't think I know that?" Joe yelled back. "We can't go any faster without flying off the road!"

Joe had nabbed a black Range Rover—sleek, shiny, low mileage, practically straight from the factory. They were driving the best of the best. Even so, Joe was pushing the vehicle's limits. The narrow road had tight turns and was covered in at least six inches of snow, more in places with snowdrifts. And the snow kept on drifting in the blizzard-level wind. There was plenty of light, but not where it mattered. Most of it was reflected back into their eyes, including the other vehicle's high beams that kept getting brighter in the SUV's mirrors.

"He's going to hit—"

The other vehicle crashed into them, and Chris was launched into the air. He smacked against the steering wheel, grabbed it, and dangled there while Joe turned it back and forth, fighting for control.

Before Joe could steady the wheel, they were hit from behind again. Joe lost his grip but Chris held tight. As the vehicle went into a spin, brakes squealed and the backside of the Range Rover bounced off something on the side of the road.

Their vehicle teetered to a stop, and the front wheels tilted up at an angle that wasn't promising. Joe revved the engine, redlining surely. Despite the smoke and the earsplitting shriek of the wheels, the vehicle did little more than shimmy side to side.

Joe paused, reversed, and tried again. The next time, they made it farther. By the third attempt, they kept inching until they were back on the road. Then Joe stomped on the gas and, after checking the rearview mirror, hit the steering wheel with his palm. "Just so you know, we lost them," he said with a wink. "They ain't getting out of that mess anytime soon!"

Chris, dizzy with relief, dropped onto Joe's hand and from there slid onto the passenger seat. There weren't entirely out of trouble, but he had to admit their escape so far had been pretty spectacular. And now they were barreling ahead in a top-of-the-line human machine with heat, gas, and no pursuers. It was almost too good to be true.

"I can see why the Range Rover is the vehicle of choice," Joe said. "This road, if you can call it that, is a mess."

Chris stood back up and looked over all the buttons and gadgets on the dashboard. "This thing is worth over eighty grand." Chris shook his head in wonder. "Joe, where did you learn to drive like that? I know you were always bold behind the wheel, but a snowmobile?"

"Aspen," he answered.

"Colorado?"

"Yeah, Rebecca's family owned a ski lodge out there."

Chris narrowed his eyes as he attempted to pull the name Rebecca from his memory bank. "Is that the rich ex-girlfriend with the daddy issues?"

Joe replied with a side-eyed glower.

"Hey . . ." Chris put his hands up to free himself from blame. "I'm just repeating what you said. I never had the pleasure of meeting her."

"Probably a good thing. She would have been all over you."

"Whatever," Chris grumbled with an eye flutter. "So who taught you?"

"Her brother, a cool guy. A crazy you-know-what, though. There was this one long weekend when we were out most of the day attempting these idiotic stunts. When we got back, Becca was finishing World War Three with her father. I missed most of it, and of course that meant I didn't love her and never defended her. Beginning of the end, really."

"Was she the reason you left med school?"

"Definitely a contributing factor." Joe checked the rearview mirror and glanced over his shoulder. Then he pressed on the gas a little harder. "Why the sudden interest?"

"I've always been interested."

Joe gave Chris another look. This time it clearly meant "liar."

"Okay," Chris conceded. "Maybe 'always' is a strong word. Can't you just tell me? It's a good distraction. Hearing about ordinary stuff makes me feel like we could return to a normal life now, after our, uh, little adventure."

"I hate to break it to you, Chris, but you were never normal."

"That's not true," Chris objected.

"Oh, please. You grew up in your room with your door locked, all alone with your crybaby rock. Mom and I sat downstairs making fun of you and your music."

Chris shrugged, neither confirming nor denying the accusation. "I was just misunderstood."

"Yeah, I'd say. Well, that's enough about us," Joe said. He then opened the flap of his snowsuit pocket. "Cassie, how are the kids in there? Everyone okay? If so, we'd like you to come out and tell us the rest of your story."

The dark-haired fairy poked out her head and allowed Joe to lift her. He set her down on the seat beside Chris. "They're fine. I think all that motion just rocked them to sleep." She stretched to loosen her cramped limbs. "As for my story, it's not that interesting."

"Oh, sure. When you were a kid, you played in dungeons and frolicked over mass graves. It sounds terribly boring."

"God, Joe!" Chris said to spare Cassie from the inquisition. "Maybe she doesn't want to talk about it!"

Protecting her was the right thing to do. She still hadn't recovered from her encounter with her mother, it seemed. Joe had no way of knowing about their narrow escape from Andromeda, and if Cassie wasn't going to mention it, Chris wasn't going to either. There was obviously a bitter history, and one Cassie would probably want to keep in the deep-dark-secrets category for now, or forever.

"What you might find interesting I don't feel is relevant to the task at hand," she added.

"How is your background irrelevant?" Joe persisted. "The same queen of darkness is trying to kill us all. Couldn't you tell us the details so we have a better idea of what we're up against?"

"Would you let it go already?" Chris chimed in again.

Joe sighed audibly. "Fine. I'll let it go for now, Princess, but I still think we should know."

With Chris and Cassie unable to see out the windows, Joe began a travel narration as they began to pass signs of human civilization. They were gloomy and desolate signs, but signs nonetheless. A shack here, an oil drum on the side of the road, the rusty shell of a pickup truck over there, and an upcoming route marker. Joe squinted at it and then slowed down in front of the sign. "Hey, Cassie, How's your French?"

"Je parle très bien le français," she said with melodic fluency.

"Good, much better than mine. Do you mind?" He lowered his hand in front of her; she stepped onto his palm, and he lifted her to the dashboard.

"Ce serait mon plaisir."

She directed them to the town of Chibougamau. As they drove, Chris and Joe spun out a plan to ditch the Range Rover and use their fairy size to acquire a car that was less conspicuous.

Once in town, Joe was about to turn into in a church parking lot when he abruptly straightened out the wheel. He then sped forward with his eyes fixed on the rearview mirror.

"What? What's wrong?" Chris asked.

"Shhh! Hold up!" He made a few turns at a ridiculous speed. "Yeah, we're being followed. It's another black Range Rover."

"What do you mean we're being followed? When did this—"

"Get in my pocket, now!" Joe shouted in response, scooping up both Cassie and Chris before they could protest. He tucked them beneath the same flap as the sleeping children. "Hold on for your life. . . ."

Joe slammed on the brakes and jerked the wheel to the left. The vehicle spun out of control and then there was the metallic crunch of vehicles colliding. Chris felt Joe's stumbling motion just before the crash, so he knew his brother was at least not lying maimed in the wreckage.

Moments later, they were falling. Chris and the others hit the ground in a tangle of legs, arms, heads, and bodies, their landing cushioned by the layers of the snowsuit. As quickly as possible, he helped Cassie and the children, now awake and amazingly calm, find their way out of the pocket. Joe had Modified and was getting the last of his fairy clothes on when they met up with him.

They all scurried beneath a car on the side of the road. Joe's stolen clothes lay in a heap nearby. They huddled behind an enormous front tire and watched four black boots and flashlight beams pass over the shattered glass from the collision, not more than a few human-sized paces away.

Their location wasn't what Chris would consider secure. With hand gestures, Chris and Joe began the debate of when to run. Cassie, however, didn't wait for the outcome. She ran to the opposite wheel and slipped between it and the curb.

Chris and Joe froze as they watched her dart into the open. Then they turned toward the boots, which no doubt belonged to a pair of Gray Coats, and followed the beams of light with their eyes. All motion remained slow and thorough.

When Cassie made it underneath the next car, she signaled for them to follow. They followed her route, two at a time—Chris and Morgan, then Joe and Ryan—and made it there, unnoticed.

The next car was farther away. They had to be much more careful. The Gray Coats had already found the snowsuit and would soon figure out that the fairy group was on the run. So Chris and the others had to move, no hesitation.

They made it to the next car, the last one before an intersection. They hugged the curb, crouched low, and rounded the corner. Then they ran as far and fast as they could. But soon the brutal wind had them staggering. They paused underneath another car to catch their breath and weigh their options.

"We need to get the kids inside somehow. We can't go on like this for much longer." Joe blew a few labored breaths over his bare hands. "At our size, we'll die of hypothermia that much faster."

"Why don't we pick a house and try to find a car," Chris suggested. "How about this one next to us? It looks like there's a television on."

"Shouldn't we pick a house without lights on?" Joe asked.

"People who aren't home don't usually leave their keys lying around."

"I meant a house where people are sleeping. Not absent," Joe retorted in his I'm-not-an-idiot tone.

Cassie pointed to the beam of light sweeping over the ground nearby. "We have to make a decision."

Chris, with Morgan in his arms, peeked out from underneath the car. He darted across the sidewalk and ran up the shoveled walkway of the one-story house. The front steps looked too steep and challenging, so he took a right turn behind a snow bank.

They all met up again beside a garbage barrel. Then as a group, they ran alongside the house and by a basement window.

Chris paused when he dragged his hand across a familiar sort of fabric on the window. "Hold on—that's duct tape! I think we can get in here."

He tried to peel the tape off the window, where it was sealing a crack in the glass. Joe and Cassie joined his efforts. But their tiny frozen fingers could not rip the weathered tape.

"Do we still have a knife or a sword handy?" Chris asked.

"We still have the sword I was using. I put it back in Cassie's bag a little while ago."

Joe turned to grab it from her. She already had the sword in her hand with the hilt propped in Chris's direction.

"Thanks."

Chris stabbed through the tape and felt warm air seeping through the crack. He warmed his fingers, but that was all he could do without breaking additional glass.

He tapped the glass lightly with the hilt of the sword and tried to muffle the shattering sound with his other hand. Since he couldn't make the sound go away, he worked quickly and chipped a triangular hole down to the window frame.

Chris eased Cassie inside first by her wrists. She found her footing on the windowsill, walked around for a moment, and then waved them inside.

Then, as light reflected off nearby windows, Chris climbed in and put his arms out for the children.

Joe hurried them inside. "Move, move, move!" he hissed as a direct beam hit the driveway.

Chris herded everyone away from the hole and as soon as Joe was inside, Chris balanced on the windowsill and pulled the loose tape back into position as best he could. He held still, not daring to breathe. The window lit up and then gradually darkened. Chris exhaled and let go of the tape.

They were out of sight and temporarily warm and safe. Even though their circumstances had improved, it wasn't by much. The darkness was almost too dense to navigate and they were stuck on a narrow ledge with no way down. Phasing back to his human self would increase the risk of discovery, but navigating the human world at fairy size would be dangerous and time-consuming. Certain challenges in both cases would be nearly impossible to complete, so they would have to find a balance.

"Wings would come in handy right about now," Joe whispered, and that gave Chris an idea.

"Cassie, do you have any rope?"

He heard her rummaging through her sack. "Here." She handed him the bundle.

"Ryan, buddy, can you do us a special job?" Chris asked.

He could vaguely see Ryan's nod.

"Can you take this rope, fly up, and find something on the ceiling to wrap it around? There should be pipes up there."

"Can I help, Daddy? Please?" Morgan asked.

"All right. I'll hold on to this end of the rope, and you help your brother carry the other end. I know it's dark, but use your hands to find something to wrap it around. Then bring your end back to me. You can see a little light coming in from the window, right?"

The children looked over at the window and agreed. Then they each picked up a handful of rope and flew off.

"Work together," Chris suggested in a loud whisper.

The twins returned with the other end of the rope a few minutes later.

"Good job, you two!"

Chris tugged on the ends of the rope, one at a time. The rope slid back and forth, but when he pulled in the slack and tugged, the ends seemed like they could support his weight.

He evened out the ends and made a knot at the bottom. Then he handed Joe a side of the rope and jumped on the other.

Joe lowered him to the floor, and they kept the rope cycling until the three wingless adults were all safely on the ground.

Chris cycled the rope back around and untied the knot. Then another idea came to him. There was flashing light above them, and he figured it was coming from underneath the basement door.

"Ryan and Morgan, where are you?" Chris asked.

"Right here, Dad," Morgan answered, only an arm's reach away.

Chris set one hand on her head and fumbled to find Ryan's as well. "Do you see that light above our heads? It's probably a door!" he said brightly. "Can you do us another big favor? Can you fly up and wrap the rope around the doorknob?"

The twins flew off together once again. The noisy doorknob rattled Chris's nerves even further, but the task was soon complete and they landed back by his side.

Then, with the children hovering beside them, Chris, Cassie, and Joe climbed, pulled, or lifted each other up the stairs. When they reached the top step, Chris sent the twins back up to release the rope. After more rattling, they came down empty-handed.

"It's stuck," Morgan explained.

"Cut it off, Chris. We can make do with what we have left," Joe said.

Chris nodded and sawed through the rope with the sword, and while he bundled what remained of it into a circle with his hand and elbow, Cassie was crouching down, trying to fit underneath the door. If she couldn't get through, then they were all likely stuck there. They might not be able to postpone transformation much longer.

Cassie kept trying in various locations, and finally, where the door met the doorframe, an L-shaped gap allowed her to slip underneath.

Everyone else came over to the spot where she had disappeared. Chris saw the size of the hole and shook his head. "You try first," he suggested to Joe.

Joe made it to the other side without an issue and Chris sent the twins through next. Then he held his breath and had to play with his angle of entry a few times, but he eventually pulled through as well.

There was a cluttered galley kitchen on the other side of the door. While Joe, Cassie, and the twins were exploring it from the ground and the air, Chris followed the house's only source of light—a television set blaring the late evening news in French.

Chris jogged to the living room and saw a man, probably in his late fifties, sleeping in a tattered recliner. He looked like a miner or a logger, weatherworn and aging gracelessly from a hard life. Chris also surmised from a shrine-like photo display on a nearby shelf that the man's wife was no longer among the living. It compelled Chris to consider his own fate for a moment. When this adventure reached its conclusion, would he be able to resume his human life where it had left off? In thirty or forty years, would he be alone on a couch somewhere counting down the days until he would see his enshrined wife again? Or was the human world forever gone to him? And if so, what would take its place? Perpetual struggle in a tumultuous new fantasy world? Ryan and Morgan—what did the future hold for them? And, well, where *was* his father after all?

The man suddenly coughed and snorted. Then his snoring pattern resumed. But the interruption was enough to jar Chris back to the present.

When he returned to the kitchen, Joe and Cassie were staring up at a counter full of clutter.

"Where've you been?" Joe asked.

"The guy's asleep. I was just making sure. How are things going in here?"

"The kids found the keys and the wallet, but they can't lift them," Joe reported. "We probably don't want anything crashing to the ground. So here's my plan. . . ."

Joe suggested with a twirl of his finger that Cassie turn around. She raised her eyebrows with what looked like a combination of impatience and disbelief, but she did as she was told and put her hands over her eyes as well. Morgan didn't pick up on the cue, so Chris covered her eyes for her. And then Joe slipped off his clothing, seated himself, and covered his own eyes.

He was getting good at Modifying; it took no more than a few seconds. In his human form, Joe began lowering items to the floor—a wad of money, keys, a miniature flashlight. Then, in the blink of an eye, he was small again. Chris envied his brother's ease with this newfound power.

Once Joe had his fairy clothes back on, he and Chris picked up the keys, Cassie carried the flashlight, and the twins each carried a side of the folded Canadian money down the hall. They brought all the items to the utility room at the back of the house.

With a running start, Chris swung the utility room door closed, then grabbed it to slow it down so that it would shut quietly. The man at the other end of the house didn't seem like a light sleeper, but Chris wasn't going to take any chances. Then, with a quick look around, he realized they were in the right place. There were clothes in laundry baskets, shoes and boots lining the wall, and a back door leading out.

Joe had already Modified again and was throwing on clothes in the corner of the room. Chris decided it might be best to join him. He sat down behind a laundry basket, put his head between his knees, covered out all light with his arms, and tried to let his mind go blank. It took a few tries; he opened his eyes to see the basket looming above him several times before he managed to let go of his thoughts. At last, though, he found himself at human size.

He dressed in layers of the old man's sturdy, warm clothing, put on some work boots, and joined Joe by the back door just as Joe was adding Cassie and the twins to the breast pocket of his flannel shirt. Then they both nodded with readiness.

Chris covered the bolted lock with his left hand and slowly rotated it counterclockwise with his right. Then he eased the door open just enough to slip through. Joe followed closely behind.

The garage was about ten paces beyond the porch. They would have to expose themselves to the street.

Chris craned his neck around the corner of the house. The driveway was dark, and there were no signs of flashlights. There were other lights animating the street in cycles, but they seemed distant and routine. So Chris stepped down, moved to the side, and signaled Joe over to the garage.

Joe knelt down and tried the handle of the garage door. It was locked. Joe fanned out the keys in the wad and began selecting ones to try while Chris kept glancing at the street over his shoulder.

Chris had never seen so many keys on the same ring before, but eventually, Joe identified the right one. The handle pulled up with a squeak and the overhead door rolled with a sound like thunder. Chris cringed and crouched down to help his brother lift it with the right momentum so that they could minimize the noise and its duration. Then, with one last look over his shoulder, Chris followed Joe into the garage.

Joe opened the driver's side door of a well-used Chevrolet Silverado, and Chris accepted the passenger's seat. Joe had proved his worth for the night with his skillfully aggressive driving.

"Give me the flashlight," Chris whispered.

"Shouldn't we go?"

"Wait a second." Chris rummaged through the glove compartment. "Here's a map. Let's figure out where we're going as long as we're still alone." He glanced in his side view mirror.

While Joe watched the rearview mirror, Chris opened the map. He found the right quadrant, he thought, but the map was in French and with little time and space, as well as bad lighting, his progress was slow.

Joe soon lifted Cassie out of his pocket. "What towns are we near, my dear?"

"There are no towns. I believe you just have to follow Route 167 south toward Lac Saint-Jean, where you pick up Route 169 toward Quebec."

"Lac Saint-Jean? That's a lake, right? I think I saw a sign for that earlier," Joe said.

Chris shook his head and continued to scrutinize the map. *Where is Chibougamau or Route 167?* "Would you put money on that? We won't have a lot of time to spare."

"If we make a right out of here, and then a right at the next street, we'll avoid the street we had the accident on and then we can circle back a ways."

"I'd like to be able to confirm that." But then Chris sighed and refolded the map. "All right. Let's go. Drive fast, but try not to stand out, unless we're being chased."

"I'm all over it. Buckle up."

Joe started the ignition and backed down the driveway. Once he rolled onto the street, he put the truck into drive with a jolt and sped off.

Chris turned around for a better look and Joe glanced in his mirror. There were flashing lights at the scene of the accident, but there were no Gray Coats in sight.

Joe made the turns he suggested and followed a sign to Route 167. Then they fled from Chibougamau uninterrupted.

CHAPTER 8
Wrath

At the main entrance to Pyxis, General Cygnus Gustave was waiting for news from Chibougamau. He had barked at every Gray Coat and soldier, told each not to bother him with guesswork or excuses, and now he was alone with his thoughts. As he played over recent events in his head, he still could not fathom how two ignorant brothers could have accomplished such an improbable escape with only the help of Andromeda's wingless daughter.

Apparently, Cassiopeia was not to be underestimated. She had that in common with her mother. Cygnus realized he should have never disregarded the princess when she disappeared. Andromeda had wanted her closely monitored, but Cassiopeia fell through the cracks. A meek and cowering runaway hardly seemed worthy of time and resources when the Extermination List was lengthening by the day.

Hours passed. Even though the air was frigid with dagger-sharp blasts of wind, Cygnus was sweating profusely. His career and probably his life depended on the two witless Gray Coats stationed in Chibougamau.

Where did this mission go wrong?

The apprehension had gone smoothly enough, with only two Gray Coat casualties. Christopher was an unexpected force to reckon with. Still, they overpowered him with relative ease. Then they all slept soundly through the transport into Canada and were well supervised throughout the queen's interrogations. The children, however, had caught them off guard. Royal Modifiers? Who would have thought it possible?

The queen was certainly a believer. In addition to her plots for vengeance, she had spent a fortune searching for Royal fairies who could also change to human size. She had gone through numerous husbands and years of trial and error in attempt to give birth to a son worthy of becoming her heir. Power and legitimacy in both the fairy world and the human world were at stake. Ironically, the family of her despised first husband had turned myth into reality without either knowing or trying.

Then, after they had all vanished from the guarded cage, the misfit group had had the audacity to enter the Aerial Palace, the most unlikely of places, and slip right through Andromeda's fingers. A jammed gate and a naked and unconscious Gray Coat later, the MacRaes had managed to hijack one of their vehicles and escape. Somehow, those Bottom-Dwellers and the broken little princess had outmaneuvered his best Crown Champions and evaded his Gray Legion. The entire mission had become a fiasco, a boondoggle, a bust, and the queen would hold someone responsible.

Cygnus's attention then shifted to the sound of approaching snowmobiles. The Gray Coat–driven machines crested the hill, and Lieutenant Crux Chevalier's battalion of the Royal Air Brigade flew in from behind. They were back, at last, but their carriers appeared empty.

Cygnus swooped up and landed beside his lieutenant. "Where are the Bottom-Dwellers? How dare you come back without them!"

"I'm sorry, sir," Crux said. "They Modified after abandoning the vehicle, and we lost sight of them. But surely they are hiding in Chibougamau. And I've already increased our numbers there. We'll apprehend them soon, General. I'm fairly confident—"

"Apprehended soon? Fairly confident? They could be halfway to America by now!"

"We'll keep looking. They'll resurface at some point."

"You had better hope they do," Cygnus growled between clenched teeth.

"General Gustave," a soldier at the entrance gate called out. "Her Majesty has requested your presence in the Strategy Room."

"I'll be there momentarily."

Cygnus walked underneath a black spruce tree and lit his pipe. While he took in a long drag, he considered flying off and never returning. If only he were a Modifier. He would be a vile, detested creature, but at least he would be able to assimilate into the human world. As a Royal fairy, where would he go and what would he do? Every decent fairy society across the globe had some of Andromeda's eyes living there. He would be a fugitive for the rest of his life. And at this late hour he would only be able to save himself. In his absence, the queen would undoubtedly kill off his entire bloodline, currently nestled in luxury on Royal Way.

The general considered his career for a moment, perhaps his only reprieve. He had helped line Andromeda's pockets with gold and riches, and had conquered any fairy clan she deemed Unworthy. His accomplishments were among the greatest of all time, yet this one misstep could taint his entire career—over thirty years of dedicated service.

He put out his pipe in the snow and returned to Crux's side. "Good luck out there. You'll need it."

"Thanks, sir."

Cygnus entered the cave and headed west on Royal Way. Then he nodded at the guards in front of the Aerial Palace. They opened the gate for him and moved aside. Cygnus opened the palace doors for himself, and as usual, the Hall of Crystal's orbiting gemstones were too bright in their display cases for his aging eyes. He squinted as he wove his way through the queen's prized possessions—diamonds larger than his head, emeralds, sapphires, fine metals worked by geniuses into shapes that seemed impossible, and one grandiose ruby prominently placed on a pedestal in the center of the hall. Most of her trophies were family heirlooms, peace offerings, or the spoils of war, though some were more magical, enigmatic, or sinister in origin than others. But that was the queen's business. Once the items were on display, they were out of his realm, and not to be disturbed, questioned, or admired too intently by anyone other than her, ever. He had grown used to passing by without interest, and palace staff seemed to do the same, the ones who valued their employment and their heads.

Then, as he made his way up the first flight of the Grand Staircase, he looked upon the sizable portraits of Pyxians honored for their greatness. Among them was a painting of his father, Cygnus Gustave III. Known as "the Enforcer," his father had seen war as a necessary means to an end. After the murder of King Canis Major V, the elder Gustave had led the efforts to annihilate Polaris. Rigel Kincaid, alias Scott MacRae, was the lone survivor. Cygnus's father had died soon after of battle-related wounds, but his legacy far exceeded his lifespan.

Cygnus bowed to his father and climbed to the third floor, East Wing. When he tapped on the Strategy Room door, he didn't receive an invitation inside. He waited, tapped again, and decided to crack the door open. Since the queen was sitting on her throne, he stepped inside. He stood just over the threshold with his legs together, chest high, and chin pointed out. "Your Excellency? You requested my company?"

Queen Andromeda picked up her dagger and began sharpening it with long, slow strokes. Every zing of the blade made the general's body tense. And the queen's wordlessness did not bode well.

"Your Excellency," he said again in a more placating tone, "we are doing all we can to recapture the MacRae brothers. They shan't get far. They are surely confined to Chibougamau."

Andromeda whipped the dagger from the sharpening stone and let it ring in the air. Then she stared at him with enough intensity to warp solid rock.

Cygnus continued the tale when the sharpening resumed. "You see, they were nearly apprehended, yet . . ." He paused, his thoughts hemorrhaged, and then he started again. "Your Excellency, we were unaware the princess was assisting them. Had we known, we would have been prepared for their bold escape tactic."

"And why, pray tell, is Cassiopeia still alive?" Andromeda inquired.

She seemed civil and calm—too calm. Cygnus sensed a trap. "Your Majesty, you requested she be closely monitored, not that she—"

"Consorting with rebels." Andromeda snickered, slowly at first, but her laugh grew hysterical, shrill, and insane. When at last her lunacy tapered off, she wiped the tears from her eyes and said, "Death would be the only acceptable punishment, no?"

Cygnus knew he was fighting for his life. "I . . . we did monitor her for a while . . . that is to say, for at least a couple of years, but our priorities changed at your request! She never appeared to be a threat—"

"Never appeared to be a threat. Hmmm . . . yes . . . that is what you would see, isn't it? An innocent young fairy, so small, so sweet, so sad," she chided like a child with her lips pouted, "just fighting to survive, live every day of her quaint little life to the fullest, with no agenda." Then she began to seethe. "But you were deceived, Cygnus, and to add to my mounting embarrassment, she is undoubtedly seducing her way into the noble hearts and virile pants of the sons of my sworn enemy. How will that make me look, my dear, tenderhearted general?"

Cygnus did not answer. He knew not to answer.

"Since an adequate response eludes you, I'll enlighten you. This debacle makes me look weak and incompetent. And you know I hate that."

Andromeda grabbed her dagger and fluttered toward Cygnus faster than his mind could process her movement.

Cygnus backed against the doors and threw his surrendering hands in the air. "Your Majesty, I will do everything in my power to fix this. You have my word and my unwavering loyalty. Give me another chance! I will make it up to you. Please . . ."

She was not taller than he was. She didn't have to be. He gave her all the power she needed when he lowered to his knees.

A nasty smile then slithered onto her distorted face.

"I beg you," he said. "Kill me quickly."

She lifted him by the chin with her cold fingertips. "Cygnus, you have served Pyxis honorably for many years. However, your shortsightedness is unforgivable. You will step down from your position and you are never to be seen in Pyxis again. Am I making myself perfectly clear?"

"Oh, yes! Thank you, Your Majesty." He lifted her hand to his lips and kissed it. "You are merciful and . . . and kind! I don't deserve your graciousness! Oh, thank you!"

"You may go," she said.

Cygnus rose to his shaky legs. And when his eyes lifted, he watched the queen's smile wither away and her expression plummet to that ghastly place known as wrath.

Pretending not to notice, he turned to leave. The door was nearly at his fingertips, but he never reached it. A sharp and staggering pain in his back had him on his knees.

And then he was falling.

"You fool! You worthless piece of filth! Did you honestly think I would grant you amnesty?"

The general tried to say no. He had known exactly what would happen before he entered the room. But he was dead in a pool of his own blood before he could answer.

***

Whereas most palace staff members performed their duties quietly, obediently, and industriously as far away from the queen as possible, Ursa did as she pleased, and tended to gravitate toward greatness. With the clever use of appropriate cleaning implements, closets and shadows, and spectacular excuses, she had made an art out of avoiding punishment for her unconventional behavior.

Just outside the Strategy Room, she was casually dusting every nook of the grand marble statue of a fairy goddess and if she kept her wings silent and her steps light, she could overhear most of what was said inside. On this particular night, she expected admonishment to be met with much groveling. And Ursa was usually right.

But, as always, her older sister, Lyra, kept interrupting her concentration. "Ursa, the furniture in the West Wing is not going to dust itself. Would you do your part so I don't have to this time?"

Lyra's disgustingly beautiful golden ringlets bounced off her back in the breeze of her departure. Ursa continued to dust the statue and didn't know why her sister had to try so hard all the time. Lyra was tall and slender, and had a pretty smile and weepy blue eyes, but if she were intelligent, she would make better use of those assets instead of her rag and dust mop. Ursa, however, would never be the angelic kind of beautiful, but she knew how to catch more than just the eye. Plus, she paid attention and spread information to the proper audience. She always had a way of being in the right place at the right time. Her skills served her well and kept her entertained, and perhaps they might enable her to escape the lowly class of her forefathers.

The Strategy Room doors suddenly snapped open. "I'm in need of assistance," said the queen.

Ursa entered quickly and curtsied. The fat general's blood was all over the floor, the walls, the doors, and there was even a streak of it across the queen's cheek.

"Find me Lieutenant Chevalier this very instant!"

"Yes, Your Majesty." Ursa curtsied again and fluttered out of the room to relay the message. As she waited for the lieutenant's arrival, she pondered her next move. She had seen and heard many foul things in the palace she had worked in all her life, but the general's execution was something else entirely. Still, she decided, spreading the news could wait. There was an even better story about to transpire.

Ursa was dusting the statue again when Crux Chevalier entered the East Hall. As he approached, she backed against the wall where the torchlight was most favorable, swept her copper-colored hair to the side, lifted her ample chest, and parted her lips. But Crux didn't even glance at her as he strode into the Strategy Room.

She released her held breath, and though she was slightly disappointed—Crux was a bulk of masculinity, with wings that could span the entire hallway, and he was filthy rich on top of that—she figured that it was just as well. Supposedly, if one believed the old fairies in the kitchen, Crux was a dangerous anomaly who preferred a challenge.

Ursa wouldn't say she was intimidated by the Brute and his boorish habits, but she was always true to herself, and her style didn't match his. She hadn't earned her reputation, one she was quite proud of, by being meek and helpless.

The door to the Strategy Room creaked closed, but it didn't quite latch shut. Ursa then noticed a scuff on the marble floor right beside the door crack. She pulled a rag from her pocket and knelt beside it, scrubbing in soft little circles while the queen was giving Crux her orders.

"For the time being, you are in charge," she muttered indifferently. "Your first order of business is to clean the mess your commanding officer left for you." Andromeda gestured to the heap on the floor, but she clearly meant "mess" in a broader context. "Have the body beheaded and post the head on a spike at the main gate. Let it serve as a warning that I do not tolerate blunders of this magnitude. Burn his residence to the ground, and finally, see that Canis Major returns from the academy. He will lead the next mission when he arrives. And, my dear Crux. . ."

As the queen rose from her throne, Ursa disappeared into the supply closet across the hall, though she made sure the closet door was slightly ajar.

"Do not fail me," the queen said as she pulled open the Strategy Room door.

Ursa saw her glance down at the body of General Gustave and then peer into Lieutenant Chevalier's eyes.

"Yes, Your Majesty," Crux responded expressionlessly.

The queen then buzzed from the room. Judging by the time it took for a door to latch shut, Ursa knew the queen had retired to her bedchamber.

Then, with an expression that Ursa could only describe as pleasure, Crux began to carry out his orders with three sword strikes to the general's thick neck. Once severed, the head dangled from Crux's grip by a tuft of hair. It left a trail of blood as Crux made his way to the door. "I could use a hand in here!" his booming voice echoed.

Hidden and content where she was, Ursa watched Lyra fly in to him.

"Get this cleaned!" Crux roared. "Not a drop of blood is to be left on the floor! Do you understand?"

Lyra's complexion matched that of the general's nearly bloodless head, but she managed an obedient nod and curtsy. As Crux left the room, Lyra tentatively knelt beside the blood and pulled out her pitifully little white rag.

At that, Ursa decided the show was over and slipped out of the supply closet. *I must start my chores in the West Wing,* she thought with a grin as she passed Lyra. But first she would stop by the kitchen and give those busybodies something new to talk about.

There was one piece of information, however, that she would keep to herself and cherish. Canis Major was coming home at last!

CHAPTER 9
Famous Last Words

By two in the morning, Joe's eyes were getting heavy. He was about to wake Chris—who after bits and pieces of restless sleep in tight quarters had Modified and disappeared beneath his pile of clothes—when Joe felt movement in his breast pocket.

"Cassie, are you awake?"

Her tiny hands pulled down the edge of the pocket and her head popped out. "Yes, I'm awake. The children are finally asleep, though."

"Do you mind keeping me company? If I have someone to talk to, I'll be able to stay awake longer."

"All right."

Joe helped her out and placed her on his shoulder. She teetered for a moment and then sat with her legs dangling against the flannel shirt.

Once she was settled, Joe took in a deep breath that hitched and shook on its way out. "I've been meaning to talk to you about something."

"Sounds serious."

"It is . . . but it's not. . . . "

"Go on," she urged.

"Well, I can't believe I'm admitting this, but Chris was right. I'm sorry for what I said earlier about your past. I've met people who've had some pretty messed-up things happen to them. But how could what you've been through even compare, right? So when you're ready to talk about it, I'd like to be there for you, all jokes aside, of course."

"I appreciate the apology," she responded. "Honestly, I'm used to the inquiries about my past. The questions don't bother me anymore. The answers to those questions, however, are best left unsaid."

Since she didn't seem upset, Joe's jovial disposition returned. "Understood. Okay, Princess, we'll keep things light for the moment. Can I ask you something slightly less intrusive?"

"I . . ." She hesitated. "I suppose that would be acceptable."

"Brace yourself for this. How old are you?"

Joe had been meaning to ask when the time was right, because he couldn't put an approximate number on her age, and that frustrated him. She looked like she ought to be still in school, but all other evidence—her language, knowledge, and poise—suggested otherwise. He thought fairies might age differently too. Perhaps they lived longer or always looked young. Did they live forever? Die of disease or old age like humans did?

"That was a disappointing question," Cassie said, "but I'm not going to give you the opportunity to redeem yourself. I turned twenty on December 6."

"Twenty whole years old!" he mocked. "And I thought you didn't look a day over sixteen."

He spied a subtle smile on her face in the rearview mirror even though she tried to curtail it by biting her lip. To him that meant she had a sense of humor. It was ever so slight, but it was there, and something he could work with. And then Joe started counting.

"So what's the difference?" she asked unexpectedly, just when he came up with the number.

He was confused, caught off guard, and that was a rare occurrence. "What difference?"

"What's the difference between our ages? I could tell you were doing simple math in your head."

How did she know that? "Was not."

"Yes, you were."

"Prove it," he challenged.

"Why is your face so red, then?"

"Fine," Joe confessed. "You win. It's five years, seven months, and nine days. I turned twenty-five on July 15."

"Twenty-five! It's no wonder you're infinitely wiser than I," she retorted. "And how old is Chris?"

"That old man is turning thirty on January 6. Do you want me to do the math on that one too?"

"No, that's not necessary."

"Nine years and eleven months, exactly, making him way, way, way too old for you."

"That's not why I—"

"Sure, famous last words." He glanced at her face again in the mirror. "And look who's blushing now."

She was blushing, like a rose, but judging by her scowl and crossed arms, her pink face wasn't just due to embarrassment.

Joe decided to back off a bit. It was too much teasing, too soon, and she couldn't handle it. "Oh, don't be like that, Princess. I was just kidding. I'm sorry, and I promise I'll be nice."

"Famous last words," she mocked back at him.

After a long pause, Joe broke the silence by picking a new topic. "What were you doing in Pyxis when you weren't busy spearheading rebellions? Wait . . . sorry . . . is that too intrusive?"

"No, that's fine. I did what I could to survive. Mostly, I was—I am—a teacher. There are no schools for the underprivileged. I helped a number of families in exchange for a small fee or something they could trade."

"Did you go to school?"

"I had a few tutors. Mostly, though, I am self-taught. I spent a lot of my youth and early adolescence hiding in the Royal Library. Later on . . ."

Cassie trailed off while Joe was checking all his mirrors. He glanced over his shoulder as well.

"What's wrong?" she asked.

"Nothing, I hope. I just noticed a car behind us, and we all know what happened last time."

Cassie knelt on his shoulder and swiveled around for a better look. "Are they gaining on us?"

"To a degree, yes. Enough to worry? I don't know. I'll try to lose them," he said, flooring the gas pedal.

The headlights behind them became smaller and fainter until they disappeared.

Joe's eyes returned to the road ahead. "Paranoia. Sorry. Looks like we're fine now. Feel free to continue."

"Where did I leave off? Oh, education. Once I was on my own, I read everything I could find. I love learning. It's the only thing I excel at."

"I'm sure that's not true."

"Perhaps, but without wings I could never do what others around me could. Also, early on, I showed no talent for magic, adding to Andromeda's mounting disapproval."

"Wait a sec. They . . . I mean, *she* can use magic?"

"She is among the few who can. The queen must grant fairies permission to practice it, though some secretly use it anyway. She wants absolute power. Therefore, magic is reserved for her or for those who serve her interests."

"That's strange," Joe said, while trying to recall his transgression with Andromeda. "I wonder why she didn't use it on us. She only used physical intimidation."

"I know little of her magic or its limits."

"Truly terrifying. Do you think my father knows any magic?"

"Again, I'm not certain. If he does, he learned on his own or from his kind. She would never allow a fairy-male to be more powerful than her."

Joe laughed. "Fairy-male?"

"Why is that funny?" she challenged. "I don't find the human words 'man' and 'woman' that amusing."

"I don't know. It's just so fairy-ish, I guess. What's a female called? Femairy?"

"No, fem-fairy."

"Ah," he said, holding up his index finger on his right hand. "I was close. Anyway, Princess, I don't think I can last much longer without sleep, even with your company. So I'll wake Chris."

"I could try to wake him," she offered.

Joe lifted her off his shoulder. "Yeah, why don't you? I don't want to hurt him or raise my voice and wake the twins."

***

Cassie was placed at the peak of Chris's pile of clothes. She rummaged around until she made a hole for herself. Careful of her foot placement, she lowered herself in.

She crouched down, felt around for him with her hands, and listened closely to the sound of his breathing. When she located his shoulder, she shook it gently. "Chris," she whispered, but he didn't stir. "Chris," she repeated a little louder.

He woke up with a start and a gasp for air. She could feel his entire body tense with the hand she still had on his shoulder.

"Sorry to wake you, Chris. Joe needs you to drive, if you feel ready."

"Oh . . . right." She released her hand when he sat up. "I forgot for a second what's real and what's not."

"I know what you mean. Sometimes the imaginary is more terrifying than the real."

"Yeah," he mumbled in exaggerated agreement.

When Joe pulled the truck over, Chris Modified to human size, redressed, and then the brothers stepped out to switch sides. Cassie used the brief moment of solitude to climb underneath the passenger seat.

"Cassie? Are you still here?" Joe asked when he returned.

"I'm here. I'm going to rest," she called out.

Joe leaned forward and checked for her by his feet. "Where are you? You can take the seat if you want."

She didn't reply. She was fine where she was and needed some time to herself.

It seemed unlikely that Chris would come to her aid yet again, but he did just that. "Joe, she probably wants to be alone," he said softly.

"All right. Offer still stands if you change your mind." With the springs over Cassie's head squeaking each time Joe fidgeted and readjusted, she was grateful to hear, "Chris, hold my shirt. The kids are still in the pocket." Then Joe's pant legs went limp as he Modified to fairy size.

Once Cassie believed he was asleep or at least comfortable and no longer able to see her, she crawled out from underneath the seat. Then she leaned against the edge of carpet by the door and slipped beneath the floor mat. The last thing she looked at before closing her eyes was Chris. He was concentrating on the open road, and his face was neutral, but his eyes were longing for something—or someone—far away.

The very nerve of Joe to suggest . . .

The last thing she, or anyone else in their party, needed was a romantic entanglement. *And besides, Chris's heart is probably the most impenetrable fortress in the history of man or fairy.*

Cassie pinched her eyes shut as if attempting to expel any further introspection on the matter from her head. The truck was dark and quiet, and Cassie, despite her mind-cleansing efforts, entered into a tangled array of memories—a dangerous place indeed.

When her eyes tore open, as if only minutes later, she was startled by something unusual to her. And clearly a significant amount of time had passed because a natural source of light was peeking through the Silverado's windows. She hadn't seen the sun in such a long time that she stood and reached for it.

Cassie dropped her hand when Chris's eyes flicked over.

"I was wondering where you'd disappeared to. You didn't have to sleep on the floor. We would have made room on a seat somewhere."

He leaned over and offered his hand to her. After she climbed on, he lifted her up in his open palm. His hand wasn't a stable surface, but even so, she stood on her tiptoes so she could see out of the front window.

"It's spectacular!" she gushed, nearly losing her balance.

"What is?" Chris pinched her feet for her and lifted her higher. "Oh, the sun. Yeah, it's nice today. I haven't seen a sunrise like that in years," he replied pleasantly, but not with the same degree of awe.

Chris's lift soon wilted and before he had the chance to abandon her on the passenger seat or some other uninteresting location, she slid down his forearm and climbed onto his shoulder.

"That's better." She stood on the tip of her toes again so she could see over the dashboard.

"Um, I guess that works," Chris said. "Make yourself comfortable."

She sat on his shoulder, delighted with the view. There was something magical about the snow-draped forest and the way the sun made everything sparkle. But before she became too enamored of the beauty, she reminded herself how cruel winter could be.

***

Later that morning, Chris was driving through the streets of Montreal. He pulled into a hotel parking garage and, with Joe's help, started watching cars and people. Since they intended to find some Americans and hitch a ride across the border, he parked in an area where there were many American license plates nearby.

"So we've got two New Yorks, one New Jersey, one Massachusetts, and a random New Mexico," Joe announced.

And then they waited, and waited some more. The cars remained dormant. The car owners were probably sleeping off their Christmas vacation hangovers.

"Look!" Joe eventually said. "Sleep-deprived American youth with a duffel bag walking toward us, three o'clock."

Chris looked over and then contorted his face with disgust. "Joe, you obviously don't have your glasses on. He's wearing a Yankees cap."

Joe gave him an are-you-serious look. "The curse is dead, dude."

"Yeah, but it's a matter of principle," he replied with his head held high. Any other proud and loyal fan would have said exactly the same thing. "What are you? A Dodgers fan now? Traitor!"

"No, I don't follow sports anymore."

"Traitor by default."

"You've lost me," Cassie announced from her vigilant spot on the dashboard. She was apparently people-watching too, or at least trying to absorb the nuances of the human world.

"Chris wanted to be the next great thing for the Boston Red Sox," Joe explained. "He was the best catcher our school ever had."

"Awww, Joe, that's so sweet," Chris said in a sappy voice.

"No, you just pay me well to say nice things."

Cassie looked even more lost than before, so Joe tried to elaborate. "Baseball . . . you've heard of it, right?"

"Yes, men hit a ball with a stick," Cassie said with surprising accuracy. "So why can't we choose that vehicle? It has four wheels and an engine."

"It would be incredibly unlucky!" Chris said with a chopping hand gesture.

"Yeah, but when we steal his car in a few hours, you won't feel that bad," Joe said.

They all watched the New Yorker open the hatch of his Toyota 4Runner. He threw the duffel bag into the cargo hold, locked the SUV with his clicker, and walked back to the hotel.

"That's a good point," Chris replied.

Joe threw one hand up in agreement. "Come on. If we wait for a guy in a sombrero, we'll be headed to New Mexico faster than you can say nacho grande!"

"Fine," Chris succumbed. "Let's get going before Mr. Yankee comes back."

Since Joe was better at Modifying quickly if he had to, the tentative plan they hatched called for Joe to stay in human form for the time being. From there they'd have to improvise.

Chris steadied himself in the Silverado and let his mind go blank. As usual, it took a few minutes, but once he had shrunk to fairy size again, he and Cassie joined the children in Joe's pocket.

Joe then exited the truck, walked over to the 4Runner, and unloaded everyone onto the back bumper.

"What are we doing?" Chris asked as Joe crouched beside the back wheel, for the most part hidden from view.

"We're waiting until the guy comes back and unlocks—"

They all jolted when the locks clicked and the rear lights flashed. The driver had again used his clicker; luckily, he had no other baggage and didn't notice the small forms on his bumper or Joe on the other side of the 4Runner.

As he started the engine and cranked up his gangsta rap on the sound system, Joe cracked open the hatch; Chris and Cassie ducked inside, the kids in tow. Then Joe disappeared and his clothes fell into a pile beside the 4Runner.

"Cass, throw me the rope! Then take the kids and hide," Chris said in an urgent whisper. He then caught the coil that Cassie threw and lowered one end to the ground underneath the hatch.

The driver rolled down his window and called to someone in the depths of the parking garage. "It should be open."

Chris panicked. He assumed the other person was on his way to the back of the SUV. Just then, Joe tugged on the rope.

Instead of the hatch, though, one of the passenger doors opened.

Chris heaved and Joe climbed as if both of their lives depended on it. The side door then slammed shut just as Joe crested the bumper.

Chris and Joe scurried deeper into the cargo hold as the hatch lifted. Luckily, the MacRae brothers were behind the first duffel bag by the time the second bag fell.

The hatch closed, the passenger got in, and the 4Runner pulled out, music blaring. Neatly hidden away from the clueless New Yorkers, the five fairy-sized figures sat in a circle, and Cassie pulled from her sack some much-needed nourishment—a loaf of bread and some jam.

Chris took a knife out of his pocket and gave it a toss. It flipped in a neat circle and he caught it by the handle. In the process he also caught

Cassie's eye. His trick made her smile. Increasing the level of difficulty, he tossed the knife in three consecutive circles. He changed the direction of rotation each time. Then he sliced the bread. Chris handed her the first piece and the knife; she spread the jam and then gave the slice to Ryan.

Once breakfast was distributed, Chris felt much better about their circumstances. They had survived a few of the most trying days of their lives. Although they had all been—to varying degrees—battered, amazed, frightened, and exhausted, their mood was surprisingly light, as if the us-versus-them scoreboard was finally in their favor.

CHAPTER 10
Proposition

Canis Major was awake early practicing for his Fencing Masters Level Practical Exam—a test he planned to ace—when an unexpected knock on his dormitory door interrupted his concentration.

He whipped the door open and was visually accosted by the detestable Crux Chevalier and three of his Royal Air Brigade cronies. "I'm busy. Come back another time."

As Canis swung the door shut, Crux shoved his foot in the crack and muscled himself into the room. "Your mother is waiting for you in Pyxis."

"I won't be a pawn in her vendetta. I have better uses for my time. You may see yourselves out."

Canis had found out late the night before that his mother had finally captured some of the Unworthies topping her Extermination List. He had nodded with dignified affirmation when word had reached him, but Canis rarely, if ever, agreed with his mother's policy choices. Following her whims, she had been squandering his inheritance. But Canis could do nothing but wait until Andromeda stepped down or died. Then, at last, he would be king! He planned to model his regime after that of the great Canis Major V, his grandfather, and hoped to bring prosperity, perhaps even another golden age, to Pyxis.

"This isn't a request. It's an order!" Crux growled.

"I don't abide by her orders," Canis said, and turned his back on his unwelcome visitors. He resumed the practice of his most advanced maneuvers with his artfully crafted sword, worth a small fortune. The majestic rubies and diamonds glinted with every slash and thrust.

"I can sympathize with your position," Crux replied, though clearly "sympathy" was not a word he understood. "However, those slippery Bottom-Dwellers have escaped, and General Gustave was held responsible. The queen demands you lead the operation to recapture the MacRaes. Her anger is unprecedented, so now is not the time to question her authority."

Canis considered which option would be most self-serving. "I'm a semester away from graduating with the highest honors. I don't want to be affiliated with her regime's failures."

"If you turn this failure into a success, you will be on your way to greatness," Crux cajoled. "You know you only have one option. The academy will let you finish your studies once the Unworthy are executed and order is restored."

Canis had to accept that Crux was speaking the truth. If he could turn this situation around, his subjects would love and respect him well after his death. He would be a Pyxian legend.

"Fine, but from this moment forward, I make the decisions. Understood?"

"Yes, Your Majesty," Crux replied.

The lieutenant played the role of a loyal servant deceivingly well, but Canis was not easily fooled. Crux was not to be trusted.

Canis took a few minutes to pack some of his belongings, and then he followed his Royal entourage out of his Regal Military Academy dormitory. They emerged from a hole in the crumbling architecture of a seventeenth-century Quebec City building and flew down to the Range Rover waiting for them on the cobblestone.

By midafternoon, they had entered the Aerial Palace in Pyxis. Canis followed Crux up the Grand Staircase but halted midair at the landing between the east and west stairs.

Crux paused in flight and turned to listen.

"Tell my mother that I'm very tired from our journey and prefer to be left undisturbed until evening. Though do make certain my chamber is tended to right away."

At Crux's weak nod, Canis nodded back once with authoritative finality. Then he fluttered to the West Wing and entered his chamber, the most lavish suite in the palace other than his mother's.

He removed his traveling clothes and put on his most flattering crimson robe. His many full-length mirrors reflected a kingly fairy-male with neat black hair, pale skin, and eyes dark as night. He used to be bony and grotesque, but maturity and a grueling fitness routine had finally given him the muscle tone that would be expected of both a prince and a military leader.

He removed his sword from his trunk and watched his body ripple with perfection as he fenced his reflection.

"You may enter," Canis commanded in response to a tap on his door.

Lyra entered his chamber with her arms full of fresh pillows, linens, and towels. She curtsied and went about her chores. And she was exactly what he was in the mood for—someone sweet, sensitive, and gorgeous.

She stripped the old linens off his bed and let the fresh ones fly high in the air. Her enticing curves begged to be touched. The academy had been all work and no play—and how he had longed for opportunities to play!

When he could no longer resist, he laid his sword on his bureau, eased up on the maid from behind, and ran his hands down her sides.

"Did you miss me?" he whispered in her ear.

Lyra swept her hair aside so that his lips could descend her neck unhindered. Then with closed eyes and a sweet sigh, she backed against him until it was gloriously uncomfortable. "Not as much as you missed me."

She had always tried hard to please him, to stand out from the others, and it wasn't even necessary. She was and always would be his favorite.

His lips continued to roam about, and his hands worked assiduously on the buttons in the front of her uniform. Gluttonous for more skin, he also unclasped the flap of fabric that connected the dress around her splendid white wings. The uniform slipped off her narrow shoulders and rested midarm.

Just as he began to cup her breasts with his hands, she slipped away and landed in a provocative position in the center of the bed. Her blue eyes, as deep and vulnerable as the day she had offered her virginity to him, expressed her faithful and unequivocal yearning.

As she finished the job of undressing herself, his robe dropped to the ground. Then he bounced on the bed in pursuit of her. They played a game of cat and mouse until he finally caught hold of her arms. She giggled and yelped in surrender when he pinned her underneath him.

His mouth overtook hers and then wandered, wild and free. She was even more delectable than he remembered, with fuller curves and softer skin, engorged and fleshy pink in all the right places.

With each kiss and stroke, her back arched, her legs slackened. A breath or two escaped her as a whimper, and without further ado Canis began satisfying his strongest craving.

Then, unexpectedly, his bedroom door swung open and hit the wall hard enough to startle the enamored pair.

"Canis," his mother hissed.

Oh, Crux Chevalier, the prince thought, *this one will be costly. . . .*

He sighed irritably and disengaged himself from his lover. "Honestly, Mother. You could knock or, better yet, respect the message I had sent to you that I did not wish to be disturbed."

"Get rid of her! We have urgent matters to discuss!"

Lyra was already redressing as if her life were at stake. With her head lowered, she sped past his mother and out of his chamber. For a libidinous moment, his thoughts followed her, summoning to mind a supply closet, her tidy little bed, an abandoned hall.

Nonetheless, he put his robe back on, tied it tightly, and got out of bed. "All right, Mother. I'm listening."

"Good. I believe you've heard the latest?"

"Indeed. The MacRae brothers have escaped."

Andromeda emitted a brief snigger. "Oh, Crux Chevalier must have left out my favorite part: your vile wretch of a half sister helped them every step of the way."

"I'm not all that surprised, Mother. Honestly, what did you expect?"

"I needed that filth out of my sight!" she proclaimed, paradoxically raising her voice and whispering. "I presumed she'd be closely observed, killed if necessary. And yet some fools are too soft to follow orders."

Canis knew he had overstepped a boundary. He decided to divert the topic away from Cassiopeia. It was too sensitive of a subject for them both. "Mother, why exactly am I here? I had nothing to do with the MacRaes' capture. I lack the details pertaining to their strengths and weaknesses."

"You were brought here to lead this mission. Now that Cygnus has failed me, you are the only one I trust to end this madness. I also have a proposition for you. . . ."

"I'm still listening," he urged, eyes wide with anticipation.

"The second they are all dead, you will get something you've been lusting for. I will step down, and you will be crowned king." Andromeda let her words sink in for a moment before pressing home her point. "By 'they,' I mean all three generations of the MacRaes—father, both sons, and the grandchildren—and your sister as well."

"If I have to kill Cassiopeia, I'm not participating—and that's final."

He paced away from his mother and removed the sword from his bureau. With the bejeweled hilt in one hand and sparkly blade in the other, he hoped his mother wouldn't call his bluff. He professed a fondness for his half sister, but he would never forfeit his future for anyone.

"Awww. Feeling sentimental, are we?" she chided. "Fine. Have it your way. She can live. You'll just be responsible for dealing with her."

"Agreed. Is that all, Mother?"

"Oh, there is one more thing. . . ."

Her hand wove through the many layers of her black gown. Her wardrobe choices were always so outlandish—the embroidered bodice studded with crystals, the skirt pouf as wide as three robust fairy-males. Every day she primped herself as if she were attending a lavish event. It had to be her way of diverting attention from her face. But Canis could see that beyond the scars her beauty had begun to deteriorate. There were deep-set trenches around her eyes and mouth that made her appear angry all the time, and outright terrifying when she smiled. No matter how hard she scrubbed, polished, painted, adorned, or outfitted herself, she couldn't remove the ugliness. Canis wondered why she even bothered trying.

Canis could have conceived three male heirs in the time it took his mother to find what she was searching for. At last, she removed a newspaper from her gown and tossed it to him. "Not that you deserve this, but you might want to follow, perhaps, your only lead."

"*The Pyxis Discourse?*" Canis's nose flared with disgust. "Why do you still read this sensationalist rubbish? You know how it upsets you."

"I like to know how my *loyal* subjects spend their frolicsome hours. And the editor, Pierre Delacroix, supposedly had a little chat with the MacRaes early yesterday morning. Read it. I also suggest you find him. And, Canis . . ."

"Yes?"

"If I were you, I would begin right away. Every second counts, and I doubt the Unworthy will be found between your bedsheets."

Canis could feel his cheeks flush. He remained silent until Andromeda had left his chamber. "Yes, *Mother*," he then said, imitating her lofty voice.

He chucked the copy of *The Pyxis Discourse* on his bed and picked up his sword. His mind was going in many directions.

I will be king!

The idea of ruling Pyxis at such a young age put a little extra swagger in his feints. After a few minutes, though, Canis grew bored of swordsmanship practice. Despite his mother's suggestion to find Pierre immediately, there was not much Canis could do until late evening. Pierre most likely did not stay in one place long due to the dangerous nature of his work. But like most uncivilized rebels, liquor and feminine company would smoke him out of his hiding place by midnight.

Canis collapsed onto his bed, scanned the *Discourse*, and thought of at least a dozen things he'd rather be doing. Less than halfheartedly, he opened to the featured article, "Christopher the Valiant Seeks Revenge."

Weeding through the long-winded paragraphs made him irritable. Although the details regarding the MacRaes were sketchy, the article did allude to "their mission" and "reconnecting with their father."

"I suppose Pierre might know something," he mumbled.

He looked up from the article when he heard a light knock on the door. It was most likely not his mother; she didn't believe in knocking. "Come in." Canis was glad Lyra had read his mind. She of course topped the list of things he would rather be doing than reading *The Pyxis Discourse*. "May I suggest you lock the door behind you this time?" He tossed the newspaper aside and patted the spot next to him on the bed. "Now where were we?" he asked as the golden-haired maid undressed and rejoined him atop the fresh linens. He loosened his robe and tried to make up for lost time, kissing, exploring, caressing. But he soon sensed a hesitancy from Lyra and bore down on her troubled lips. "Don't fret, love. You have no need to fear her."

Lyra gave him a slight smile, and when he kissed her again, her mouth and body were more receptive.

Canis didn't think twice about his mother's directive to begin his search for the MacRaes at once. He was confident he could please her and still have time to please himself.

CHAPTER 11
Homecoming Party

By midmorning, the MacRae brothers had pulled some more Modifying tricks during a gas-station stop and were now in control of the Yankee fan's 4Runner, heading south through New York. The sparkling morning had turned overcast, and a wintry mix was falling. Ryan and Morgan had grown bored and tired; the combination led them to sleep soundly in Joe's pocket as the highway miles rolled on. If Cassie's silence was any indication, she had found a nook to rest in somewhere amidst the cargo in the backseat, but Chris couldn't tell for sure. Since they left Pyxis, she seemed to listen more than speak, though it was clear she was oblivious to nothing.

The plan Chris and Joe had made so hastily as they sped through the Adirondacks had been to head to Westport, Connecticut, where they would make contact with their mother's sister, Gretchen. It wasn't a great plan—they had never even met their aunt—but it was the only plan they had. But when they reached Albany, Chris changed his course.

"Hey, we were supposed to go south there," Joe said, craning his neck and pointing over his shoulder.

They were now heading east. "I didn't miss anything," Chris said evenly.

"I thought we were going to Westport."

"We are, just not first."

"Then where are we going?"

Chris didn't answer. He intended to return to Salem, Massachusetts, and his home—or what remained of it—and Joe would figure that out soon enough.

"Are you fu—" Afraid he might wake and startle the children with his choice word, Joe edited the statement he was about to make. "Are you bleeping crazy? Why would you want to go back there?"

"I need to know."

"Okay, I get that. But, here, the guy left his cell phone in the car. You could try calling—or maybe just googling the news—instead of taking us, uh, to a place we may not want to go right now." Joe picked up the phone from the cup holder and started pushing icons.

"I don't want to find out anything from the freaking Internet! All right?"

Joe indelicately chucked the phone back where he'd found it. Then, with an exasperated sigh, he crossed his arms and stared out his window.

Chris glanced at the clock, 12:15 p.m. He knew that Joe, no matter how out of sorts, could deprive himself of technology for only so long. They had been out of the loop for more than three days and the suspense was probably killing him. Now that the suggestion of reconnecting with their own world had been made, Chris expected his brother to last no more than five minutes. Sure enough, at 12:19, Joe picked up the phone again and started fiddling with it. And almost as soon as he did, Chris snatched it out of his hand, rolled down his window, and threw the device onto the highway.

"What'd you do that for?"

"Two reasons," Chris said. "One, I don't want you to know either, even if you don't tell me. And, two, we did just steal a car. Can't the cops track us with those things?"

"I wasn't going to check," Joe said. "The last thing I want to do right now is give you bad news."

Chris knew he was at fault—he had hollowly agreed to a plan and then changed it without consulting anyone else—but he was infuriated all the same. Part of what had propelled him forward in Pyxis was the possibility that Alana was still alive. Yes, it was stupid and dangerous to go back—there were other ways for him to learn the truth—but he had to do it. And Joe, though right in theory, should understand this. But it seemed he had grown too used to taking care of himself, by himself.

"Can I talk now or are you going to rip my head off?" Joe asked, breaking the long silence.

"You mean talk me out of going where I have to go?"

"Good. So glad you brought it up. We shouldn't go there because—"

"I never said *we* were going anywhere. I'm going alone."

"Whatever," Joe retorted. "Still a bad idea because, A, the evil winged ones might still be there; B, the police, and maybe the FBI, will be all over the place; and, C, I don't think you can handle it right now."

"Law enforcement should scare off the Gray Coats, and I am going to go in as a fairy so that the cops won't know I'm there. And I have to handle it sooner or later."

The two brothers said nothing more. The air in the 4Runner grew uncomfortably thick, like the pressure was slowly increasing. Everyone in the car could probably feel Chris's tension—for him, with him, and because of him.

Soon he turned up the hard rock on the sound system. Despite the sleet and freezing rain, the needle on the speedometer edged toward ninety-five.

"If you stay below ninety in this weather, we should be fine," Joe mentioned sarcastically.

Chris didn't react. He was in another place.

***

The drive along the Mass Pike was uneventful. Then, once they were in Salem, the twins awoke and recognized their surroundings. They buzzed around with more and more excitement at every turn Chris made.

Morgan landed on her father's shoulder. "Daddy, are we going to see Mom soon?"

Joe gave his brother an I-told-you-so look.

"Mom isn't home today," Chris said. "I'm going to try to find out where she is, though."

"Oh," Morgan replied. "Is she at work? I want her to see my new wings."

"I don't think so."

Morgan sulked for a moment but soon fluttered off and joined Ryan, who was now playing a game of tag with Joe's palms.

About a mile away from the house, Chris and Joe got out of the car and switched sides.

"Don't you want to get a little closer to the house?" Joe asked with his elbow leaning on the open driver's-side door.

"I'll walk the rest of the way. It will be safer for all of us if you stay here," Chris replied from the sidewalk. He stared in the direction he intended to travel.

"Walking could take you the rest of the day," Joe pointed out.

Chris's eyes shot back in his brother's direction. "I'll hitch a ride somehow."

"What are we supposed to do while you're off playing spy?"

Chris was already exhausted from hashing out what he considered needless details. "I don't know! Go to the museum!"

Joe scowled. "Where do we meet you, then, and what time?"

"I'll be back in a few hours. How about right here?"

Chris turned then and stood silent, refusing to answer any more of Joe's persistent questions. A few seconds later—Chris was finally getting used to Modifying with ease—he disappeared into his clothes and redressed in his fairy attire.

As miniature Chris emerged, Joe removed the human clothes from the ground without comment or even a glance, and then he slammed the vehicle door shut.

Chris lingered in the middle of the sidewalk as he watched the 4Runner disappear. It took a passing car and a shudder to spur him into motion. He jumped to the road and jogged toward his house alongside the curb. When a traffic light turned red, he caught hold of a mud flap on a low-riding sedan and held on until close to his destination. He let go before the car made an undesirable turn and continued jogging for the remaining blocks.

Before he rounded the last corner, Chris glanced over the curb and captured his first view of the house. It was a white Victorian built in the late nineteenth century. He always admired its quaint charm. In the chilly light rain, however, it looked as gray as the sky. The yellow crime scene tape further marred its appearance.

Chris felt as if a noose were tightening around his neck. At first, he forgot why he wanted to put himself through this. He briefly considered turning back. Then an inner, almost supernatural force drove him forward.

Once he reached the house, he hoisted himself up the shallow steps with a run, a jump, and a climbing lift. At the top, he leaned beside the door and waited.

When the door opened, a state trooper stepped out. Chris sneaked inside before the door slammed shut. Then he crouched behind a snow boot by the radiator.

There were at least half a dozen people inside his living room. They were violating every corner and shadow, every book and photo and knickknack, every bill and receipt.

He had to remind himself that the police were not the enemy. They were just doing what they were paid to do. An evil-fairy invasion wouldn't exactly top their list of plausible explanations for the bloodbath in the bedroom.

Just as he was about to move closer to hear their subdued chatter, the front door swung open again. Chris dodged back behind the boot.

The young man in a cheap suit approached the older, heavyset investigator holding the clipboard.

"Did you discover anything unusual today?" the younger of the two asked.

"No, not yet."

"Do you still think he killed her?"

Dead. She was dead.

"There's no doubt in my mind," the older one said, with a thick Boston accent.

"Shouldn't we wait for forensics to confirm that before we write this guy off?" said the younger man, obviously a rookie. "I mean, he never even had a speeding ticket."

"Nah, I've got a hunch. Seen it all before."

"You have to admit it's strange that his brother and father are missing."

The older man shrugged. "His father has been gone for about four years, and his brother's probably shooting up in some drug den. My guess, a coincidence."

"I hope we find the kids in time. Only four years old . . ."

"You hang on to that hope, kid. You're gonna need it."

Chris couldn't listen or even function after that. The colors in the room became hazy, furniture looked like it was hanging from the ceiling, and voices sounded muffled as if coming from under water.

She's dead, and they think I'm her killer. . . . They think I murdered my wife and kidnapped my own children. . . .

Chris had to sit or he would have fallen down. He wondered what he'd done to deserve this. Everything had been taken from him. Alana—he would

116

never hear her voice again or feel her touch. There would be no more laughing together while watching bad movies or comforting each other after bad days at work. Picnics, movies, road trips—no more. There would be no more fights and no more making up. On top of that, any hope of a normal life for his children evaporated in front of him like a splash of water in the desert. The humans would want blood from him for a crime he did not commit. He would spend the rest of his life on the run, hiding from humans, hiding from fairies.

Like a vigilant sheepdog, his anger corralled all the erratic facets of grief deep inside of him and pushed outward a bitter numbness that at least enabled his feet to move, his mind to zoom in on one goal—going forward. Chris decided to collect a few items and leave his old life behind. He was a MacRae—a fairy, a warrior—and would avenge his wife to the death.

He hustled to the staircase when the timing was right. The wood trim on the wall allowed him to walk to the second floor without the need to climb each stair one by one.

Most urgently, he, Joe, Cassie, and the kids needed money. Continuing to steal cars would attract unwanted attention, and stealing food—even if only just enough to feed themselves at fairy size—would be dangerous and time-consuming.

Alana had had a rainy-day stash that she'd tried to keep secret from him. He always knew it existed, though. It was tucked inside an old pair of sneakers in a shoebox in the master bedroom closet; the police may have seen the shoes but may not have looked inside them.

Luckily, the bedroom was empty. The police had already cataloged the area, it seemed. Everything was tagged, marked, torn apart, and then put back to a police standard of neatness.

As Chris moved closer to the scene of the crime, he turned away from the bloodstains on the throw rug. Even though he diverted his eyes, he couldn't erase the memory of the intruders, the baseball bat, the struggle, and the fall.

If only . . .

Why hadn't his father ever told him anything? Not even the slightest hint! No "By the way, Chris," or "I hate to break it to you."

Standing in the open space between the bed and the closet, Chris suddenly heard a familiar buzzing sound. His head snapped toward the hallway. There he spotted a winged fairy hovering along the ceiling, headed in his direction.

Chris was in very real danger once again. As he'd told Joe, Modifiers in their human state would stay away because of law enforcement. But fairies, winged or not, would be as inconspicuous as he himself was. Plus, they had swords and armor, and the Royals could get a bird's-eye view.

At least Chris had the home-field advantage. He scurried to the cracked-open closet and, even in the dark, easily found the money. It was too bulky to carry in his current form, so he needed some way to make it manageable. He unlaced a sneaker and wrapped the bills in a tight roll, securing them with the shoelace.

He lifted the ends of the lace over his shoulder and peeked out the crack. The flying fairy was circling his bedroom. After a couple of rotations, the fairy went back into the hall.

Once he could no longer see or hear the other fairy, Chris ran toward the hall. He was a few steps past the doorway when the buzzing sound returned and slowly increased in volume. Believing he was still unseen, he ducked into Morgan's bedroom.

Thankful for once that his daughter was a messy child who never put her things away, Chris found plenty of places to hide among the toys as the fairy whizzed past the door. While he waited, he realized some of the objects strewn around Morgan's room might be useful: doll clothes, a doll purse that had a strap he could throw across his shoulder.

Chris added the clothes and the roll of money to the purse and then climbed into a toy bin on a low shelf to search for anything else that might come in handy. On his way back down, his foot nicked a pink ball with bells inside. It bounced to the hard wood floor and rolled all the way to Morgan's open door.

Buzzing. It grew louder until Chris heard it ringing in his ears like a thousand bees. He ducked behind a teddy bear just as the Royal fairy moved into the room with his sword drawn.

Chris rummaged through his pockets for his knife, but both were empty. A string of expletives went through his head. He'd toyed with the knife when they'd had breakfast, and it never found its way back into his pocket.

The Royal paced around, sword elevated and ready. He was heading in Chris's direction. Then there were approaching footsteps—large ones. The fairy ducked behind a toy less than one human pace away from Chris.

An officer pushed Morgan's door all the way open with his foot. He entered the room with his gun pointed. After scanning the room and the closet, he put his gun back in its holster. Then, by the doorway, he squatted down and picked up the ball. As he rattled it a couple of times, his walkie-talkie crackled to life. "All clear?"

The officer stood back up and tossed the ball into the bin. Then he detached his walkie-talkie from his belt. "Yeah, looks like a toy fell. I swear this place is haunted."

The voice chuckled and said, "Yeah, no kiddin.' Wonder why that is?"

The officer then left the room. Chris remained motionless, and so did the other fairy. Time ticked by. Chris muffled every breath and tensed every muscle.

Then the fairy did something Chris didn't expect. He simply flew out of the room. And Chris wasn't going to stand around and wait for him to come back.

The hall was empty, so—with the doll purse strapped to his back like a hiker's pack—he ran toward the stairs. Before he made it there, the buzzing sound approached again. This time he ducked into Ryan's room. Over his shoulder, he saw three fairies fly by. As soon as they passed, Chris knew he didn't have a moment to lose. He ran to the stairs. Instead of walking carefully down the trim, he slid down it and used his feet to gain more speed.

He made it to the pile of boots by the door, but he stopped and circled, not knowing where to go next. When the three fairies hovered to the ceiling above the stairs, Chris darted behind a police detective's laptop bag. He didn't want to risk running anywhere else. So he unzipped the bag and climbed in. The computer would eventually exit the house. He just hoped it would be sooner rather than later.

CHAPTER 12
The Deal

Prince Canis Major, Lieutenant Crux Chevalier, and three Crown Champions began their quest to find Pierre Delacroix in Pyxis's South End. They harassed the poor, the drunk, and the homeless. When the subjects of their interrogations were rude or unhelpful, the ruthless quintet used threats of death to loosen their tongues. A number of suggestions led them to the Dark Nebula, a grimy tavern by the West River.

They entered the hole in the rock and secured a table by pulling out their swords. Even the toughest patrons moved aside.

While Crux and the soldiers took a seat, Canis lowered himself onto the corner of the only remaining chair with extreme caution. He didn't want to soil his hands or clothes on anything unsavory.

A scantily clad barmaid soon hovered over to their table. "Can I get you Royals something?"

Crux spoke first. "Yes, we need some information—"

"Crux, please. Be pleasant," Canis interrupted. "Let the lovely fem-fairy get us some cold ales before we get to know one another." He tossed in her direction a gold coin and his best debonair smile.

The barmaid gaped at the gold in her hand. She pocketed the coin and returned promptly with five mugs.

"You can keep the change," Canis said. "Now, your name is . . . ?"

The barmaid turned back toward him, cautious and uncertain. "Gemini."

"Ah, yes. Lovely. Gemini, are you aware of the goings-on in this fine establishment?"

Gemini pursed her lips to the side when he used "fine" to describe her place of employment. "I suppose you could say that."

"Well then, we were told Pierre Delacroix frequents this place. Are you acquainted with him?"

Gemini gulped and fiddled with the sloppy, strawlike hair by her ears. "I've heard of him."

"Where can we find him?" Crux chimed in abruptly. He leaned so far forward, straining to hear her answer, that he looked as if he might hover off his chair.

Canis lifted his hand in front of him, certain this fem-fairy required a more subtle approach. "Gemini, any information you can give us would be greatly appreciated. Have you seen him here lately?"

Her eyes wandered, pointlessly, guiltily. "I said I've heard of him. I wouldn't be able to pick him out of a crowd, though."

A clear lie, Canis thought. He moved his face into the torchlight. "I'm confident you can do better than that, Gemini. Where can we find him?"

"Sorry. Pierre doesn't tell anyone where he's going these days." The barmaid turned away.

"Wait!" Canis commanded. He pulled a handful of gold out of his pocket. "Can you venture a guess, love?"

She turned back around. "You can ask the Banker," she replied as if hypnotized, her eyes fixed on the gold. "He knows everyone. He's sitting in the back corner."

"Now, was that so hard?" Canis asked. "We are through with you, Gemini. You may go."

He gave her one additional piece of gold and thrust the rest back in his pocket. "Crux, come with me," he ordered. Then he said to the others, "You three, stay here and try to stay awake."

Canis fluttered over to the Banker with Crux at his side.

Grotesquely fat and with more hair in his nose and ears than on his spherical head, the Banker was playing cards with a grubby lot of miscreants while two fem-fairies, nearly half his age, lounged next to him. Judging by the greens sticking out of their scant clothing, he had his particular way of keeping them close—a way that certainly had nothing to do with his appearance.

Canis cleared his throat to get his attention. "Are you the Banker?"

"I am." The fat fairy's eyes were slow to lift as if heavy with irritation. "What business brings you here?" He returned to his task of dealing cards, unyielding to the interruption.

"My name is—"

"I know who you are, Prince Canis Major," the Banker interjected after glancing over Canis's face. "I see the family resemblance. Why is it you seek my company?"

"I've heard you are the fairy to see for my particular situation."

The Banker paused in his dealing, narrowed his eyes as if he'd lost count, and then collected the cards back into a pile. "That being?"

"I need to find Pierre Delacroix. Anything you can tell me will be lucratively rewarded."

"I see." The Banker whispered to his neighbor, who nodded, and then, a few nods later, the others left the table. Then the Banker gestured to the empty seats. "I may know where Pierre is. I may not. Unfortunately for you, I am a rich man already and, with favors only *he* can provide, Pierre pays me to *not* know where he is, if you follow."

Canis leaned back in his chair and scoffed at the Banker's blatant lack of fear and respect. "Don't play games with me. You may be powerful in your own realm, but even you are expendable."

The Banker chuckled. "Are you threatening me? It would be extremely unwise to do me harm." He twisted his jeweled rings around on his stumplike fingers. "Surely, fairies of your upbringing realize the threat of an angry mob. I cannot emphasize enough that I am the life force of Pyxis. I am the one who essentially controls this place. You may think you have all the power with your gold and your mercenaries, but without me, commerce would stagnate, currency would dry up, fairies would grow even more hungry and uncivilized. Is that something your mother's floundering administration can manage right now?"

"All right. You've made your point," Canis growled. "You have no interest in our gold, then?"

"No, it would take more than gold to capture my interest," the Banker replied as his attention turned elsewhere.

A group of giggly, intoxicated fem-fairies entered the tavern and caught the Banker's eye. And at the moment, Canis Major narrowed in on the fat fairy's biggest weakness.

"You seem like someone who can always make a deal," Canis said in a tone meant to massage the Banker's masculine ego. "All we want is a street address. There has to be something we have that you want in exchange."

"There is something that comes to mind. . . ."

"Name it!" Canis demanded.

"Your sister. After her whole wedding fiasco, your mother surely wouldn't mind if she rejoins my staff."

"My mother wants Cassiopeia dead, but she won't mind if we turn her over to you instead of killing her. There is, however, one tiny problem. Cassiopeia ran off with those abhorrent MacRae brothers. Recapturing them is our top priority, and I'm sure you can guess who potentially knows where they are. . . ."

The Banker's watery jowl practically fell to the ground. But then he regained his composure and his face hardened. "How do I know you will follow through with your end of the bargain?"

"You'll have to trust me," Canis said. "Besides, it seems like getting answers out of Pierre is in both our best interests."

"And what about her servitude papers? If she abandons her assignment again, I want to know that she'll be arrested and returned to me."

"I'll sign them myself. They'll be delivered upon her arrival. Her rights will be yours to protect."

The Banker massaged his stubbly jawline for a while, and then gave his assent with a nod. Canis brought his head down to hear his whisper.

"The headquarters for *The Pyxis Discourse* recently moved into one of my buildings on Le Noir Alley, number 11," the Banker said. "A fire destroyed the structure a few years ago, but the cellar is undamaged. There is a trapdoor entrance buried under a rock pile at the back of the ruined building. It may seem locked to an ordinary prowler. The lock is faulty, however. You can wriggle it open with patience and strong hands. Pierre arrives at precisely four o'clock in the morning to prepare the printing press. At six o'clock, the *Discourse* is ready for distribution. Pierre doles out responsibilities and disappears until early the next morning."

Canis stood up and offered the Banker his hand to confirm the transaction. "It was a pleasure doing business with you, sir. I will look back at this day favorably when I am king."

The Banker returned the handshake with a firm grip. "Please find me as soon as your mission is complete. There will be penalties to endure if you keep me waiting."

"You have my word."

***

Pierre Delacroix glanced up from beneath his hooded cloak and saw a green flag waving in the watch station. He scoured the street for stray eyes, just in case, and then dashed across Le Noir Alley with stringed bundles of paper dangling from his index fingers.

He slipped into the passage next to the *Discourse*'s headquarters, a boarded-up building with a crooked and filth-covered number 11 hanging above what was once the side entrance to a brothel, he recalled with a smile. For some reason, the number was moving with a metallic squeak, an odd occurrence in a zone of the cave so deep and sheltered. He made a mental note to remove it. If he intended to keep headquarters there for any duration, he didn't want the building to have any distinguishing features. Otherwise, the burned-out shell was perfect for his purposes. Because of the fire, there were no functional stairs, walls, or eaves, but the previous occupants had built the cellar like a fortress—windowless, waterproof, soundproof, fireproof—and there was only one way inside it.

At the back of the building, Pierre teetered over the labyrinth of flat rock slabs. He knelt down and moved the slab with the smooth edges aside.

He fiddled with his key in the lock. It sometimes gave him a moment of trouble, but not usually more than that. It popped open just before his frustration set in.

Pierre lit the candle waiting for him on the first step of the stairwell and balanced it on top of his paper. He could barely see over his pile as he eased down the narrow passage.

He counted the steps—nine—and at the bottom he took three more steps to his worktable. There, he set down his pile and immediately flexed his cramped fingers.

The candle continued to flicker, he noticed, even though it was no longer in motion. Out of the corner of his eye, he saw a shadow swell. He turned his head and spotted the whites of two eyes. As his body shifted toward the stairs, he crashed against armor. He was dangling in the air by a chokehold an instant later.

Fighting to free himself, he kicked over the candle. The squeeze around his neck strengthened until it became impossible for Pierre to move or even breathe. Then he lost consciousness.

***

When he came to, Pierre wasn't sure where he was or what had happened; the dark was absolute and the pressure on his airway remained firm. But the strike of a match brought him back to full awareness.

A fairy, all in black, moved with slow deliberation to the scraps of torchwood heaped in the corner of the room. He lit a fire, and upon his return, his malicious face came into view. "Pierre! We've been looking all over for you," the black-clad fairy chanted as if they were old friends.

Pierre's eyes wobbled around the cellar. He saw the red, the blue, the starred shields, the long swords. He was outnumbered by five, more than that if he considered their might and armor. "You bastards!"

Pierre tried lifting his feet and using his weight to weaken the chokehold. But the bulky arm around his neck squeezed tighter. He had to set his feet back down or he would have passed out again.

The fairy in black hovered up and landed on the ground in front of him. His teeth glinted in a mocking smile. Pierre had only one recourse: he spat in his enemy's face.

As soon as the gob hit the Royal's pale cheek, Pierre was slammed down onto the table. His wriggling wrists were pinned against his back.

"You should learn some respect," his punisher growled. Pierre's head was then knocked against a pile of paper with a sword-clasped fist.

The fairy in black pulled out a handkerchief embroidered with gold thread and wiped his face clean. "I wouldn't have done that if I were you. Do you have any idea of whom you are dealing with?"

"You are a *fiend* just like your foul mother," Pierre said coolly.

"Crux, punish him for his sharp tongue," Canis Major instructed with an accompanying sweep of his hand.

While the soldiers held Pierre in place, the notorious "Brute" peeled his right hand away from his body and secured it against the table.

Pierre watched the blade rise and fall. Then his hand exploded with pain. While he screamed and writhed, wondering how much of his hand he'd lost, his severed pinkie was shoved in his mouth.

"Now, Pierre, we would prefer to act civilized, if only you would cooperate. You have information we want. It's as simple as that."

Pierre spat out the finger. "I know nothing."

Canis lifted Pierre's head by his hair. "I don't believe that to be true. Where did the MacRae brothers say they were going?"

"I don't know to whom you are referring."

Canis slammed his head into the table with enough force to make papers fly. "Pierre, I'm no fool. I read your article."

"I write a lot of articles," Pierre retorted defiantly.

"I am particularly interested in the article about 'Christopher the Valiant.' Do you recall?"

"I . . . I . . . fabricated the entire thing. I never met him."

"Liar! Witnesses all over this disgraceful end of the city have suggested otherwise." Canis reached for Pierre's bleeding right hand, clamped it down, and lifted his sword. "I will give you one last chance. Tell me where the MacRaes intend to go, or you will lose the entire hand." Canis's arm slackened for a second while he snickered. "A handless writer. How very tragic."

While they all chuckled at his expense, Pierre squirmed with desperation, trying to free himself. But the clutches all over his body tightened to the point where it hurt to twitch. He had to yield.

Hyperventilating from terror and overexertion, he weighed his options carefully. He considered telling them nothing. He would lose his hand, probably his life, but he would die honorably as a martyr for his cause. If instead, he told them what he knew, there was a slim chance they would let him go. He would then continue fighting against injustices like these.

Pierre made his choice. "Connecticut. They have an aunt on their mother's side who lives in Connecticut. She might have information about their fairy heritage. And that's all I know. They didn't confide in me with the specifics."

"I knew you would submit, Pierre," Canis said with eerie serenity as he slipped his sword back into its sheath. "You reek of cowardice and are about as loyal to your cause as I am."

Two of the other soldiers put their weapons away as well, and the oppressive pressure against Pierre's body eased. "I gave you what you requested," he said, emboldened by the reprieve. "So set me free!"

Canis moved closer to Pierre's face and stared at him, coldly expressionless. "Finish him," he growled with demonic fervor.

A decisive blow was administered to the back of his neck. Pierre watched Canis Major wipe splattered blood off his pale cheek with his handkerchief. Then the editor of the *Discourse* saw no more.

***

Devastating news would reach the South End in a few hours, although not in print. The white paper that should have been covered with florid words in black ink was drenched instead with Pierre's blood.

CHAPTER 13
Memory Lane

While Cassie and Joe were waiting in the winter dark for Chris to arrive, Cassie was alternately entertaining the twins and listening to Joe talk. She played her best games, smiled, and made a few halfhearted comments when the conversation required them, but her thoughts were not inside the vehicle.

Hours passed. Once the twins had fallen asleep and Joe had dozed off, Cassie climbed onto the dashboard for a better view of the street. At first she sat cross-legged. Then she lounged on one hand. A little later, she was lying on her stomach. Her cheek was resting on the back of her hand, and her feet were swinging up and down. She never meant to, but she fell asleep watching and waiting.

A few hours later, a car zoomed by with music blaring. The motion rattled the 4Runner and snapped her back to wakefulness.

Why did I let myself fall asleep? she wondered, half panicked.

Cassie slid off the dashboard, walked along the passenger side armrest, and turned to see the dashboard clock. 4:02 a.m.!

She eased herself onto the passenger seat and bounded over the center console. "Joe," she called while tugging on his shirt. "Wake up!"

He didn't respond. She kept trying—she yelled, she shook his clothes, she jumped all over his leg—but she could not get him to stir. As a last resort, she took a sword from her sack and stabbed through the denim of his pants. This time she successfully startled him.

Joe's groggy eyes gradually focused on her. "Ow! What was that for? You know, you're not the first small one to stab me."

"Have you seen what time it is?"

Joe squinted at the digital display. "It's 4:06." He shifted the sweatshirt he was using for a pillow and shut his eyes again.

"And?"

He peered at her with one eye cracked open. "What?"

"Where is Chris?"

He closed his eyes again, but this time he was smirking. "I don't know. He's not here yet?"

Not amused, she stabbed him again, harder and deeper than the first time. "Do you think I would be asking if he were?"

"Ow, stop doing that! Princess, it sounds like you're panicking. Do us both a favor and stop. And it might help to breathe. . . ."

She gasped out her held breath, though she continued to panic. "Shouldn't we try to find him? He is about eight hours later than he said he would be. What if he's in trouble? What if the Royals have found him? What if he's stuck, or hurt, or . . . or . . ."

As her mind jumped to the most unthinkable scenario, tears were pooling in her eyes. They were about to spill into a humiliating cascade of despair.

"Let me reiterate: breathe. You don't know Chris like I do. He doesn't handle bad news well. He would need some time to himself."

"That could be one theory. And then there are my theories."

Joe grunted and grabbed his already disoriented hair. "We shouldn't even be having this conversation. We could be starting some secret fairy society in the mountains of Nepal by now. But no. We're waiting in a cold car, at four in the morning, right in the heart of danger all because Chris is too stubborn to listen."

Cassie climbed off Joe's lap. Arguing with him was time-consuming and futile.

"C'mon, Princess, don't be like that. Don't let the joking fool you. I'm worried too."

On the passenger seat, she grabbed her sack. "That's why I'm going out there to find him."

"You're not going anywhere!" Joe scolded patronizingly.

"Watch me."

129

Cassie climbed onto the armrest by the window. While she was trying to figure out how to open the door, Joe picked her up by the back of her cloak and brought her to eye level. "You're staying here and that's final!"

She thrashed around and tried to squirm out of her cloak. "Put me down!"

"Aren't you a feisty thing today? Don't make me put you in the glove compartment." He pointed his finger at her as a warning.

"You will do no such thing!"

"Will you calm down?"

She refused to answer.

"Can I be the voice of reason for one second?"

"Reason," she said coolly with her arms crossed, "can be a crutch for those who lack empathy."

All of the good humor drained from his face, and he set her down in the cup holder, but not with the delicacy to which she was accustomed. Then his head turned toward the window. "We'll give him a little more time. If he doesn't come back before dawn, I'll go find him. *You* shouldn't be wandering around in a world you have no experience with. *You* don't know the neighborhood and the house like I do, and you never know what's still lurking around. It's just not safe."

Cassie slumped into the cup holder until she could no longer see Joe and he could no longer see her. If she remained quiet and out of sight, she thought Joe might mistake her silence for compliance. She really intended to wait him out. He would go back to sleep soon enough.

But perhaps it didn't matter. There was a tapping noise on the passenger side of the car. Joe leaned over and opened the door. "Speak of the devil . . ."

Chris, still in fairy form, jumped from the curb to the floor of the 4Runner. "We should get out of here," he said as he removed a size-appropriate bag from his shoulder.

Joe slammed the door behind him. "Yeah, you don't say," he said. Then, in no particular rush, he buckled his seat belt, started the ignition, turned down the sound system, and took a sip of his beverage.

"Now, Joe!"

"All right!" Joe slammed his foot down. The wheels squealed as the 4Runner burst into motion. "We lose almost a whole day because of you, and now we're suddenly in a hurry?"

Chris didn't respond. Instead, he climbed into the passenger seat and collapsed to a sitting position by the seat's back. After staring blankly for a while, he pulled in his knees and covered his face with his arms.

Joe was the first to interrupt the weighty silence. "Do you mind telling us why you're eight hours late? Cassie was starting to hyperventilate."

"That's not true," she mumbled from her hiding spot. She was neither loud nor convincing.

Chris rose to his feet. "I'll be right back," he said as he disappeared into the backseat.

After he had Modified into human form and dressed, he leaned his head into the space between the seats. "I was stuck in the trunk of a state trooper's car. By the time I managed to get out, I was miles away."

"Better to be in the trunk than in the backseat with handcuffs. How'd you get in the trunk anyway?" Joe asked.

"That's another interesting part of the story. There were fairies still in the house. I climbed into a laptop case so they wouldn't see me. I knew at some point I would get back out of the house."

Joe peeked over at the sleeping nest the twins had made for themselves out of extra clothes on the passenger seat. Then he lowered his voice to a whisper. "And Alana?"

"Dead," Chris whispered back. "And, as if that isn't bad enough, they think I killed her, and our kids. Because *I'm* the deranged psychopath."

"I am so sorry, Chris," Cassie said, this time loud enough for him to hear.

"Yeah, me too," Joe added.

"Talk about something else now, please." Chris said. "Anything else."

Judging by Joe's pained facial expressions, he had trouble thinking of something else to discuss under such immense pressure. "Do you know where we're going?"

"Yes. Westport."

"I'm aware of that. I'm even driving in the right direction now. But do you have an address in mind?"

"I think I remember how to get to Gretchen's house," Chris answered.

"Wait. You've been there before? When did you ever meet her?"

"I never said I met her. We drove by her house once." Chris shrugged. "This isn't exactly a cheerful story either."

"When you said 'we,' did you mean you and Mom?"

"Yeah, we took a road trip there once. I guess our grandfather disowned Mom when she married our father. Did you know that?" Chris asked.

"I think I remember her mentioning it. I used to wonder why we didn't have grandparents like other kids in our neighborhood did."

"Yeah, well, Mom supposedly didn't speak to her sister after being disowned, so I'm guessing Gretchen sided with Grandpa. But once Mom found out she had cancer, she made contact."

Though Chris paused, Cassie found herself hoping he would continue. She was intrigued not just because the ongoing MacRae family saga was not dissimilar to her own familial misfortunes but also because this was one of the longest explanations Chris had ever given. He was either at peace with his beloved mother's death or was doing whatever he could to keep his mind off Alana. Cassie had a strong sense that his candor was due the latter.

"It was through email, I think," Chris went on. "When her health started slipping, they arranged to meet and she asked me to go with her. Why Gretchen didn't drive up to Salem instead, I don't know. . . .

"So, anyway, Mom was feeling okay in the morning, but that changed as the day went on. We made it all the way to the house and waited outside. She thought the nausea would pass, but it didn't. It was just over a year ago. I remember it being December because I was staring at Christmas lights for what felt like forever. The lights in this neighborhood were a bit unreal, like a winter wonderland.

"We never did get out of the car, and Gretchen never came out to meet us. Mom asked me to turn around and so I did. She said we'd go another time, but we never made it back there. And Gretchen didn't come to the funeral, either. No card, nothing."

Joe kept his eyes fixed on the road for a long time. Then he shook his head, subtly but with resentment, and his eyes pointed toward the rearview mirror, apparently to look his brother in the eye. "Why didn't you ever tell me this?"

Chris returned the look with his eyes bulging and he lifted a questioning hand in the air. "There wasn't much to tell. We went for an unproductive road trip to Connecticut and back. And besides, if you called more often, there are a lot of things I could have told you." Then he looked away.

"Last time I knew, phones are bi-directional," Joe said, now his eyes bulging.

"Sure, but I was busy with a wife, the kids, a thankless job, our sick mother, bills, a will, hospitals, insurance companies, blah, blah, blah, yadda, yadda, while you were off living the dream in Cali."

"Trust me." Joe's full attention returned to the road ahead. "My life there was no dream."

"Then why didn't you come back home?"

"You never asked me to."

"Did I really have to? Wasn't it obvious Mom wanted you to come back? You never heard her all those times she said 'Joe, I miss you' and 'Joe, it's not the same without you'?"

"She was never honest with me about her health. You should have told me how bad things were getting."

"I did!" Chris snapped.

"Yeah, but by then it was practically too late!" Joe sighed and his knuckles clenched on the steering wheel. "At least I made it back in time to say good-bye."

"Whatever . . . New topic . . ."

Chris leaned back and disappeared into the darkened backseat.

Joe's eyes flicked to the mirror again. "So are you going to be pissed at me for the rest of our lives?"

"I'm not pissed. At least you had an address and phone number. If there's anyone I'm pissed at it's . . ."

Cassie was still in the cup holder, hugging her knees and hanging on to the brothers' every word. Disappointed that the conversation seemed to have reached its conclusion, she stood up and cleared her throat, ready to be loud and clear. "What was your mother like? I apologize for the intrusion. Yet, I thought, perhaps, I could redirect the conversation to the good times."

"Wise move, small one." Joe looked down at her for a lingering moment. "Our mother—Skylar was her name—was an average-sized woman, but she had a presence about her that made her seem more domineering. Don't get me wrong, she was friendly to almost everyone she met unless she had a reason not to be. She had a high threshold, but if you ever crossed over the line, man were you in trouble! There was this one time, during a little league baseball game—I think it was a championship game or something, right, Chris?"

"Uh-huh," he agreed from the backseat.

"Well, there was this obese kid who didn't listen to his coach on third base, and he rounded the turn for home plate. Chris was the catcher, and he had the ball right there and the kid should have just accepted the tag. But the kid plowed into Chris like he was going for the kill. Chris would have landed on his back or shoulder or even his neck if he hadn't thrown his hand down. Even the spectators heard the bones in his wrist break, and my mother sprang into action like a lioness protecting her cub. I wanted to hide under the bleachers. I imagine my father did too. He tried to calm her down, but she didn't relent until the officials kicked the kid out of the game and probably baseball, maybe even society, for the rest of his life. Then she bossed the paramedics around like she was a doctor."

"That wrist still isn't right," Chris added. "I was lucky it was my left hand or my baseball career would have ended at thirteen."

"Did you play baseball as well?" Cassie asked Joe.

"A little, but I was always small for my age, and had bad eyes. I was more of a theater nerd and a musician."

"Oh, what instrument did you play?" Cassie asked, with genuine curiosity.

"Percussion. Piano or keyboard mostly. Do you play an instrument, Princess?"

"I can play anything with keys or strings, though for me an instrument's purpose is to accompany my vocals."

"Oh, yeah? A fairy princess with a voice like a bell? There's one I haven't heard before. Do you want to sing something for us? A little impromptu concert? *Mi mi mi miiiiiii, you you yooouuu,*" he sang in a hideous parody of a soprano. Then he bit his lip, and thankfully stopped singing. After that, and not a moment too soon, he quieted the chuckling. "Sorry. I'm done now. Since we're halfway there and the sun hasn't even risen yet, where should we go?"

Chris leaned back into the gap between seats and looked over Joe's shoulder. "You should put some gas in this thing. That orange light has been on for a while now."

"We've got plenty of time left. Do you happen to have any money in that cute little bag of yours?"

"Yes, as a matter of fact." Chris grabbed the pink doll purse from the front seat and pulled from it a wad of money. Then he set the purse inside the empty cup holder beside Cassie. "There are also some girl's clothes in there if you want to take a look, Cassie."

She nodded and pulled out three dresses. The first was simple and gray, the second a rich green color, and the third floral with a white background.

She held the tiny dresses to her body, estimating their likelihood to fit. They were oversized, but not by much. She could easily fix them with the needle and thread she'd brought with her. She started right away on the floral one. It had the most beautiful print she had ever seen.

"Should we find a gas station and something to eat?" Joe asked. "I'm famished. How about you?"

"Yeah, I suppose. We better pull off now or we might have to push this thing," Chris said, pointing to a sign on the road.

"All right already about the gas! You were never one for living dangerously, were you, Chris?"

"Don't give me a lecture about dangerous. I was in Iraq for how many years? And besides, driving with an empty gas tank isn't dangerous. It's just stupid."

Joe rolled his eyes but pulled off the road without comment.

***

By midmorning, Chris was navigating the streets of Westport with prudent impatience, past shops still busy with holiday commerce, luxury cars—stopping, parking, idling—and chic pedestrians, scarfed, coated, and hatted, strolling about in the light snow. The shopping bags, the smiles, handshakes and hugs, the jingle bells, and the music were all part of an unreachable illusion. And for Chris to witness love and happiness on the morning *after*—it was a form of cruelty he had never experienced before.

He kept on, gained speed, and once the downtown shopping area was behind him, he turned into a residential neighborhood and brought the 4Runner to a crawl with a gasp of relief. "This is it, I believe."

Chris parked the car on the road in front of his aunt's house, just beyond the half-circle brick driveway, and watched Joe's eyes go wide in the side window's reflection.

"Holy mother of pearl! That's not a house. It's an estate!" Then Joe bobbed his nose toward the Long Island Sound. "Wow, right on the water too. Look!"

"Yeah, that's great," Chris said without really looking. He dragged the key from the ignition one notch at a time.

"Okay. I admit it," Joe said, catching Chris's hesitation. "Even I'm a little intimidated. I mean, what do we say? 'Good morning. We're your estranged nephews. And here are your grand-niece and grand-nephew; don't

135

mind their wings. Oh, and this little princess here—she doesn't take up much space. Mind if we crash at your place while you cough up your family history?' "

"Or how about, 'It would have been nice if you had come to your sister's funeral.' "

"No offense, Chris, why don't you let me do the talking? You can just smile and nod."

Chris gave Joe a sideway glance.

"All right, just nod then."

Joe evaluated the mansion one last time and then opened the car door. "I feel kind of bad. We look like slobs wearing these college kids' clothes. It hardly seems appropriate considering the venue."

"Who cares?" Chris replied. "On second thought, maybe it's good that you care. You might actually fit in with the Wakefield side of the family."

With Cassie, Morgan, and Ryan tucked away in their pockets, the MacRae brothers stepped past the open gate and onto the driveway. The closer they moved to the house, the more luxurious it seemed. It had slate-gray siding with elaborate white trim around every window and door. There were white porches and balconies circulating around the house, with patio furniture covered and secured for the New England winter. For late December, it looked picturesque as the rough and turbulent sea crashed on the nearby rocks. On a warm summer evening, with the sun hiding behind wispy clouds low on the horizon, this location could have easily been one of the most spectacular places to live on the East Coast.

They climbed onto the gleaming scuff-mark-free front porch, rang the doorbell, and waited for what felt like an eternity.

Finally, they heard footsteps. Both Chris and Joe exchanged one last desperate look that said, "Is it too late to run screaming in the other direction?"

A slight woman in her fifties wearing a trendy yoga outfit opened the door. "Can I help you?" she snapped with her spindly arms tight over her chest.

"Hi, my name is Joe, and this is—"

"Oh, my God!" she said, after taking a better look at them. "How could I not immediately recognize you? Christopher, right?"

Chris raised his eyebrows with nervous surprise. "That's right. You can call me Chris." He unhooked his thumb from his pants pocket and offered his hand to her.

Gretchen brushed Chris's hand with her fingertips. "Chris, wow, you look almost exactly like your father did all those years ago." She let go of Chris's hand and turned to Joe. As she took his hand in both of hers, she stared into the eyes that were almost identical to her own. "And Joseph. You look like your mother, with the dark hair and the blue eyes."

Joe shrugged and flashed his teeth in a grin worthy of a politician. "You look more like our mother than I ever will."

This was true. Gretchen was a little taller and more slender than their mother had been, but she had similar features.

"So what brings you boys to Connecticut? It's obviously not the weather." Gretchen pulled the two halves of her zip-up sweatshirt over her stomach and shivered in response to a gust of wind.

"Sorry to drop in on you like this, Aunt Gretchen—" Joe began.

"Please, just call me Gretchen."

"Okay, Gretchen, but we were wondering if you had a few minutes to clue us in on some miscellaneous family details. Our parents didn't talk much about their past, and now we're curious," Joe said, commendably revealing neither too much nor too little.

Gretchen opened the door a little wider. "Sure, come on in. I was about to make myself a soy breakfast smoothie. I know. That doesn't sound at all appealing. I could make some coffee, if you'd like."

Joe looked to his brother for confirmation, which Chris supplied with a slight upward head bob.

"That would be great. Thanks," Joe replied.

They followed her through the double doors, passed another set of double doors, and emerged into the main foyer. Natural light flooded in through the tall, narrow windows. The ceilings were multitiered, two or three stories high, and the staircase in the center of the hall seemed the perfect spot for making a dramatic entrance.

As they headed to the nearest doorway, Gretchen secured her loose hair into a messy knot with an elastic. The sight of her neck reminded Chris of his own fairy mark—the four black dots in the shape of a diamond—and he didn't notice anything like that on her.

Is she human or . . . ?

The kitchen was spacious, modern, and sparkly clean, like something out of a home magazine. Chris and Joe took a seat in the sunny breakfast nook while Gretchen prepped the coffeemaker and began pulling containers out of the pantry and refrigerator. "My housekeeper made her famous granola yesterday. It's fantastic. There's fruit salad and yogurt as well."

Gretchen brought the food over and set down a pint-sized pink concoction, presumably her smoothie, at the head of the table.

Chris pretended to nibble at the granola, and while Gretchen headed back to the counter, he dropped a few pieces into his breast pocket. The twins were inside it, moving around a little too much. He had to lean his chin on his palm so they would remain undetected, but after a few attempts to angle himself away from direct view, he decided their motion was still too bouncy. Even though the T-shirt he had on underneath his flannel shirt was in need of washing, he removed the flannel and draped it over the back of his chair. The twins fluttered to the floor and were out of sight unless Gretchen happened to peek under the table. Chris just hoped they would stay there, but once he accepted the potential that they wouldn't, he could feel his pulse begin to beat against his temples.

"Did you two have a nice Christmas?" Gretchen asked as she took her seat.

Joe smirked and bit back a laugh. "Mine was interesting, to say the least. How about yours, Chris?"

Chris was not amused and gave Joe a look to let him know. Then he lied through his teeth. "It was all right. And yours?"

"Christmas was quiet without my girls around. They're in the French Alps with their *father*."

Chris could tell by the way she said "father" that there was a divorce or a separation involved.

"We have two cousins, right?" Joe asked.

"Yes, I have two daughters. Victoria is eighteen and Anne Marie is sixteen. Don't you have children, Chris?"

"Yeah, Morgan and Ryan. They're twins and four years old."

"Your mother always mentioned them in the emails she sent me. Gushed about them is more like it. You didn't want to bring them along? I love kids."

"They're home with their . . . *mother*." Chris accidently let a note of misery slip out.

Gretchen peered at him with confusion that bordered on suspicion. Then her eyes dropped to his scabbed wrist and zoomed in on his ring-free finger.

Joe, thankfully, disrupted the tension when he cleared his throat. "How are your parents—our grandparents—doing?"

After one last wary glance at Chris, her attention returned to Joe. "Mother lives in her own little world, and Father just recently passed."

"Oh, I'm sorry," Joe said, and Chris forced himself to nod in agreement.

"No need to be sorry. He led a full life. He was ninety-one years old and a tough old bird until his last dying breath. And he never would have admitted this, but once he heard your mother had died, he seemed to lose the will to live."

Joe's eyes lit up when the conversation took a desirable turn. "Why is that? I thought he and Mom hadn't spoken since before our parents' wedding?"

"That's true. He was determined never to speak to Skylar—your mother—again. But if she'd made the first move, he probably would have forgiven her. And when she died, the hope of reconciliation must have died with her."

"I don't understand. What did she do that was so unforgivable?"

"Father adored Skylar. He wanted only the best for her and had plans that did not include her marrying a mysterious fisherman with no family and no money. When she appeared and announced she intended to marry Scott MacRae, Father threatened to disown her. She didn't seem to care." Gretchen gave a small but shrill laugh.

Chris wanted to walk out of the room.

"That was the last time she and Father ever spoke," Gretchen went on. "Neither Father nor anyone else among us could figure out why she made the choice she did. We had to assume she was pregnant. Why else would she marry . . . ?"

"Some nobody?" Chris chimed in, not caring if he came off as rude. He found Gretchen's implication insulting. Chris had done the math before; his mother had been pregnant when she eloped with his father, and he was that baby.

Gretchen glared at Chris suspiciously once again. "What I was going to say was 'so quickly,'" she corrected loftily.

"Sorry," Chris mumbled, even though he wasn't.

After an uncomfortable silence, Gretchen got out of her chair with an abrasive screech. "Coffee. I forgot about the coffee. How do you take it?"

"One cream, one sugar," Joe said.

"Black," Chris said simultaneously.

When Gretchen returned, she handed a delicate china cup and the matching saucer across the table to Joe. Then she clunked Chris's down in front of him. The coffee sloshed over the edge, onto the saucer, and dripped next to the pink flowers on the tablecloth. The oblong mark stood out like a dash of blood on a white bandage.

Even the thought of blood made Chris woozy. Blood had flowed so freely over the past few days—out of his wife's throat, down his wrist, out of that fat Gray Coat's bloated abdomen. All of a sudden, Chris's greasy breakfast from a few hours earlier made his stomach flip from testy to uproarious. He forced a few slow, deep breaths to subdue the ravaging nausea.

It's just coffee. Try to relax.

Chris closed his eyes and reached for his wedding band with his shaky hand. He felt nothing and vowed never again to reach for his ghost of a ring.

His eyes startled open when Joe nudged him with his foot underneath the table. Joe gave him a what-is-your-problem look, and then Chris's eyes met up with Gretchen's. Her eyebrows were high too. Chris looked back to Joe and hoped his brother could recognize the cry for help.

"How did our parents meet anyway?" Joe asked a good question with even better timing. "It seems unlikely she would just show up in Gloucester one day and meet a handsome stranger."

Gretchen cradled her tiny coffee cup in her hand. "That's pretty much how it happened. Skylar was teaching at the time and took her seventh-grade biology class on a field trip there. Apparently, one of her students went missing. The one who found the missing girl was, of course, Scott. They never told you that story?"

"They probably did, but like most teenage boys, we tuned them out when they started reminiscing. But now that they're both gone . . ."

"I've been meaning to ask you about that. Have you heard anything from your father lately?"

"No, and that's one of the reasons we're here," Joe said. "We want to find him and hoped you might be able to tell us something we don't already know."

"I barely knew him," Gretchen claimed. "Your mother began to email me only in the last few years. I missed your whole growing-up years. When she and I started to communicate with each other after all that time, she mentioned your father had left, but she was pretty vague about the details."

"Do you still have any of those emails?" Joe asked. "Even something minor could help us."

"I think so. I don't usually erase anything personal. I'll see if I can print them out for you."

"That would be great! Thanks, Gretchen. We knew we could count on you," Joe said with a wink.

Gretchen smiled with a quick giggle as Joe slathered on the charm. "I'll be right back."

Once Gretchen was out of sight, Joe smacked Chris in the back of the head.

"Ow! What'd I do now?" Chris said.

"Could you act any more dark and suspicious? Honestly!" Joe threw his hands in the air.

"I can't help it. The woman hates me. I can already tell."

"I wonder why, jackass!"

Chris just shrugged. What he wanted more than anything else right now was to be alone.

Joe crouched his head into his shoulders, raised his eyebrows, and put his hands back up in the air, this time in surrender. "All right. I get it."

"I don't think you do," Chris replied solemnly.

"Yes, I do. Can you at least try a little harder to act like nothing is wrong? If Gretchen senses something's off, she might not—"

"Fine!" Chris interrupted, not needing or wanting a lecture on how to behave. "What do you think so far anyway?"

"I think she has human written all over her. I hope these emails pan out, or this trip is a dead end."

"I agree about the human thing. Hey, let Cassie out. I have a question."

Joe leaned over in his chair and peeked out the doorway. Then he pulled Cassie from his pocket.

Chris rested his head on his folded arms so he could see her and hear her better. "Cassie, the marks on the neck . . . Do all fairies have them?"

"Fairies in Pyxis either have wings or they have a mark, but not both. The fairy marks vary in pattern depending on your ancestry." She swept her long hair off her neck and turned around. "Look, I even have one."

Chris glanced at her mark. It was a star shape, but it wasn't the same as the sigil he'd seen tattooed on the Gray Coats. Her star was symmetrical, much more elaborate, and with its shading and intricate patterning, it looked better than any tattoo or mark he had ever seen.

"Does Gretchen have a mark?" Joe asked.

Chris removed his head from his arms and leaned back into his chair. "I checked her neck when she was pulling her hair back. I don't think there was anything there, but it all happened so fast."

"Assuming Mom was human because her sister most likely is, you do know what this could mean, right, Chris?"

"No, but I'm sure you'll enlighten me."

"Your kids. Get them out for a second."

Chris set Morgan and Ryan on the table and checked their necks. "They have wings and the mark, our mark. The diamond. Strange, right? Now reason through it with me. Say Mom was human and Dad has the diamond mark. That's why you and I have it, too. And the diamond would be dominant. Now, if Alana was human, then where would the kids have gotten the wings? Assuming what Cassie told us is true, their type of fairy was considered 'legendary' before we showed up in Pyxis. And the wing trait was inherited along with our mark, possibly making the children truly unique. Back to our mother—if she was this weird type of fairy, wouldn't we also have wings?"

"So Alana is—was—a fairy? Is that what you're saying? I mean, what would the odds be? Alana and I, both of us fairies without knowing it, and her type so rare that they practically don't exist, and we just so happened to marry each other?"

"I know it sounds a little far-fetched, but it's the simplest explanation."

"And can we really use human genetics to explain fairy traits when there's clearly magic involved?"

"I don't know for sure," Joe admitted. "But science works in this case. We might as well stick to what we know. And geographically it makes . . ." His voice tapered off to a whisper and he didn't get a chance to finish.

Chris and Joe stashed Cassie and the twins back in their pockets. Then Gretchen reentered the room, sat back in her chair, and placed a stack of paper on the table. "So, your mother mainly talked about her progress and setbacks with radiation and chemotherapy . . . and her grandchildren," Gretchen said, skimming the emails. "But, oh, wait! Here she mentioned your father in one email from around three years ago: 'Scott has been gone for over a year now, and I miss him tremendously. I know I don't talk about him much, but I need to get this off my chest. When he left, he said he needed to take care of some business about his past. He never said how long it would take. I suppose I should have asked, right? He wanted me to go to Hawaii with him. I chose to stay behind. I figured he would be back in a month or so. I wish he would call, write, or give me some indication he is even alive. He doesn't even know I'm sick. Don't get me wrong, Chris and Alana have been wonderful. They have moved into my house with their new babies, and they take turns helping me with my doctor appointments, but they cannot replace him, and I'm starting to feel like my days are numbered.' "

Gretchen stopped there and looked up. "I'm sorry. I know this can't be easy to hear. I think this is the only time she mentions him. But here." She handed Joe the emails. "You can look them over when you're ready."

Joe quickly wiped his eyes dry with his thumb and forefinger. Then his rare show of emotion was over. "Thanks."

Chris was not tearing up but staring into space, something he did when he was trying to avoid boiling over with anger.

"Well," Gretchen said, "Are you boys headed back to Massachusetts tonight?"

"No, we're traveling around right now—a male-bonding road trip. We haven't decided what our next destination will be," Joe lied convincingly enough.

"If you want, you could spend the night here so you can get a fresh start in the morning," Gretchen offered.

Chris shrugged and Joe said, "Are you sure? We don't want to impose. You've helped us so much already."

"Don't be silly," Gretchen said with a dismissive wave. "Here, I'll show you the rooms you can have."

Their aunt led them from the kitchen and climbed the stairs. They followed her around a corner and down a bright hall decorated with nautical artifacts, photographs, and oil paintings. She opened the last two doors. Chris took the closer of the two rooms. Joe took the one at the end of the hall.

Once Gretchen left them alone to settle in, Chris closed his door and let his kids fly out of his pocket. Then he collapsed on his bed. Indoor plumbing, hot water, bedsheets, and a few minutes of television would be much appreciated comforts, even if only for one night.

He covered his head with his arms to block out the excess light and he fell almost instantly asleep.

CHAPTER 14
House Guests

Chris awoke to the dull sound of piano music. The digital clock on the nightstand read 5:30. He'd slept through most of the afternoon, and it was already dark outside. He sat up and flipped on the bedside light.

Morgan then landed on the pillow beside him. "Daddy! You're finally up."

"Sorry, kiddo. I'm a little tired today. Hey, where's your brother?"

"There he is. See?" Morgan pointed to a small blob in the corner of the room by the ceiling. "Are we going to find Uncle Joe now? And the princess? Do you think they hear the music too?"

"Uncle Joe is probably playing the music." Chris waved Ryan over to the bed. "Yeah, we'll go see them, but I want to talk to you first," he said as Ryan landed next to his sister. "Why don't you two sit down?"

It was time to tell them about their mother, but he didn't know where to start. He looked down at his two fairy children. Sitting, they were no larger than half dollars with wings. Their eyes, though, were as thoughtful and expectant as always. They may have known more about what was going on than he'd initially thought. Chris was just too preoccupied with his own misery to notice theirs.

"Is this about Mommy?" Ryan asked with the threat of tears already in his voice.

"Yes."

Morgan began sniffling and her eyes quickly filled with tears. "Did the bad men in our house hurt her?"

Chris nodded, not able to speak the words.

"Is she dead?"

Chris was caught off guard by Ryan's question. He had not been sure if his children were old enough to understand the concept of death. That was why he had hesitated to tell them in the first place. But they were growing up fast, maybe even faster due to all the things they've seen and heard. And they had a right to know the truth. Chris nodded again, this time with tears in his own eyes. "I'm sorry. You just have me now."

Ryan looked angry, disappointed maybe, but Morgan flew up and hovered beside his face. She cupped one of Chris's tears and lifted it from his cheek. For a moment, she held on to the bead of water as if it had mystical powers and then she let the droplet fall to the sheets. "Don't cry, Daddy. She'll always be with us."

He smiled ruefully and wiped the lingering tears from his eyes. "I hope so, and that's just what I needed to hear." He opened his palm for Morgan to land on. "I love you," he said as he lifted her to eye level. Then he opened his other hand for Ryan. "Love you too, Buddy."

Ryan sighed and then took his place in Chris's hand.

"And don't you two forget it!"

After that, they all needed a few moments to compose themselves, longer than that really, but they had to continue to carry on like nothing was wrong. Chris had to admit his children were much better at the façade than he was.

With his kids in his pocket, Chris followed the music to a den behind the main stairs. He went inside and leaned on the side of the grand piano.

He stared at Joe's fingers gliding across the keys until everything went blurry. He zoomed back in when he saw movement from the piano's music stand. Cassie was sitting there with her legs dangling in front of her. When her eyes met his, she waved at him and Chris smiled back. Then Chris looked into the hall for signs of Gretchen and didn't see any.

"Look who finally decided to join us," Joe said.

"Sorry, I fell asleep. I didn't even hear the piano until a few minutes ago. What'd I miss?"

"Not much. Gretchen had to run an errand and then was going to pick up dinner. I'm just entertaining the princess here. What do you think of jazz, small one?"

"It makes me want to dance," she replied as her feet kicked back and forth. Then she looked at Chris intuitively as if to say, "Is everything okay?"

Chris forced a quick smile and then turned to Joe before she could figure out more. "Does Gretchen know you're in here?"

"No, but I don't think she'll send me to bed without supper for playing the piano. Relax, Chris."

"I am relaxed," he insisted. "All right, fine. I'm a little on edge," he conceded. "Do you think we're safe here for the night or should we take off while she's gone?"

"I think we'll be fine until morning." Joe ended his song and started to play a louder, more upbeat tune. "You do know where we're headed tomorrow, right, Chris? Aloha, baby!"

Chris wasn't convinced. "You really think he's still in Hawaii?"

"Well, there are a few reasons to look into it."

"What reasons are those?" Cassie shouted so they could hear her over the music. "I'm a little lost, as usual."

"Gretchen mentioned it, obviously, and we lived there for a summer about . . ." Joe lifted his eyes to the ceiling as he tried to recall how much time had elapsed.

"Thirteen years ago," Chris said for him without the need to think.

"Chris remembers," Joe continued, eyes back on the princess, "because he met Alana there. My guess is some of these things are connected. And if it doesn't pan out, Hawaii is a much nicer place to waste time than New England in the winter." Joe changed the mood and speed of his music again. His new song was slower and less cheerful. "Before we jump on a plane, I think we should first discuss our goals for a second. What is it we want to accomplish? We could just find a secluded place to live, or Chris and I could return to the human world. We would just have to be more careful. Cassie, you could be our secret pet."

Cassie folded her arms and looked away from Joe's shameless grin. "I will never be anyone's pet."

"I can't return to my life in Salem," Chris said. "I'm now a wanted man. It would be easy to disappear, but what then? I can't raise my kids in hiding. I want my freedom back, and I won't have that until I deal with Andromeda. There is no way we can accomplish this on our own. Joe, if you're not interested in fighting anymore and just want to go back to California, I completely understand. I don't want to go to Hawaii, but I have to see this thing through to the end, whatever that end may be."

147

"I'm with you, Chris," Cassie announced. "I'd never experienced freedom and though we are in a race against time and evil, I now have a better sense of what it could be like if victory were ours."

"Well, when you both put it like that, I'm in too, all the way," Joe said.

Everyone tensed when a door opened.

"Gretchen's home. Back we go, Princess," Joe whispered as he put Cassie in his pocket.

A few minutes later, as Joe was playing some jazz again, Gretchen wandered in. "Dinner is here," she said, then leaned on the piano next to Chris and listened for a few minutes. "I see you have your mother's talent, Joe. But she preferred Beethoven."

"I can do Beethoven." Joe gave her a confident smile and started to play the first movement of Beethoven's Moonlight Sonata. "I don't get to play that much anymore. I am a little rusty, but it's like riding a bike."

"If that's you when you're out of practice, then I'd be glad to hear you when you *have* been practicing," Gretchen said. "Well, the sushi is in the kitchen whenever you're ready to eat."

"Thanks, Gretchen. We'll be right in," Joe said, continuing the sonata.

She stepped away from the piano and left the room at a perky pace.

Chris grimaced once she was out of sight. "Sushi? You didn't campaign for something better?"

"Does it look like she eats cheeseburgers?" Joe asked. "Son of a fisherman and you won't eat sushi. Figure that one out."

They soon joined Gretchen in the kitchen and took the same seats they'd had earlier. Beverages, plates, napkins, and chopsticks were distributed.

While Chris tried to consume a few pieces of sushi with the help of copious amounts of sparkling water, Joe was entertaining his aunt with funny stories from their youth and adolescence.

After dinner, Joe and Chris pitched in to clean up—the housekeeper was off until after New Year's—and then they chatted around the piano for a couple more hours before they went to their rooms.

Chris put his children to bed in the nightstand drawer. After a hot shower, he returned to his room, turned on the television, and appreciated an hour or so of feeling normal before he turned out the lights.

***

In the room next door, Joe was preparing a place for Cassie to sleep on the window seat. He stacked books into a pile so she could have some privacy, and lined up cotton balls and washcloths for her to use as a bed. Then he set her down behind the books. "All set, Princess?"

"This is perfect. Thank you."

"Well, um, good night, then," he said, suddenly feeling awkward. He tried to think of a catchy one-liner that would give him an excuse to Modify down to fairy size and enable him to join her even if it was just to talk. But everything that may have worked in the real world seemed oddly out of context in his predicament. "Yeah, holler if you need anything. I can't promise I'll hear you, but you can always try."

She sat down on the cushion and brought her knees to her chest. "Good night, Joe."

Joe sensed the closure in her voice and motioned with his hands that he was leaving. After he shut off the lamp, he collapsed onto the bed and looked toward the moonlit window. He wished for a few minutes that he could see Cassie behind the books, but soon enough sleep subdued his curiosity.

***

Gretchen woke up in her master suite, overheated underneath her thick comforter, her mind whirling with memories stirred up by the arrival of her guests. The digital clock on her nightstand read 2:50. She tossed and turned for a while but couldn't get back to sleep. She admitted defeat and switched on the television. As she was flipping channels, she was startled to see her nephew's face on the news. Recent pictures of his wife and children followed.

Then she remembered Chris's scabs and yellowing bruises, his poorly explained missing children, his lack of a wedding ring, and his weird behavior.

He could be a murderer, and he's in my house. . . .

***

Cassie shuddered underneath her washcloth covers, awake because of another nightmare. In the three nights since they'd left Pyxis, her odd, disrupted sleep had been filled with such dreams. It was as if her mother had a found a way inside her head. Andromeda was clawing around in there, leaving her signature in the color red.

149

Cassie was afraid to go back to sleep but was struggling to stay awake, so she dragged her bed closer to the window. She lay back down and stared at the sky. The nearly full moon seemed to light up the entire world with cool tranquillity. As she tried counting the stars, she had never felt tinier or more insignificant. Her eyes soon closed again. She kept opening them with great effort. Open, closed—and there was her mother's ghastly face, her long nails poised to do harm. Open! Cassie gasped for breath, but her racing heart demanded more and more air. Her lungs could hardly keep up.

Cassie stared at the stars again and calmed herself by focusing on Joe's rhythmic breathing and the whir coming from the heating vent. Open, closed—this time she could barely hear her own chilling scream over the sound of shattering glass. Open! She sat up, hugged her knees, and wrapped the washcloth over her shoulders. Then she rested her chin on her knees, but her stubborn eyes refused to stay open.

In a state of half consciousness, she heard another unsettling sound—a dull mechanical drone. An automobile, she realized, without opening her eyes. She should have been used to that sound by now, but something wasn't quite right. The noise of a moving car should peak and then gradually disappear. For some reason, though, the hum was steady and joined by a choir of others, each with its unique intonation.

She lifted her heavy eyelids and saw three black vehicles in front of Gretchen's house that definitely had not been there before. Smoke was pluming from their tailpipes and then, abruptly, the noise and the smoke stopped. At first, nothing happened; no one moved, and that included Cassie. She was frozen still. But then men with weapons in hand emerged from the vehicles with the coordination and discipline of an army. They hustled silently toward Gretchen's house, crouching and using hand signals.

Cassie sprang to her feet and ran to the edge of the window seat, nearly forgetting it was a long way down. She circled back along the outer edge and checked for alternative ways to the floor. There was nothing. The nearest piece of furniture was a few human strides away.

"Joe!" she screamed. The cavernous room swallowed her voice. She yelled again using her hands to amplify the sound. His rhythmic breathing didn't pause.

Desperate now, she reconsidered the distance to the floor and scanned the area one last time. She finally noticed the curtains tied to the side of the window. They nearly reached the ground. She ran over to them and fumbled with the sheer fabric until she found the edge. She latched on to it and slid to the floor.

She sprinted toward Joe's bed and made one last attempt to wake him. Again, he did not stir. He had his head buried beneath the covers and was facing the center of the bed. She had to accept that she was wasting time and decided to move on. She slipped underneath Joe's door, ran along the hall, and then slipped underneath Chris's.

Chris was facing the edge of the bed. His elbow was hanging off the side and he had his hand tucked under the pillow. His sleep seemed restless, his breaths shaky and intermittent.

"Chris," Cassie called from the floor.

His eyes pinched shut more tightly in response to her voice. Then he shifted to his back.

"Chris!"

Even from the floor, Cassie felt him jolt awake. He rolled back over to the edge of the bed with open eyes. Within a few seconds, he was reaching for her. "What's wrong?"

"S-W-A-T," she spelled for him. "What does that mean?"

Chris's wide eyes made an explanation unnecessary. He carried her in his loose fist into Joe's room.

"Joe!" he said loud enough to jar him. Chris gave him a firm shake, too. "We've got trouble. Get up. Hide!"

Joe lifted himself in bed, though not with any urgency. "Oh, for the love of God! What's wrong now?"

Chris crouched and scurried to the window to confirm Cassie's report. "Just Modify. Now!"

Joe vanished as directed, and with Cassie still in hand, Chris darted into the hall.

On the lower level of the house a door opened, then Gretchen's voice shouted, "They're upstairs." The sound of heavy feet moving spurred Chris's jog into a dash.

Once inside his room, he shoved Cassie inside the top drawer of the nightstand where Ryan and Morgan were sleeping, and pushed the drawer closed to a crack.

From within the drawer, Cassie could only count Chris's frantic footsteps—far too many, for far too long.

Cassie's hands flew to her mouth when she heard and angry voice say, "Put your hands up! Nobody Move!"

Just when Cassie believed Chris wasn't able to Modify in time, she saw his legs dangle over the side of the drawer. He slipped inside. It was dark, but not dark enough for her adjusted eyes. It shouldn't have come as a shock that he'd be naked, and she should have been prepared to shy her eyes away, but that didn't happen, not fast enough. While he rummaged with his fairy clothes, every muscle in her body constricted. All she could do was pinch her eyes shut and hope the suffocating feeling would pass. And despite all her worries, fears, and the dread of discovery, she couldn't make the image of him go away.

Her eyes sprung open when Chris grabbed her arm. He brought her to the darkest corner and then dragged the bed he made for his children to the same place, with them still sleeping peacefully within it. As time ticked by, his labored breathing became slower and calmer. It became easier to hear the men in the room. Their rapid footsteps gradually became more distant.

"Well, that was close," Chris finally whispered.

"Do you think they're gone?"

"They'll filter out slowly, check all the rooms and outside, but when they can't find me, they'll be back sniffing around for clues. So we should get out of here. This is one of the first places they might check."

"And then what?" she asked.

"I don't know. I don't have any answers right now."

***

By dawn, five scared-silent fairies were underneath a display case in Gretchen's long, well-lit second-floor hallway. They were waiting for an opportunity to make progress toward the stairs, but the humans had been stomping by nonstop for hours.

"Do you think it's safe to move yet?" Joe whispered to Chris when the hall finally cleared.

"I think so."

Chris was darkly contemplative for a while, trying to come up with the most efficient way to escape from his aunt's house and get to an airport. There were fewer options than he would have liked. Still, he crunched ideas and tried to come up with a fresh perspective. The weather, although not as bitterly cold as in Chibougamau, was still on the uncomfortable side. They would have to find an empty house that had an available car and unattended keys. That would require time-consuming trial and error. On top of that, people would be on high alert with a murder suspect in town.

"Why don't we see if Gretchen can help us so we're not wandering around the streets of Westport all day?" Joe said, breaking into Chris's thoughts.

"Yeah," Chris agreed reluctantly. "We need to at least warn her. I don't want her death on my conscience."

Chris peeked out from underneath the display case. The closest piece of furniture was a decorative table by the staircase, about ten human-sized paces away. He ducked back under when two men in suits rounded the corner.

"That is one long walk," Chris complained once the detectives went into the bedroom.

When the hall cleared again, Chris squatted down to give the twins instructions. "See that table by the stairs?" They peered out and nodded. "I want you to fly over there and then hide underneath. Can you do that for me?" They nodded again.

Chris looked left and right one last time. Then he signaled for the twins to fly. Chris, Joe, and Cassie hunched over and watched the children flutter over to the table faster than the three of them could have ever achieved on foot.

Joe darted out next. Then Chris looked to Cassie. She was lingering by the wall, immersed in shadow. Her silence hadn't concerned him until now. He walked over to her with a halfhearted smile and put his arm around her shoulders. "C'mon, this is child's play compared to what we've already been through."

"Oh, I'm fine," she said falteringly. "Well, no, I'm not. What concerns me is that I didn't grab my sack in Joe's room. It has all of our weapons, supplies, clothing, food. . . ."

Chris hunched down and looked back at Joe's room. He heard voices originating from that direction. "It looks like we're gonna have to cut our losses. I still have my bag. There are a few things we can wear, and there's some money left."

"Sorry," Cassie said with her eyes averted to the floor. "I should have remembered to grab it."

She really was sorry, too sorry under the circumstances. She was acting as if he was going to yell at her, or worse. He didn't want her head to hang low on his behalf, so he tapped her underneath her chin. And then she looked up at him with her wide, pensive stare. "It's all right. You were a little preoccupied saving our tails again. You're one up by the way."

A little cheer came to her eyes and it took away a layer of darkness. "I'm a light sleeper and thankfully you are as well. Joe on the other hand—"

"Could sleep through a nuclear holocaust. He has always been like that. Are you ready?"

Chris checked to see if Joe made it to the other end of the hall. He had, and was waving them forward.

"Ready as I'll ever be," she said.

"I'll be right behind you."

Cassie glanced at him over her shoulder. He gave her a reassuring nod and then she ran out. As promised, Chris followed closely behind.

Everyone reconvened underneath the table, and then Chris instructed the twins to fly to the first floor and hide under or behind the nearest obstacle. When their wings stopped buzzing, Joe, Cassie, and then Chris stumbled down the slippery ledge between the iron banister and the steps while holding on to the lower rail of the banister. They all met up again behind the potted palm tree beside the stairs.

"Where do you think Gretchen is?" Chris asked.

"I'm not sure," Joe said. "Why don't I try to find her by myself? I'll be back in a few minutes and then we can all go talk to her together. Or I'll talk and the rest of you can be, say, visual aids."

"Okay. Whatever. Just hurry!"

Joe ran into the kitchen first but soon returned. He shook his head and then went to the back hallway, past the piano room, and disappeared behind the stairs.

After several long minutes he reappeared, motioned silently, and led the fairy crew to the living room. They tried to stay inconspicuous by the wall, circumventing or going underneath furniture in their path. But they had to walk along the open floor to approach Gretchen on the couch.

When she spotted their movement along the floor, Gretchen retracted her legs and retreated into the cushions of the couch. Coffee sloshed out of the cup in her hand. She hunched over for a better look with her mouth gaped open.

"So, uh, our story is a little more complicated than what we told you when we got here yesterday," Joe shouted.

"What . . . ?" Gretchen breathed.

"Well, you see, it sounds ridiculous to admit this out loud, but Chris and I are technically fairies—and so are his children, here, Ryan and Morgan—and we have our father to thank for it. Oh, and this other fairy here is Princess Cassiopeia of the fairy city of Pyxis."

"This is a ludicrous . . . dream . . . ?" She pinched her eyes shut, and when she reopened them, she pressed her lips into a firm line, clearly frustrated that the reality in front of her had not changed. "He . . . he . . . killed his wife!" She pointed at Chris.

"I didn't kill her!" Chris roared. "She was murdered by our father's enemies!"

"How can . . . Why should I believe you?"

Chris could feel his face burn red. His lips twitched, close to spurting some choice words, but Joe gave him the signal to back off.

"Gretchen, please, I know this is a lot to take in. But we're in danger, and now that the whole world knows we're here, you're in danger too."

"Me? Why?"

"As Chris said, our father has enemies, and those enemies not only killed Alana but also captured us. We escaped, and they are following with the intent to kill us, along with anyone involved. They can turn from fairy size to human size and back again, just like we can, which only makes the danger to you greater," Joe said in a level tone that allowed the outlandish story to penetrate his Westport aunt's understanding. "Trust me. I don't mean to give orders, but you need to get us out of here. We need to get to the nearest airport as soon as possible."

"The police are crawling all over this place," Gretchen sputtered. "Do you really think they'll let me drive away right now?"

"We have to find a way," Joe continued softly. "You should get out of here too, until this all blows over. Call your daughters and tell them to stay away as well."

Everyone froze as footsteps fell along the hall. Gretchen threw her legs in front of the fairies.

"Is everything okay in here, ma'am?"

Gretchen looked up at the stocky man in the suit and gave him a fake smile. "All is well."

"Is there someone you were talking to?" the officer pressed.

"I was talking to myself. I do it all the time. No one usually worries until I start answering myself," Gretchen said archly.

The officer's condescending eyes had a hint of amusement in them. "May I talk with you for a minute?"

Chris realized the situation was heading in the wrong direction, and directed everyone underneath the couch.

"Do you mind if I use my own bathroom first?"

The officer clearly sensed the shift in her demeanor; she was probably angry and frightened when she had opened the door to his team a few hours ago, and now she was being flippant and coy. "Why don't I escort you?"

"Is that really necessary? Honestly, the thanks I get for alerting the authorities! You treat me like a child in my own house! Hopefully, for your sake, my lawyer doesn't have to hear about this!"

Chris let out a nervous breath. There was hope for Gretchen yet.

"Ma'am, calm down!" the officer insisted. "There's no need to take that tone with me. Meet me in the kitchen when you're ready."

Once the officer left the room, Gretchen reached under the couch. "Just so you know, I'm doing this for my sister and not for you—and definitely not for your father."

"That's cool," Joe replied as she shoved them all in the pocket of her zip-up sweatshirt.

The five fairies clung on tight as Gretchen strode down the hall, entered the bathroom, opened the window, and climbed through. There was one large thud to the ground, some jogging through the cold of the yard, some stair climbing, and then a knocking.

A door creaked open. "Gretchen? How are you?" a woman asked in a grandmotherly voice. "Is everything all right?"

"Fine. Linda, I need a favor. . . ."

Gretchen spun an incredible story to her neighbor that explained away the SWAT team and resulted in being handed the keys to Linda's black Mercedes. She proceeded calmly to the garage, backed the car down the drive, and drove off past the police cars.

Once they were rolling along, Joe crawled out of her pocket first. "Gretchen, you were incredible! I couldn't have done better myself!"

She let out a deep, dramatic breath. "Remind me again why I'm doing this?"

"Because we're your nephews and you love us?"

As Chris stepped out of Gretchen's pocket, he noticed that she looked annoyed rather than amused. Joe's charm wasn't nearly as effective now as it had been the day before. With one wrong word, their aunt could change her mind and scuttle his and Joe's quest to find their father.

"All right," she said once her knuckles unclenched a bit. "I want a better look at you."

Chris was happy to oblige and raised the edge of her pocket. Morgan and Ryan flew out and spiraled around each other. Then they hovered just below the ceiling of the car.

"Chris's children can fly?"

"Yeah, isn't it amazing?" Joe replied.

Finally, Chris helped Cassie climb out. With Joe leading the way, they jumped from Gretchen's lap to the cup holders in the central console. They lined up within Gretchen's sight, but not in her way.

Gretchen's eye wandered over to Cassie. "So you're a princess?"

Joe and Cassie exchanged looks. They both started speaking at the same time. "She's—"

"Yes, as Joe told you, my name is Cassiopeia, or Cassie for short. And, Gretchen, it's a pleasure to finally meet you. Thank you for assisting us. Words cannot express how grateful we are."

"Beautiful and polite. You could teach these boys a few things." Gretchen glared in Chris's direction. He chose not to glare back. Instead, he looked to the cloudless morning sky outside of the passenger's side window. "How do you know my nephews?"

Cassie exchanged another glance with Joe. "We met a few days ago in the city where I am from."

"She's technically . . . kind of . . . our ex-stepsister," Joe added with a chuckle. It was the first time anyone had expressed the odd and twisted terms of the relationship.

"You'll have to explain that one to me," Gretchen said, shaking her head.

Joe enlightened her to some extent until Chris cut him off. "Gretchen, I hate to be the prince of darkness here, but the less you know the better. Also, as Joe said back at your house, it's extremely important for you and your daughters to disappear for a while. Don't say anything to anyone about us. You're not potentially in danger. You *are* in danger."

"Fine, Chris. I understand," Gretchen claimed.

Her offhanded tone, however, suggested to Chris that she didn't exactly grasp the concept of danger.

***

After she returned to her neighborhood from the airport, Gretchen parked the Mercedes back in Linda's garage and spent the rest of the day drinking herbal tea and nibbling on this and that at her neighbor's house. Most of the police officers had left, the commotion had died down, and Linda had accepted the odd story, which Gretchen continued to spin out and mix with other tales and bits of neighborly gossip. After the winter sun had set, Gretchen wished Linda a "Happy New Year" and left the house out the back door.

For most of the day, Gretchen had been considering her nephews' advice and changing it to suit her needs. She could have disappeared from the airport, as they'd suggested, but she wouldn't have gotten very far without some of her personal belongings. Her best idea was to sneak into her house and get a few necessities—like her wallet, a coat, and her cell phone, all of which were located in the hallway connecting her garage to her kitchen. She would be careful to avoid law enforcement. If they spotted her, she would make up a good excuse, call her top-of-the-line lawyer, and would be free to do as she pleased by morning. As for the vaguely described enemies of her dead sister's absent husband, how threatening could they be, especially with the police still on guard at her house?

She speed-walked along the water's edge and threw her hood over her head. The evening sky was clear, though the weather was far from calm. The icy wind swirled off the Long Island Sound and pierced right through her sweatshirt. With the frequent, powerful gusts, she had difficulty walking in a straight line.

Gretchen passed the dock at the edge of her property and turned away from the water. Her frigid extremities, the uneven sand under her feet, and a burst of wind suddenly brought her to the ground. Her ankle twisted with a crunch.

"Great," she mumbled to herself. "A trip to the emergency room is just what I need right now."

She maneuvered herself into a sitting position and tried to rotate her foot in a circle to assess the damage. The pain made her wince, but her violent fits of shivering propelled her to get up anyway.

Gretchen hobbled in a circle. With her head down, she concentrated on careful foot placement. Then she noticed a shadow from the moonlight. She glanced up and saw two legs. Startled, she brought her head up with a snap. She gasped and collapsed again.

"Officer, I can explain," she said before she noticed the figure's strange attire. Then three other figures emerged from the darkness. They all wore helmets and long gray coats, and did not change course when she spoke to them.

"Stay back. Or . . . or . . . I'll scream!"

Their progress toward her remained constant.

"Please, I—"

She pushed onto her feet and tried to run, but she was grabbed from behind. There was a hand over her mouth before she had enough air in her lungs to scream.

Gretchen was carried to the outer edge of the dock and pinned down by her throat. Frigid water seeped into her hair. The pressure on her windpipe was strong enough to fog her vision. Her whole body began to tingle.

"That's quite enough. We don't want to kill her prematurely," a tiny but proud voice scolded.

The pressure on her throat eased enough for her to gasp for air.

Gretchen watched a fairy hover onto the palm of one of the gray-clad figures. "You don't seem surprised to see me, so I'm sure you know why we're here," the winged fairy said. "Did you help the MacRaes escape?"

"No. I called the police, but they escaped on their own."

"You're lying! Make her cooperate!" the fairy ordered.

The behemoth holding Gretchen's throat picked her up by the ankles and propped her body over the water.

"Wait! You're right. I did help them escape."

Gretchen was clunked back onto the dock, close to the edge. And the timing was ominous. A larger-than-ordinary wave crashed over the dock and saturated her clothes, right down to her socks.

She coughed and sputtered to bring up the salt water and was shaking even more uncontrollably. Her body temperature was dropping dangerously low.

"Where did they go?" another winged fairy yelled.

"I don't know exactly," she whispered between chattering teeth.

The second winged fairy, brawnier and scarier than the first one, hovered in her face. His snake-like tongue flicked into the moonlight. "Do you realize your life is at stake and the lives of your children? Victoria and Anne Marie . . . am I correct? We already know they're in France."

"You're a monster! Don't you dare lay a finger on them!"

Gretchen wanted to protect her nephews, but she wasn't willing to risk the lives of her own children. She also felt she'd acted beyond what was required of her and that Chris and Joe had a significant head start thanks to her. She convinced herself not to feel guilty.

"If I tell you the truth, will you let me go?" she asked, playing for time.

"You have my word," the haughty one replied.

"Your word," Gretchen said with a bemused grin. "Well, I took them to the airport. They are trying to find their father in Hawaii."

"Where in Hawaii?"

"I don't know." Gretchen looked frantically from one angry face to another. "Really, I don't! You have to believe me!"

"Kill her," the scary one ordered.

"Wait! I had your word! I told you what I knew! Please!"

"You had his word," the one grunted while pointing to the other, "not mine."

The figures in gray lifted her off the dock. With her mouth tightly covered, her scream was barely more audible than a hum. She attempted to kick and flail, but she was too numb. They slit her throat and threw her into the Long Island Sound. After a few strong waves, her body was adrift.

And the only solace was that Gretchen had been so cold that she hadn't felt the pain of her own death.

CHAPTER 15
Aloha

Suitcase-hopping through four different airports without detection was a feat of courage, perseverance, and quick wit. Once safely over the Pacific Ocean, in the baggage compartment of a plane headed to Honolulu International Airport, the five fairy travelers had a chance to rest and regroup.

Chris put himself in charge of coming up with a plan. Compared to his brother, he was more knowledgeable about the city of Honolulu, the neighborhoods, and the roads because he had lived in Hawaii on two separate occasions, both times when he was an adult, or close to it anyway. Joe, not quite able to relinquish control, was walking around on a map of Oahu, chiming in occasionally as Chris guessed where their father might be.

"Who knows if he's even in Oahu?" Chris suddenly complained, glancing at another, less detailed map that included the other Hawaiian Islands.

"We'll cross that bridge when the time comes," Joe said. "For now, I say we track down Alana's family. Do they still live in Manoa?"

"Her sister Simona does." Chris walked over to the residential neighborhood on the map. "I might recognize the street name if I see it."

"What about her brother or mother?" Joe asked. "You used to be friends with Kale, right?"

"Yeah," Chris replied grimly, "but that was before I became involved with his sister. Now he'll want to kill me more than ever. And her mother—

let's just say she severed ties with reality a while back. She's in some nursing home in Honolulu. I think Simona is our best bet."

"Aren't there two others?"

"Kale, Alana, Simona, Jasmine, and Bane," Chris listed, in order of their birth. Saying their names made him realize how long it had been since he had seen anyone in Alana's family, other than Simona. She had been able to visit a few times in Massachusetts, while Jasmine and Bane never could, and Kale never would. The last time Chris had been in Honolulu, Jasmine was wearing braids in her hair and Bane was barely more than waist-high, with dimples and a near toothless smile. Now they would both be teenagers. Chris wondered if he would even recognize the two youngest if he saw them. The thought made him cringe with sadness and remorse. Alana had never had the opportunity to visit her family after the twins were born, and Chris felt partially responsible. She never had enough money, or his candid blessing to use the money they could have borrowed or scraped together. And now she was gone.

"Do you think it is their mother or their father who has the fairy blood?" Joe wondered.

Chris shuddered out of his reflective silence and his eyes zoomed back in on the map. "I'm guessing their father. He has been MIA since their childhood. Catching on to a pattern like I am?"

"Yeah, deadbeat fairy fathers and the dysfunctional families they left behind."

"Yup."

Joe pointed to their old street with his foot. "Hey, here's where we used to live."

"Yeah, I saw that already." Chris continued to scour the map a few inches away, his frustration peaking. "I know it's right around here! Why can't I—" He was interrupted by a nudge in the ribs. "What?" Then he looked where Joe was looking.

Oh, he thought.

Cassie had emerged from her solitude wearing a perfectly tailored, form-fitting jungle-green sundress, courtesy of Morgan's doll collection and Cassie's own needlework. Long robes, cloaks, and multiple layers of clothing would not be necessary in Hawaii.

While the fairy was pinning her dark hair into a neat bun, Morgan and Ryan circled around her, trying to engage her in their merriment. They couldn't control their laughter and excitement. It didn't seem to matter that they were in the cramped cargo section of an airplane. Their play suggested they were already frolicking in a mystical fairy paradise. And the fairy princess who ruled over that euphoric land was kind, virtuous, and *entrancing*. Her trim legs, graceful arms, and newly revealed curves were nothing to frown on either.

She must have felt the brothers' eyes following her. Her smile faded, and her step lost buoyancy as she came toward them. "What's wrong? Is there something wrong with the dress?" She looked down, smoothed the seams, and checked for flaws. "I could change back into—"

"No, no . . . ," Joe started.

"Don't," Chris continued.

"You look fine."

"Perfect."

"It should be warm . . ."

"Very warm . . ."

They stopped jabbering like idiots and tried to act natural by continuing about their business. Chris considered himself crazy for even looking. Cassie wasn't the type to draw attention to herself, but then again, she didn't have to. Any man, fairy, troll, ogre—whatever—would notice her anyway. She was that pretty. So Chris forgave himself for the momentary lapse of judgment and vowed not to let it happen again.

"It's warm now!" Joe tugged at his collar. "Is it hot in here or is it me?"

In fairy form, both Chris and Joe had only their heavy Pyxis clothing. They had taken off the excess layers hours ago but still had on their animal-hide pants and the long-sleeve white shirts. They had the sleeves rolled up on their forearms, but still it was hot.

"No, it's not you," Chris whispered as an aside to his brother. "It's hot in here all right. And nice save."

Joe did a quick raise of his eyebrows and suppressed a smile. And Chris had yet another reason not to look; Joe had essentially claimed dibs on Cassie on day one.

"Aha! I found it!" Chris tapped the correct street with his foot. "I think the house number is ninety-one. Alana had me mail a Christmas card there only a few weeks ago."

Joe swayed a little where he stood on the map. "Do you feel that? I think we're losing elevation."

"Let's get our stuff together," Chris said. "The suitcase behind us belongs to someone staying in Waikiki. That's close to where we're going."

Chris, Joe, and Cassie gathered everything useful they'd found and put away some of the things they did not intend to carry. Then they tucked themselves and the children into an empty side pouch of the suitcase as the plane touched down.

***

They were picked up, tossed, rolled and bounced within their pouch, but they arrived safely at the hotel. Luckily, the owners of the suitcase ignored the side pouch during their unpacking and shoved the bag along with several others into a corner of the room. By the time the room was quiet and they felt it safe to emerge, it was late evening and not the ideal time to be making unannounced visits. So Chris and the others opted to hide underneath the bed until morning.

At sunrise, the human inhabitants left the room. Joe and Chris Modified and put on some of the tacky Hawaiian clothes they found in the room, tucking Cassie and the kids into the pocket of a colorful shirt. They strolled out of the hotel, figuring that in this tourist haven their bare feet and oversized clothing wouldn't attract unwanted attention.

With Chris's cash, they hit the tourist shops first. The brothers bought a backpack and human-sized flip-flops to use for the time being and fairy-sized doll clothes for themselves to use for later. Then they purchased some fruity pastries for breakfast and headed to the beach.

The day was young and the beach was not yet crowded. They found a secluded spot, flopped onto the sand, and lifted Cassie and the twins out of their pockets.

"The view is spectacular!" Cassie gushed from Joe's palm.

He handed her a large crumb of a pineapple strudel. "That's the good ol' Pacific Ocean. Doesn't it make you wonder why anyone would want to live in New England, or Pyxis for that matter?"

"I have never seen anything like it." While she ate her food, she stared at the waves breaking on the sand and took notice of the sunbathers enjoying the morning on the beach.

"Are we ready to see Aunt Simona?" Chris asked his kids once breakfast was winding down. The warmth of the sun was improving his mood and energy, and he intended to get everyone else motivated as well.

"We just got here," Joe complained.

Chris stood up, added the twins to his pocket, and brushed off the excess sand from his clothes. "Get your sorry you-know-what up. This isn't a vacation, Joe."

"Well, it should be one. We could use it." Joe lay back on the sand and put his arms behind his head. He closed his eyes and looked intent on wasting the day away, lounging in the sun.

Chris had to nudge him with his foot.

"I'm coming. I'm coming. Keep your clothes on." Joe sat back up irritably. "Do you have a plan or are we just going to show up?"

"I'm going to Modify, like we talked about last night. You should keep me out of sight for a while," Chris said with unusual patience. "Simona will have gotten the news by now, and if she thinks I murdered her sister, she may not be that helpful. Do you think she'll remember you?"

"Oh, she'll remember me."

"How do you know she'll—" Chris mouthed the word "oh" when he saw the grin on Joe's face. Then Chris smiled, nice and broad. "When did that happen?"

Joe turned bright red all the way to the tips of his ears.

Chris squatted back down and looked to Cassie. "Awww, isn't Joe cute when he's embarrassed?" Chris chucked a seashell at his brother to piss him off even more. "Oh, Joe, I do wish you would teach me your ways."

Joe gave him a look, stood up, swatted off the sand, put Cassie in his breast pocket, and then attempted to smack Chris in the head. But Chris was quick and Joe only ended up grazing Chris's scalp. "Like you ever needed any help."

"She's married now with kids, so don't expect a heartfelt reunion," Chris crooned unscrupulously. He evaded another smack with fancy footwork.

"I hope she didn't marry that tool she brought to your wedding," Joe said. "That could be awkward."

"So it was at my wedding. No wonder no one could find either of you when it was time to give the toast."

"Hmmm . . . ," Joe mumbled, chuckling to himself, apparently lost in a moment of nostalgia.

Chris moved close enough to give him a small push forward. "Come on, Don Juan. Let's get a cab."

***

165

With Chris and the others stuffed in his pocket, Joe strolled along Simona's street until he came to house number ninety-one. It was a duplex with two mailboxes by the curb.

Joe glanced at the names listed on the mailboxes. "What's her last name now?"

Chris's head popped out. "Kai."

"This is the place, then."

"Good luck." Chris ducked back in.

While walking across the lawn dotted with weeds, wildflowers, and tufts of long grass, Joe regretted accepting the leadership role in the meet-and-greet portion of the plan. He thought Chris should be the one to flounder and fall. Simona was his sister-in-law after all. Although she might think Chris had killed her sister, Joe knew she wouldn't be particularly happy to see him either. There had been no fight or anything along those lines, but back in the day Joe had said, with sweet pillow talk in her hotel room, that he would call her sometime and would visit her in Hawaii. Joe never did, though. He was still having too much fun in college, and she lived on the other side of the world.

Joe tried the doorbell a couple of times. He wasn't convinced it was working, so he knocked instead. When he heard the scamper of children, he pounded louder.

Finally, Simona opened the door. She squinted in the bright morning sun and gave him a quick glance, then a confused do-I-know-you look.

Joe was surprised that Simona didn't recognize him. Then he accepted that he was roughly five years older and wasn't wearing the glasses that would have made him instantly recognizable—not to mention what he'd been through in the past week.

"Hi, Simona. Long time, no see . . ."

His voice apparently congealed everything for her because her expression went sour. "Joseph MacRae . . . you are the last person in the world I would ever have expected to see here."

"Really? The last? I figure there would be a lot of people more unlikely than me—say, um, the president of the United States. Or, well, maybe that's not a good example." He tried to win some approval with a wink and a forced smile.

Simona crossed her arms. "Especially since the police have been crawling all over this place. Maybe I should call them." She then slammed the door in his face.

"Wait!" Joe pounded on the door. Despite his instinct to abort the mission, he pressed on. "Please, Simona, open up! I have something to show you. There is so much more to the story than the police could possibly know. Chris didn't kill your sister. And I can show you something that will make you believe me."

There was a long pause and then a scratching sound came from the other side of the door. Simona opened the door a crack with the chain lock connected. "Fine. You have two minutes. If I'm not convinced, I slam the door back in your face and call the police."

"It won't even take that long." Joe reached into his pocket and pulled out Cassie, Chris, Morgan, and Ryan. The twins buzzed out of Joe's hand and circled over his head.

"Mind if we come in?" Joe asked, now confident she would say yes.

Simona's jaw dropped and so did the chain lock. She opened the door and let Joe into her cluttered living room.

Cartoons were blaring on the television and there were toys all over the floor. A baby girl no more than a few months old was fussing in a baby swing. Then two little boys rampaged down the narrow hall in front of them. The older of the two was trying to hit his brother with a foam baseball bat. They jumped on furniture, leaped over toys, and almost knocked down the baby swing in the process. Simona had to throw herself across the room to prevent the swing from falling. The baby's fussing escalated into a full-blown wail.

"Sorry. It's a little chaotic here." She popped a pacifier into the baby's mouth, shooed the boys out to the backyard, moved some toys out of Joe's immediate vicinity, and nervously tucked some loose black hair behind her ears. "I wasn't expecting visitors."

"No big deal. We're used to chaos."

Simona's eyes returned to the four little people. "What are they?"

"They—we—are fairies. The good news is, you're probably one too. The bad news is, you're probably one too *and* there are other fairies trying to kill us. All of us," Joe said matter-of-factly.

She squinted one eye and then the other. "Fairies? Seriously?"

"I know. I felt the same way."

In Joe's palm, Chris signaled to the backpack, where Joe was carrying his human clothes.

"Is it all right if Chris joins us now? He wanted to stay out of sight for obvious reasons, but now . . ."

"That's really Chris there in your hand?" Simona paused indecisively. "What do you mean by 'joins us'?"

"Uh, where's your bathroom?" Joe asked.

Simona, in a sort of daze, gestured down the hall. Joe ducked into the room she pointed out and closed the door.

"I had just been assuming he was guilty," Simona continued, speaking through the closed door, "but the police have lowered his status from 'suspect' to 'person of interest.' I guess they found blood from two unknowns. Alana's murder could have been staged, but the new evidence did cast some doubt on their wife-killer theory."

"Well, that's good news," Joe called out, emerging from the small room. "But it's not like either Chris or I can resume our normal lives anyway."

Simona's eyes narrowed.

"May I sit?" Joe asked, heading back to the living room. "We'll explain. But let's not get too comfortable."

Simona began skipping over toys on the way to the couch, but she stopped when Chris stepped from the hall into the living room. They stood there, just staring at each other, as if waiting to see who would break first.

"I am so sorry," Chris finally said. "Sorry I couldn't save her."

Simona's tearful nod seemed to exonerate him from blame. She sat down on the couch and let Chris put his arm around her. She leaned into his shirt and cried harder.

Joe looked at Cassie and saw her tearing up as well. "Are you going to be all right, Princess?" he whispered.

Cassie sat down in his palm and hid her face from him. And then Joe shifted his weight, feeling out of place. He had liked Alana—her personality was more like his than like Chris's—but there wasn't a lot time for a mourning session.

Through the shades on the front window, Joe saw three men strolling along the sidewalk in front of Simona's house. He took in a relieved breath when he saw their bright clothes. The next men who passed, however, could be wearing gray.

Eventually Simona pulled herself away from Chris and went into the bathroom. She returned with a box of tissues and finished wiping her face dry. With a few last sniffles and quavering sighs, she put the tears on hold.

"So you're fairies. You'll have to explain that one to me. . . ."

Joe looked to see if Chris wanted to answer. Chris urged his brother to answer for him with an upward nod.

"See Morgan and Ryan?" Joe began. "They have wings. We think the only way they could have inherited them is from their mother."

"You came all the way to Hawaii to tell me I might be a fairy too?" Simona kept her eyes on the twins flitting around her living room. Their antics had caught her baby's attention and were keeping her amused in her swing.

"No, there's a lot more to it than that," Joe assured her. "We're running for our lives and looking for our father. Have you seen him?"

"Your father?" Simona said, turning her puzzled face to Joe. "I barely knew him. I don't even remember what he looked like. Why do you think I would have any idea where he is?"

"Clues have indicated he's in Hawaii somewhere."

"Sorry. I hate to say you've wasted your time, but . . ." Simona looked deep in thought for a moment. "Wait a sec. My mother. You've heard she's in her own little world, right? But sometimes she rambles on about my father. Supposedly, he 'flew off' to be with 'his kind.' I thought she believed he was an alien or something. Do you think maybe her rambling could tell us something?"

Joe and Chris exchanged looks. Simona's story corroborated their theory that her father was a fairy.

"Do you think we could speak with her?" Chris asked. "Who knows? Maybe your father and our father know each other. They might even be friends."

"We could try. I'm overdue for a visit. It's been almost a week."

"Chris, before we make any more plans here, do you want to warn her, or should I?" Joe asked.

"I will," Chris replied. "Simona, I don't want to scare you, but there is a good chance Alana's killers are only a few steps behind us. If I were you, I would leave your house for a while and find someplace safer to stay."

"My family is in danger? Why? What did we ever do?"

"These killers want our father and anyone connected to him—which we believe means even people remotely connected to him—dead. The have shown that they will not hesitate to kill innocent people, like Alana. Please take this seriously. We'll even help you pack and get everyone out of the house."

"So have I—and my kids and my husband—been in danger all along or just since you two knocked on my door?" Simona rose from the couch and began clearing a path through the clutter of the room, her confusion and sadness and anger all boiling over into a flurry of activity.

It was Joe's turn to speak. "All along, most likely—and all the more so if your father and ours actually do know each other."

While Simona made a phone call to her husband, Joe and Chris took inventory of the household items the Kai family would need to go into hiding with three small children, grimaced at the size of Simona's car, and scanned the street for suspicious activity.

Without any conversation beyond what was necessary for getting the children ready to leave and loading the car, they packed up in less than ten minutes. And then the sedan was in motion.

***

Canis Major and his army had received word that Christopher's wife had a sister in Hawaii. Within minutes of their arrival in Honolulu, they descended upon her home. It was empty, though, and it appeared she had left in a hurry. There was an open suitcase on the floor and a baby swing in motion, the timer still on. Neighbors said they'd seen two men helping Simona and her children into her blue Honda with at least a week's worth of luggage.

With no further leads, the group returned to their luxury hotel room. They were waiting for word from Pyxis. Canis needed information from the Royal Library, specifically from the maps Andromeda and her father had created during the Golden Age. These maps allegedly contained detailed notes regarding fairy populations around the world.

Canis had a general knowledge of fairy clan whereabouts in North America and Europe, but he was unfamiliar with the island populations of the South Pacific. If Scott MacRae was in Hawaii, he was probably living among one of the clans, perhaps building an army of his own.

The possibility remained that Andromeda's research was incomplete. If so, then Canis and his army would know no more than the MacRae brothers did. However, if the maps provided a couple of facts—clan leaders, their history, their approximate locations—then Pyxis would have a distinct advantage.

Canis was becoming more irate with each passing second. This was his mother's war, and yet she hadn't gotten her facts together. And the MacRaes were no doubt in hiding already or following leads of their own.

Finally, there was a rap on the door. A Gray Coat dressed as a hideous island native accepted a wax-sealed envelope. He opened it and handed Canis the tiny letter inside the larger one.

My Prince,

I ran into that witless wonder you sent into my library. Had I not intervened, he surely would have burnt it to the ground!

Regardless, I am the only one who can provide what you need. As you are aware, the research regarding fairy populations around the world is nearly complete. Unfortunately, the only information we have about the South Pacific is merely legendary. Although my father's regime conducted preliminary searches there, they never captured and questioned any inhabitants.

We do know there are two neighboring clans hidden in Oahu's Ewa Forest, named after the Hawaiian gods Kāne and Kanaloa. There existed only the Kanaloa until an oppressed subpopulation broke away, forming the Kāne. The two populations have been at war ever since. There are also two populations living on Hawaii's big island called Pō and Ao. We know less about these clans. If my beloved ex-husband is hiding among these populations, I would hypothesize he lives among the Kāne. He always had a propensity to align with the tyrannized, but don't rule out any of the others until we know more.

You will need to search the Ewa Forest far and wide. I have assigned more soldiers to this mission to enable you to do so efficiently. They should be arriving by nightfall.

Canis, I have also amended your mission. I want you to verify the existence of Royal Modifiers. Find a fem-fairy of breeding age who is capable of bearing what we desire. Marry her, and your sons will have powers beyond your wildest imagination.

Canis had to pause there. He loathed the idea of being told whom to marry, but he had to comply if he wanted his mother to concede the crown. Still, he did not intend to end relations with Lyra or her sister, Ursa. They were inferior by birth, but luscious distractions nonetheless. Unless he could find a wife who met his mother's criteria as well as his own, he would have to call on the maids and on his other lovers all the more often. "Anything you wish, Mother," he mumbled bitterly to himself.

Otherwise, correspond with Pyxis daily. I want to know every detail of your progress. And, Canis, you have made noteworthy progress with this task, but do not become overconfident. The MacRaes have an obscene amount of luck on their side. Fortunately, you have superior training, an army that will triple in number by evening, and a good idea of where to start looking. I have high expectations this mission will come to a speedy resolution. DO NOT FAIL ME.

Best Regards,
Your Dearest Mother

Canis folded the letter and returned it to its envelope. "Bring me the map," he commanded.

A winged fairy brought the map over and Canis pinpointed the Ewa Forest. They were now in much better shape than they had been previously. Still, they would have to sift through many miles of territory to find that wretched King of the Unworthy.

CHAPTER 16
Departure from Reality

Simona impressed Joe and Chris by deftly ushering her children into the house of her mother-in-law, Mrs. Kai, and spinning out a story about urgently needing to visit her own mother at the hospital. Once outside again, she conferred with the fairies on their next move. The small group decided it would be best for Cassie to wait with Ryan and Morgan in Mrs. Kai's garden while Simona took Chris and Joe with her in her purse. Simona and the MacRae brothers then left for the Aloha State Care Center.

After parking her car, Simona strolled along her usual route past visitors, doctors, and employees. She cradled her purse under her arm like a newborn baby and made an extra effort not to bump into anything.

While tapping her impatient foot, she waited for the slowest elevator ever built, or so she believed. When the doors opened, she walked inside with throngs of other people. Pushed against the wall, she stared at the changing floor numbers and had the uneasy feeling that all eyes were upon her.

On the fifth floor, she arrived at the security desk and signed the visitor logbook. The security guard buzzed her in. "Thanks, Paul."

"Have a good one," he replied.

Simona tucked her arm over her purse again and headed toward her mother's room. When she arrived, her mother, Mikala Jokura, was rapidly flipping through a magazine. She did not acknowledge Simona's entry.

"Hi, Mom!" Simona said with exaggerated cheer. "How are you feeling today?"

Mikala did not look up. "No, not feeling good today."

"Why, what's wrong?"

And then Mikala started to cry.

***

Chris could hear the crying and wondered how things were progressing otherwise. He couldn't make out any words, so he propped up Simona's wallet and climbed on. Once he was closer to the zipper, he began to catch more of what they were saying, but it didn't matter. His former mother-in-law seemed to be obsessing about fictitious people and highly questionable events.

"How's it going out there?" Joe whispered.

The wallet started to wobble. Chris jumped down into a pile of loose items—a few coins, a gum wrapper, and a chapstick. "Not well. Her mom is crying."

"Yeah, I hear that. What's she saying?"

"Nothing solid yet. It sounds like Simona's about to mention her father."

"What's wrong with Mikala anyway?"

Chris thought about it for a second. Alana used to talk about her mother frequently. He remembered only half listening and now he felt guilty for not knowing more. "I really don't know. Why do you ask? Do you have any doctor tricks you could use?"

"No, I was just making conversation. It's sort of a hobby of mine to diagnose people. Like you, for example—"

"Shhhh!" Chris said suddenly. "Joe, do you hear that?"

"Hear what?"

Chris attempted to prop up the wallet again, urgently this time. "How come no one can ever hear it but me? The buzzing . . . from wings!"

Joe climbed onto the pack of gum next to him. "I hear it now as well."

"Help me get out of here." Chris waved Joe forward. "Hold this for me."

Joe propped up the wallet on its tall side and held it steady. Chris climbed back on top of it. The zipper of the purse was slightly open at the edge, and Chris could just reach it. Bright sunshine flooded in as he pried the zipper open.

His head popped out. The purse was on the floor next to Simona's chair. She was still attempting to console her mother.

Between sobs, Chris heard the buzzing sound again. It was louder than before. His position allowed him to see only the ceiling and the doorway behind him. The sound seemed to be coming from the window on the other side of Mikala's bed.

Chris considered climbing out of the bag and exploring the room. It would be a dangerous move, but he felt confident Andromeda's agents couldn't have tracked them down so soon even if Gretchen had ratted them out. He was about seventy-five percent committed to getting a better look when he saw a fairy zip across the room by the ceiling so fast it almost seemed like a glitch in the fluorescent lighting. The fairy then landed on the floor by the door and looked over every corner of the room.

Chris ducked down and froze. Most of the Pyxians he had seen were pale to the extreme, so when he caught a glimpse of the fairy's tan skin, he scrambled to get out of the bag.

"Chris!" Joe hissed in response to his brother's movement.

Chris ignored him and pursued the Hawaiian-looking fairy into the hallway. "Wait! Please!"

The fairy spun around and coasted to the ground. Then he whisked Chris beneath an abandoned janitor's cart by his arm. "Are you trying to get us all killed?"

"No, I'm sorry . . . I just . . ." Everything suddenly clicked together. Alana had long kept an old picture of her father in her wallet. She would occasionally pull it out and, with stars in her eyes, her wish was obvious—that one day she would see her father again. "You're my father-in-law, aren't you?"

"Yes, I am. Kimo Jokura. And you must be Christopher MacRae. I'm sorry we meet under such dire circumstances. I just heard the news. . . ."

Chris nodded and joined Kimo in what he recognized to be a moment of silence. Joe then appeared underneath the janitor's cart and joined Chris's side.

"And you must be Joseph."

"That's right," Joe replied cautiously.

Kimo wasn't a large fairy, but every word he said sounded harsh and brought no cheer to his expressionless face. "Your father will be pleased to know you've made it to Hawaii."

Chris and Joe exchanged looks of relief. Ten minutes ago, the probability of a family reunion seemed low. Now finding their father appeared more likely than ever.

"Can you bring us to him?" Chris asked.

"Yes," Kimo said. "You will have to enter our world under the cover of darkness, keeping your fairy form. It's safer that way. Have Simona bring you to Komo Mai Drive in Pearl City. At the gate to the Ewa Forest, walk three thousand paces due east in a straight line, no talking, no light. I will meet you in that spot at three a.m. tomorrow. Don't be late. And tell Simona to get a hotel room with her in-laws. Have her contact Jasmine and Bane and move everyone to safety. Tell her to use the cash I set aside and false names. And, Christopher, I would suggest your children stay behind with them. I will do everything I can to protect them."

At Chris's nod, Kimo Jokura lifted off the ground and buzzed away.

"He's a little intense," Joe blurted after he disappeared around the bend.

"Did you catch everything he said?" Chris asked in a panic. "I think I remember everything, but just in case—"

"Don't worry. I won't forget," Joe said with unusual calm.

When they returned to the room, Simona was on her feet and giving her mother a hug. It was the right time to get back inside her purse. Visiting hour was over.

***

Beneath a starry Hawaiian sky, Simona drove her Honda down Komo Mai Drive under the speed limit to the point at which the road ended. She parked and took a deep breath.

"I'm sure we'll be fine. Everything's okay," tiny Chris reassured her.

Simona was more terrified than everyone else combined, and she had been on the run for less than a day, not a full week as Chris and Joe had been. She was still acclimating to her new reality, and poorly at that. "How do you know you'll be fine? And if everything is okay, why do I feel like this?"

"If you're nervous, you can stay in the car. We can walk the extra distance," Joe said.

"Out in the open like that? No way!"

Chris glanced at the clock on her dashboard. *1:04.* Then he looked up at her expectantly with raised eyebrows, and his hand went to the hair at the back of his neck. He was clearly urging her to pull it together and hurry. "Let us know when you feel ready."

Simona took one last shaky breath. "All right. I'm ready."

"Good," Chris replied a little too quickly. "We can do this. And Simona . . ."

"Yes, Chris?"

"Thanks for all your help, and for watching Ryan and Morgan."

"No problem. It's what Alana would have wanted." She checked all her mirrors and saw only parked cars and dark houses.

"I'll be back to get them as soon as we get things situated," Chris added.

"Take your time."

"Thanks, and please be careful."

"I will. Same to you."

Simona dropped Chris, Joe, and Cassie into her purse and stepped out of the car. She tried to walk casually, but every noise frightened her. When she could feel danger all the way to her bones, her pace quickened into a run.

She reached the Ewa Forest gate and checked over both shoulders. The street was still. The only sound came from the rain forest. The chirps and hums reassured her everything in the world she knew was in its proper place. On the other hand, she realized how artificial her sense of security might be. Nature's symphony could easily drown out all sound of approaching evil.

Simona squatted down in front of the gate and reached into her purse. She moved items out of the way as quietly as she could. Then she lifted Chris, Joe, and Cassie into her hands, and while doing so, her weight shifted into the gate. It made a short metallic grunt. Everything after that remained motionless except for their wary eyes.

Nature's hum continued, uninterrupted.

***

With their traveling sacks over their shoulders, the three wingless fairies stood side by side and looked upon the towering forest with dread. Three thousand paces seemed like an incredibly long distance in the dark and at their size.

Enemies or predators could be lurking anywhere—behind rocks, beneath plants, or in the airspace. And though Chris had spent the better part of the evening making a miniature spear for himself out of volcanic glass, they were otherwise without weapons.

Simona was gone, Chris noticed over his shoulder, and there was no turning back. So he aligned himself with the center of the gate and started his paces. Cassie and Joe followed. They walked on a well-worn dirt path for the first hundred paces. Then the dirt path veered to the left and their due-east paces led them into long grass and then thick jungle foliage.

Chris grabbed Cassie's hand, and Cassie grabbed Joe's. The ground was slippery with mud from a recent downpour. When Chris tripped, they all stumbled. While he struggled to see in the dark of night, he also had to worry about what he could hear. There was definitely a buzzing above them. But with so many other sounds in the jungle, he knew nothing for certain.

"What number are you on?" Joe whispered to Chris when they stopped to assess how to get around a rock.

"One thousand eight hundred seventy-two."

"I'm on one thousand eight hundred ninety-three," Joe countered.

"And I'm on one thousand nine hundred eight," Cassie added.

"We obviously have different pace sizes," Joe said. "How will we ever know where to stop?"

"Maybe we'll just know," Chris stated, wanting to finalize the discussion.

"And we were supposed to walk in a straight line. I doubt that has happened, hence Mount Kilauea in our path."

"It's not that bad. I say we go over it."

"Not that bad? It may not be that tall, but it's steep and smooth. How on earth are we . . . ?"

Chris tossed his brother a tendril from a plant growing along the rock wall; at their size, it was as good as a stout rope. "Stop yapping for once. Let's go."

Once on top of the rock, they were relieved to see that the other side appeared much more steplike. They climbed down with relative ease, all still counting their paces.

Chris initiated the hand latching again and they continued walking. After several hundred more paces, the walk seemed less daunting. The numbers in Chris's head were climbing quickly. The ground was flatter, grassier, and not as rocky or muddy, but the group was also more exposed. And just when he became aware of how exposed they were, Cassie became a deadweight.

Chris swung around, but he couldn't figure out why she had stopped. The slivers of moonlight didn't help his vision. He tried to walk on, pulling her by the hand, but still she wouldn't move.

Chris remembered Cassie acting like this back when they were escaping from Pyxis, right before Andromeda made her dramatic entrance into the dungeon. Coincidence? Maybe. But then he thought of the SWAT team incident at Gretchen's house in Connecticut. Cassie, a palm-sized fairy in an alien environment, had managed to warn everyone in time to disappear. She seemed to be able to tell if danger was imminent. Chris thought of the question he'd asked her when they first arrived at the Aurora Borealis in Pyxis—*How did you know I wouldn't kill you?* She had replied, *Because I didn't feel afraid.* It was a strange answer, he'd thought then, but now he could guess what she'd meant. Overall, he considered her current behavior a bad sign.

Chris now had enough nerve to whisper into her ear. "What's wrong?"

Joe edged in, and the twig he stepped on let out a snap. "Sorry, that was me. What's going on?"

"They're here," Cassie murmured almost inaudibly.

The three of them pressed their backs into a triangle and waited for the jungle to tell them something. The sound of buzzing came from all directions, neither strengthening nor weakening. The drone was constant. They waited. No change. They waited longer.

Chris squeezed Cassie's hand and tried to press onward. She didn't budge. Just as his balance recovered from his ineffective tug, he heard *bzzzz* right above his head.

They crouched down and, as one, ran. They followed along a fallen log and dodged leaves and branches.

Chris stopped when his feet splashed in water. Joe and Cassie plowed into him. He waded a few steps into the stream, but stopped when he decided the current was stronger than he was. To get across, he would have to Modify, and that would be too risky if enemies were watching. Plus, Kimo had told them to stay in fairy form.

Chris turned around and urged Joe and Cassie back onto the bank of the stream.

"What now?" Joe said, checking over his shoulder.

"Maybe this is where we're supposed to stop."

"Do you think we're that lucky? We lost the count and the exact direction."

179

Chris's eyes swept from left to right. "Even if we're slightly off, it looks like we would have run into this stream anyway."

He decided to wait and see, so he led the way to a crevice in a rock that was shielded by a fern. Chris was the last to enter the hideout. He sat closest to the opening and kept watch.

"Okay, Princess, what was that all about back there?" Joe whispered.

"You heard the buzzing," she replied, ever so softly.

"You obviously heard it before we did!"

She didn't answer.

"Well?" Joe demanded.

No response.

Joe let out a loud sigh. "Your silence is so mind-boggling sometimes."

"Silence, under these circumstances, cannot be overvalued," Cassie said. "You might want to try it."

Chris muffled a laugh. He enjoyed the princess version of "Shut the hell up." It appeared that Joe had met his intellectual match and, in Chris's opinion, he was not faring well. And maybe it was just a flare-up of sibling rivalry, but Chris preferred it that way.

Chris then watched Cassie's dark silhouette shoot straight up. If he could see her eyes, he was sure they would be as wide as globes. "Someone's coming," she whispered.

"Is this princess intuition again or a real threat?" Joe asked.

A shadow was cast over the entrance to their hideout.

"Quickly, join me," they were instructed with a harsh whisper.

They climbed out, one at a time, as Kimo Jokura flew to the top of a boulder by the stream. He turned in two full circles. The first time, his eyes scanned the ground and the stream. By the second turn, he was checking the trees. Then he closed his eyes and whispered, "Two, one, nineteen, fifty-four."

"Isn't that . . . ?" Joe whispered to Chris.

"Yup, Mom's birthday. Very original, Dad."

Kimo fluttered to the water's edge as the earth began to rumble. When he moved aside, there was a hole in the ground by the stream. Without a word of greeting to Chris, Joe, or Cassie—without any reaction whatsoever to their having made it to this meeting point—Kimo signaled for them to crawl inside.

Chris went into the hole first. He pushed through the tight space in absolute darkness. He could tell the hole had widened into a tunnel when he could no longer feel his body scraping along the walls.

He rose to a crouch, and within a few waddled steps, he could stand with a slight hunch. He moved forward until he was sure everyone else had enough room to stand.

Then he felt a pop underneath his feet, and slowly, waves of light—purple, blue, and green—oozed up both sides of the tunnel. The light met at a domed ceiling but remained fluid. When Chris moved his arm, the colors flowed along with it. And when he touched the wall with one finger, it was as if he'd thrown a stone. The colors rippled away from the impact.

"I think we can safely add this to our list of new experiences," Joe said from behind.

Kimo brought everyone back to reality with terse instructions. "Walk to the end of the tunnel. It should take about six hours. I will meet you on the other side."

"Wait. You're not coming with us?" Chris asked.

"No, and you shouldn't worry. The path is direct and invisible to outsiders."

Without a good-bye or good luck, Kimo turned and left. A few moments later, the opening to the hole closed over with a *thwop*.

And then Chris started walking. Cassie was close on his heel.

From the rear, Joe said, "Let the psychedelic journey to fairyland commence!"

Chris laughed aloud this time, and it felt good.

***

Canis Major joined his soldiers and demanded an immediate briefing. "If they were here, why are they not in our possession?"

"They vanished, Your Excellency, right underneath the water," replied the nearest Crown Champion. "Then we saw a Royal emerge from the ground. He headed north."

Canis squatted and splashed the water from side to side with his hand, attempting to reveal the secret. There was no hole, no dent, not even a ripple in the silt.

He presumed magic of some kind had enabled their escape, but he considered other possibilities as well. "Lead a group downstream. They may have found something to float on. And you"—he pointed to another able-bodied Crown Champion who seemed sharp and ambitious—"lead a group north. See if you can catch up with the Royal."

Other fairies flew or marched in to catch the tail end of Canis's orders. This included Crux Chevalier and his battalion of mercenaries, wingless and slow.

"The rest of you are to establish camp," Canis Major ordered. "This exact location is to be discreetly monitored—day and night, rain or shine. Is that understood? They may emerge at any moment, and we will not let them escape again."

As his fairy army dispersed, Canis continued to analyze the area where the Unworthy had vanished. Creating a disappearing, reappearing tunnel would require magic beyond his capabilities. Dismantling one would be even more difficult. He would have to figure out the password.

He suddenly felt the urge to fly to the boulder beside the stream. With his hands up and eyes closed, he hoped to dissect from the wind any magic words still lingering.

CHAPTER 17
Mutual Understanding

The morning rays of sun refracted through the prismatic tunnel walls and provided a myriad of colors that Cassie had never seen before. Shades of blue from the sky and green from the jungle were prevalent, but there were unusual shades of pink and purple there too.

When not captivated by the magnificence of her surroundings, her thoughts were vacillating, high and low, light and dark. She was doing her best not to let the conflict show. She kept her expression neutral and hoped her eyes would not betray her.

Joe, unable to stay silent for any duration of time, gradually quickened his pace to match hers. He nudged her and smiled. She smiled back. Her attention then returned to Chris's sure footsteps, now a few more paces farther in the distance. It was unlikely he would even look back.

She tried to purge the ache from her chest with a sigh, but it was as if her throat were closing over. The wisp of breath that did escape was merely a sad quiver.

"Princess, you're awfully quiet today," Joe said.

It took a moment for his statement to register. "Am I?"

"What are you thinking about right now?"

Recapture, likelihood of premature death, and . . . your brother . . . just to name a few things . . .

"Don't hesitate. Just say it," he urged.

"Oh, nothing really," she lied.

His mouth twisted with dissatisfaction. "I'm not buying it."

Cassie decided to trigger Joe's monologue mode. It would be a good distraction and would keep him content for a while. "Why don't you tell me why you decided not to become a doctor? It seems the occupation would have suited you."

Until this point, Chris had seemed silently immersed in his own troubles. But then he slowed down and made their single-file line into a more of a cluster. "That's an excellent question, Joe," he said. "You wasted a lot of money when you dropped out of med school, and it wasn't your money either."

Joe went rigid, from eyes to jaw to shoulders. Normally, his anger was the stewing sort, a slow smolder, but that didn't mean he was above the emotion. He could mask even fury and rage with a poignant quip and a forced smile, but he couldn't make all signs of it recede.

Cassie worried that too much provocation could result in an explosion. Everyone had a limit, a threshold that should never be crossed. And at this stage in their journey, she didn't want to cause conflict on a topic so inconsequential. "I'm sorry," she said. "I should never have asked. It's not my concern."

"Don't be sorry. It was a fair question," Joe said with the fake smile Cassie had anticipated. "And for the record, it was money borrowed against the equity on my mother's house—a house neither my brother nor I will ever go back to," he said while looking at her, though the words were clearly pointed at Chris.

Chris stepped ahead of them again. Then he shrugged as if the answer were inadequate but not worth the fight.

"Well," Joe started, sounding calm and reasonable, yet lacking the same level of good humor as before. "There was a combination of factors. I hated spending twenty hours a day memorizing material that I no longer found interesting. And then there was Rebecca. I know I mentioned her not too long ago. Do you remember?"

"Yes," Cassie replied. "You were with her in Aspen, Colorado, and that was where you learned to drive a snowmobile."

"Right," he said. "Good memory. Well, it was a full-time job trying to keep her happy. Um, let me rephrase that. It was a full-time job keeping her *stable*. We moved in together, had the same friends, saw each other night and day. It all fit together for a while, but then our grades started slipping, and she just couldn't cope. Her cries for attention just pushed me away. I rediscovered my creative side, music and such, and started hanging out with different people. And Becca hated that. Then an acquaintance of mine was writing a screenplay. He liked some of my ideas and asked if I wanted in on the project. This was after I found out I was on academic probation. I could have worked it out, but I decided to move from San Francisco to Los Angeles. Then all of a sudden I was a screenplay writer, and a struggling one at that, and that's when life really got out of hand."

"Joe?" Cassie asked before he had a chance to move off topic.

"Yes, Princess?"

"What about Rebecca? She didn't want to go with you?"

"To L.A.? No. I didn't ask her to."

"Did you love her?"

"Of course I did, but—"

"You loved her and were with her for over a year, yet you didn't even consider marrying her?" Cassie frowned. If Joe knew the meaning of love, he would not have followed his "Of course" with a "but." She would have been more satisfied if Joe had said no.

"Marry her!" Joe replied with jovial outrage. "That's a bit old-fashioned don't you think?"

"Joe, look who you're talking to," Chris chimed in.

Joe didn't even acknowledge Chris with a glance. "I was only twenty-three."

"Chris was approximately the same age when he married Alana," Cassie pointed out. "Right?"

"I was twenty-four," Chris answered.

"Chris was an aberration," Joe shot back quickly.

"I heard that," Chris said.

Cassie wasn't going to back down until Joe explained himself better. "Joe, you lived with Rebecca. She counted on you to be there for her, and you abandoned her when she needed you?"

Joe emitted a scornful laugh. "I don't know why I am even attempting to explain this to you. You're obviously out of touch with the human world."

"Try me," Cassie said. "Maybe I'm not as out of touch as you believe."

"Okay, relationships can be messy."

"Aren't they always, in every world?" she challenged.

"Rebecca . . . had too many family issues," Joe said carelessly, thoughtlessly.

Cassie spun around and looked him dead in the eye. "Don't we all?"

Joe looked startled at first, and then a grin sneaked onto his face as he raised his hands in mock surrender. "Look, I know the future Mrs. Joseph MacRae is out there somewhere, and Becca just didn't fit the bill. We can't all be as fortunate as Chris and find 'the one' at seventeen years old. Many of us require a lot more trial and error. Some more than others. And what about you, Princess? Any wedding bells in your future?"

"No, not even remotely," she murmured through a sigh. "I don't think I'll ever get married."

"Really? Why is that?"

Because a wedding dress would be inviting bloodshed . . . like last time . . .

"I don't think it suits me," she replied, intentionally vague.

Joe's eyebrows lifted as if he were waiting for her to say more.

"I mean, the wedding part, not necessarily the marriage . . . The whole thing seems overblown," she continued. Her response wasn't a lie per se, and she hoped it would satisfy him.

He quickened his pace and put his arm around her back and onto her shoulder. "Maybe you just haven't found the right guy," he said with a wink.

Cassie leaned in toward Joe but was more confused than comforted. "Joe, why do you keep doing that with your eye?"

"Wink, you mean?"

"Yes."

Chris was apparently still paying attention because a chuckle burst out of him. "Yeah, Joe. Why don't you tell her?"

"Hey, that's enough out of you," Joe said to his brother, clearly not amused. "I wink automatically when I'm joking with someone. It's like I'm letting you in on a little secret."

"What's the secret, then?" Cassie asked. She watched his eyes switch from calculating to self-assured. She could almost watch the witty remark write itself on his face before the words came out.

"Princess, if I have to explain it to you, maybe you weren't deserving of the wink. I take it back."

"You can't take it back."

"I can do what I want," Joe said lightly.

She sighed with frustration this time. "You are impossible."

He squeezed her shoulder tighter and said, "I know. I get that a lot."

"Hmmm . . ."

She rolled her eyes. *I wonder why?*

They walked along with his arm around her shoulder for a while. As she was wondering how to politely disengage, the tunnel began to narrow. And then Chris slowed down.

"As much as I hate to break up the love fest back there . . . ," he began.

"Love is not quite the word I would use." Cassie pulled out from underneath Joe's arm and took a few fast strides away from him.

"There's only love, Princess, only love. You just have no sense of humor," Joe said.

She shook her head and crossed her arms but decided not to give him any further satisfaction. She let him have the last word—this time.

"We're here," Chris announced. He fumbled around the arched wall blocking their path. His hand disappeared into the sea of colors. There was an audible sucking sound and he whisked his hand back out. "It's a door. I just can't figure out how to open it."

Joe joined his brother's side and stuck his hands into the wall. "It's a weird sensation, but it doesn't hurt."

Chris put his hands back in. Together they pushed, pulled, and poked along the adjacent walls.

Eventually, Joe sat down and Cassie took a seat next to him. Chris struggled for a few more minutes and then took a seat facing them.

It was best for them to wait and see. Kimo had said he would meet them on the other side. Although he was gruff and intimidating, his word seemed ironclad.

"We're going to see Dad, allegedly," Joe said to Chris. "What do you think that will be like?"

"I don't know. It's hard to say," Chris replied. "What do you think?"

"It will certainly be uncomfortable."

"Are you going to be the good little golden child or give him the verbal lashing he deserves?" Chris asked.

"Huh," Joe said as he considered his options. "That's a tough one. I haven't decided yet. And are you going to keep your cool or kick the bloody pulp out of him?"

"We'll find out soon enough, I guess." Chris looked to Joe, raised his eyebrows, and smiled a roguish smile.

Then they both laughed.

"That's what I'm afraid of—your spontaneity on these matters," Joe teased.

Their laughter seemed to signal that they had recovered from their tiff and were united against a common adversary—their father. Scott MacRae certainly had many apologies to make.

The moment of levity was brief, however. A hazy figure swooped in from the sky and landed in front of the impassible wall. There came a click, and a blast of humid air rushed in. The colors shielding the wall did not vanish but became more transparent.

With Chris in the lead, they pressed through what remained of the strange shell.

"There's a wooden lever on the ground by the exit," Kimo informed them once they emerged. "I thought you would have been able to figure that out for yourselves."

He walked away from the tunnel, and after exchanging looks, Cassie, Chris, and Joe followed him silently.

Cassie would have been speechless regardless of any surrounding conversation. Outside the colored tunnel, she couldn't tell if she was still on planet Earth.

She had never believed paradise existed, but her senses now told her otherwise. Bright green grass; trees with broad leaves interlaced with flowers in deep purple, orange, sunny yellow, pink; birds and winged insects flitting from one bloom to another—all of it beneath a cloudless blue sky. Beams of early morning light were filtering through the flora, and the moist air seemed to warm her from the inside out. She could not have imagined a more wistfully romantic setting. It was as if she had been reborn and life was full of possibilities rather than boundless tragedies.

Soon the sound of falling water captured her attention. As they wove through the lush terrain, the sound grew louder. She finally caught a glimpse of a magnificent waterfall. At the top, the water rumbled over the edge with power, but as it hit the jutting rocks and vines, it became a misty spray and a stone-bound cascade.

She refused to walk any farther until she saw where the water pooled. Water had never been pleasant or inviting before. In Pyxis, the West River was a sure death for the fairies it swallowed. And the dank trickle accompanying the city's borders was a foul warning to reconsider any unauthorized journeys.

Since the ground was soft and Chris's steps were marking the course, she made the gutsy choice to veer toward the water. It was meant to be a quick, solitary endeavor, but Joe's footsteps remained in stride with hers.

"Is everything okay?" he asked.

"Perfect," she replied without slowing down or looking back.

"Are you coming, then? We're going to lose Kimo."

He stopped walking, and she paused to answer. "You can go on without me. I'll find my way."

"I'm not going without you, so come on!" he chided, making a dramatic sweep with his arm.

As she darted away from him, a sound blipped from his mouth. She was out of range before she could receive his full-fledged protest.

Cassie breezed through the sprawling fronds and scaled a rock at the edge of the lagoon. The brief detour was worth the sprinting she would have to do to catch up with the others. It was the perfect time of morning to see the sunlight hit the mist at an angle to make rainbows. With no time to spare, she memorized the position and shade of every color. She wanted the image to be just as vivid in her dreams, the kind of dreams she hoped to wake from with a smile.

When she returned to the place where she'd forked off, Joe was still waiting for her. He immediately grabbed her wrist, giving her no choice but to stumble along, though with each step she grew more and more resentful. She wasn't a child, and hated being treated like one. And even a child could have found the way back without assistance. Her footsteps in the mud were impossible to miss, and so were everyone else's.

They weren't too far behind, and soon Chris was in sight. Joe pulled Cassie in front of him and finally released her, yet he continued to march her forward with his hands on her shoulders. And of course, Chris glanced back at them in time to witness the tail end of her humiliation.

"Where did you two crazy kids wander off to?" he asked.

"Someone, who will remain nameless"—Joe's head bobbed in her direction—"went on a sightseeing expedition."

"I told you to go on without me," she whispered through clenched teeth.

While Cassie was making sure Joe could not misinterpret her fury, Chris began walking backward. "I've been meaning to say this all day. You two should totally duel it out, and may the best fairy win." He then turned his back on them and took a few long strides ahead. "And I would definitely put money on the good-looking one."

"He means me." Joe coughed in amusement, yet to Cassie's oversensitive ears his tone was painfully smug.

189

"No, I didn't!" Chris shouted over his shoulder.

Cassie raised one eyebrow. Then she pushed past him, purposefully bumping his elbow. And, easy as that, Cassie's dampened mood no longer existed. In fact, she had to force herself not to smile. Despite her efforts, she knew she couldn't effectively remove the elation from her face. Her silent revelry lasted until Chris reached the crest of a hill. She took her place beside him.

Buried beneath a thick bed of Hawaiian tree ferns was a long fairy-sized hut with a steeply pitched roof covered in coconut husks. Kimo charged toward its bark door without hesitation.

When Joe joined Chris and Cassie, the three of them exchanged nervous glances. After three years of bitterness, this encounter was not likely going to be something to smile about.

***

As Kimo knocked on the door, Joe stumbled down the hill. Chris urged Cassie to go next with a nod, and after a deep breath, he plodded toward the hut with heavy, reluctant steps.

"Do you think he's here?" Joe whispered over his shoulder.

Chris shrugged, and then Kimo knocked again. His first knock had been loud enough to scare off some impressively large gnats and mosquitoes, so Chris couldn't figure out why no one had answered yet. Maybe Scott wasn't there. Was he out for a pleasant stroll, whistling that tinny fisherman's whistle, still pretending his family didn't exist?

At last, Scott MacRae, now the size of a fairy, eased the door open a crack, as if expecting the boogeyman. "Hello, Kimo," he said. Then his one visible eye widened and the door flew open. "Well, boys, this is a surprise!"

He sounded exceedingly happy, as if receiving holiday visitors. Chris wasn't convinced the sentiment was genuine. His dad had been impassive even during the best of times, so his present vibrancy was out of character.

Scott glanced at each of them while sporting a close-lipped smile. "Welcome back, Kimo, and thanks for bringing my boys and . . ." He looked to Cassie with his eyes narrowed as if recognized her, but was unable to piece the entire tale together.

"Dad, we found you . . . finally. . . ," Joe said, interrupting Scott's moment of uncertainty and Cassie's chance to offer a reluctant answer.

Though Joe's sarcasm was unmistakable, Scott didn't seem to notice. "I'm glad you did. It's been a long time!" He grasped Joe in a quick hug. They released each other, and then Chris begrudgingly made eye contact with his father. "Chris!" said Scott MacRae.

"Dad," Chris replied flatly.

There was an awkward moment in which Scott held his arms out and Chris had to decide whether to accept his father's hug. But Chris's eyes dropped abruptly and the moment was over, the decision made. When Chris looked back up, Scott's hand was on Joe's shoulder, and they were walking into the hut together, side by side, father and son.

Kimo stepped inside next, and Chris expected Cassie to follow suit, but she remained by his side. She was looking up at him expectantly, as if waiting for his go-ahead. He started to give it to her with a smile, half real and half forced. Then he realized his smile probably looked the same as his father's. He put an end to it quickly and gave her a nod.

Her responding smile was subtle, amused, but thankfully understanding.

"Welcome to the Kāne society," Scott exclaimed proudly as they entered.

The hut was extremely primitive inside—dirt floors, scantly furnished eating and living areas, and nonexistent embellishment. Other than a fireplace, a rack of weapons by the door, and a couple of alcoves without doors, there wasn't much else to see.

"Did you enjoy the wormhole?" Scot went on, turning to Joe.

"You mean the LSD-inspired tunnel that brought us here?"

Scott chuckled. "I designed it myself so I could travel between worlds at the speed of a Royal."

"That's awesome," Joe gushed. "And you can totally tell you peaked in the 1970s."

Chris's hands started shaking, even when he balled them into fists. *So much for that verbal lashing . . .*

As Scott made small talk with Joe and Kimo, Chris was distracted by his father's physical appearance. He seemed well, tanned and fit. Chris would have preferred he look worse. He had barely aged a day, whereas his mother had aged a lifetime in her last year. Scott was also leaner than he remembered. His hair was much different too. It used to be similar to Chris's shade of dark blond. Now it was lighter, longer, and with the addition of a neatly trimmed beard. Chris found the beard the most irritating. His mother would have never let him get away with wearing one in either the real world or fairyland.

He zoned back into the conversation just in time to hear Scott say, "I'm sorry I couldn't make it to your mother's funeral. I was—"

"Sorry? You're *sorry*?" Chris interrupted. He pointed at his father and looked to Joe. "Did he just say he was sorry?"

Joe's eyes bulged out and he shook his head, as if to say, *Don't do this.*

"Yes, that's what I said," Scott answered in Joe's place.

Chris shoved past Joe's outstretched arm and pushed his father in the chest. Chris had the advantage—strength, speed, motivation—and Scott stumbled backward. One more push and Scott could have easily been toppled. But Kimo grabbed Chris from behind.

Chris wasn't prepared for or knowledgeable enough to counter Kimo's precise and effective martial arts maneuver. So his cheek hit the ground with a flesh-smashing thud.

His hands were pinned, his body immobilized. "Get off me, you son of a bitch!"

Chris thrashed around in defiance. Then his former father-in-law applied even more tension to his overextended shoulders. He started hyperventilating, and the pain was enough to bring tears to his eyes.

Just as he feared he would never be able to use his arms again, Chris heard, "Stop! You're hurting him!" The voice was distinctly feminine, though very frightening. "Hasn't he endured enough violence for one lifetime? And now so bountifully bestowed by his own family."

Chris strained to see his unexpected defender, the tiny fairy princess, beautiful as always, but potentially lethal, like a poisonous flower. All eyes turned to her.

Scott called off Kimo with his hand. Then he backed away from Cassie, cautiously, with his hands up in surrender. "Calm down, Cassiopeia." He had figured out her name, no formal introduction required. Her anger must have brought out something in her face that he recognized and subsequently feared. "No one is going to hurt him."

"He should show his father some respect," Kimo grunted as he released Chris's arms.

"His father will have to earn some," Cassie spat. There was enough ice in her voice to chill the room.

At first, Chris wasn't sure he liked that Cassie had to come to his aid. She put his indecision to rest, though, when she crouched down and offered her hand. Illuminated by a halo of light, she helped him to his feet. No one had ever defended his rash behavior before with such poignancy and grace. He had no idea what he'd done to deserve her allegiance.

His eyes locked onto hers. He had never really looked into her eyes before. They were a deep, rich brown, but there were also tiny flecks of purple in their depths. Strange, otherworldly. She wasn't human—but then again, neither was he, not really.

Can you hear me?

Her eyelids contracted inquisitively.

Chris couldn't make himself look away; he actually forgot there were others in the room. Then an exaggerated, interruptive cough pierced his concentration. Chris didn't know who it was, didn't care, but Cassie's eyes shifted to Joe.

"I think what Chris is trying to say, in his not-so-subtle way," Joe explained, "is that Mom died last March. And he was not thrilled that he had to watch her die by himself. Not to mention that his wife was murdered almost right before his eyes, and he and his kids were dragged from their home and put in a cage." Joe's lilting voice belied his anger. Clearly, his apparent acceptance of their father had been an act. "So thanks for the heads-up about that psycho ex-wife of yours."

"I can and will explain everything soon," Scott replied. "For now, settle in and make yourselves comfortable. And know that you're safe here and among friends."

Comfortable . . . safe . . . friends . . .

The words should have provided Chris with some relief, but he was dizzy, drained to the point of emptiness, and had an overwhelming urge to flee. Too much heat, too much family, too little space.

He sneaked outside and walked away from the hut with no destination in mind. Soon though, he felt a pull. His father had been born in Nova Scotia and had settled in Salem, Massachusetts, and worked as a fisherman. What did Chris have in common with his father other than appearance? Not much, he believed, except for a love for the water. Chris had been practically born with gills.

He kicked off his doll-size sandals and stepped into the lagoon. It was a water-loving fairy's nirvana. The cool, clear pool rippled rhythmically as the cascade tumbled into it. Paradise even had a scent. The pink wildflowers nearby seemed to consume the direct morning sunlight, and, in return, filled the humid air with their praises.

Even knee-deep, the water was wearing away the sharp edges of his mood. He was about to take his shirt off and dive under when he heard a voice.

"Are you going to be all right?"

Cassie's concern was even more soothing than the water. And only a few minutes ago her angry voice had instilled fear in the hearts of the haughty and the powerful. The discrepancy was enough to tie his tongue and confuse his male pea brain.

"I'll make it," he eventually replied.

To avoid looking at her—worried she could read his thoughts—he waded in deeper, nearing the waterfall. But out of the corner of his eye, he noticed her toes still on the bank. "Do you not you like the water?"

Her head popped up. "No, it's beautiful. I could stand here and watch the waterfall all day. I would rather not be submerged in it, however."

He chuckled because he found it funny that for her, water was the bad guy. Then he understood. Water to a cave-dwelling fairy from the far north was probably linked to cold and gloom. He recalled how enchanted Cassie had been, just the day before, at her first sight of the ocean, and he realized she had probably never gone swimming in her life. "It's not that deep here, and the slope is gradual. And besides, I've already scanned the area for swamp monsters."

Cassie stumbled backward, and the color drained from her face. "Swa-swamp monsters?"

Chris muffled an outburst of laughter. "That was a joke. You were supposed to giggle. Not run away screaming."

"You may want to laugh at my expense, I see. Unlike you, I grew up believing in fantastical creatures because I am one. I'm fairly certain you didn't even believe in fairies eight days ago."

"That's true. I guess anything is possible, so I should watch my step. But if you'd like to take your chances and join me . . ."

Cassie lifted her hand and held it underneath her chin indecisively. Before she could make a decision, Chris's jaw clenched and his spine tightened. Cassie must have noticed this abrupt shift because her head snapped toward the reason.

Scott joined them by the water's edge. Chris turned his back and his attention returned to the silt underneath his feet.

"Cassiopeia Labelle," Scott said, nodding to her.

"It's nice to officially meet you, Mr. MacRae," Cassie said formally. "I apologize for our misunderstanding earlier. I—we—have been through quite an ordeal in the past week."

"I completely understand."

"And if you don't mind my asking, how is it you know who I am? You left Pyxis long before Andromeda married my father. I am surprised that you know the name Labelle."

"I recognized you, eventually. You look like a Labelle crossed with a Sauvageau."

"Did you know my father?" Her excitement suggested that she herself knew little of her father but was eager to know more.

"Yes, I did. Perseus was a friend of mine. I did my best to stay in touch with him, to get a better idea of your mother's transgressions. The last I heard, he was married to her and expecting the birth of his child. He must have been in trouble or he never would have. . . And then after your birth . . ."

Cassie nodded. "I know the rest," she said sadly.

For her sake, Chris stayed nearby. Then he remembered Andromeda's nickname—Black Widow. He hadn't given much thought to Andromeda's other husbands, besides his own father, and should have realized that Cassie's father had been among the queen's victims. And if this Perseus Labelle was one of Scott MacRae's friends, he wasn't just some power-hungry fool who got what he deserved. Perhaps Perseus had been small in stature, intelligent, and soft-spoken, just like his daughter, and maybe he would have adored her, given her everything she ever wanted, if he had been allowed to live.

"I'll tell you more about him sometime," Scott continued. "But for now, would you mind if I talk to my son?"

Cassie sought visual confirmation. Chris gave her an upward nod, and then, like a dignified princess, she bowed her head and walked away.

For a few painfully silent minutes, Chris paced around in the water. He was going to listen to his father's side of things, but he didn't intend to make it easy. He waited, leaving it to his father to speak first.

"So how did Cassiopeia end up joining you in Pyxis?"

"You knew we were in Pyxis?" Chris asked.

"I assumed so when Kimo told me about Alana's death. The American media may have labeled you as 'missing,' but I knew who was responsible for your disappearance, and in fact I thought I would never see you or Joe again. I feared the Gray Coats would kill you. But then I heard you were in

Connecticut. I couldn't predict where you would go from there. But I stayed optimistic you would make wise decisions and go into hiding, here or wherever."

Chris realized his father must have been at least a day or two behind the current information. Even if Scott had wanted to help, he and Joe had been going in and out of worlds too quickly. If Scott joined the chase, they might all still be chasing. Fortunately, the chase was over. Or, at least, one part of it was.

Chris sighed and said, "Cassie helped us escape from the queen's guards in Pyxis. I don't think she meant to join us for the long haul, but Andromeda chased us out, literally on our heels. After everything we've been through, I'm just as amazed as you are that we made it here alive." He paused, and for the first time looked at his father directly. "And what about you? What's your story?"

"What do you want to know?"

"Everything. For starters, why did you abandon our mother, your wife?"

"The truth is I never should have gotten involved with your mother. After having been married to Andromeda, I had a bad taste in my mouth and was prepared to remain, in human form, a bachelor forever. Then your mother found me, not the other way around, and she changed my outlook on the world. I knew early on that I couldn't live without her. When she told me she was pregnant, I was thrilled but terrified. Alone, I was vulnerable. With a family . . . ? Well, I lived every day in fear for your lives—yours, your brother's, hers. You probably never noticed me looking over my shoulder, wondering if and when they—she—would find us. In downtown Salem, I always checked the lampposts. It was the most likely place they would hide. The coast was clear until a few years ago. Andromeda's Royals were there, watching the crowds go by, and my eyes may have lingered on them too long. Since you and your brother were fairly self-sufficient, and out of Massachusetts, and Skylar was healthy—I had no reason to expect that she'd become so ill so quickly—it was the right time to remove all traces of my human existence and return to the fairy world. I came here, to a place with common goals and a growing army.

"All those years ago, I brought your mother and you boys here to Hawaii because of a legend I'd heard, one about fairies that could both fly and change form. I assume you've heard about them by now—the Royal Modifiers. I was curious to see if I could find any before Andromeda did.

Amazingly enough, I rented a house for us in the same neighborhood as the Jokuras. Kimo didn't live there anymore, but he kept an eye on his family, especially his daughters. And Alana was suddenly spending a lot of time at our place. One night, I glanced at the kitchen light—a nervous habit of mine—and saw his silhouette. I acted as human as possible. Then when I left the room, I hid against the wall and threw a tablecloth over him when he came out. After I introduced myself, I set him free. It wasn't an instant friendship, but we grew to trust each other.

"When I returned a few years ago, I joined Kimo's efforts to rebuild the Kāne Army. They had come a long way since the first time I was in Hawaii. And they—or we, I should say—continue to make progress. But even to this day, the Kanaloans, our northern rivals, keep pushing for absolute control of the Ewa Forest. We've attempted to negotiate the terms for peace, but repeatedly, they choose war.

"As you probably know by now, your mother *was* human, and I did offer to bring her to Hawaii four years ago. I would have done everything to make her comfortable and keep her safe in some nearby town. But she decided to stay behind because she was in love—"

"With who?" Chris asked angrily and in disbelief.

"Two dimple-faced toddlers," his father countered. "Yours, I might add."

"Well, Mom needed you at home. You had to have known that, even while you were off gallivanting in the jungle."

"If that's what you think, I am highly disappointed. . . ."

Chris shook his head and shot his eyes to heaven. He couldn't believe his father was acting so self-righteous when he was clearly in the wrong.

"I thought you, with your military experience, would understand," Scott continued, "that sometimes we need to leave those we love behind to fight for what's right. The fairy world is a treacherous one. Pyxis is among the most powerful of the fairy kingdoms, yet there are others out there. Some of the fairy leaders have a reputation to make and uphold; comparatively, they would make Andromeda seem benevolent."

"I'll take your word for it," Chris replied. "But I still don't understand why you never told us. If I had known you were being hunted, that my brother and I were identifiable because of the fairy mark you gave us, and that my children—those lovable toddlers—would get caught up in all of it, then I would have been more careful. And Alana would still be alive."

"I am sorry," Scott said softly. " I never said anything, not even to your mother, because I assumed you would be safer without knowing the truth. Unfortunately, I underestimated Andromeda's self-propulsion toward revenge."

"And you couldn't find the time to make an appearance at Mom's funeral?"

"I know there is no excuse that could compensate for my absence. But I found out about her declining health too late. And the army I was heading was embroiled in an ugly border dispute."

"You're right. Even that excuse isn't good enough. She was your wife, and I had to take care of everything. While Joe, in the meantime, was too busy being Joe."

"Chris, I appreciate all you've done and understand why you're so resentful. I just hope, sooner or later, you can find a reason not to hate me."

"I don't hate you," Chris admitted. "I just need . . . some time."

"Fair enough."

Chris didn't want to be angry at the world anymore. But things in the future had to be different. "From now on, could you do us a favor and let us know anything about your life that might, even in the remotest way, have a bearing on ours?"

"I will." Scott's voice cracked on those two words.

Chris stopped pacing and stared at the waterfall. His father entered the water at his side. Looking away from each other, they stood in silence, yet for the first time there was an inkling of mutual understanding. They had more in common than their appearance. And though they knew they were not free to choose a life without struggle and heartache, they still had a lot to be thankful for. Their unyielding dispositions would put them at odds, same as always, but at least they would no longer have to wage war on injustice entirely alone.

CHAPTER 18
Bedtime Story

As Scott MacRae walked back to his hut that evening, after spending the day seeing to the details regarding everyone's safety, he felt for the first time in years that he could breathe a little easier. Skirmishes with the Kanaloans had been small and isolated in recent months, and the northern border of Kāne territory had been unexpectedly quiet. Prince Haipo, the new Kanaloan leader, seemed to be more moderate than his ailing father. Perhaps they were only a few negotiations short of a lasting peace treaty. And then the civil war might finally be over.

The Pyxis Problem, as he called it, also seemed like less of a problem now that his boys had found their way. Back east, Gretchen had disappeared, as advised, and her family was still out of the country. Most of the Jokuras were safe as well and would be moved into the Zone of Protection soon enough. The only exception was Mikala. She had to remain in the hospital. Andromeda might eventually make the connection to Hawaii, but Mikala didn't know enough to be a vulnerability and her room was now being protected by the Kāne Army. Pyxis would not be able to get to her without a fight.

When Scott returned to the hut, the smell of a home-cooked meal made his stomach grumble. In the cooking area, there was a pot of stew simmering over the fire and a loaf of bread baking on the hearth.

They had all been busy, he noticed. Cassiopeia was stirring the stew, and his sons had sectioned the hut into rooms and distinct areas they were calling the kitchen, the dining area, and the den. Curtains quartered off areas that would require privacy, like the bedroom and the bathroom. The bare ground was even covered with a few handwoven rugs. Scott recognized the reedy material they were made from—the long grass that grew beside the hut.

"Who made the rugs?" he asked Chris as he stepped into the dining area.

Chris flipped over the chair he was building, wriggled the posts stabilizing the back of it, and when he decided it was sturdy, he pushed it underneath the table. Cassiopeia then came over and set some wooden bowls down on the table. When she walked away, Chris's head bobbed toward her to answer the question. Then Chris gave a shrug that suggested he was just as astonished, but his beaming face suggested something else.

The fairy princess could cook a meal with only a few ingredients, make rugs, pull off daring rescues, scare grown fairy-males into doing her bidding, and look flawless all the while. She was almost too good to be true. And Joe was acting like her shadow, helping her, adding a clever quip at every opportunity, and Chris couldn't even allude to her without grinning.

Scott would give her the benefit of the doubt for the moment, but would never trust a Sauvageau. The ice crystals in her veins would surely trump any good she had inherited from her father.

Since the hut was big enough for only two or three inhabitants, Scott set up a tent for himself outside. He then pulled a bottle of red wine from a storage bin beside the hut. When he returned, supper was ready to serve. They all took seats and portioned out the stew, the bread, and the wine.

"This wine is pretty decent," Joe said while swirling his goblet. "Did you make it?"

"Make it?" Scott chuckled. "No, I bought it in Nohea. There's a marketplace there. I would have bought more if I knew I was having company."

"There's a marketplace?" Chris asked.

"Yeah. It's a couple of hours northwest of here. You should check it out sometime."

After dinner, they cleared the plates from the table, keeping only their goblets with the last of the wine, and settled back into their seats.

Scott was the last to sit down. He knew his sons needed to hear more about fairies and their family history, but he decided to listen to them chat. He had a lot to learn about them too.

Scott wasn't surprised that Chris seemed more volatile than ever. His well-being often mirrored the world around him, and that world had crumbled. If others suffered, he became one with their pain. Scott remembered how his elder son had been when times were good. He would occasionally kick back, laugh, and let his charisma shine through. Usually though, Chris was too introspective and guarded to get along with. He had been that way since childhood. But from time to time, he would lower his guard. Once someone earned his approval, he was loyal to a fault.

Joe, on the other hand, was as variable as the weather and just as hard to predict. He was always intelligent, driven, well rounded, and well liked, just as his mother was. Anything he touched turned to gold. If he picked up an instrument, he could play it. If he read a book or a play, he could immediately recite lines from it. He could ace tests without studying, make friends without trying, and then replace those friends with new ones as his interests vacillated. California and life outside of academia had seemed to change him, though. From what Scott had heard, he became a wanderer, floating from one whim to the next. If Joe wanted to succeed in the fairy world or the human world, he would have to find his focus.

When the conversation hit a lull, Joe looked over. "So, Dad, is now a good time to tell us your story?"

"As good a time as any." Scott took a deep breath and ran through his mental catalog of experiences. "Any place you'd like me to start?"

"I think you should start from the beginning," Joe said.

"Like where he was born?" Chris asked Joe. "Or the beginning of time?"

"I feel like I should have asked this a long time ago, but, Dad, where do fairies come from?" Joe asked in a childish tone.

Scott recognized his son's inability to take anything too seriously. "That's a place to start, and it would explain some of the social differences between Royals and Modifiers."

"Sounds perfect, then," Joe said, and Chris nodded in agreement.

"Well, one myth says that fairies came from outer space. . . ."

Joe leaned back in his chair, crossed his arms, and let out the chuckle of a skeptic. "You have to be kidding. Outer space?"

"Don't almost all myths begin in the heavens?" Scott challenged.

"Then you should have said that. Outer space is different."

"Do you want to hear the myth or not?"

Scott watched his sons exchange doubtful looks. Then Cassiopeia leaned forward, her face aglow with candlelight. "Your father is right," she murmured sweetly. "There are alternative theories, but our mythology regarding the earth's colonization involves a pioneering duo. After years of retelling, they inherited the names Cassiopeia and Cepheus from Greek mythology. They named their oldest daughter after the galaxy from which they came, Andromeda. As for the exact reason for their departure from the Andromeda galaxy, I would imagine your father's version of the story is different from the one I've heard."

"How so?" Joe asked.

"I'll let your father tell his version, and then I'll clarify any discrepancies."

"Cassiopeia is indeed correct," Scott said. "There are different versions of the story. In the version I heard, the legendary Cassiopeia was in love with a fairy named Cepheus on their native planet. However, Cassiopeia was married to King Phoenix. Cassiopeia and King Phoenix were both Flyers, or what Pyxians refer to as Royals. Cepheus was from the enslaved Modifier class, wingless and half giant, and thought to be inferior in all ways. But Cassiopeia despised her husband and began an affair with Cepheus. When King Phoenix found out, he threw a lightning bolt at their love nest. A piece of their planet containing that nest was sent into orbit. The lovers landed on earth near what is now Domrémy-la-Pucelle, a tiny village in the Lorraine region of France. They eventually had several offspring; each child could either fly or change form, but not both. Europe had its own mystical creatures, and after many centuries, the mating among fairies, humans, elves, sprites, nymphs, and so on generated the distinct populations we have today. Is my retelling close to your version, Cassiopeia?"

"For the most part, yes, although there is one major difference. I was taught that Cepheus kidnapped Cassiopeia and threw the cataclysmic lightning bolt at Phoenix. In that version, the Modifier is the villain."

"You don't really believe all of that, do you?" Joe asked.

"No, I don't," Scott said. "I think fairies evolved as a human subpopulation. It's a matter of genetics. Still, many fairies believe the myth religiously. It's the reason why Royals and Modifiers hate each other in the more traditional societies like Pyxis, and it explains why many fairies and landmarks are named after celestial objects."

"Do you mind if I elaborate?" Cassie asked when Scott grabbed for his goblet. He gestured for her to take the floor while he finished the last of his wine. "My version of the myth has also validated the maltreatment of Modifiers for centuries. Many Modifiers live in Pyxis, yet the Royal class will never accept them, regardless of their worth. There are strictly enforced mandates instructing Modifiers where they can live, eat, socialize, learn, and so on. Depending on the severity of the violation, punishments can range from imprisonment to death."

"Dad, why did Andromeda marry you, then, if she considered you inferior?" Chris asked. "And why did you marry her?"

"Isn't that the million-dollar question?" Scott plopped his empty goblet down on the table for emphasis. "I should first tell you about where I grew up. I was born Rigel Kincaid in a small coastal community called Herring Cove, south of Halifax, Nova Scotia. My mother was actually the MacRae. So anyway, my family and other Modifiers belonged to a secret society of fairies called Polaris. It was nestled in the high rocks just beside the ocean, and . . . it was beautiful. But our lifelong enemy—Pyxis—was aware of our existence. There was war, war, and more war dating back as far as the establishment of Nova Scotia. When I was young, the Pyxian king at the time, Canis Major V, was especially aggressive toward us. He didn't even have a good reason. We were peaceful, appreciated our isolation, and had a love for the sea, not for gold. So we assumed they picked fights with us like a bully at a playground— domination for the sake of domination. Our society was small compared to Pyxis, but we maintained our sovereignty. We knew enough protective magic to keep Polaris safe.

"One day, my father, King Naos, received a letter inviting him to come to Pyxis. Peace negotiations were supposedly the main order of business. My father accepted the invitation and brought me along on the journey north. My father and King Canis Major came to an agreement with deceptive ease. As a gesture of peace and prosperity, they arranged my marriage to Andromeda. I didn't love the idea, but then I met Princess Andromeda at our engagement ball. Foolish as it may seem now, at the time I thought she was. . .well. . ." He shrugged instead of saying beautiful or gorgeous, too ashamed to say the truth. "I asked her to dance with me and became even more . . . charmed, let's say. She was worldly, elegant, and said just enough to intrigue me. As the ball was winding down, she took my hand and led me to a quiet hallway. Suddenly, she backed me against the wall and kissed me. Her kiss was intense, almost forceful, and then over so quickly. She left me there, breathless and confused, but begging for my wedding day."

The wine was gone, so Scott poured himself a goblet of water and took a gulp. "Are you three bored yet?" he asked, but then he noticed their transfixed faces.

"I was losing interest for a few minutes, but now you're about to get to the good stuff," Joe replied.

"I'll try to be more entertaining for you in the future," Scott said flatly. "Trust me when I say this story only gets better. My father and I returned the next morning to Polaris. I spent the next month preparing to leave home; part of the bargain was that after the marriage I would settle in Pyxis. The plan was for me to return to Pyxis on my own, with my family following in time for the big day.

"As for the wedding, I anticipated a grand affair, something even bigger than the engagement ball. But my family never arrived. Andromeda wasn't even there. The ceremony was a dry business, undertaken in the presence of her father and a few intimidating members of the Royal Air Brigade. They forced a quill into my hand and shoved me into a chair next to a table on which lay the marriage contract. I had a feeling my blood would have been spilled right then and there if I refused, so I signed my life away. Then they brought me to a room in the North Wing of the Aerial Palace, a level lower than the staff quarters, and locked me in. I had only my trunk of personal items for company.

"For weeks, I was not allowed to leave that room. Servants did bring me food, but other than that, no one, not even my wife, came to see me. I began to wonder why my father and King Canis Major found it so important that I marry Andromeda.

"One day, I was feeling rebellious and at last managed to sneak out of the room. I went exploring only so long as I dared. When I returned— unnoticed, I thought—I saw that my things were in slightly different places than they'd been when I left. My trunk was at least still locked and magically fortified on top of that, and I had the key in my pocket.

"A few days later, there was a knock on my door just as I was getting into bed for the evening. I couldn't mask my surprise when I opened the door and saw Andromeda there. She asked if she could come in. I started spewing questions, but she didn't care to answer any. Without detail, she blamed her father for the many injustices I'd suffered, and the next thing I knew, she was undressing herself."

"And you were dumb enough to take that bait?" Joe chided.

"After a month alone in a cold, dark room, you would have done the exact same thing," Scott replied. "Any guesses why she was really there?"

"She was sent there to seduce you," Chris answered. "She wanted the key."

"Yeah, but what did you have in your trunk that they were after?" Joe asked. "Cassie, I remember you mentioning a magical artifact. Was that it?"

Scott left the table and rustled around in the room behind one of the curtains. He returned a few moments later and plopped a blue hardcover book onto the table. It had tattered edges and a loose binding that made the browning pages jut out on different planes.

They all glanced at the title and then looked up, waiting for an explanation. The gold block letters on the cover, faded with time, said MAGICAL MECHANICS.

Chris's face contorted with outrage. "That's what this is all about? A book? Everyone is fighting for, dying for this dusty piece of—"

"This is not just any book," Scott interrupted before Chris's anger had a chance to escalate. "Consider it Polaris's magical bible."

"It sounds like a physics book," Joe added. "Just like 'classical mechanics' or 'quantum mechanics.' "

"In a way, it is. It describes how to manipulate the motion of objects and magical energy."

Cassiopeia's expression was the first to switch from mystified to enlightened. She was quick and astute, and probably knew better than anyone how deceitful and manipulative her family could be. "Am I safe to assume that tricking you into marrying my mother was the only way my grandfather could have gotten access to this book? And that once the book was in his possession, he would have held the secrets of your society's defenses?"

"Yes. That pretty much sums it up. There were about a dozen other magical guidebooks in my trunk as well. But Pyxis's Royal Library held tens of thousands of books, so I didn't grasp the power or the rarity of this particular one."

"Why did the Pyxians go through so much trouble, though? Why didn't they just take the trunk and the key? Or kill you?" Chris asked.

"I don't know. I suspect they wanted to plan a secret attack on Polaris. The Aerial Palace is leakier than Swiss cheese, so if word escaped that I was dead, then Polaris may have found out beforehand, in which case all bets were off. Since the Royals could never harness the magic, they needed time to understand it. Does that make sense? Do you have any better theories?"

Chris shrugged but didn't answer. Joe stayed silent as well, so Scott picked up the story where he left off.

"Months went by, and Andromeda's visits became longer and more frequent. And one night she had a servant bring us a nice dinner and a bottle of wine. I remember becoming tired all of a sudden, and then I don't remember anything else. I woke up the next day feeling weak and nauseous. I foolishly blamed it on the wine.

"Day after solitary day passed, but Andromeda never returned. Before long, I started going stir crazy. Even though I wasn't supposed to leave my room, let alone the castle, I stopped obeying the rules. Strangely, no one seemed to care where I was or what I was doing. It was as if they considered me dead already. One day, I was wandering around the Main Street of Pyxis and decided to get a late lunch at a tavern. Cassiopeia, you'll like this part of my story because this was the day I met your father."

"Perseus Labelle, right?" Chris looked to the princess for confirmation.

She nodded and Scott said, "Yeah, that's right."

"How did you know that?" Joe asked.

"I'm not psychic." Chris and Cassie exchanged a quick smile. "They just mentioned it when you weren't around."

"Oh." Joe's eyes narrowed as if he were coping with the disappointment of knowing something last. "So what about this Perseus Labelle?"

"Well, Perseus was reading at a table across from me. When two barmaids with trays collided, I used my abilities to stop the falling plates and cups midair, and I returned them back to their trays. While everyone else was staring at me, my bookish neighbor came over and introduced himself. He asked me where I studied 'mechanics.' I told him my father taught me in Polaris. From that, Perseus had figured out who I was and said he considered it an honor to meet me. I was shocked to hear that from a Royal. They weren't all hateful bigots, I learned. And he was obviously brilliant. He rattled off various uses, pros and cons, theories and philosophies about magical mechanics. He had to leave soon after that, but he invited me to his family's estate on Royal Way for dinner that evening."

"Does that mean he was an aristocrat?'" Joe asked.

"Yes, the Labelles had family money and they led everyone to believe they were of the royalist school of thought. However, they were among the minority of intellectuals who secretly chafed against the king's administration. His father and brothers were considered the pioneers of what they termed the 'cerebralist' movement, which is not to be confused with the 'radicalist' movement started by the poverty-stricken intellectuals of the South End."

"Sounds messy," Chris complained.

"It was and still is, but I won't bore you with political philosophy. So I visited Perseus when I could sneak away, and we often practiced magic together. He was extraordinarily talented with traditional sorcery and was on the verge of cutting-edge discoveries in alchemy that could have rivaled modern medicine. He attempted to teach me what he knew. I tried my hardest, but I didn't have his gift. Most fairy magic was beyond me. I ended up sharing what I knew about mechanics. He was the only Royal I ever met who could practice it. And if King Canis Major had ever found out, we would have both been in trouble. The administration would have considered it treason. So we were forever bound by our secret.

"One day, Perseus asked me how to do something beyond my abilities. I told him I would check with my mechanics book back at the castle. The color drained from his face. He'd never imagined that I'd have brought the book to Pyxis. He conveyed to me how dangerous it would be if the book got into the wrong hands. I assured him that no one in Pyxis besides himself knew anything about it. I mentioned the enchanted trunk and showed him the key around my neck. Then it hit me. I recalled the night with the goblets, the seduction, the deep sleep, and Andromeda's disappearance. I ran back to the castle and checked my trunk. The book was gone!

"I paced. I panicked. I needed that book back before it was too late. But I decided not to do anything rash. My plan was to familiarize myself with the territory, find Andromeda and follow her. I wanted to figure out what she and her father were up to, retrieve the book, and return to Polaris. I soon realized they often convened in the Strategy Room with General Cygnus Gustave III and their highest-ranking officials. On that first night, I tried to get into the room after it cleared out. The door, of course, was locked. Late the following night, I brought some tools with me and a potion Perseus made me that would soften the metal. A few of the longest minutes of my life passed while I was trying to open that door. At last, I made it inside. I found plenty of incriminating evidence—maps of Herring Cove with their notations, their agendas, and a paper trail for the financing. Unfortunately, the book wasn't there. I was about to give up for the night when the door flew open. To my horror, Andromeda was standing on the threshold with the book under her arm. We stood there, face-to-face, sizing each other up. Her nose flared with a level of animosity I've never seen anyone else possess. I quickly realized she would kill me before she surrendered the book. She pulled out her wand, and I got ready to protect myself from anything she conjured up—"

"Sorry to interrupt, but how could you defend yourself without a magic wand?" Joe asked.

"With traditional sorcery, you need a magical implement such as a wand or a scepter, a pendant or a ring, or something along those lines. Magical mechanics requires only your mind."

"That's convenient," Joe said. "Okay, feel free to continue."

"I'm almost done. I promise," Scott reassured his listeners, since they appeared to be getting tired. "She flung a lightning-bolt curse at me. I deflected it easily. Then she threw a ball of fire. I bounced it onto the table full of documents. The papers burst into flame. We seemed to be at an impasse, but the fire was sweeping toward me first, and she was blocking the only exit. So I charged forward and she spurted a fiery red poison at me. I flung it back into her face. She screeched in pain, loud enough to wake the dead, and tumbled to the ground. The poison sizzled into her skin and gown. I should have killed her while I had the advantage. I thought about it, but I felt too much pity for her. I merely grabbed the book and ran. Midsprint down the East Hall, I saw the king rounding the corner. Before he had the chance to pull out his scepter, I knocked over a display case of weapons on top of him. I heard he died a few hours later."

"With the book under my arm and only a few gold coins in my pocket, I fled to the South End. I escaped through the caves but nearly froze to death there in the far north of Canada. It was mid autumn. At any rate, I made it back to Herring Cove about a week later. Polaris had been burned to ashes, every member slaughtered."

Scott paused.

"I cobbled together a new name for myself, Scott MacRae, and disappeared into the human world. However, I never intended to leave the fairy world forever. There was, and still is, unfinished business."

Scott stared at Chris until their eyes met. There was just a brief moment before Chris looked away, but Scott could see his determination to make things right. Chris would fight to end the Sauvageau dynasty, or would die trying.

Scott's eyes then wandered to Joe. His younger son was curious and paying attention, but he clearly didn't have the same commitment his brother did.

"Andromeda survived her wounds, of course, and became queen of Pyxis at nineteen years of age. Her first act upon taking the throne was to have our marriage annulled, or so I've heard."

"On that note . . . ," Joe said, getting up from the table.

"I can tell you three are worn out. Why don't we stop there for the night? We can discuss Andromeda's administration with clear heads some other time."

Chris stood and yawned, and then helped the princess from her chair. After their long day and the revelations of the evening, they were all ready for a night of solace, if only they could keep thoughts of Andromeda at bay.

CHAPTER 19
Rivalry Revisited

Before the sun had a chance to rise, Chris abandoned his unsuccessful attempts to go back to sleep. The mat he was trying to sleep on was about one notch more comfortable than solid ground. Plus he was sleeping next to Joe, not exactly Chris's idea, but until they made more grass mattresses and put an addition onto the hut, the sleeping arrangements would have to suffice. If he could find the time and if their stay was longer than a few days, then he had big plans for the place. The homestead needed to be big enough for three generations of MacRaes and the princess.

After spending a few minutes shifting and realigning his bones, he crawled over his dead-to-the-world brother, who just so happened to have all the blankets coiled around him.

Chris went to the kitchen area looking for something to eat. He peeked inside various sacks and canisters—flour, dried fruit, sugar, leftover bread, jam, and dried meat.

He was slicing himself a piece of bread when his father came through the door. Scott looked like he had already been awake for hours. His heavy breathing, loose stride, and damp clothes suggested he was just returning from a workout. Chris vowed that this would be the last day his father would ever outdo him.

"Good. You're already up," Scott said in a low voice. "Is your brother awake yet?" He stroked his beard and squinted over at the lifeless bundle in the corner of the room.

Chris raised his eyebrows in disbelief that his father just asked that. Surely, he remembered that Joe and morning didn't go together. "No, I'm pretty sure he's still asleep."

"Well, wake him. We have to be there in less than an hour." Scott strolled over to the shelves. He grabbed an inconspicuous sack and began munching on what looked like candied pineapple. His father always did have a strange obsession with the fruit. A fresh supply of pineapple was probably among his top reasons for abandoning the North Atlantic.

"Where is 'there'?" Chris asked just before his father walked out.

Scott turned around and rested his arm on the partially open door. "You're going to start training with the Kāne Army today."

"Oh," Chris replied, surprised.

"Are you all right with that?"

"Absolutely! This is just the first time I'm hearing about it. Do they train nearby?"

"Yeah, the training field is just outside of their base camp. It's about a ten-minute walk. So get ready, and meet me outside." He nodded and left the hut.

Once Scott left and reality set in, Chris developed a nervous pit in his stomach. Whenever physical activity was called for, he pushed himself to maximize his performance. Today was no exception. He wanted to shine like never before.

Chris paced around itemizing and prioritizing everything he needed to accomplish. He was about to sit down and eat his breakfast when his brother's snoring changed his course. Since rousing Joe would be arduous and time-consuming, Chris made it a priority and nudged his brother with the side of his foot. "Joe."

Joe rolled away from the unwelcome assault and pulled the blankets over his bed-matted hair. Chris nudged him again, harder.

"Huh?" Joe grumbled in response.

"Get up. We have to leave soon," Chris said in a firm whisper.

Joe lifted his head off the pillow and squinted toward a glassless window. "It's still dark out. Go to hell," he replied like a grizzly bear. His head collapsed back down and he pulled the blanket over it.

Chris squatted and shook his shoulder. "Come on. Get up, or Dad's gonna like me better for once."

"Ten more minutes," Joe mumbled. "Or better yet, how does an hour sound?"

Chris chuckled. "Do I look like an alarm clock?"

Joe didn't answer, but he curled into a ball and rolled away from his brother.

Then Chris went to the kitchen, returned with a bucket of water, and dumped it over Joe's head.

Joe sprang to life and conjured up the most disgruntled of faces. "You rat bastard! I hate you."

Chris considered Joe about as intimidating as a lapdog—noisy and feisty, but not life-threatening. Chris rumpled Joe's wet hair and said, "Yeah, but I *wuv* you." He moved before Joe could slug him.

"Don't talk to me!" Joe said with his unwelcoming palms up. Then he stood and rubbed his eyes. "Why on earth are you so chipper? It's really irritating this early in the morning."

"Me? Chipper? You're obviously mistaken."

"You should be shaking with fear." Joe bobbed a scolding finger at him. "Payback is going to be a real bitch!"

"If I had boots, I'd be shaking in them."

"You just wait. It will be messy and embarrassing."

Chris gave him the "whatever" eye flutter. "C'mon. Get changed. We begin fairy boot camp in half an hour."

"Oh, joy. I can't wait. I knew there was a great reason why I should be awake."

Joe untangled himself from the damp blankets and changed his clothes. Then he slumped over to the table and joined Chris for a quick breakfast.

They were about to head out when Joe pointed over his shoulder to the bedroom area, dark and curtained off. "Is she still asleep?"

"Yeah. She's still in there. I assume she's sleeping."

"Should we wake her and let her know what's going on?"

"Let her sleep," Chris said. "She was awake most of the night."

While Chris was tossing and turning, he was in good company. There were a few stretches of time where she was quiet, but they were interrupted by gasping, twitchy movement, and the occasional whimper. He had a feeling her quiet periods were because she was awake, not asleep.

"We should at least leave her a note."

Joe found a pad of paper and a pencil, then he sat at the table and put the end of the pencil to his mouth. His hand was positioned to jot something down, but he waited, as if for inspiration, and then the pencil end returned to his mouth.

"It's not a freakin' love poem. Give me the pencil." Chris's hand shook impatiently. Joe didn't hand it over, so Chris snatched it and started writing. " 'Dearest C-a-s-s-i-o-p-i-a,' " he mockingly read out loud as he wrote.

"It's p-*e*-i-a," Joe corrected disdainfully.

Chris gave Joe a slanted glance but wedged in the *e*. " 'Went to train with the army. Be back later. Love, Joe.' " Chris then slapped the pen down next to the paper.

Joe's mouth gaped open. "How dare you sign my name to that artless atrocity?"

Chris ignored him. "Let's go. We're late." He left the hut and met up with Scott by his tent.

"Where's Joe?" Scott asked.

Chris swiveled around and squinted at the door he had left open on purpose. "I don't know. I thought he was right behind me."

As they waited, Chris suspected that Joe was rewriting the note to Cassie. Why else would he be taking so long? He could be there all day drafting the perfect prose. It would need to be witty as well as informative. But jeez! They didn't have all day!

At last, Joe stepped outside. And the smug look on his face made Chris a little uneasy. Whenever Joe said something like "Payback is a bitch," he meant it. But Chris didn't ask. He didn't want to know.

Joe's look turned serious and professional as soon as Scott looked over. "Where to?" Joe asked.

Scott handed them swords and gestured for them to follow. "This way."

"Is this your sword?" Chris flipped the weapon back and forth in his palms and then slashed it through the air. It moved impressively fast, and the swooping sound was clean and crisp. He liked the feel of the sword as well. It had a practical hilt, fit perfectly in his grip, and was surprisingly lightweight for its length.

"Yeah. I'm not using it much these days, though. It's yours now."

Joe struggled to match their stride. "What about this one?"

Scott glanced over. "That's mine too."

Joe's sword was smaller, blunter, and didn't look nearly as lethal. "It might be yours, but it's not *yours*. Is that right?"

Scott didn't answer. And except for Joe's scowl, he didn't protest.

Soon Chris heard the clanging of weapons and the jungle opened into a clearing. There were dozens of fairies in uniform—loose green knee-length pants and brown sleeveless tunics. They were chatting, warming up, and dueling in the trimmed grass. The majority of them had wings; some were even sparring while in flight. It would have made sense if there were two separate groups, winged or wingless, but they were all intermingled and seemed equally skilled and socially compatible. They did stop what they were doing, however, and gawk.

Chris watched Joe give everyone a polite grin and a nod of acknowledgment. Chris tried to do the same, but he didn't think he pulled it off. He was only making the effort because he was among friends. Yet the word seemed foreign to him. Maybe it had been too long since he had bothered making any friends. Whatever the reason, or the excuse, he felt like the new kid on the first day of school. And there was little hope he would blend in.

His anxiety had a chance to subside when the others resumed their activities. Without any instruction to do otherwise, Joe and Chris started warming up together with some light swordplay.

As the day progressed, most fairies went about their business with only occasional glances in their direction. But throughout the sparring, an outdoor lunch, a brief free time, and then more sparring, an imposing figure on the opposite side of the field kept glowering at them. Chris pretended not to notice.

But Joe kept casually peeking back when he could get away with it. "Hey, Chris," he said as the large fairy stopped his workout to speak with Kimo Jokura. "Isn't that Kale, Alana's older brother?"

"Yeah, that's him all right," Chris replied with undisguised contempt.

Joe jabbed him in the ribs with his elbow. "Aren't you going to say hello?"

Chris pulled his head back and raised his eyebrows as if to say, "What? Are you nuts?"

"So that's a no, then?"

"More like a 'no way in hell.' Are *you* going to say hello?"

"He's not my brother-in-law!" Joe said with both fear and awe. It was no surprise to Chris that Joe was eying him warily. Kale had the wingspan of a hawk and outweighed him by a Cassie-sized fairy, maybe more.

"If he knows about Simona," Chris chided as he squeezed Joe's bony shoulder, "you are in deep shit!"

"Yeah, I was young, but I do vaguely recall what you went through."

"Hmmm," was Chris's only reply.

Kale finished the conversation he was having with his father. Then he stared in their direction as if he knew they were talking about him. Kale and Chris's glares crossed paths and lingered there a moment too long.

"I wonder why he's here?" Joe asked. "He's obviously been here a long time. And his sisters didn't even know they were fairies."

"I've been wondering the same damn thing." Chris had taken Kale's presence as a slap in the face. If Kale had given Chris some kind of warning, months, if not years ago, Alana might still be alive. But Chris decided this was not the time or place to make a scene. "Come on," he said to Joe. "Are you done yet? I want to forget about him by kicking your ass some more."

Joe sprang into ready position and pointed the tip of his sword at Chris's abdomen. "You will do no such thing! En garde!" Then Joe started marching closer.

Chris ducked out of the way of his lousy swing. "Watch it, Joe! You could take someone's eye out with your aim." Then Chris easily found his rhythm and Joe had to stumble backward to keep up.

They practiced for a while longer, but the day was growing warmer and Joe was losing his ability to take anything seriously.

Chris made the most of his complacence and knocked the sword out of Joe's hand. "Is that the best you can do, rookie?"

"You haven't seen anything yet!" Joe picked the sword back up and lifted it over his head. He started swinging it around like an inebriated ninja. "Waaaa . . . waaaa. Who's the rookie now? Yeah, that's what I thought! You're terrified of me!"

Chris leaned back and tried to keep a straight face, but he couldn't take things seriously with his substandard partner acting like a clown.

"Joe, can you come here for a second?"

They both turned toward their father's voice. He was holding a red ball in his hand, about the size of a baseball. He tossed it straight up and caught it.

Joe shrugged at Chris and then jogged to the edge of the field.

"Should I come too?" Chris shouted after them.

"I'll work with you later," Scott replied and then they disappeared into the jungle.

They left Chris there alone and confused.

**

Joe and Scott found a secluded spot in the shade. While Scott continued to toss the ball to himself, Joe stood there waiting for an explanation. When he didn't immediately receive one, he said, "Dad, if you want to play pitch and catch, I think you have the wrong son."

"Humor me for a few minutes."

"Sure," Joe replied tentatively.

"I have a feeling that learning to fight with a sword is a waste of your time."

"Thanks for the vote of confidence."

"That's not what I meant. I just know how your mind works. Stay right there," Scott instructed.

Joe watched his father walk away and then turn back toward him. Before he could figure out what his father's plan was, Scott threw the ball at him hard and fast. Joe threw his hands up for protection. The ball bounced off his right hand and hit the ground.

"Ow!" Joe shook his hand and brought his stinging fingers closer to his face. He wriggled them to make sure they weren't broken. "You could have waited until I was ready!"

"The point is to be ready before something hits you."

"Okay." Joe picked up the ball and tossed it back to his father. "Now I am ready. Where does that leave us?"

"Try to block the ball before it hits you," Scott explained.

"I did that already and I have the jammed finger to prove it." Joe lifted his hand for demonstration.

"Only don't use your hands," his father added.

"What? How would I . . . ? This is a magical mechanics thing, isn't it?"

Scott didn't answer, but his amused expression answered the question. He threw the ball again, equally hard, and Joe resisted blocking the ball with his hands. But it hit him in the stomach instead.

Joe hunched over. "This is really fun and all, but I don't think this is working."

"Yes it is. You just need to focus."

The pain was making Joe testy. "Focus on what?"

"Blocking."

"Could you be a little more specific?"

"Here. Let me demonstrate."

Scott threw the ball into the air. Just before it hit the ground, it hovered there, motionless. When Scott's eyes dropped from the ball, it continued to fall to the ground.

Wow.

Joe realized that he might be able to use magic, too. His mood brightened, and the pain that had been unbearable just moments ago suddenly went away. "Can I try that—the pop-fly approach and not the Joe-is-bleeding-internally method?"

"Deterring pain should be your biggest motivating factor," Scott replied matter-of-factly as he tossed Joe the ball with a lax arm. "And by the way, I already know you can do it. Things used to mysteriously break when you were angry. Your mother joked that the ghosts in the house were sympathetic to your plight."

Joe thought back to a recent event—the Christmas party at Walt Burbank's house in California, when the light bulb had burst in the room he was in and then later that night in the hallway of his apartment building just before he was captured.

So I performed magic before without knowing or trying? he marveled.

Joe closed his eyes and visualized the ball his father had thrown to him—color, size, weight—as well as the environment—wind, air friction, gravity. Then he threw the ball upward and opened his eyes just when the ball was about to land. But the ball never hit the ground, not until he allowed it to. When the ball rolled to a stop, Joe looked up at his father.

"Very good!" Scott gushed. "I'm impressed."

Joe could no longer control his smile and felt giddy, like a child. "Can you teach me more?"

"I will. But first, as your father, I should warn you: this is some powerful stuff. My advice is to treat it like an animal. Be careful what you feed it, keep it contained, treat it well, or—"

"Dad," Joe interrupted. "I get it. Be responsible. But hey, if you think about it, magic can't be any more dangerous than me with a sword."

Scott chuckled. "That's for damn sure."

Joe laughed too, and then he tossed the ball back to his father, ready to learn the next skill.

***

Chris was in the shade, sitting, taking one sip from his canteen at a time, and pretty much dawdling to pass the time, not sure where to be or what to do. He ended up just watching the Kāne Army obey Kimo's barking war cry. The man he'd known simply as his father-in-law was often addressed as General or General Jokura, and Kale was either by his side or strutting around correcting sword positions; checking neatness, posture, attitude; and, in Chris's opinion, flaunting his number two status.

After a while, Chris grew restless, but he had already surpassed that awkward moment where he ought to join the others.

Soon, though, Joe sneaked up behind him and slapped him on the back. "New lesson. You need to throw this at me as fast as you can." Joe handed him the ball.

"I like this lesson already."

"I knew you would."

They stepped into the bright afternoon sun. Joe jogged backward and when Chris stopped shooing him farther away, Chris threw the ball at him fast enough to snag a runner stealing second base.

Rarely in his baseball career had Chris missed that throw. He wouldn't have missed it this time either, but the ball acted as if it hit an invisible wall. As it bounced in the opposite direction, its lightning-fast momentum was reduced to a wobbly hover. Then it hung in the air, motionless, and in the blinding sunlight the red ball glowed like a planet in orbit.

"How did you . . . ?"

The ball dropped to the ground and Joe's eyebrows then bobbed up and down. "It's magic."

"Why did he teach you and not me?" Chris wondered out loud.

Joe shrugged while his narrow eyes peered at the rustling grass at the edge of the clearing. And then he smiled. "Look who's here."

Chris looked over and saw dark hair, pale skin, piercing eyes. Cassie didn't exactly blend in with the vegetation. "Mmmm . . . she shouldn't be here."

Joe grandiosely motioned for her to join them. "Why not?"

Cassie stepped into the light of the sun. Her lavender dress, a new one he'd never seen her wear before, fell just at the knee. But as she walked toward them with cautious grace, the air-light skirt moved with the breeze, exposing a hint of thigh. Her arms were bare to the shoulder, and when she lifted her hand to secure a loose strand of hair, she revealed more of her slim profile than she may have realized. She didn't seem to notice the sweaty, muscle-clad warriors stop what they were doing, but Chris certainly did. Their eyes were devouring every speck of her bare skin, and if their stupid grins were any indication, their minds were quick to fill in the blanks, painting a crisp image of what they couldn't see.

"Um, I don't know," Chris answered sardonically. "Maybe because we're surrounded by hungry flies and in walks the honey."

"Chris, this is one of those times where you should lighten up or you'll go into cardiac arrest!"

Instead of lightening up, Chris doled out death threats with his eyes. And if the soldiers were too dense to miss his face, they would undoubtedly notice his clenched fists.

"And what is going on with you two lately?" Joe continued. "She's your bodyguard. You're hers."

"Nothing!" Chris blurted too quickly, loudly, and defensively to be believable.

He knew it too, and Joe called him on it. From fluttering eyes to twisted lips, Joe's whole face demonstrated his doubt and irritation.

"Nothing," Chris whispered to correct himself.

And then Cassie was close enough to hear them. When she lifted her face, she made eye contact with Chris first. Her smile was subtle, yet her delight practically sparkled in the sunshine.

Before Chris had the chance to greet her, he heard his name called. Scott was waving him over to the edge of the field.

"Keep an eye on her," Chris warned in his brother's ear, and all he could give Cassie was a quick wave as he passed.

Chris joined his father, and then Kimo and Kale came over. The conversation initiated by Scott was brief. Kimo nodded, Kale nodded, and before Chris could come up with a decent excuse to decline, he was following Kale to the center of the field.

Chris was supposed to be improving his swordsmanship with a more challenging partner than Joe had been. But after Chris blocked a few of Kale's aggressive maneuvers, Chris realized they were dueling. And now that the whole army had cleared off the field to watch, he really wanted to win.

"So, Kale, how long have you known?" Chris asked as he made his first counterattack, which Kale parried.

"A couple of years," Kale replied offhandedly as he lunged forward.

Chris dodged Kale's thrust and took a side swing at Kale as his balance recovered. "And you didn't feel like telling the rest of us?"

Kale avoided Chris's swing by lifting into the air. When he landed, they paced in a circle around each other, crossing one foot over the other as they decided how to proceed. "I was sworn to secrecy. My father never wanted his daughters involved in this life. And besides, it's not like you and I were ever on good terms."

"Still, it would have been nice," Chris said. "You sister might still be alive had we known we were fairies."

They circled to avoid each other, tension mounting with every step. Then Kale unexpectedly lowered his sword and glanced over to the edge of the field. "Who's the girl?" His eyes went beady with greed and lust, and his chest puffed out as if he were somehow worthy of her.

"I don't think you're her type," Chris taunted.

"And what type is that? She's not into tall, dark, and handsome?"

"More like rude, cocky, dumb as hell . . . Want me to continue?"

Kale responded with his fiercest attack yet. Luckily, Chris was able to deflect Kale's sword to the side. With their glares locked and blades crossed, they pushed against each other until they were both shaking with rage and overexertion.

"You know what?" Chris asked in a low, caustic tone. "On second thought, you should totally go for her. And I'll laugh when she brushes you off like a bug on her shoulder."

Kale threw his shoulder into their impasse and knocked Chris back a few steps. Then they prowled around each other again.

"I think I'm too late anyway," Kale said as he launched another attack. "It looks like she's into *you*."

Chris sensed a trap and didn't fall for it.

"No, I'm serious," Kale continued. "She's staring at you. I swear! Only you. She's practically undressing you with her eyes. . . . Oh my God, she's . . . "

Chris only meant to glance. He could have gotten away with that, but his attention was zapped away from his control.

Cassie was talking to Joe, giggling, happy again, and Joe had never looked more self-satisfied. They had eyes only for each other, or so it seemed.

Suddenly, Chris's sword flew out of his grip and Kale's in-flight body blocked out enough sunlight to fog Chris's vision. Then with a two-footed kick to the chest, Chris was falling backward. He landed with full force on his tailbone.

Kale touched back down and backed away with a haughty look on his face. Then he turned around and lifted both swords to win audience admiration for the victory. Then he threw Chris's sword back at him, hard and fast. The blade landed in an upright position in the ground between Chris's thighs, purposely a little too close.

"I'm sorry," Kale chided with his head cocked to the side. "My mistake. It looks like your brother got to her first. So how does it feel to be second best?"

Chris would have loved to knock Kale off his high horse, but no words came to mind. Kale didn't wait around for a response either, and he made sure to kick dirt at Chris when he strutted past.

Chris's dust-clouded eyes followed him. Kale joined his fellow Kāne soldiers and received various congratulatory gestures—back slaps, high fives, mock punches. It was enough to make Chris sick to his stomach.

Soon Cassie and Joe came over and offered Chris a hand, but he refused to accept their help. "Thanks, but this is humiliating enough as it is."

"Eh," Joe said with a dismissive wave, "practically no one noticed."

Chris pulled his sword out of the ground and stood, wincing. "Don't bother lying to make me feel better. It's not helping."

"Does it help that I think Kale is a loathsome bully," Cassie added, "and that I detest everything about him, including the ground he walks on and the air he breathes?"

Chris put his arm around her shoulders. "That does help. Thank you!"

They all laughed.

Chris found it amusing that Cassie was carrying Joe's sword with two hands as if it were too heavy to carry with one. In a surprise maneuver, he nicked it and sprinted out of reach. He no longer cared who was watching. Laughter, in this case, was the best medicine as well as the best revenge.

"Christopher MacRae! You give that back!" Cassie shouted, all smiles.

"I'll give it back, but you'll have to fight me for it."

He edged away from her, balancing the two swords in the palms of his hands. When she dashed forward, he smoothly bounced both swords toward the opposite hand, snagged them by the hilts, and dodged out of her reach.

"Awww," Chris said with a fake pout. "Is that the best you can do?"

"C'mon, Princess," Joe put in. "Sic him! Wipe that smile off his face. Here—you go this way, and I'll go that way."

"Oh, so now you're ganging up on me? It doesn't matter. I'll still crush you." Chris took a few more paces and started swinging his swords. "Whaaa. . . whaaa."

"Hey! That was only funny when I was doing it!" Joe lunged at his brother but missed.

"No. You're wrong. It's still funny."

Chris backed right into Cassie's open arms. She squeezed his waist from behind while Joe jumped for his sword. Chris was quick to swivel around, and then Cassie was jumping for the sword. He held it just out of her reach and raised it every time she bounced.

"C'mon, shorty, is that all you got?"

She paused for a second with a look of good-natured frustration. He thought she was about to give up, unwilling to encourage his uncouth behavior. But then she took a loud breath and launched her attack. She didn't have the strength to bring him to the ground, but she certainly had the enthusiasm. With Joe's help from behind, they almost had him.

Chris glanced away from the struggle just long enough to make sure Kale was watching. And he was. Oh, yes he was.

When it appeared Cassie had had enough, Chris bowed and presented Joe's sword to her. She had earned it. Then he put her in a loose headlock and the three of them started walking off the field, rosy-cheeked from the heat, the activity, and the laughter. And Chris glared at Kale and his cronies with his dignity restored.

Kale was sitting against a tree root, stewing toward a boil. His followers were scared silent, but watchful, holding their breath, waiting for Kale's reaction. Would he snap?

Chris recalled seeing Kale like this the day Alana told him she was moving to Massachusetts. Only Alana's tears prevented bloodshed and some very choice words.

Kale took an exaggerated swig of water from his canteen as if to emphasize that he was lubricating his vocal cords. "It's no wonder my sister's dead," he shouted. "Her husband could have defended her, but I bet he cried like a baby and begged for his own life."

A little voice in Chris's head told him to let it go, but sometimes he didn't feel like listening to that irksome voice of reason. He removed his arm from Cassie's neck and clenched his fist around his father's sword hard enough to make his knuckles white.

"Chris, don't do anything—" Joe began.

Chris catapulted his sword into the crowd. The knocking sound of the hit and the ring of the blade had the crowd gasping and stepping aside. Chris's sword was embedded in the tree root disturbingly close to Kale's left eye.

"Stupid," Joe finished in a voice as dry as desert sand.

Chris was initially pleased with himself. "What? I wasn't actually going to hit him."

"You could have taken off his head!"

"Joe, when I throw something, I don't miss."

"Okay, Chris. You keep telling yourself that."

Not rallying any support from Joe or Cassie, Chris ducked his head and continued walking off the field. He didn't have to look up to know everyone was sending hate in his direction. Kale was the general's oldest son, the pride and joy of the Jokura family, and Chris had pulled a stunt that no one in his right mind would even consider. Chris knew he should have regretted the choice he'd made, but he didn't, not for a moment. Kale had had no right to speak to him like that.

Chris glanced up only once and captured the ashamed glare of his father. Then he averted his eyes and disappeared into the jungle. He arrived at the hut many long minutes before anyone else did. The extra minutes didn't help, though. He was still charging around aimlessly when Cassie and Joe sneaked inside.

Then the door flew open with a bang. "Chris. You. Me. Outside. Now!" Scott led Chris farther away from the hut than necessary. "Well?"

"Well what?"

"How about, for starters: Well, what were you thinking?" Scott continued.

"Nothing! I mean, I was thinking Kale got exactly what he deserved. You heard what he said!"

"Life isn't always about getting even! You could have killed someone, and we need allies here, not more enemies. If you feel you can take on the evils of our world with only your sword and your pride, go right ahead, but the rest of us know better."

"Look, Dad, I never planned to make enemies. I was fine avoiding Kale. And then you came along and paired us up. There's bad blood between us. Don't you remember? So why would you put us together with swords in our hands?"

"I thought you might learn something if you were challenged," Scott explained. "And I don't care what happened in the past. Exhibit some self-control, and fix this so we can move forward. I want you to apologize to Kimo and Kale and resume your training, or you might as well pack your bags."

Chris could tell his father was serious. He wasn't quite ready for banishment from two worlds. "Fine. But I'm not happy about it."

"And no more horsing around with your brother. Finally, tell Cassiopeia to stay away. She's obviously too much of a distraction."

"Why do I have to tell her that?"

Scott gave Chris a look that said, *Obey, or else.* "I have to go smooth things over, and you'll do the same in the morning, after you cool off. I'll be back later. Try to stay out of trouble."

Scott disappeared into the deep green of the dusky jungle. The sun was about to abandon them for the day. And Chris could already feel the loss.

When he returned to the hut, Joe and Cassie were making dinner together like an annoyingly cute married couple. But they did both pause to exchange nervous glances.

Chris pretended not to notice and pulled a seat out from underneath the table. He sat down in it backward with his arms resting across the back.

Then Joe strolled over and leaned on the table with both hands. "So what did Father Dearest say?"

"The usual. I'm stupid and irresponsible, and if don't apologize I'll get kicked out of fairyland."

"You may have to apologize," Cassie said from the kitchen, "but I'm not about to. Tomorrow, I'll give this Kale figure a piece of my mind."

She handed Joe four plates and returned to the kitchen. And she did not look back. She had no reason to suspect the course the conversation was about to take.

Chris followed and watched Cassie add greens, spices, and flower petals to a bowl. She sniffed and then measured each item in her tiny palm, not a granule shy of perfection. But she must have felt his nervous energy because she set down the long stems and looked up at him before he was ready.

"As much as I'd love to see you put Kale in his place . . . ," Chris fumbled. "I'm sorry I have to say this but . . . Scott thinks you should stay away from the training grounds."

"Why? What did I do?"

Chris put his hands up to placate her. "Nothing. Not at all, it's just—"

"Shouldn't I be trained for battle?"

"No . . . I mean, yes, by all means, except that—"

"It's because I'm a fem-fairy, isn't it?" she said.

Chris sighed and ran his fingers through his hair. He was trying to tread lightly on this issue. "Well, that's part of it."

"What's the other part?"

Chris looked to Joe for support. With his arms crossed and body slouched in the most distant chair, Joe only gave him a you're-on-your-own look.

"Don't worry about it. It's not that important." Hoping that would end the discussion, Chris walked to the fireplace. He squatted down and checked on the fire, but he could feel her eyes follow him there and knew she would demand more from him.

"Maybe to you! What did he say?"

Chris stalled as long as he could by prodding the fire. "Please keep in mind I am just the messenger. If you really want to know—"

"I do."

"He said you're a distraction."

"What a sexist thing to say!" she quickly retorted.

"I-I know," Chris stammered. "I didn't say I agree with him."

"And what am I supposed to do while you two learn how to conquer the universe? Sit pretty, make meals, tidy the kitchen?"

He didn't answer.

"In case either of you have forgotten, I rescued you from Andromeda's guards, and I led you out of Pyxis. I have proven myself capable of a great many things, and my part in this battle should not be small! If you fairy-males could stop being so 'distractible' and exhibit a hint of discipline, then you might accomplish something as well. Perhaps we'd be able to win some of these wars!"

Cassie vanished behind the curtain of her room while Chris just stood there, stunned and speechless.

With one arm, he leaned on the wall over the fire. He stared at the flames as their heat and volume tapered off. When he turned to walk away, a piece of paper fluttered off the mantel. He would have overlooked it, but there was something familiar about it. It was the note he had written to Cassie that morning. Joe had doctored it up to make it as humiliating as possible. Below all the hearts and the "I love you," Joe scratched out his own name and put "Chris" at the bottom.

Out of the corner of his eye, Chris saw Joe shrink in his chair. Chris wanted to yell, explode, something, but he knew that Joe was the only one who wasn't mad at him.

Give it a day or two, he thought. *That'll probably change too. . .*

Chris crumpled up the note and chucked it into the fire. The paper caught the flames and gave the entire room an extra burst of light. Then he stormed out of the hut and went straight to the lagoon.

He dived, swam, then broke the surface, and when he looked up at the purplish sky, Chris wished he never needed air again. Underwater, his heart rate slowed, his muscles and joints felt free, and his many misdeeds in life seemed less significant.

He dived again and held his breath for an uncomfortably long time before surfacing with a gasp. Then he repeated the submerging and resurfacing process until he was ready to face his extreme new world with a clear head.

CHAPTER 20
Apology Accepted

Cassie was cold. Her cloak provided little protection from the brutal Canadian wind. Wherever she ran, the wind chased her. As it tossed and pulled her cloak away from her body, she could feel the burn of the wind on her bare legs.

And then snow began swirling all around her. The drifts piled high on the sides of her path, creating a maze of white walls.

With the snow strengthening the wind, and the wind strengthening the snow, she had to keep running. There was warmth somewhere. She just had to find it.

Only the starry night sky provided any solace. She could see Orion, the hunter, the colors of the aurora borealis, and in Ursa Minor she saw the twinkle of Polaris, the North Star. And then she regained her sense of direction.

Go south. . .

She turned her back on Polaris. Soon the wind died down and the snowflakes turned into works of Mother Nature's genius. She looked up at the bluish-white moon and spun around. The blanketed treetops, the snow, the stars, and the sky spun with her.

Still dizzy, she cupped her palms and lifted them to the sky. A snow crystal landed in her hands. She brought it to her lips, closed her eyes, blew it into the still air, and made a wish. For the first time ever, she knew exactly what she wanted.

Cassie almost awakened with the wish still on her lips and in her heart, but she held on a little longer, knowing it was a risk. A dream this good wasn't meant to continue.

When she opened her eyes again, she saw a hut of twigs jutting out of the snow. There was a fire inside. She could see it flickering through the rude walls.

The stiff breeze at her back made her shiver. Behind her, there was only cold, wind, and darkness. The choice was simple, if it even was a choice. Whatever was inside the hut, the pull was hard to defy.

She opened the tree-bark door. Christopher MacRae, Son of Grace, had his back facing her, but he turned when the wind rustled his clothes. In the crook of an arm was a baby boy with a head of golden curls and deep brown eyes, the perfect union of father and mother.

Cassie untied her cloak, and Chris hung it up for her next to the fire. In a panic, she glanced down to see she was wearing very little else. It was no wonder she had felt the wind so strongly on her legs. Though she matched Chris's attire in theme—rustic, primitive, homemade—her clothes didn't suit her the same way. He looked handsome and natural in the leathery grays and browns. Her dress exposed most of her legs, but otherwise, it was baggy and too wide for her shoulders. She thought it made her look young. But Chris smiled at her as if he didn't notice, and stroked her bare arm in a way that said she was beautiful no matter what she wore. Then he kissed her forehead. His lips were warm and full of want.

"The little prince wants his mother," he whispered as he shifted the baby into her arms.

There was no sarcasm in Chris's voice. Their child was a prince.

And when he placed the baby in her arms, she could feel her left hand heating up. The warmth increased and the orange glow from the fire seemed dull in comparison to the bright and pure yellow light. Its source seemed to be underneath the baby.

She shifted him into her right arm. Then she lifted and turned over her hot and heavy hand. On her ring finger, a smooth stone glowed like a piece of the sun. Slowly, the glow dimmed to reveal a yellow sapphire. But as she lowered it back toward the baby, the light from the sapphire returned and strengthened.

Strange. . .

Her hand returned to where it was apparently supposed to be, holding her son tight to her chest, and in the heat and the light, the baby drifted to sleep.

On the other side of the fire, there were animal-skin blankets on the ground and a cradle beside them. She kissed her baby's rosy cheek and set him in his cradle. He whimpered for her, so she sat beside him and rocked him back to sleep.

Mesmerized by her dimming ring, she started when she felt Chris's lips on her shoulder. They moved to the base of her neck, and her body tensed with need. Gradually, her racing heart and shallow breathing made her feel light and carefree. Every time they touched, hands or lips, the pace quickened, and move for move, she was his equal. They were a jumble of arms, legs, blankets, strings, buckles. Then with his fervent tug, the dress that made her feel so undesirable was over her head and tossed aside.

228

And then. . .

Cassie forced herself awake. Her body was in tight knots from her throbbing temple all the way down to her pointed toes, but she couldn't bear to watch, to feel, to be *with* him any longer.

She had never had a dream like that before, and it was incredible, but she knew it was about to end badly. Andromeda would come with her army, and they would burn the hut to the ground or take Chris and the baby. . .

Andromeda would turn the baby over to the Brute, and the smell of innocence would rile the demon inside of him.

But all of that was in Cassie's mind, not in the dream, and she tried to appreciate the dream for what it was—a beautiful tease. Chris might never be able to love again, and if he could, that love would not be given to her. Cassie's mother had been the cause of his suffering. How could he ever move past that?

Her sigh was loud enough to hear outside of her room, but it didn't matter. The hut was empty. She had heard the MacRaes leave hours ago. Wherever they were going for the day, she wasn't invited, not even to watch. She could waste the day with more sleep if she wanted, but idleness wasn't something she was used to.

Now that the MacRae brothers were reunited with their father, her work was done and they had no further use for her. It would be best to say good-bye.

She would leave, she determined, but not today. Chris's birthday was in two days, and she wanted to give him something to remember her by.

Cassie dressed and left the hut. After finding a suitable stick, she chose a sunny spot in the jungle. She worked continuously for many hours, and whenever she felt sad or lonely, she would break the silence with a song.

Will your strong embrace
mend my. . .

She paused when she heard a twig snap. "Is someone there?"
No one answered.

Her first thought was that someone was sneaking up on her, and only one name came to mind. "Joe, is that you?" She wasn't going to let him scare her.

There was some rustling, and then Chris pushed through the grass. "Good guess, but no. It's just me."

"Oh," Cassie said as she fumbled to hide what she was doing. She also turned her head away from him because she didn't want him to see the layers of embarrassment piling up on her cheeks. The last and heaviest layer of red that was hot enough to feel was a result of the dream. Even hours later, she remembered every detail. . . the golden hue of the baby's curls in the yellow light, the scent of the fire that seemed to cling to everything, the feel of the clothes, the blankets, Chris's bare skin—and his touch, heated, determined, loving.

"You don't have to stop singing. You sound nice."

"You were listening?" she groaned.

"Briefly, yes. Was I not supposed to?"

His amused smile made her shrug and squirm. "So what brings you here, Chris? I didn't expect to see you until tonight."

"I went to the hut for a bandage." He held up his right hand, showing patches where the skin had been rubbed away. "And then I followed the sound of your voice."

The sight of his blood replaced all of Cassie's uneasiness with concern. "That looks painful."

"It is, but someone I know suggested I 'exhibit a hint of discipline' and not be 'so distractible.' So I've been practicing with blisters, apparently for a while." He analyzed his palm and winced as he flexed it. Then, flourishing the bandage, he sat down on a stone near her and attempted to wrap his right hand with his left. He struggled, though, to keep everything tight and together. As he was wrapping his palm, a strip by his wrist dangled loose. He tried to correct the flaw but ended up unwrapping the bandage all the way.

She came over to him and lightly took his hand. "Here. Let me help. I insist." After a minute or so, keeping her eyes on the bandage as she wrapped it, she said, "I'm sorry. I said many things I shouldn't have. And I wasn't referring specifically to you."

Chris propped his hand up on his knee. "No, you were right. Everything you said was true. I was distracted yesterday, and I let Kale get to me. So I'm the one who should apologize. Is there anything I can do to make it up to you?"

She worked the cloth around his wrist and then carefully across his bloody palm. "Your apology is enough and much appreciated. You don't need to do anything beyond that." She pulled the cloth snug, but not enough to be uncomfortable.

"We have been running in fear for our lives ever since we met. Maybe we could do something . . . fun . . . for a change. Joe and I will take a day off and . . . and . . ."

Cassie could almost see what he saw: the lagoon, Honolulu, the ocean. She didn't know for sure, but she almost felt as if her thoughts and Chris's were in tune somehow. Then his mind zoomed in. The visual clutter, the erratic noise, went dark and silent, and then she could hear a high-pitched ring. "We can go to that marketplace my father mentioned. We'll make a day of it!"

She had to silence her mind before she could answer and she tried to act natural, say what she was supposed to say. "That would be nice."

Cassie tied the bandage in a tight knot below his knuckles.

He opened and closed his fist a few times and twisted his wrist. "Remind you of something?"

Her eyes met his briefly and then they dropped back to his hand. "The first time we met."

"One of the most life-altering days I'd ever had," Chris said with a sigh.

"I would have to agree," Cassie said.

"Yeah, and I bet you regret getting involved."

"Untrue. I have no regrets." Their eyes met again. When she felt herself blush, she looked down and caught a glimpse of peeling skin on his left hand. She lifted it and uncurled his fingers. "This hand is on the brink of destruction as well. Have you been training with both hands?"

"Why use one sword when you can master the use of two?" His sarcastic half smile told her was trying to be funny, not arrogant.

"I don't know. You tell me."

"I'll be able to conquer the universe in half the time, obviously," he said.

"I believe you're laughing at my expense." Cassie tried to maintain a serious expression, but the harder she tried, the more she smiled.

"Since we're on good terms again, can I make a request?" Chris asked.

"Anything."

"Will you sing your song for me? It was hard to hear the words, but the melody was haunting."

Cassie had never sang for an audience before and could already feel her throat going dry at the thought. But had just told Chris she'd do anything he asked, and she'd meant it. She wandered away from him and turned her back. After a shaky gulp and a deep breath, she began her song.

Will your strong embrace
mend my weary soul?
Can it shelter me
from eternal cold?

Love's emerging as a bud
craving kiss of light.
Who shall guard that fragile bloom
if plucked by winter's bite?

Blindly I will carry on,
not living but enduring.
Though colder, wiser than before,
my hope is everlasting.

Good-bye until the day
when flesh is warm no longer.
Meet me on the other side,
where love will make us stronger.

When she turned around, he was on his feet, and gently studying her.

"That really is your song, isn't it?"

"Yes." She had composed it, words and melody. "Did you like it?" she asked, though she couldn't look at him. Realizing their time together was about to end, she was more skittish than ever.

What exactly will good-bye entail?

"It was just what I needed to get through the day. Thank you." He glanced back at the clearing in the grass and said, "I should get going."

She brought her head up. "So soon?"

"Yeah," he said, his voice changing back to its usual brusqueness. "I have a rematch with Kale. We've made nice . . . for now. But everyone is still watching, expecting me to mess up somehow, and this time it won't happen."

"Oh, all right. You should go then," she murmured.

She gave him a weak smile. Then he stepped closer and rubbed his knuckles on her cheek. She was too shocked to blink her wide eyes. But she didn't flinch. For once, her reflexes betrayed her.

"You should stay out of the sun."

"Why? I like the sun."

"And it likes you . . . too much." He moved his hand from her face to her bare shoulder, which had turned pink, and lightly pressed his thumb down as he stroked it. "That's going to hurt later."

"It is?"

He nodded and brushed a loose strand of hair off her shoulder.

"I'll stay out of the sun, then, if you insist," she said.

"I do. And please be careful out here." Chris's narrow eyes scanned over the bushes, the grass, the rocks, the tree limbs. There were tiny, colorful birds chirping a merry tune, but he didn't seem to appreciate any creature that could fly. "If anything ever happened to you, I would . . . "

"Don't worry, Chris. I'll return to the hut soon."

"Good." He tapped her underneath the chin and smiled again. "I'll see you later."

She watched him disappear, but in her thoughts he was still present.

Cassie sat back down in a shady spot this time and found the piece of sandstone she had been using earlier. She continued smoothing down the wood into a shape she hoped would be recognizable. Yet the work was more taxing than before.

Chris had given her much to think about and maybe even a reason to stay in Hawaii, just a little longer.

CHAPTER 21
Dangerous Territory

Nohea Marketplace wasn't what Chris imagined. When he and Cassie and Joe arrived late the following afternoon, there were crowds of fairies bustling through the canopy-covered booths and open-faced island huts, but that wasn't what concerned him. He had gotten used to the idea that he wasn't human, and seeing fairies with wings no longer fazed him. But in Nohea, bizarre was apparently the norm. The colors and patterns were bright and wild. Though most of the fairies resembled tiny Polynesian humans, Chris was dwelling on the faces that didn't even resemble faces. Some were tattooed and pierced with sharp objects in a way that looked painful and grotesque. And then a fairy-male passed by whose face was half covered in what looked like dragon scales.

Chris stared until another sight drew his attention: two short, wide creatures with large hairy ears and noses, and disproportionally short arms and legs. They were waddling along enjoying a long skewer of meat and vegetables from a nearby food stall.

He rested his hand on the hilt of his sword just in case.

After the ugly creatures passed, Cassie squeezed his arm and stood on her toes to say, "Gnomes, and plump enough to be harmless. You only need to be wary of the thin ones."

On her other side, Joe took a step ahead and turned to see them both. "Chris, at this point, how can anything surprise you?"

Joe and Cassie were both smiling at him. He forced a tentative grin back, but it didn't ease his tension. The marketplace was busy enough to lose each other if they were careless. And there could be enemies nearby, some of whom might be looking for them.

After wandering around for a while with no destination in mind, Cassie glanced back at Chris. Then she grabbed Joe's elbow and led them both to a spot between a spice tent and a bakery booth.

"Chris, is everything all right? You look unwell," she warbled kindly as if he were on his deathbed.

"She's right, Chris. You look like crap," Joe added with much less sympathy.

"I'm fine," Chris claimed, and it was close to being true. He was in a secluded place, and the smell of fresh bread was overpowering the exotic spices, so he was almost back to his normal self—cautious and watchful with a good dose of paranoia. Nothing he couldn't handle. So he ignored their scrutiny, took a gulp from his canteen, and then pulled their shopping list and the wad of orange-edged bills from his pocket. "Where should we go first?" He handed a third of the manako notes to Joe.

Joe glanced at the list and flicked the paper where it said flour and yeast. Then he flipped through the Kāne money. And just as he had earlier that morning, he chuckled when he saw the sketch of General Kimo Jokura in the center of the fairy currency. The picture looked just like him; the eyes even had the right combination of ferocity and impatience.

Chris handed the rest of the bills to Cassie. He had seen enough of his former father-in-law lately and didn't need to carry his heavy essence in his pocket. The day at the market and therefore the spending money were meant to be for her.

Cassie was reluctant to take it, but Chris insisted, so she shrugged and placed it in the plaited bag at her hip, one she must have made herself. It was too elaborate to have been made by anyone else.

While Joe took a place in line at the bakery counter, Cassie pointed to the tent across the way and grabbed him by the wrist. Chris pointed in the direction they were headed, and when Joe looked over, he nodded.

Inside the boutique, the colorful clothing looked like a work of art. While Cassie gravitated toward the fem-fairy side, Chris remained by a table with simple-looking shirts. He was checking out a black tunic, similar in style to the white one he was already wearing, when Cassie sidled up beside him. "You should choose forest green."

Chris dropped the shirt back on the pile. "I don't really need anything."

"You should get it." She held the green shirt underneath his chin. "It brings out the green in your eyes."

He squinted one eye and then the other. "My eyes are brown."

"No, they're hazel."

"I think I would know the color of my own eyes," he bantered.

"Chris, I don't think you are nearly as observant as you think you are."

"Not true."

"Sorry, I'm not swayed." Then she turned her back and covered her eyes with her hands. "Do you even know the color of my eyes?"

"They're so brown they're almost purple," he said immediately.

"So you do pay attention." She twirled back around like a dancer and ended up closer than she was before.

"Yes, I do, but that was way too easy. Your eyes are piercing enough to bore a hole into something, especially when you're angry."

"And what about when I'm not angry?"

Chris tapped her on the nose. "Now you're just fishing for a compliment." He quickly sought to rectify the awkward moment he'd just created. "All right, you win. My eyes are hazel. I'll get the green one."

He tucked the shirt under his arm and followed her to the back of the tent. She browsed racks for a few more minutes and kept returning to the dresses. The dress that made her eyes light up was pink. When she held it to her body, it brightened the hue of her lips and brought out the rose in her cheeks. He liked the dress she was wearing, white with blue and purple flowers, but this one looked like it was made just for her.

He nodded his approval, and they paid for their purchases at the front table, then left to find Joe.

There was no longer a line at the bread booth, and Joe was not in sight. Chris and Cassie wandered around a small area, then broadened their search. They traveled all the way back to their starting spot and turned around. The crowd had thinned considerably, so Joe shouldn't have been that hard to find. But they made it to the other end of the market and there was still no sign of him.

There was a patch of long grass acting as a gate at the end of the market path. Chris heard faint tropical music coming from somewhere beyond. Joe may have wandered over there.

While Cassie moved the grass aside so she could peek through, Chris began to visually backtrack through the market. He whirled around when he heard Cassie gasp. Joe had sneaked up beside her and tucked a tiny pink plumeria behind her ear.

"Where have you been!?" she scolded. "We were starting to get worried!"

"I finished the list by myself so it wouldn't take all day." Joe lifted the three bags he was carrying for her to see. "Come here, both of you. I found something fun to do."

Joe led them through the long grass toward the music. The grass soon flattened into a circular clearing. The calypso band, the warm breeze, the glow of the early evening sun set the mood for dancing and romance.

Numerous young, starry-eyed fairies ebbed and flowed like grass in the wind. Some were even fluttering in the air around each other as if partaking in a magical mating ritual.

Chris's hand went into the back of his hair and he shifted his weight toward the area where they entered. If he'd had a watch, he would have checked it. "This is nice and all, but I think we should get going."

Joe dropped the bags by Chris's feet. "Why? What's the hurry?" He removed the flower from Cassie's ear, put it between his teeth, and danced his way over to the center of the action before Chris had a chance to protest.

To Chris's surprise, Cassie remained by his side. Maybe she wasn't much of a dancer either. Together, they watched Joe choose one partner after another, dancing until he was receiving praise, and compliments, and a lot of laughter.

"Is he always like this?" Cassie asked.

"Pretty much. You should see him once he has a few beers in him."

Her giggle tapered off to a silence that was more uncomfortable than usual. Then she took a breath. It sounded deep enough to be revitalizing. "Do you dance, Chris?"

"No!" he blurted. "It would take a lot more than beer to get *me* out there."

"Oh," was her only reply.

By the time Chris realized why she was asking, Joe was staring right at her. With the flower still in his mouth, he lifted his arm and curled his finger. But she shook her head and waved him off.

"Awwww, c'mon," he shouted, head cocked to the side.

Soon there were a few other fairies smiling at her, hooting and hollering. "Dance with him! Dance with him!"

When she still would not join in, Joe danced his way over to her and grabbed her by the hand.

"I can't dance," Cassie said as she resisted his pull.

Cassie threw Chris a desperate glance over her shoulder. Chris grinned and shrugged, and then felt a pang of remorse when she took her place in Joe's arms.

At first she paid more attention to her feet than anything else. But soon her inhibitions were no longer holding her back and her grace and talent had a chance to shine through.

Joe dipped her, spun her around. They made a great pair, and Chris felt more alone than ever. He spun his thoughts out into the future. He would always be the widower, the outsider. The happy couple would tolerate him only because he was family. But they would always gaze at each other with mutual pity in their eyes. *Poor Chris. If only he was as happy as we are. . . .*

When the upbeat music stopped and a slower song started to play, another fairy took Cassie's place in Joe's arms.

Cassie bowed her head graciously at her replacement and offered what looked like words of encouragement. Then she waved good-bye and wove her way back in Chris's direction.

Soon Chris noticed that she had a shadow, a fairy-male with enough metal piercing his face and body to be a hazard in a lightning storm. He grabbed her wrist and when she turned toward the tug, he grunted something to her with his shoulders puffed out and muscles flexed. Chris thought he might be delivering some poorly rehearsed pickup line.

Oh, you look familiar. Do you fly here often?

She shook her head and pointed over her shoulder.

Denied! Ha! Take that!

Whatever she said should have been enough to send the pierced fairy on his way, yet he did not let go of her hand. He plastered on an abhorrent excuse for a smile and started to say something else.

Chris's weight shifted to his toes, but he forced a deep breath and settled back on his heels. He had to remind himself that it would be best to wait. If Cassie could handle the situation herself, he should let her.

She shook her head again. The pierced fairy pulled his face back in stubborn incomprehension and then tugged her closer. When his hand went for her face in an aggressive attempt to entice her, Cassie flinched, then stepped away from his touch and twisted her wrist free. When she turned, she smacked into Chris's chest.

"Oh, I'm sorry. I . . . "

Chris barely noticed her flushed cheeks or her stammering because he was too busy giving the fairy who wouldn't take no for an answer a look that said cease and desist.

Like a coward, the pierced fairy dropped his eyes, mumbled something under his breath, and then flew off.

Chris's unforgiving stare followed him until he was out of sight. Then his attention was back where it belonged—with Cassie.

They were the only two stationary objects in the clearing. And though they were facing each other, her eyes were deflected down and to the side. He had no idea what Cassie was thinking—shame, embarrassment, fear, relief, loneliness? But she looked sad, so he grasped the tips of her fingers.

He lifted their hands and twirled her in a slow circle. Then their hands settled, his on her waist, hers on his shoulders, and the music sent them into orbit.

"So you got me out here," he said when he caught her eye. "You and that fairy pincushion."

"It certainly took you long enough."

He tried to find the words to explain why he'd waited, but she was smiling and had a playful twinkle in her eyes, so it really didn't matter. And though her eyes dropped away from his face, he saw the strange flick of purple inside them again and couldn't stop staring. "They're soothing."

She looked back up. "What's soothing?"

"Your eyes. When you're not angry, your eyes are soothing. Remember when you asked earlier?"

"I haven't forgotten."

"Whatever is in there, it's magical and it's working. See how calm I am?"

He must have said something right. She pressed against him, linked her arms behind his neck, and rested her head on his chest.

His body went rigid and his heart started beating with so much nervous energy that he worried she could feel it pounding against her. He should have stepped away from her, made some excuse. He knew he was treading in dangerous territory, but he couldn't deny himself the rush. His hands moved to her lower back and kept her close.

He rested his chin against her forehead and escaped outside of himself. He became someone who believed in a place where there would be no more fighting. Then he could love again as if it were the first time, freely, openly, fearlessly.

But the moment passed quickly. There was no such place, in this world or any other world. And the sudden stab of guilt, as well as the suspicion he was being watched and judged, made him aware that happiness wasn't his to have. It belonged to someone else.

Chris opened his eyes and saw Joe there, waiting. Joe raised his eyebrows when he was finally acknowledged. "Sorry to interrupt. Are you two ready to go?"

Cassie withdrew from Chris's clutch, and her cheerful glow vanished.

A buzzing then filled the air, and a new gang of fairies was dropping in from the sky like a swarm of black locusts.

"Who are these flying pieces of trouble?" Chris asked aloud.

"No idea," Joe shouted, "but let's get out of here!"

They grabbed their bags and scurried toward the grassy exit, but they weren't the only ones who were beginning to flee. There was pushing, screaming, fluttering. The pollen and dirt clouds the chaos stirred up made it hard to see, to move, and to stay together.

The three of them somehow managed to escape to the marketplace. There was more room to breathe, but the danger was just as real. Knifed-up canopies dangled from their splintered bases in booth after booth. Some of the dark-winged fairies were looting the marketplace, and knife fights were in progress all around.

Chris pulled out his sword and led the way toward the market gate, beyond which lay the way back to one of his father's magical wormholes. They were nearly free when Chris heard a slash and felt a disorienting burst of pain on his left side. Then Cassie was seized from his protective huddle.

A winged fairy with a bald round head was dragging Cassie away by the wrist. Her arm squirmed wildly, and she was digging her toes into the ground hard enough to leave furrow marks.

Her will to resist gave Chris and Joe enough time to launch a counterattack. Chris was closest to her and grasped her by the waist with his free hand.

To avoid the swing of Chris's sword, the bald fairy released Cassie, but his malicious smile suggested he wasn't about to surrender his prize, not without a fight.

As Chris stepped in front of Cassie, Joe crossed his arms and gave their enemy a challenging stare. Some kind of invisible energy popped forth, and the bald fairy spiraled into the sky as if caught in a cyclone.

Joe's magic had solved one problem but potentially created new ones. Allies? Enemies? It was hard to tell the difference among the circus show of fantastical creatures. Chris, Joe, and Cassie scurried from the market path into the brush and then the full-blown jungle. They ran without a word until they made it back to the wormhole. Once inside, Chris finally had a chance to check on the nagging source of pain.

The back of his shirt was torn and covered in blood.

CHAPTER 22
This Means War

Joe wasn't too concerned. Chris's knife wound was just a scratch. And he was certainly getting enough attention for it.

Cassie had torn the hem of her dress and was stumbling beside Chris, putting pressure on the cut. And Joe, the third wheel, lingered behind them, pretending he wasn't paying attention to their conversation.

They had been talking nonstop since they left the marketplace, or that is, Chris had been talking about himself. And did Cassie mind? Of course not. She was firing off one personal question after another. And Chris was telling her things Joe had never even heard before.

"Hey, Joe, what do you think that was all about back there?" Chris unexpectedly shouted over his shoulder. "Do you think there was something we could have done?"

This was Chris's first effort to include Joe in the conversation and the only reference so far to the skirmish at the marketplace, which could have had dire consequences. "Don't know," Joe replied curtly.

Cassie, then, replied without hesitation in Joe's stead. "Chris, the scene was anarchy. The territory and its inhabitants, as well as the attackers, were foreign to us. It would have been a challenge to differentiate allies from enemies. Before we could even find our bearings, you were injured. Your well-being became the priority. I'm sure your father and General Jokura would agree. Though I'm now certain that with the right care your wound will heal nicely with minimal scarring, the same cannot be said for some of your previous injuries."

"Yeah, I know. My back's a mess."

"Where did this scar come from?" she asked.

Joe noticed the smooth redirection of the conversation back to Cassie's top priority—poor mistreated Chris.

"This big one here?" Chris grabbed a fistful of material at the back of his neck and lifted his shirt to just below his shoulder blades. He craned his neck around to see which scar she meant. Apparently, there were a number of them.

She nodded.

"It was a third-degree burn."

"Does it still hurt?"

As Cassie brushed her fingertips over the distorted skin on his back, he took in a sharp breath.

Cassie pulled her hand away, and Chris started to laugh. "No, it doesn't hurt."

"That wasn't funny!" She smacked him lightly on his forearm.

"Ow!" Chris yelled as if she'd broken his arm, and this time both of them burst into laughter.

Joe genuinely missed his broody, miserable brother. This new Chris—cheerful and flirtatious—was getting on his nerves. If he stayed on his current course, he would be insufferable.

"Was the burn from when you were in the army?" Cassie asked further.

"Yeah, there was a roadside bomb in Iraq. It sent all sorts of fun things flying at me. I'm not exactly sure what caused the burn, but it scorched my skin until I was able to get my shirt off, no small feat with other injuries." He pointed to his right forearm, his left wrist, and a white spot on the side of his neck. "My shirt must have caught on fire, or maybe it was a hot liquid or chemical. I don't remember. The details are fuzzy."

"I feel awful you had to endure all of that," she gushed.

Joe couldn't believe the whole battle-wound thing was working on Cassie—like magic, and not the kind Joe had.

"The physical injuries weren't that bad," Chris continued. "They were painful for a while, but the aftermath was worse—insomnia, nightmares, what-ifs. A friend of mine, who was standing right next to me, died in that explosion. The difference between my life and his death was determined by a fraction of a second. It's impossible to understand, unless you've experienced a moment like that."

"I have, though," Cassie replied, "more than once."

Chris just looked at her, with the type of silence meant to encourage her to elaborate. But her head dropped, and eventually his did too. She wasn't going to say anything more, not even to him.

And luckily for Joe, he didn't have to endure any more boring war stories. The hut was in sight.

"I can't believe we're here already," Chris said as he placed his hand on Cassie's shoulder. "The walk was a lot faster the second time."

"I wonder why?" Joe mumbled under his breath. *Time must fly when you're the center of the universe.*

Chris moved the ferns aside so that Cassie could walk by unhindered. The two of them stopped before they reached the front door and glanced at Joe as if they were waiting for a moment alone. But Joe wasn't going to give it to them. Whatever they were going to say to each other, Joe was going to hear it. He leaned his back against the side of the house and waited in the darkness.

Cassie finally removed the torn piece of fabric from Chris's wound and shrugged. "Will you be all right?"

"I think I'll make it," he teased. "And sorry about your dress. You didn't have to do that."

"I wanted to."

"Well, thanks. Good thing you just bought a new one."

Then he guided her to the door with his hand on her shoulder. He was about to follow her inside when Joe cleared his throat. "Chris, can I talk to you for a second?"

Cassie turned around and looked to Chris. He gave her quick nod, which she understood as, "Go on without us." She stepped inside and eased the door shut with a subtle click.

Joe saw firelight filter through the closed shutters and heard her footsteps fade away. Then he led Chris away from the hut anyway, just in case. What he was about to say was not meant for her ears.

When he stopped walking, he didn't say anything. He just paced around and brushed plant debris out of the way with his feet.

Soon Chris made a what-do-you-want gesture with his hands and eyes. "Joe, say what's on your mind already."

"Well, if you insist," Joe said. "You seem to be moving on quickly."

"What's that supposed to mean?"

"You heard me!"

"I'm not moving on! I danced with her for two minutes and then told a couple of stories. I was being nice when you decided not to be."

"Danced?" Joe snapped back. "If that's what you call it! But I couldn't tell where she started and you ended. And since when do you dance anyway?"

"Since . . . since now, okay?" Chris stammered. His face was red and his hands were shaking. "And since when did you get so possessive? I didn't know you had exclusive rights."

"I don't! I just thought you realized—"

"Realized you've been panting after her since day one. Yeah, hard to miss."

Joe stepped closer to him. "Then why don't you back off?"

"I didn't do anything wrong," Chris stated, "so I don't need to—"

"Oh, Chris, did it hurt? Oh, Chris, can I touch it?" Joe said, imitating Cassie's voice and batting his eyelids. "You may not have done anything yet, but you *want* to."

Joe stepped forward and looked Chris right in the eye. He wanted Chris to snap. He wanted to get hit, the harder the better.

But Chris unexpectedly stepped back. "You know what?" he said calmly. "You don't deserve her." Then he turned and walked away.

"Yeah, well . . . ," Joe called after him, trying to get in the last word. But the door of the hut had slammed shut before he could finish.

Neither do you . . .

***

Canis Major scheduled a briefing session at dawn on the sixth day since their arrival in Hawaii. The first two of the four battalions he had sent out had not yet arrived even though the sun was clearly visible on the horizon. These missions were under Lieutenant Crux Chevalier's authority. They were the most dangerous and included the most soldiers. Therefore, they were most likely to be newsworthy.

Every moment Canis waited was a moment wasted. He decided to start without his lieutenant.

"You there, go first!" Canis commanded the leader of the third battalion. "Give me an update on your progress."

"I'm sorry, Your Majesty. There is no news to report. We've explored upstream and downstream many times as well as the surrounding forest. I'm sure you are aware the original tunnel has not reopened. If there are other tunnels, we have not yet discovered them."

Canis had an urge to slit a throat or two to express his disapproval. But that was what his mother would do. Instead, he scowled and looked up at the sky. He hoped the fading morning stars could hear his request for patience and self-control.

"How about you?" Canis asked the fourth battalion. "Any word from Pyxis?"

"None, Your Majesty. They have no further information."

This time when Canis looked up, he saw Crux's phalanx descending toward the ground. The soldiers landed, two at a time, and took their stance behind the two other battalions. And the Gray Coats marched over in their fairy state a few moments later and stood behind everyone else.

Crux was the last to arrive. He took his spot on Canis's right side.

"Nice of you to finally join us," Canis hissed at Crux. After a rough estimate, Canis realized the group was short in numbers. "Where are the others?"

Crux stood tall and stepped forward with his chest out. "They are pursuing a small cluster of Royals north."

Canis straightened his posture too, reaffirming his place as number one in command. "Other news?"

"Mikala Jokura is dead," Crux informed him, "but killing her was more of a challenge than we anticipated. Arrows came down upon us as soon as we entered her room. We lacked adequate numbers to overpower the well-hidden assailants, so I ordered a Gray Coat to dress like a doctor. Mrs. Jokura was poisoned."

"Casualties?"

"Three Reds, six Grays. Ten others were injured."

"And the other Jokuras?" Canis asked.

"They've abandoned their homes. We are still in the process of questioning friends and neighbors."

Canis sighed loudly through his nose. "That's it? That's all we've accomplished in six days? We've killed one deranged woman. Did you extract any information from her first?"

"No. Once there were casualties, it became a mission of retribution rather than inquiry."

The prince and the lieutenant both turned their heads to the sound of the fourth battalion approaching from behind. From what it appeared, they had two prisoners with them.

Crux cracked his knuckles.

At Canis's feet, the Crown Champion commander pushed to the ground two bound and gagged adolescent Royals—a girl and a boy. "We were able to catch two, Your Majesty. Two of their companions evaded capture."

"Good work," Canis said. "I applaud your success and diligence. I will likely reward you with a promotion."

The commander lowered to one knee and bowed his head.

"Have they spoken yet?" Canis asked.

He rose to his feet. "No, but we haven't been particularly persuasive. We wanted to bring them to you without delay."

"Wise decision." Canis looked up. "Crux?"

Crux pulled out his hunting knife, the one most useful for interrogations. He kept it either rusty or bloody at all times, and the teeth of the serrated edge were large enough to see from a distance.

Tears were already falling from the prisoners' dirt-stained faces. As they twitched and thrashed, the heavy rope coiled around them was strangling the flight out of their moth-colored wings. There was already cosmetic damage; their wings would forever be ugly. If they continued to struggle, they would be eroding away their own wing function.

The great Canis Major would choose death over living with mangled and flightless wings. He was amazed that his prisoners didn't seem to respect flight with the same reverence.

Canis squatted and looked into the boy's fearful brown eyes. "What is your name, and what clan are you from?"

Crux grabbed the boy by his hair and cut the gag from his mouth. Then he propped the blade against the boy's upper lip, just below his nose.

The shaking boy glanced at the girl. She warned him not to talk with a quick shake of her head.

Crux slashed his blade across the boy's lip. "Do you think your mate is in charge here?" Then Crux moved the blade to the boy's throat.

The boy's lip began to drip blood. "She's . . . not my mate. She's my sister."

Crux's eyes roamed over her and then loitered around her exposed belly button. "She's *very* pretty. . . ."

When the girl's sobbing escalated, Crux prowled closer to her.

"Not yet." Canis stayed the lieutenant with his hand up, then looked back at the boy. "We don't want to hurt either of you, but I asked for your clan and your name. Don't make me ask a second time, or I will allow my lieutenant here to do whatever he sees fit." Canis looked into the eyes of the deranged beast beside him. "And trust me, he has no boundaries."

Canis had to stand to reassert his place. After a heated silence, their interlocked glares dropped and Crux crouched back down next to the boy. "Will this loosen your tongue?"

The boy winced when Crux's blade was back against his throat. "My . . . my . . . sister and I are Kanaloan. We're fairies from the north. Our names are Pono and Luana."

Canis scowled at the unkempt appearance of Pono's sister as he recalled his mother's request. "And what is your kind? Are you among the legendary Royal Modifiers?"

"We're Royals. The Royal Modifiers are rare. General Jokura and his son are the only ones I know of."

Canis felt relief surge into his lungs as he inhaled. He might not have to marry a fem-fairy from this primitive jungle clan after all. "Nice to meet you, Pono. I am Prince Canis Major, and this is the Pyxis Royal Army." He gestured to the others. "Do you know why we're here?"

Pono's eyes darted from side to side and then to his sister's gagged face. Finally, he looked at Canis and nodded. "You're looking for Scott MacRae and his family."

"Indeed. How well informed you are. And if you know where he is, it would be best for you to speak up."

"I believe he is an adviser for the Kāne Army." Pono pressed his lips together in a firm line. "I would tell you how to find him if I knew. His army killed my older brother, and when I am old enough, I will join the Great Army and avenge his death. But ever since Scott brought his black magic here, we have been unable to locate their base."

Canis began hovering in wide circles with his hands linked behind his back as he tried to recall what his mother had taught him about magical mechanics. She had focused on the sorcery tactics required to battle those who were practiced in the art. Long ago, Pyxis had won the battle against Polaris by knowing enough about its inhabitants' magic to work around it. Unfortunately, only those Modifiers who possessed the diamond mark seemed capable of wielding the power. Canis realized they might have to wait for those aligned with Kimo Jokura to reemerge from the tunnel, and there would be no telling when—or even if—that would happen. The MacRaes might not ever leave their protected zone.

Canis then stopped his circling and landed. "How would you go about finding the MacRaes?" he asked Pono.

"The MacRae brothers were spotted in the Nohea Marketplace yesterday," the young fairy said. "One of them was getting cozy with a pretty, wingless fairy not from around here."

Canis was slightly encouraged by this news, but he was appalled as well. Crux's pursed lips demonstrated that the same thought was crossing his mind.

Getting cozy? Canis thought. His sister Cassiopeia had helped the MacRae brothers escape Pyxis, and that was bad enough, but a romantic involvement would put her life in danger. Andromeda would not tolerate it for an instant. He tried to shake off the unsettling notion so he could finish the interrogation. "Where is Nohea? Is it protected?"

"Nohea is a merchant village that sprouted up along our southern border, technically on the Kāne side. Everyone is peaceably welcome, in the village doctrine, but we want the area back under Kanaloan control, even if Prince Haipo refuses to go to war over it. I would suggest you send your warriors there, and if you want to find the MacRaes you could also patrol the area around their tunnels."

Canis's spirits lifted. "Tunnels? There are more of them?"

"Other than the one right here," Pono said, bobbing his head toward the stream, "we expect there are at least three others; one near Nohea, one that goes north through our territory, and one that heads east to the ocean. We wish we knew more about them too. But they are used so infrequently and in such secrecy, it's a challenge to figure out where they open up or how they work."

"I would still like to know their approximate locations," Canis said, pleased the captive boy was talking so openly. "Furthermore, I assure you, no harm will come to you or your sister if you fulfill my final request. I would like you to take me to your leader. I will bring him gifts, and perhaps we can form an alliance."

Pono looked to his sister again and she nodded this time. "Emperor Ailani has resigned from public life because of his health. His heir, Prince Haipo, is our new leader."

"Thank you, my young friend." Canis rummaged through the pocket of his vest. He pulled out a sack and opened it in front of Pono to reveal the gold and jewels inside. "Here is a token of my gratitude." He added the sack to a pouch on Pono's belt. Then he addressed his army: "The Fourth Battalion will accompany me north. The rest of you will continue your searches and report back here at dawn." He glared at Crux. "And don't be late."

CHAPTER 23
Unraveled

Chris wasn't one to make a big deal out of his birthday. He didn't want anything special, didn't expect anything, but it was his thirtieth birthday. At the very least, he hoped someone would remember.

But the day had turned into evening, and the evening was nearly over. He hadn't even seen his father or brother all day.

When Chris returned to the hut, he had to duck out of the way of a floating book. Then he had to wait for a bowl with a wooden spoon to pass by. It wasn't exactly the "Welcome home, happy birthday!" he expected.

Chris understood why his father selected Joe to be the magician, yet it was still irksome. While Chris was training with the army, sweating in the heat of the Hawaiian sun until he couldn't see straight, Joe was likely in cool shady spots moving little twigs and flowers with his mind. And from a tactical standpoint, it seemed to him that he and Joe should be trained in both areas. If Chris knew how to use magic, wouldn't that give him a greater advantage over his enemies in a battle? And Joe learning how to use a sword couldn't hurt either.

So Chris hung his weapons and armor on the rack, determined to ask his father for his first lesson in moving things with his mind.

When Chris spoke up, Scott gave him an I'll-humor-you pat on the back and put him in the corner of the room with *Magical Mechanics*. Then Scott left the hut for a moment and returned with a green leaf about the size of a sheet of paper.

Chris set the leaf on the floor and read the first page of the first chapter, "Simple Lift." The initial read-through didn't go well. The wording was archaic and technical, and he got nothing out of it. He gave the page another attempt, and then another. When he thought he had the basic idea, he pointed all his mental energy at the leaf. Nothing happened—no lift, no swirl, no rustle, not even a twitch!

It wasn't helping his confidence that Joe had all four chairs and the kitchen table floating in the air. Then Scott suggested that Joe flip the chairs over and stack them on top of the table. Joe performed the task flawlessly.

"Now the candles," Scott said.

Joe lifted the room's candles into the air while he simultaneously lowered the chairs into their positions underneath the table. He set the candles down in a perfect square on top. He added the plates, goblets, and silverware with amazing control. Next Joe levitated a pitcher over to the table and poured water into each goblet without missing a drop. At last, he set the pitcher down between the candles. The table looked prepped for a romantic dinner by the ceiling.

Then Scott came over to check on Chris's progress. His unhelpful suggestions made Chris want to shred the leaf into a thousand pieces and throw every fragment into the fire.

Scott sighed and shook his head. "Chris, you seem like you've had enough for one day. Why don't you call it a night?"

"Giving up on me already?"

Joe joined Scott's side. They both looked down at Chris and then exchanged condescending glances.

"No, I get it," Chris said as he rose to his feet. "He's brains, I'm brawn. So why don't I go play in the jungle with the other gorillas?" Then Chris charged over to the front door.

"Chris, it's not like that!" his father called after him.

Chris slammed the door shut. He didn't want to hear any more lies.

It was like that. And it had always been like that.

***

Cassie, reading one of Scott's reference books behind her curtain, heard the heated exchange and the slamming of the door.

Wolu—*walrus*

Wōwō—*to bellow, roar*

Once she'd committed the last word the Hawaiian-English dictionary to memory, she clapped the book shut and set it back on the bookshelf. Then she peeked around her curtain. Joe and Scott had resumed their lesson. They were lifting furniture, clearing out the cabinets, and making quite a racket.

It looked as if they would be working their magic for a while, and even if they stopped for the night, they still had to put the contents of the hut back in order.

Cassie had never been skillful in the realm of magic and could therefore sympathize with Chris. She decided to find him. He might appreciate some company on his birthday, and this seemed like the perfect time to catch him alone, an opportunity she had waited for all day. She grabbed a lantern and a wrapped bundle, and slipped out of the hut. She guessed that Chris had headed to the lagoon.

Cassie knew the way there, or at least she thought she did. She had never wandered around at night, though. As she stepped away from the safety of the light from the hut, she realized her intended journey was a much better idea in theory. The flora were tall, thick, convoluted, and menacing. And though the harmless insects had fascinated her during the day, they were now creepy, massive, and incredibly fast! When she spotted the back end of a centipede slither by, three words came to mind: *venomous, nocturnal, carnivore.* Her tentative steps switched to a sprint.

Then she saw the water and, better yet, she saw him. Four stones, each one successively larger, led to the tallest, widest, and most deeply embedded stone, a miniature mountain with a sizable drop to the lagoon. And at its steep edge, Chris was chucking pebbles into the waterfall.

For a few moments, she felt safe and comfortable just watching. From a mild distance, she could appreciate the simplicity of her admiration. Staying there, hiding, waiting, or considering a hasty retreat would be something a young girl would do. Thanks to her mother, she had matured early, as a means of survival. The phase between childhood and adulthood had never existed for her, so she was ready to move forward, take a chance, step out of the safe zone and into the unknown.

***

Chris noticed a lantern in the distance. It was bobbing a bit but didn't seem to be getting any closer. "Is somebody there?"

Then the lantern did move closer, slowly and tentatively. "It's me," said a gentle voice.

"Oh."

A nervous lump lodged itself in his throat. He tried to get rid of it by swallowing. But doing so only created a new lump in his stomach. After what Joe had accused him of the night before, most of which he denied, he was now alone with the fairy princess.

This is a test, he decided. Some higher power was testing his willpower and judgment. And that power was laughing at him, knowing he wasn't good at tests.

"Expecting someone else?" Cassie said when she appeared by the lowest rock.

"No . . . well. . . yes." Chris skipped down and helped her up. "I thought you might be my father, coming to share wisdom," he said, deepening his voice with sarcasm. He took her hand and helped her over a deep gorge. "Or Joe, coming to . . . well, I don't know. Remind me again of his purpose?"

"To provide the great earth with intelligence and wit, deep and vast as the ocean," she said as they climbed upon the highest rock, "and to bestow upon us . . . *humble* us . . . with other praiseworthy attributes, numerous as stars in the sky." She spun around in a circle with a giggle while gesturing to the heavens with both hands.

"Yeah, that! How could I forget?"

Chris glanced at the dress Cassie had bought at the market—the delicate pink fabric light against her sunburned skin, now turning to a tan. He made an effort not to glance again, but the image was ingrained, the damage done. A cold sweat broke out on his palms and lower back.

He took a seat at the rock's edge and let his legs dangle over the side. Then he leaned back on his arms and took a deep breath. When he looked over his shoulder, she was still at the far end of the rock, tiptoes pressed into place, her wide eyes seemed fixed on something present—a rock, a ledge, the dark space over the water—and distant—the debilitating memory of something or someone.

Her fear of the water put his angst into perspective. The *will I, won't I, can I, should I* seemed of little consequence in a world where tomorrow was no guarantee. What she needed more than anything was a friend, and he could be that for her.

254

When Cassie realized he was watching her, she smiled and sat down in the spot where she'd been standing. Then she adjusted her skirt around her legs until she looked like a flower without a stem.

"So you don't want to watch the prodigal son get his merit badge in magic?" Chris asked, keeping to the safe topic of his brother.

"No, playing with a gorilla sounds much more fun."

He grimaced over his shoulder. "Hey, that's not nice."

"In all seriousness, Chris, try not to take it personally. Magic has a certain mystery to it. Although it's possible to overcome any shortcomings with hard work, in most cases you're either born with the ability or you're not. In fact, can you guess which category I represent?"

He pushed away from the ledge and turned to face her. "Team gorilla?"

"Ha," Cassie retorted. "And I thought Joe was the funny one."

"Oh, so Joe's the funny one too!" Chris threw his eyes to heaven. "What does that make me known for? Temper tantrums?"

"Do you really want to know?"

"Sure, why not? But be nice. I have a fragile male ego."

"I'll try to keep that in mind." She paused and bit her lip. Finally, she said, "From my perspective you are full of passion. You say exactly what you feel. You do exactly what you are compelled to do. When you are upset, or angry, or frustrated, you act without thinking rather than think without acting. Some, perhaps, would call you impetuous or reckless. Others might call you brave."

Chris raised one eyebrow, impressed. "I think I know what your fairy superpower is."

"What do you mean?" she asked.

"You're eerily perceptive sometimes, and you have a way with words. You can describe a head case like me and make it sound like poetry."

"You're not a head case. And perceptiveness and poetry won't save any lives or win any battles."

"They might be more useful than 'acts without thinking,'" Chris replied, mocking her voice.

"I'm not convinced. I'm not allowed to train with you, and I'm not brilliant like my father or like Andromeda in any way—"

"Thankfully! I can't imagine a Cassiopeia/Andromeda duo—the world as we know it would be over!"

Cassie laughed. "I suppose we may find out some day if my 'fairy superpower' can pull any weight in the war against evil."

———

"You never know. You might surprise yourself!" he responded brightly.

"I hope so."

Cassie then stood, the flower of her dress settling around her knees. "I'll be right back. I have something for you." She skipped down the rocks and disappeared into the reeds by the side of the lagoon.

Chris stood, too, as Cassie climbed back up the rocks with something tucked underneath her arm. Whatever it was, it had flowers braided around it. He reached out to help her over the last stones, but instead of taking his hand she placed the long bundle into it.

"That," he said, "looks like a baseball bat."

"It is," Cassie said.

"Nicely done! May I?" he asked untangling the flowers from the smooth wood.

She nodded and returned to her previous sitting position. "Happy birthday."

Chris took a few practice swings. "Thanks. And how did you know it was my birthday?"

"Joe mentioned it."

"I'm sure he also mentioned that turning thirty makes me an old man." Chris had a feeling he didn't want to know, but that was the exact reason he should probably ask the dreaded question, *How old are you?*

"Let me save you the trouble," Cassie said as if reading his thoughts. "I turned twenty on December 6. You are nine years and eleven months older than I am."

Chris felt like he got the wind kicked out of him. He pulled himself together with a few choking breaths and threw a pebble into the air. He hit it into the high trees and lost sight of it in the darkness.

"Does that bother you?" Cassie asked.

He shrugged, not knowing how to answer at first. A ten-year age gap was at the high end of being socially acceptable by human standards, but in the fairy world, age might not have the same meaning. And what Cassie lacked in years, she made up for in life experience.

After his brother had accused him of moving on too quickly, Chris had been up most of the night, sleepless with a combination of anger and guilt. Was Joe right? After all, Alana had died and he had met Cassie less than two weeks ago. At last, Chris had decided that he hadn't chosen to move on from Alana. Cassie had simply come along and demonstrated both compassion and understanding, and this whole experience was something beyond his, or her, control. And then he had fallen into a peaceful sleep.

He didn't know how much time he had. Even if Andromeda never found them, he was training for the very real possibility of a full-blown fairy war in the Ewa Forest. Every day was a gift, and he might as well spend as much time as he could with someone who made him happy.

"No," he finally said. "Unless it bothers you."

"Not in the least."

"Well then, I guess we can be friends."

"Friends," she repeated.

"Right," he said, and then he presented the bat to her, ready to start a friendly game of pitch and catch. "Do you want to try it?"

Her eyes widened. "I don't know how."

"I'll show you."

Chris waved for her to come closer.

She took the bat and held it in both hands, one on top of the other, and with her elbows locked straight.

He stood behind her, pulled the bat closer, and separated her hands. "Are you right handed?"

"I usually write with my right hand because it is more efficient. Faster, you could say. But the handwriting that results from my left hand is more pleasing to the eye. Then there are other circumstances where I prefer my left hand. It really depends on what I'm doing."

He chuckled under his breath.

"Right's fine," she corrected simply.

"Good!"

Chris squared off her hips and lifted her right elbow. Then he went in front of her. He turned and lifted her chin. Their glances bumped into each other as he removed his hand from her face.

He deflected his eyes to her hands, and once he was done repositioning them, he jumped back to finish the lesson. "Look to the left, bend your knees slightly, and keep your legs shoulder-width apart."

Chris walked a few paces away to get a better look at her stance and laughed aloud once he saw her. Then he walked back over.

"I'm glad I entertain you," she huffed as he readjusted her hands again.

"The bat is bigger than you are. You need to choke up a bit and put your hands closer together so it's not flopping all over the place."

"Better?"

He stepped away again. "Looks much better. Now you're ready to hit something."

"Are you really going to throw something at me?"

"Isn't that the point?" he asked with his hands in the shape of a W.

She didn't look too sure.

"Come on. I'll be careful." He picked up a pebble. "It's a good stress reliever. You'll see."

He found a good spot and threw the stone toward her, slow and underhanded. She swung hard, but missed.

"See? It's not that hard!"

"I didn't hit anything yet!"

"Yeah, but that was a decent swing."

He picked up another pebble and tried again. This time she made contact. She hit it high and to Chris's right side. He tried to jump for it, but the rock flew behind him.

"Not bad! Isn't baseball fun? You'll probably be spitting, swearing, and—my personal favorite—heckling your opponents by the end of the night."

"I'm not sure about that." She returned the bat to him and sat back down.

For a few minutes, he tossed rocks to himself and hit them into the darkness. When he had had enough, he took a seat on the rock next to her.

"Well, thanks for remembering my birthday and for the gift," he said, balancing the bat on his palm. "At least somebody remembered. If Alana were still alive, I'd probably be at a party in my honor right now. She liked parties more than I ever did."

"I would imagine it's difficult to be back in the place where you met. Everything must remind you of her."

"Definitely," he said, purposefully evading elaboration and still maneuvering the bat around in his hand.

"Do you want to talk about it?"

He stabilized the bat with a squeeze on the bottom and gave her his full attention. "Why? Is it sharing time?" He raised an eyebrow.

"Perhaps." She raised an eyebrow back at him.

"Does that mean you'll tell me your story?"

"Why? Will you tell me yours?"

"Maybe. I'll let you have one question." He pointed the bat at her good-naturedly. "And in exchange, you can tell me something I want to know."

"Is it imperative we bargain over questions?"

"Don't try to distract me with words like 'imperative.' Do we have a deal or not?"

"Yes, but I want to go first."

When she smiled and laced her hands beneath her chin, Chris lost the nerve to challenge her. "Okay."

"Here we go. How did you and your wife meet and fall in love?"

"Wow. You get right to the point. But first, I should warn you. I'm not much of a storyteller. Whenever anyone asked us how we met, Alana always told them, every funny and embarrassing detail."

"I'm sure you'll do fine."

He nodded once before he began. "So my dad brought Mom, Joe, and me to Hawaii that infamous summer because he knew some retired fisherman—I forget his name—from Massachusetts who owned a tour boat out here. I know now that that was a cover story. Anyway, the exact reason why we were here isn't important.

"I hated it here at first. Back home I was supposed to be training for my last year on the baseball team. Instead, I was stuck in a place where I had no friends and nothing to do except work for my father.

"But Hawaii started growing on me. It helped when I found some other kids to hang out with. We spent most of our free time on the beach. One of the guys I saw a lot was Kale. Remember him?" Chris asked, elbowing her.

"How could I forget? You were friends with him?"

"Sort of. He was the pack leader, so I had to tolerate him if I wanted to stay in the group. And occasionally this mouthy girl would pop up to give Kale and some of the other guys a lot of grief. I found out it was his sister."

"Was it love at first sight?" Cassie asked.

Chris gave a slightly self-conscious chuckle. "Um, I don't know. Not really. She was cute and all, but not what I thought was my type. And I was a little jaded, to be perfectly honest. I'd had a few bad experiences back at home. But that's another story.

"One night, I left the beach and ventured into a tourist trap to get something to eat. I was walking along, minding my own business, when I passed by a group of security guards harassing this girl. I recognized her, so I stopped. They were accusing her of stealing something. But it was obvious they were just giving her a hard time for the sake of giving her a hard time. So, blah, blah, blah. Damsel in distress . . ."

Cassie had unlaced her hands and now had two fingers on her cheek, one tapping. "Damsels in distress . . . hmmm . . . Is that your specialty?"

"Naturally," he said. "They are my greatest strength and my greatest weakness."

"So what did you say to the guards?"

"I said if she stole something, they should prove it or let her go. They mumbled something about checking the security camera, then they scattered and went back to work, and I use the term 'work' loosely.

"I ended up buying Alana some ice cream and walking her home. She was a lot different from the New England girls I knew, in a good way. It was really more her than me, but I felt funny when I was with her. We played off each other's comments like a comedy routine.

"After that, we started spending a lot of time together. First, just as friends. But Kale saw things differently. The next time I saw him, I got a fist in the gut and a death threat from his posse. So those friends I made? Gone. Even Mikala—Mrs. Jokura—disliked me. She called me 'haole' all the time. It's an insult. I forget the exact translation."

"In simple terms, it just means 'foreigner,' " Cassie answered quickly. "But it's used in a pejorative sense for white people in general, especially whites who are at cultural odds with the native Polynesian people."

"Right." Chris pulled his head back, confused as usual. "How did you know that?"

She dropped her eyes and mouthed a couple of words as if scolding herself. Why? He didn't know.

Chris shrugged once he realized that she wasn't going to answer. He didn't want to push her too hard or in the wrong direction. "After that, I was going to call the whole thing off. I didn't want the drama. There were only a few weeks left of summer anyway. I thought it might be a good idea to say good-bye early. I thought Alana would understand too. But then, one night, she had a fight with her mother—about me—and showed up at my window in tears. We did talk a little, just not about good-bye. And then, one thing led to another . . .

"Of course, we fell asleep and woke up at the crack of dawn to the sound of Kale banging on the front door. My parents, thankfully, managed the situation and asked him to leave, and Alana was able to make it back to her house unseen. But her family knew she'd been with me anyway.

"Now that my family knew something was going on, I got a long lecture about it. But at least my parents didn't think it was that big of a deal. My mother liked Alana and had seen what she called positive changes in me, so at least she was on my side.

"When the summer ended, Alana and I did say good-bye, and I promised to keep in touch. Obviously, I kept my promise. We talked on the phone almost every night. I even wrote her a few letters. Can you imagine me writing letters? It was my mother's idea. She said it was romantic . . . and cheaper than all the phone calls. After I graduated from high school, I moved to Hawaii to be with her. We rented this horrible shack for a while and even had roommates to deal with. We struggled to get by, but we had a lot of fun together—too much fun. That was the main reason we struggled. We would drink ourselves silly with our coworkers, locals, tourists, whoever, go home, sleep it off, drag ourselves through whatever restaurant job we had, and do it all again the next night.

"Since Kale and Mikala never warmed to me and Kimo was never seen or heard from, we eventually decided to move to Massachusetts and our lives became much more tame. She wanted to go to nursing school. I played a little minor league baseball, but the money was terrible. So before long, I joined the army.

"A couple of years later, the twins came along. I wanted to be a part of their lives, so I left the army as soon as I could. And while I was struggling to find my place in the world, my mother was diagnosed with cancer. She died, and then . . . well . . . you know the rest."

He threw a stone into the waterfall and waited. He waited for Cassie to say something, waited for that cleansed feeling that should have come from talking, and while he waited, he wondered if he was prepared to hear her story, one that was not likely to lift his mood either.

"Thank you, Chris," Cassie said quietly. "You didn't have to tell me all of that. And you are a great storyteller." She gave him a genuine smile. "Hmmm . . . I suppose it's my turn to answer your question now, unless you've changed your mind and you'd rather we discuss something else," she blurted all in one breath.

He threw her a scolding glance. "Nice try." Then he tried to put together a good question, something that was simple and direct but that would draw out as much information as possible. "Well, on our first night here in this haven, we heard the story of my father and your mother. But we didn't hear anything about you and your mother. What was it like being Queen Andromeda's daughter and how did it all end?"

She sighed. "I knew you were going to ask something like that. And before I answer, I have to be forthcoming. What I'm about to tell you is not particularly pleasant."

"I appreciate the warning, but I still want to know."

"When I was born wingless, my mother of course had no use for me whatsoever. I was raised in the Aerial Palace and given a Royal education, but mostly out of her sight or hearing. I knew nothing about your father or my father or, indeed, little about anything else. My only friend was a boy about my age, Phoenix, the son of a groundskeeper. We ran and played together in many dark, mysterious places, and no one other than palace staff ever took notice of us. Still, as I grew, my mother apparently came to believe there was a slim chance I could be of use to her: an arranged marriage with a foreign Royal would have increased her wealth and power. The day I turned sixteen, she came to my room before I was even out of bed, grabbed my jaw, and eyed my features. 'It is time,' she said. She'd chosen a husband for me: Lord Vulpecula, a fairy from Imperio del Fuego, a Spanish empire too powerful for her acquisition. I started to protest, but she then told me that if I didn't obey, she would make sure that Phoenix would be burned and would never rise from the ashes. I was stunned. I had no idea she even knew I had a friend."

Cassie stopped and shrugged. Then she took a gulp and continued. "I'd lived my whole life in the shelter of the palace, so no one beyond its walls knew that I was not a Royal. My mother had deceived the Spanish fairy lord about my status. When the day of the wedding arrived, fake wings were pinned to the lace beneath my dress. But the wings were heavy with jewels, and the lace tore, stitch by stitch, with every step I took toward the horrified groom. I kept walking despite the gasps, the snickers, and the whispers. I was naïve enough to believe Vulpecula might marry me anyway. I lifted my chin and forced a smile. But he wasn't smiling back."

"I guess that explains your aversion to weddings," Chris said when she paused.

"Yes," she replied simply. "Shall I continue?"

"Go ahead. I'm listening."

"After the groom soared off, I somehow managed to find my legs. I ran to find Phoenix before my mother did. I'd never told him his life was in jeopardy; I suppose I thought that if I obeyed my mother, she would leave him alone.

"To my dismay, his room was empty. I was about search the grounds for him when I noticed a marble box on the floor with its cover ajar. I stepped a little closer and saw smudges of blood on the stone. I don't know what compelled me to look inside. There was a note signed, 'Best Regards, Your Dearest Mother.' My friend's ashes were to have been placed among the wedding presents. Obedience aside, he was dead already."

"Did you love him?" Chris asked.

"What? Oh. Did I love him? Yes, the way a lonely and unwanted child loves the only constant in her life."

"That's sad. I'm sorry."

Cassie stared into space for a moment, and then closed her eyes. When she opened them again, she turned back toward Chris. "Do you still want to hear the rest?"

"Only if you still want to tell me."

She nodded. "From there, I had to decide: live or die? To live, I would have to run, hide, struggle, find my way in a city that was not kind. It would have been easier to die, but I chose life. I went back to the North Tower to shed my hideous wedding dress and pack some of my things. I lost many crucial minutes removing the tangled lace. It was as if I were ensnared in the wretched thing! Once I had changed clothes, Andromeda hovered into my room. Her open wings cast a shadow over me. Every lantern dimmed to a glowing wick. I turned and backed away from her. Then my legs gave way. I caught myself with my hands and tried to scramble to my feet, but . . ."

"I get the idea," Chris said. "You don't have to go on if you don't want to."

She shrugged and fiddled with a loose strand of her hair.

"You survived to tell the tale. Once you escaped, things could only improve, right?" Chris asked, hoping Pyxis hadn't been as cruel to her as her mother had been.

"For the most part yes, though I did spend a couple of weeks begging for food. When I thought I would die in an alley somewhere, a fairy known as the Banker hired me as a private tutor for his children. He was proud of the name he had earned, but allowed me to call him by his real name, Scorpius.

"In the beginning, he was good to me, and told me what I needed to hear—I would be safe, supported, and my mother would never have to know. And I believed him.

"I considered myself lucky, and I worked hard to earn his praise. His compliments were many. I was the smartest fem-fairy he had ever met . . . I had a keen sense for politics . . . the children were making such remarkable progress. I could do no wrong. But the whispers . . . every time I entered a room, they stopped, and when I left, they started again. They were like a familiar song. I had heard them all my life, but I thought I had finally escaped them.

"Then, late one night, I heard a light shuffling outside my bedroom, too soft to be an adult, too loud to be dismissed as my imagination. I cracked open my door and saw a child from the kitchen standing there. Dusty, they called him. I asked what he had hidden behind his back. He revealed a book and his intentions. He wanted me to teach him to read, in secret. He offered all the coins in his pocket—a sad pittance, nothing more. The only payment I asked for was the truth. Why were there so many secrets?

" 'There are many things the Banker would rather we not discuss,' Dusty said, and he showed me the scar beneath his ear. 'His rings leave their mark,' he warned. I listened in shock to the rest of his story. He was supposedly Scorpius's bastard child. What was worse, his mother, a scullery maid, had been beaten to death because she'd found solace in the arms of another fairy-male. 'He's always kind, at first, to the pretty ones,' Dusty continued. 'Until they are round with child. Then he moves on, but both mother and child will always belong to him.'

"From that point on, I avoided Scorpius as best I could. I was determined to be the exception, not the rule. My plan backfired, however. If he failed to come across me during the day, he requested my presence in his office late at night. The meetings seemed to last forever even though the business portion of the conversation ended quickly. He showed me his extensive library, his awards, his trophies, and he bragged about his net worth. His hand always seemed to end up on my shoulder and his eyes had this unnerving way of wandering all over me. In essence, I endured more than I should have.

"He was in no hurry—the pursuit seemed to thrill him—but day by day, his advances grew more brazen. He made it clear that I 'owed' him something."

"Jeez!" Chris interrupted. "If I'm ever in Pyxis again, where do I find this guy?"

"That's very chivalrous of you, Chris, but he never had a chance to carry out his intention." She brought her knees to her chest. One of her hands then cradled her neck as she stared at the waterfall. Her hand dropped, and finally she looked at Chris. "I was saved. That's all that matters. Dusty was my little hero. He knocked over one of the Banker's trophies at a critical moment. I was able to sneak away. And I don't know what ever became of Dusty. . . .

"I left in the middle of the night but had no place to go. I traveled from one slum to another, and fell deeper and deeper into despair. Then I became sick one day and collapsed. When I awoke, Carina's wide green eyes were there to greet me. She and her sister, Vela, called me princess and never left my side. I found out later that Vela and Carina's mother had once been one of my nursemaids back at the Aerial Palace.

"Then, when I was well again, I worked around the clock to repay my debts—cooking, cleaning, teaching, sewing. I slept on the floor with Carina and Vela's children until I could afford my own room. But I missed them once I left. They were the closest I had to a real family. And in that time, I also met Pierre Delacroix and his associates. They cornered me one day and bombarded me with inquiries. At first, I hesitated to say much. Speaking candidly would be asking for trouble, the kind punishable by death. But once I heard some of their stories, the harder it became to do nothing. We began talking about rebellion. Given what we were up against, our efforts to organize one were almost laughable. But, then again, my mother has put so many fairies in a position where they have nothing left to lose . . . same as me." She stopped, looked down, and did not continue.

Chris threw pebbles into the waterfall until he felt her hand on his shoulder. "You're quiet. What does that mean?"

"I'm thinking," he replied.

"What are you thinking, Chris?"

He shrugged. "I'm just trying to take it all in. Take it in, and not put my fist through something."

She suddenly covered her face with her hands. "I knew I should have kept this to myself. I apologize for upsetting you."

He shot to his feet and paced away from her. "There's no reason you should be apologizing for anything!" He turned back around and saw tears in her eyes. "Hey, I'm sorry I yelled." Then his hand dived into the hair at the back of his neck, and when he sat back down, he let out a deep sigh. "Thanks for answering my question."

She glanced at him through the heavy gloss of water in her eyes. When she looked away, she let her tears fall. "I'm glad you asked it. I feel better— liberated, I suppose. I would prefer there be no secrets between us."

She captured her tears with her index finger and thumb. Her eyes seemed to stay dry after that, but she was still visibly distressed. Her sad story was by no means over. Her mother's army was looking for her at this very moment, and they weren't going to give up until they found her.

Chris picked up his baseball bat. He stood and hit stones into the darkness harder than he had before. His anger put some extra momentum into his swing. Soon he stopped and held the bat in the palms of his hands. Some of the happiest moments of his life had occurred while he was holding a baseball bat, but his most recent experience in doing so now overshadowed the others. "It's hard to believe I can pick up a bat right now," he muttered.

"Why is that?"

"Because baseball is the reason Alana is dead."

Cassie stood and moved to his side, unaware or somehow less afraid of the precipice by the water. "How so?"

"The night I was abducted, I pulled out my bat from underneath the bed and used it against one of the Gray Coats. Alana was murdered to punish me."

"Chris, please don't blame yourself. You did what you could to protect your family."

"I know, but I still feel . . . responsible."

Chris sniffled and, for the first time since the evening he told his children about their mother, felt hot tears building in the corners of his eyes.

Cassie took him by the hand the way a child might grab a parent, or the way a friend might show solidarity. But then she slid her fingertips between his and squeezed his hand as if she would never let go. And whatever she was doing to make him feel calmer, it was working, and working well.

He could have stayed there, hand in hand with her, for a long time, but thunder was rumbling in the distance. Drops of rain began sprinkling dots on the rocks.

"It is beautiful here," she said as she watched the waterfall tumble over the embankment.

"What? Oh. Beautiful. Right."

Chris wasn't looking at the view. He was staring at her lips. They were slightly apart, just shy of a pucker. He forced his eyes away—rocks, leaves, vines, water, *anywhere* else.

As the drizzle changed over to a tropical shower, Cassie swung their connected hands back and forth. "Shall we return?"

"Why? Are you going to melt in the rain?" He lifted her arm over her head and pulled her close in a dancelike maneuver.

Her back rested against him and his arm settled at her waist. His other hand sneaked across her waist as well. She was secure in his arms. He closed his eyes and enjoyed a slow, deep breath. The scent of her hair was intoxicating. He could practically taste the sunshine. After many days and nights of clouds and unrelenting darkness, she was the first ray of light to break through. He had the choice to bask in its glow or remain immersed in shadow.

Then, just as his lips were about to fall toward the soft skin between her shoulder and neck, there was a loud clap of thunder. With it came the memory of Andromeda's cruel whisper.

She'll unravel you. . . .

Chris's arms dropped. Cassie's head and shoulder snapped in his direction. He slipped, they collided, and Cassie lost her footing on the edge of the rock.

He lunged for her hand as she slid over the side. Then his feet started sliding. He glanced at her terrified face and then at the water below. He tightened his grip because he knew where they were about to end up.

She splashed into the lagoon feet-first and he had to twist to the side so he wouldn't land on top of her. But his grip on her wrist was locked shut.

Chris stopped their plummet just below the surface. He couldn't see much, but he could feel the waves of her panic. He yanked her closer and gripped her underneath her arms. Then, with one firm scissor kick, he brought her to the surface.

While Cassie was choking for breath, he towed her over to where he could stand. He put her head over his shoulder and pounded her between the shoulder blades with the heel of his palm.

She started coughing. He breathed a little easier, too, once he knew she would be all right.

"I am so sorry. That was my fault," he said. When her coughing subsided, she eased away from his shoulder. Then Chris leaned his forehead against hers. "Hey, you're supposed to exhale, not inhale."

He lifted his head, expecting to catch her smile. But she still looked terrified. There was only one other time he'd seen her so frightened, and that had been in the presence of her mother. "Are you okay?"

Her eyes were darting all over the place. "I'm not certain."

"Is it the water? If you want, we can get out." He took a step toward the shore.

"No!" Her whole body tensed around his. "It's not the water—or not just the water."

"It must be me, then. Am I really that scary?" he mumbled.

Her chin and eyes dropped as she shook her head. Then she adjusted her legs around his waist. Her body came closer, her face rose to eye level, and when she lifted her chin back up, those wide, vulnerable, beautiful eyes met his. And then he kissed her, because he wanted to, more than anything, and because he was tired of waiting, tired of worrying about all the reasons to wait.

Oh, hell, just because!

Chris dived in, full force, put everything he had to give into the kiss, and Cassie kissed him back, tentatively at first, but soon her response matched his in strength and vigor. Like the water and the rain, her lips, her hands, her whole body flowed with him, around him, into him.

He pulled her closer. Then his hands slid up her thighs. They would have continued on their quest for more skin, but her dress was bunched between them. He wrestled with it, and felt victorious when the skirt of it floated to the surface. Then she declared victory by crossing her arms at her waist and lifting the dress over her head. She set it aside and rejoined his lips.

He had pictured her naked before on more than one occasion. He was troubled, not dead, not yet. And she was almost naked and would be very soon. The wrap-around strips of fabric she had been using for a bra and underwear were slipping loose with his persistent handling.

One thing was certain. She had been holding back, hiding under the rags, because the body she kept hidden underneath was petite yet buoyant and bursting with youth and curiosity. And he was on a mission to free her, expose all skin.

Her hands grew more demanding as well. The were underneath his green shirt, the one she liked so much, though now she was intent on making it disappear.

Together, they pulled Chris's shirt over his head, and as she drew closer, he went to work on his trousers, eager to connect with her, if only their stubborn clothes would ever, just, fully, unravel.

There was that word again, back to haunt him. . . .

As the last of their clothes ebbed free, Chris hooked his hands under Cassie's arms and pushed her away.

Looking down to catch his breath, he could feel her searching his face for an explanation. He didn't have one, and didn't look up when she placed her hand on his cheek, though he did spot an approaching lantern over her shoulder.

Chris didn't have to see a face to know who was there. He could already feel the burn of his brother's jealous glare and hear the ring of resentment in his words.

The desperate search for the dress and the shirt and the trousers began. They grabbed at fabric and tried to determine up from down, in from out. Once they were at least covered, Chris towed Cassie toward the shore, and when he set her down in shallow water, she lost her balance. He had to grab her arm to steady her.

They made a last effort to reorient their sopping-wet clothes, and then they lifted their faces into the blinding light of the lantern.

CHAPTER 24
Insight

Joe wasn't naïve. "I've been looking all over for you two," he said, giving his brother a knowing smile. "Am I interrupting something?"

Chris deflected his eyes.

"It's such a perfect night for a swim," Joe added, gesturing to the rain.

Cassie glanced at Chris and then stepped in front him, all poised, chin up, and ready to defend him as if she were his lawyer. "I slipped and fell into the water and I went under—"

"Yeah," Chris interrupted. "She should learn how to swim if she's going to stay in Hawaii with us." The words sounded harsh and ungrateful, and right after he spit them out, he stomped into the jungle.

What a jerk . . . a coward . . . a liar . . .

And Joe hoped the young fairy Chris had just disrespected, in so many ways, would realize that. But she was staring after him with tear-filled eyes.

"What's wrong with him?" Joe asked in a voice in between sincerity and scorn as he stepped into the water and offered his hand to Cassie.

She shrugged and then took his hand, and for a fraction of a second, she gave Joe her eyes. "I think he needs to be alone right now."

She seemed to be hinting at the dual meaning of alone—the here-and-now version as well as the long-term form of alone. Maybe she was starting to understand that he wasn't a good choice for her and never would be.

Joe put his arm around her shoulders and walked her back toward the hut.

More than anything, he wanted to believe Chris's explanation for their being in the water, clutching each other. He knew in his gut, though, there was more to the story. Then Joe felt something strange on Cassie's shoulder, and when he lifted the lantern, he saw that the seams of her dress were showing.

Joe forced himself to breathe as anger welled up in him, anger directed only at Chris. Joe considered the princess young and impressionable, and his brother the villain for taking advantage of her.

After a long, silent walk, Joe and Cassie approached the light of the hut. When she was about to open the door, Joe grabbed her hand. "Can I talk to you for a second?"

"I'm not sure this is a good time."

She tried to hide her tears by wiping them away with the same motion she used to tuck her hair behind her ears.

There were many things he wanted to say, but he knew it would be best to bow out gracefully, for now. "I just wanted to say, if you ever change your mind, you know where to find me."

She squeezed his hand, then let herself inside.

Joe was slow to follow. The thin hope that he still had a chance with her vanished as soon as she walked away.

By the time he stepped inside, Cassie had already disappeared behind her curtain, but she was hard to ignore. Her muffled sobs were at the peak of his consciousness even after the lanterns were out.

He had a feeling it was going to be a long sleepless night, for everyone.

***

Chris plowed through the rain and thick underbrush in full darkness. He didn't intend to stop until he was lost. Very lost. There was no way he could return to the hut and look anyone in the eye.

She'll never forgive me. Neither will he. . . .

He hated himself for what had happened—his lack of control and then his harsh fits of uncertainty. As much as he wanted to deny it, though, he and Cassie had shared a moment. He had received a taste of bliss. He knew it would be smart to spit out its sweetness, but he wanted not only to savor it now but also to have more of it.

The slippery conditions soon brought Chris to the ground with a muddy slide. He decided not to chance going any farther into the jungle.

After he propped a shelter of branches and leaves over his head, he huddled into a ball underneath and tried to rest. Eyes open, eyes closed. It didn't matter. He couldn't get her off his mind. Her heartbreaking story, the magnetic pull of her eyes, and lush surroundings had made him forget who he was, where he was, what century he lived in!

Chris lay on the wet grass and clenched his teeth. He tried to clear her from his head, but his imagination was a wild and uncontrollable beast. More than anything, he wanted to hold her underneath the stars and kiss her until he restored her faith that goodness could exist in the world.

Hours passed, and in a state of light sleep, Chris entered into a dull, monotonous dream. The lush green of a jungle against the backdrop of a purplish heaven streamed past as if he were flying.

But his dreamy self was not content or captivated by the beauty of his imagination. Chris might as well have been wandering through outer space. Nothing looked familiar. He was lost and alone. Then he started to feel uneasy, like he was center stage in front of a tough audience. His worries were unfounded, although he was being watched.

"She's cute. You should totally go for her."

Chris turned toward the familiar voice. "What?" He squinted into the dreamy haze. "Alana, is that you?"

"That's a tough question to answer." She met him in his arms for an embrace. "I could be paying a visit from the afterlife, or perhaps I'm a figment of your imagination. Either way, you look like you need someone to talk to."

His hug lifted her off the ground. "You have no idea," he replied as he lowered her back down.

"Then start talking!" She poked him in the chest. "First of all, what has been up with you lately? I haven't seen you this irritable since game seven of the 2003 American League Championships!"

He grabbed her hand and they sat down together on a rock. "That was one somber night in New England, wasn't it?" He elbowed her in the side.

"Yes, but I'm not here to talk about baseball, Chris. What's going on with you?"

He paused with a sigh and then opened his mouth to speak before he had a clear answer for her. "I don't know anymore. I definitely haven't been myself. That's kind of obvious, right? I used to be relatively stable and now I'm argumentative and hot-tempered and . . ." He sighed again, louder this time. "I miss our old life. Things were so much simpler. In this world, every day is a struggle . . . with family, with myself . . . my anger . . . my guilt. And now there's even more going on. That's why I'm hiding from everyone, especially from the fairy I can't stop thinking about. I can't believe I let myself fall for her so soon."

"These things happen sometimes, so don't beat yourself up over that kiss."

Chris looked down in shame. "Kiss" was, by far, an understatement. His wife of five years shouldn't have had to witness it even if she was truly sympathetic.

"She's sweet and she'd be good for you. I can tell. You need each other. You understand each other. Don't worry about what I might think. I want you to be happy. You deserve to be happy. And besides, she saved your life. And Ryan's and Morgan's lives. She's earned major brownie points in my book."

"Yeah, but I don't think I'm ready. Not the way she needs."

"I think she realizes that. She'll wait, don't worry."

"How do you know that?"

"C'mon, Chris! Are you that blind? She's in love with you. She listens to every word you say, doesn't miss a single facial expression or tone in your voice. And it's been like that ever since she wrapped up your hand the first time, back in Pyxis!"

"That early?"

"Yes, that early," Alana droned mockingly. "And from that day on, she's looked at you as if there's no doubt in her mind. Chris, I might be your past, but she's . . ."

Chris shrugged. "The future."

"Maybe," Alana said with wistful optimism as if she really meant yes.

But the more Chris thought about it, the more doubt he had. "It's still so hard to believe. I made such a lousy first impression and was such a mess. I don't even think I was capable of being nice to her for at least a few days."

"She loves you! She's a fairy princess with a dark past, on the brink of maturity, who has craved practically since the day she was born the love of a strong, handsome, yet sensitive prince. Do you catch my drift, or would you like me to draw you a flow chart?" Alana asked with her trademark sideways glance.

"No, I get it. But what about Joe? He was all 'love at first sight' over her, and he's usually much more cautious and calculating. And all this time, I thought Cassie would choose him. Until recently, I might have been okay with that. I mean, my kid brother is good at everything. He flirted with her endlessly until he got a whiff that I was interested. Joe might not believe this, but I never meant to deceive him. Things just happened, and for whatever reason, she made her choice. I can't exactly be with her, though, if he's going to hate me forever."

"If you steal her away, he'll resent you, no question. He's not as perfect as you think and has many of his own insecurities. Exactly how upset he will be and for how long? I couldn't tell you. He has his own tough choices to make."

Chris then remembered again Andromeda's prediction. *She'll unravel you, and your brother, and lead you to your demise.*

There were so many things Chris wanted to tell Alana, but he needed insight more than anything else. "Andromeda," he stated as if one word could say it all. "Cassie's going to 'unravel' us? Why did the queen say that? And how true were her words?"

"She's the queen of manipulation. She's only right if you let her be. Whether or not Joe gets 'unraveled' depends on him."

"I suppose, but it really messed with my head—and continues to." Chris shook his head. He couldn't talk about his problems any longer or he was going to implode. So he turned to his wife. He was pleased she looked happy, and noted something new about her. "Thanks for listening to all that, but that's enough for now. What about you? How are you adjusting to your new existence? I see you've finally found your wings."

"Yeah, how do you like them?" She twisted them in his direction.

"They're nice and they suit you. I wish you were still around. You could be our secret weapon. The ultimate Royal Modifier—ready to kick some fairy ass!"

"Is that the only reason you want me around?" she asked, sounding uncharacteristically vulnerable.

"No. I miss you." He put his arm around her neck and kissed her forehead. "You were my best friend and, at times, my only friend. And I'm sorry I was pulling away from you before you died. I was too selfish to realize that you were also going through a difficult time. You had every right to be frustrated."

"I'm sorry too. I should have been more patient. I should have accepted that you deal with your problems differently than I do."

"I was just trying to protect you."

"And who was supposed to protect you?"

He shrugged and his eyes fell, heavy with sadness. The last few months they had been together, he had taken her for granted.

Unexpectedly, Alana pushed his head to the side and ruffled his hair. She brought back a hint of cheer. Chris smiled at her and said, "So, since you're here, do you want to fool around for old times' sake?"

"Sorry, hon. As much as I can tell you need some, this is not that kind of dream."

"Dammit! I thought I'd ask, just in case . . ."

"Chris?"

"Yeah?"

"I have to go now."

"What? Why? Please stay. You just got here! There is so much more to talk about. I don't think I can do any of this alone!"

"Yes you can. Try to pull yourself together." She rose from her seat and hovered in flight. "Things are only going to get more difficult. The war has only just begun. You need to stay strong and stay focused. You will definitely be tested in ways you never thought possible."

He sprang to his feet as she gained more distance. "What things are going to get more difficult? Tested how? I don't understand! Please give me some clue!" His voice rang with so much desperation he sounded like someone else.

"Chris, I love you," Alana said as she flew backward into a halo of light, "and I will always be around if you need me. . . ."

"Wait! Alana!" he shouted. Chris began to run after her, but she vanished like mist in the heat. "I love . . . you . . . too . . . ," he called out, his voice tapering off. He realized, once again, that he was brutally alone.

He ran with heavy steps looking for her, wishing he were faster, wishing he too had wings. But his feet kept getting tangled in vines, weeds, and nettles. The harder he struggled, the more black and malignant the plants became. First his ankles, then his wrists, and at last, he was tugged to the ground by the waist.

Just before he crashed in the mud, Chris's eyes snapped open.

CHAPTER 25
Oh, Brother

With her face pointed toward the tropical midday sun, Cassiopeia closed her eyes and breathed in the salt-spray air until she felt satisfied, and then she exhaled. She turned toward the ocean and became entranced by the perfection of the day—balmy and cloudless.

The steady breeze made her loose hair and knee-length white dress swell weightlessly. With her arms out, she floated to the water's edge and let the gentle waves lap over her feet without any reservation. And then she saw him.

After one last strong and graceful pull through the water, Chris was on his feet. As he moved through the waist-deep water, he was beaming at her as if she were the only answer. And she couldn't take her eyes off him either.

She stepped into the water to greet him, eager to be in his arms. He stopped just shy of her reach and held his arms out and to the side. As she stepped forward, he suddenly ducked his shoulder and lifted her over it. He spun her around in circles until she was dizzy and giddy with laughter.

When he'd had his fill of fun and games, he set her down where the tide met the sand. She leaned back and he propped himself over her. Then he gave her a kiss that said, "I love you more than I ever thought possible."

Water lapped over them and they swelled closer together as the kiss intensified. When the water withdrew, Cassie felt Chris's hand graze her leg. It started by the side of her knee and slid higher and higher. . . .

Cassie could hear the real-life rain falling, see the gray morning light through the slits in her eyes. But she squeezed her eyes shut before the tears had a chance to fall again.

She drifted back to sleep, and instantly regretted it.

An angry wave crashed on top of them as soon as her dream eyes opened. Chris sprang to his feet and helped her to hers.

She huddled in Chris's embrace as black clouds rushed in. They annihilated every sunbeam, suffocated every speck of blue in the sky.

The ocean waves continued to crash on the beach with a deafening roar, each one larger than the one before. Chris and Cassie stumbled farther up the shore, but they never seemed able to escape. The safety and protection of their jungle paradise was never within their reach.

Then a wave appeared on the horizon that looked large enough to dissolve the entire world. At its peak, Andromeda surfaced with her scepter in hand.

Lightning lit up the sky and flew from Andromeda's scepter. With each flash and crash, the tsunami sucked in more water, growing higher and angrier as if it were feeding off Andromeda's fury and Cassie's fear.

Bound by water to a narrow strip of sand, Chris and Cassie had no place left to go. When it seemed as if they would die in each other's arms, Chris's sword swept onto the shore. He dived to catch it and then disappeared into the frothy base of the colossus.

Cassie screamed for him to return, but the whir of the glacial wind swallowed her voice. She pinched her eyes and let forth a screech, painful with desperation. When her eyes opened again, only the turbulent sea remained . . . no tsunami . . . and no Chris.

She had to find him, so she rushed into the water. Immediately, her feet were ungrounded, her arms heavy and useless. So every wave overpowered her, every current pulled her under. Only love kept her from drowning. But even love had its limits.

After one violent wave rumbled over her, she spotted what looked like a raft. A surge of hope helped her reach it. She had half her body pulled onto it when she sensed something wrong with it. She could feel its evil.

She was about to abandon it when a marble box arose from the center. The slab of rock on top of it rattled, scraped, and clanked around as if something were boiling below it. As the heat and pressure built, blood began to bubble over the side of the box like hot lava. Then a grotesque object with five appendages escaped the box and oozed toward her. The blue sapphire wedding band on the fourth appendage was the only thing that made Chris's severed left hand recognizable. As she opened her mouth to scream, a hand with sharp claws clutched her around her mouth and . . .

Cassie woke up with a gasp and a jerk that shook the whole hut. *She's going to take him from me. . . .*

With more tears and a hitched breath that barely resembled a sigh, she settled back down and stared at the rafters. *Not today,* she assured herself. *And not unless she gets through me first.* She listened to the rain rap against the coconut-husk roof, but before long she shot up again.

On her feet an instant later, she went over to the curtain, wondering if Chris had ever returned the night before. She had remained awake most of the night, waiting. With a subtle peek around the edge of the curtain, she saw only one lump on the floor, and that lump had dark hair.

Before the new level of worry had a chance to set in, the front door opened. At first glance, she thought it was Chris, but realized it was Scott as he entered the living space.

She released the curtain and took a quiet step backward, feeling some relief. Scott would at least be concerned about Chris, and he had the resources to do something about it.

It didn't take Scott long to realize what she realized—one lump, not two. Through the crack in the curtain, she saw Scott crouch down and shake Joe's shoulder with a firm grip.

Joe lifted his head and then cringed away from Scott's candle. "What?"

"Where's Chris?"

Joe sat up and glanced at the empty spot beside him. "I have no idea," he stated with a contemptuous shrug. "He stormed off last night and never came back."

"Why? This is not the time to be wandering around alone. What did you say to set him off?"

"What makes you think I said anything?"

There was disdain in Joe's eyes that went deep. It wasn't just about Cassie. It couldn't have been. She had never made him any promises or given him any indication she was interested. Until his confession the night before, she even believed the feeling was mutual. So his anger toward his brother seemed irrational yet terminal, like a disease that would eventually kill him.

Scott suddenly shot back up to his feet, and after an aggravated sigh, he shouted, "Foolish. Both of you!" The front door slammed on his way out.

Cassie's heart sank to a new low.

***

Chris *was* lost.

He tried to find his way back to the hut at the first sign of light, but he came to an opaque boundary, cloudy with pastel colors. He knew not to step

278

through it or he might not be able to return. For a second, the thought appealed to him. He could find the twins and escape, be human again.

He retraced his steps, eventually heard the sound of falling water, and followed it to the lagoon. He was covered in mud from head to toe, so he figured a rinse in the water wouldn't hurt, and he was also worried about his birthday present. The baseball bat might have fallen into the water when he fell in with Cassie. She had worked hard on it, so the least he could do was look for it.

As he expected, it wasn't on the rock where they had been sitting the night before. So he dived into the water. He made a few attempts to find it in the grass and the muck, but he couldn't see very well. He decided to look another day, when the sun was out. After that, he had no more excuses. He had to stop stalling and return to the hut.

Chris held his breath for a moment, then exhaled and pushed the door open.

Joe was the only one in sight.

Great . . .

He was browning toast over the fire and did not turn to look. Chris avoided eye contact as well. Just when Chris believed he might be able to go about his business without incident, Cassie popped out of her room and took a seat at the kitchen table.

She didn't say anything and only cast an occasional sad glance in his direction, but her presence set the mood—tense and instigative, worse than he ever remembered.

Joe set his toast down and spread his honey with exaggerated movements, suggesting to Chris that the silent treatment was about to end. Chris tried to brace himself for the worst.

"Hey, Chris. You might want to try sleeping sometime. You never know. It might grow on you."

Chris didn't acknowledge his brother in any way. A witty retort was not worth the brainpower. Instead, he grabbed a rucksack off a hook on the wall and dropped it in the empty corner by the front door.

He began to pack—weapons, a change of clothing, rain gear, and the necessities for building shelter. Then he grabbed the canteens and headed to the kitchen area. As much as he wanted to avoid it and them, he couldn't leave without food and water.

Joe clunked his plate on the table but never sat down. His prowling stance indicated that eating a hot breakfast was not a priority. "You're such a mess sometimes, Chris, it's almost endearing."

Chris glanced down at himself. His clothes were still covered in mud and grass stains, and light brown water was running down his arms and legs, leaving little puddles everywhere he went.

He shrugged and kept moving. *He's not worth it. Ignore. Avoid. You'll be out of here in ten minutes, so keep your cool. . . .*

Out of the corner of his eye, he saw Cassie tap Joe on the arm. Then she shook her head and her eyes flared. It was a warning—leave Chris alone—and a smile started creeping onto his face. Chris made the smile disappear once his face was in full view, but Joe's scowl suggested he had seen it anyway.

Chris walked past Joe and slipped into the washroom. He cleaned up, changed his clothes, and hoped that when he stepped out Joe would be exercising more restraint. But Joe was there waiting for him, blocking his path. Chris shouldered him out of the way, hard enough for Joe to get the message.

Joe stumbled backward and ricocheted off the flexible wall, but he managed to mumble, "It appears you want to pin everyone against the wall these days for one reason or another."

Chris swiveled around, grabbed Joe by his shirt, and pressed him into the grassy structure high enough so that his feet dangled and with enough force to partially embed Joe's body. "Yeah, including you, because you can't keep your filthy mouth shut!"

Cassie's chair fell when she stood with a gasp. Then the front door opened and closed with a slam.

"Boys!" Scott yelled. "Could you act like adults for five consecutive minutes?"

Chris let Joe drop and walked away. "I have to get out of this place," he said to his father.

Joe stumbled to catch his balance and then straightened out his shirt in a huff.

"Where? Why?" Scott scolded. "There was more bloodshed in Nohea last night."

"I'll take my chances." Chris glared at Joe. "And besides, I'm going south. I need to get the kids. Simona can't watch them forever. And Kimo said yesterday I should get it done while everything is still quiet."

"It's not quiet anymore, Chris," Scott warned. "I just found out Mikala is dead. There was a skirmish in her room two nights ago. The attackers retreated, but your mother-in-law died a few hours later. It's true the Kanaloan Army is suddenly getting more aggressive, but we also have to consider Pyxis. Andromeda's forces may have followed you here."

Chris sighed. "Then I should hurry."

"Can you hold off for a day or two until we have a better idea of what's going on?"

"No." Chris replied flatly. He walked back over to the racks and added two swords to his belt. He was more determined than ever to leave—and by himself.

"Chris!" Scott gave him a disapproving headshake. Then he sighed, as if in surrender. "If I can't change your mind, then all I can ask is that you and Joe go together. You'll be safer, and you could spend the next couple of days working out your differences."

"I'm not going anywhere with him until he apologizes!" Chris said to Scott.

"For what?" Joe blurted defiantly.

Chris gestured toward Cassie.

"I didn't mean it like that!" Joe claimed.

Cassie shrank in her chair.

"Joe, you were never a very good liar."

"Fine. I'm sorry, Cassie, that Chris misinterpreted what I said."

"That was so heartfelt it almost brought tears to my eyes," Chris retaliated.

"I have an idea," Scott said to interrupt the painful scene. "Why don't you all go? Cassiopeia, you can make sure these two behave themselves. But before you go, Chris, can I talk to you for a second . . . alone . . . outside?"

Chris followed his father out of the hut. The air was heavy and the misty drizzle wasn't at all inviting.

"What now?" he grumbled once they were out of eavesdropping range.

"Be careful out there."

"Is that why you brought me out here in the rain?" Chris asked. "I know it's dangerous to go anywhere around here. I'll be careful."

"And," Scott continued, "I don't know what exactly is going on, and I probably don't want to know, but don't let her come between you and your brother."

Too late, Chris thought. "Is that all?"

"No, there's more. Come here." Scott led Chris even farther away and lowered his voice. "I didn't want to say anything before. Now I feel I have to. You should be much more wary of the princess. Always watch your back."

Chris bit back a bitter laugh. "Wary? Are you sure we're talking about the same princess?"

"She's trouble, dangerous even! Look what she has already accomplished. You and Joe are about to rip each other's heads off. "

"That somehow makes her dangerous?"

Scott scowled. "When Kimo had you on the floor the other day, did you see the way she looked at me? I feared for my life!"

"She was trying to protect me!" Chris was shouting now. He couldn't help it.

"Okay," Scott whispered, lifting his hands to conciliate. "It's possible she was trying to protect you. But think about it. Could she be securing your trust for other reasons? Did you ever think she might be skilled at manipulation, like her mother?"

"I don't believe it! You don't know her or what she's been through!"

"I don't mean to upset you. I've just noticed you've let your guard down with her, and that's uncharacteristic of you. Please employ some caution. And try to interpret her carefully delivered words and noble gestures from another perspective."

"Thanks, Dad. Great advice, as always," Chris replied curtly. "Is that all you need to say?"

"Yes. You can go now."

Chris walked back to the hut, and then paced in front of the doorway to collect his thoughts. At first, he intended to dismiss his father's warning. Cassie had never indicated that she had a deceitful bone in her body. But then sharp pangs of suspicion started chipping away at his certainty. Both Chris and Joe had grown to trust her. As a result, she knew most of their family secrets. And all things considered, wasn't their escape from Pyxis just a little too easy?

Chris tried to push the doubt from mind and blasted through the front door. "So who's coming?" he said brusquely. "I'm leaving in two minutes with or without you!"

Joe glanced at Cassie reproachfully. "We both are."

Chris didn't acknowledge the response and, once he'd finished gathering supplies, simply walked out the door. He wasn't going to wait or coddle anyone. It was up to them to keep pace.

Cassie and Joe had caught up by the time Chris reached the entrance to the tunnel. "Two, one, nineteen, fifty-four," Chris said clearly. It was an easy password for him to remember, and would be for anyone else in hearing range as well.

The hole opened up. Chris stepped inside and charged forward. For a while, he was far enough ahead to feel alone. But soon he heard light, rapid footsteps and uneven breathing.

"Chris?" Cassie called after him.

"Yeah, what's up?" he asked as if nothing were amiss between them. He resumed his brisk speed.

She jogged along at his heel. "I'm sorry about last night."

"Don't be. There's nothing to be sorry about."

"Then why are you angry with me?"

"I'm not."

"You won't even look at me!"

Chris paused and glanced at her over his shoulder. She was right, and she deserved an explanation. He wanted to put his arm around her and explain what was going on in his head. But Joe was gaining on them. "It's complicated. I think you realize that." He turned forward and resumed his pace.

"Yes, I do," she said, stumbling along. "But that doesn't change the way I feel about you . . . ," she replied, her voice trailing off to a doleful whisper.

Somehow she knew exactly what to say to make him feel like a heartless jerk. Even if her words were as genuine as they sounded, he didn't know how to respond, and soon she stopped racing to keep up with him.

Chris hated that he had to deny her like this after imagining what it would be like to love her, have her, be with her. He had thought they could let pleasure triumph over the obstacles that lay ahead. The obstacles were daunting, however, and growing in number every time he tried counting. The warning from his father was the latest addition. He may have been able to dismiss his father's words of advice had it not been for Andromeda's prediction.

She's dangerous. . . . She'll unravel you. . . .

***

The day dragged on.

And the sun never made an appearance. Without it, the swirling colors of Scott MacRae's tunnel were muted against the backdrop of rain and thick gray clouds.

Joe maintained an uncharacteristic silence, and Cassie occasionally let out a muffled sob. When at last Chris met the barrier of their exit, Cassie wiped away some lingering tears and followed him to the outside.

***

Immediately, Cassie sensed the air was heavily laced with danger. She gasped. The trees and vines above her were spinning, collapsing. Still, she walked on, following Chris, but every step felt like a mistake.

Then she saw *them* flitting between the branches. She could barely mutter, "Chris," before the first Crown Champion landed in front of him.

Chris stepped back and drew two swords. Joe and Cassie backed against him.

More and more soldiers rained down on them. Their mercenaries, Modified to human size, marched in as well, forming an impassable outer circle.

Without taking his eyes off the enemy, Chris grabbed Joe around the neck and whispered, "Run with her. Get help."

As soon as she overheard the words, Cassie ducked and darted. She slipped past the soldiers, and dodged the giant feet that stomped down to block her.

Under a log, through a tuft of grass, and then she checked over her shoulder. Joe was the only one following her and she reached a speed she'd never used before, never needed before.

When she arrived at the stream, she stopped and looked back. "Joe?"

He was no longer with her.

Cassie hesitated, just a moment, knowing her priority was escape even if it meant leaving Joe behind. She had to find the tunnel again before it was too late.

Her instincts told her she was a little west of the opening, so she followed the water east. Soon she saw the boulder; she was in the right place.

Running toward it, with the password on the tip of her tongue, she felt a hard strike on her back and fell on all fours. As she tried to rise, she skidded in the mud and landed back on her knees.

Then Crux Chevalier, the Brute, landed in front of her. He had swords, weapons, metal dangling all over him, but from his belt he pulled a blood-caked hunting knife.

"Cassiopeia . . . darling! Oh, how I've missed you!" he bellowed while grabbing for her hands.

He caught one of her hands, but missed the other one. She swung her palm up and smacked him across the cheekbone.

His face contorted with ugly amusement. Then his smile faded and his lips twisted. He squeezed her trapped wrist until she buckled from the pain. With his free hand, he slapped her back. She saw stars and all she could hear was rushing water.

When her eyes fluttered open, his face was in hers, his hot breath in her ear. She tried to squirm her hands free, but they were pinned over her head. Her body was trapped underneath his. The more she struggled, the harder he pressed against her.

Then Crux brought his blade into view. He traced her eyebrows with the tip. Then he dragged it around her left ear and down her neck. Cassie winced when her skin broke.

There was a growl of pleasure low in his throat. And with his long forked tongue, he caressed the blood oozing from her wound.

His tongue worked its way down her throat, while his blade dragged down her left side. The point dug into the side of her knee. And there it waited, the pressure and the sting increasing while his carnal appetite gained momentum—biting, licking, panting with frenzy. Then he drew his blade upward in a hard quick slash.

The pain was too much. Her mind broke free from her trembling, earthbound body. She was at the lagoon with Chris, her lips on his. The love she drew in from his kiss was stronger than any sword, more powerful than any enchantment.

She almost believed she was dead. The moment was too perfect, too vivid, and too romantic to be invented by a mind still attached to a body.

Then a familiar voice whisked her back into the present.

"Crux! That is quite enough!"

Crux's head turned from her, but her agony did not ease. The serrated edge was digging into her skin well below the neckline of her dress. And then his lips fell to her ear. "Now I'll always be close to your heart." He dragged the blade up her chest, the motion slow and deliberate. "And the heinous MacRae you long for will never know, because he'll be dead."

Crux then yanked Cassie to her feet.

"Hello, sister," Canis Major said curtly when he landed beside them. "The MacRae brothers have been subdued. Lieutenant Chevalier, after you bring her back to the ambush site, I want you to lead the mission to find Scott MacRae and his allies. I'll send word if I can persuade them to talk. Unless, perhaps, Cassiopeia can enlighten us now in exchange for some preferential treatment?"

She kept her eyes down and watched the blood run down her leg and onto her foot. The tiny red puddles seeped into the damp earth.

Then Crux's arms sprang on her like a trap and flung her body against his. "We can make her talk now!"

"I don't think that is necessary," Canis replied with a tone of haughty command. "She requires a softer hand. I assure you, she'll talk when she's ready. Now take her away!"

Crux nodded, then slid his savage hands around her rib cage and lifted her off the ground.

While her feet dangled, she slipped off one of her sandals. It was her one last, desperate effort to secure help.

***

Joe glanced over his shoulder.

"Keep walking!" one of his captors grunted immediately.

After a blow to the back the head and a harsh tug forward by his bound wrists, he stumbled to keep his footing, but the glance was worth it. He saw only red and blue shields and gray giants, and that meant there was still hope.

Maybe she got away. . . .

Cassie was moving fast and seemed to get past the whirlwind of falling fairy soldiers. Joe couldn't keep up with her, and while he ran out of options, hopelessly surrounded, she slipped beneath the leaves and disappeared like a breeze.

The rain suddenly paused and a shadow hovered over him. Joe's chin lifted, but then he had to crouch as the fairy over him swooped past his head.

He landed a few steps ahead and began to march at the front of Joe's escort regiment. And then Joe saw that the massive beast of a fairy was half carrying, half pushing a tiny fairy in a gray dress.

Joe's heart sank.

"Shall we call you *General* Crux Chevalier?" the soldier beside the large fairy asked.

A bunch of the surrounding soldiers snickered.

"Any day now," Crux's voice boomed. "We will all receive many accolades once I have my say." Suddenly, he swung Cassie to the side and pressed her against a rotted tree trunk.

Cassie turned her face away from him and closed her eyes, but her trembling shook loose a few tears.

Even as Joe was being roughly handled, he noticed the blood on Cassie's dress. There was a stain over her heart, and dabbles and smears across her skirt and down the side of her leg.

Once the other soldiers took their gawking positions behind him, Crux pulled out a bloody knife. He lifted the point to Cassie's eye. Then his arm retracted and muscles tensed. His hand swung fast, and the knife stopped just shy of her eyeball.

More snickers erupted.

When he had the full attention of his cronies once again, Crux delicately, sensually, lifted a tear from Cassie's cheek with the tip of his knife. Then he tasted the symbol of her fear and pain with the tip of his forked tongue.

"I think now is the perfect time to convey how lucky you are, Miss Cassiopeia. Lucky your brother was around to intervene. Because I was just getting started. Next time . . . I'll finish." Crux swung her back into his clutches and resumed walking.

As he came closer, he looked right at Joe. There was a hint of red in his wild eyes. Next, he slicked his serpentine tongue over his bloody teeth and lips, and made sure to throw an elbow into Joe's mouth when he passed.

Joe didn't hunch or cower, even though the pain told him to. He spit the blood on the ground and fought against his restraints as hard as he could, but he was no match for the shackles or for the dozens of pushing and pulling soldiers.

For his newfound magical powers to have the biggest impact, he needed to keep surprise in his favor.

Before long, Cassie slipped from view, but she was all he could think about. He tried to process everything he had seen and heard, and what he already knew about her, which wasn't much.

And one word kept coming back to haunt him.

Brother? Cassie has a brother? How come she never mentioned that?

***

Chris could only watch and wait for the others, though he hoped they wouldn't return.

After he fell to his knees in surrender, he was stripped of his swords and weapons, bound by the hands, and placed inside a glass jar topped by a lid punched with air holes. Trapped inside his glass prison, he couldn't even hear what orders were being given. Enemies as far, high, and wide as he could see—their lips moved, their hands pointed—but the acoustics of his glass prison made their voices inaudible.

But he wasn't fortunate enough to be left in silence. He had two Modified Gray Coats inside the jar with him. They paced around, ready to strike him if he so much as twitched. And their predatory breathing was almost as loud as Chris's pulse.

As his guards—inside the jar, outside the jar—passed by, he caught glimpses of others beyond them. The view came only in flashes, but Chris saw what he needed to. Joe and Cassie had been captured as well.

At the first sight of Cassie's blood, Chris's eyes immediately collided with the shameless and knowing stare of the soldier holding her by the hair. The sneer on his face made every hair on Chris's body stand up with rage. Then after a deep laugh that found its way inside of Chris's head and a brief, snakelike flick of tongue over his teeth, the soldier pushed Cassie into the mud with brutal and unnecessary force. Another soldier pushed Joe beside her. Then a Gray Coat scooped them up and dropped them into the same jar as Chris. They both landed with a bone-jarring clunk.

Chris had to dodge and evade the grasp of the two Gray Coats inside the jar to get closer to them.

"Sit back down!" one of them shouted.

Undeterred, Chris stumbled toward the center of the jar. "Are you both all right?"

"Sure. Peachy." Joe rose to his feet and wiped blood from his lip with his sleeve.

"I'm fine," Cassie muttered at the exact moment Chris had to dive underneath a tackle.

By the time he was on his feet again and had a chance to look to her, she had moved farther away. With her arms crossed over her chest and shoulders, she eased into a sitting position by the glass wall. She unfolded her arms enough to cradle her knees and then she buried her face. She may have tried, but she couldn't conceal the blood from him, not entirely, because it was everywhere.

While the Gray Coats herded Chris and Joe away from Cassie, Chris was jumping to see over their shoulders. "Then why are you bleeding?" he shouted to her.

One of the guards pushed him to the ground and gave him a backhanded slap across the face. Chris glared at his punisher and then strained to get a better look. But she was just a tiny trembling blur in the distance.

"Why is she bleeding?" Chris hissed to Joe.

Joe shrugged, but the lack of shock in his expression suggested a higher awareness.

"You know something! Tell me, Goddammit!"

"She fell. I saw it," Joe whispered.

"Quiet!"

The Gray Coat closest to Joe grabbed him by the front of his shirt and dragged him to a new location. Then the jar lifted off the ground and daylight was taken from them as they were put into some kind of bag. Even in the absolute blackness, Chris couldn't erase from his mind the sight of Cassie's blood. At this point, he could see no way around it. Red would be the color to seal their fate.

***

Hours passed, maybe a day and night, maybe several days and nights. At times, there was only a feeling of steady motion, at other times upheavals, but at no point could they tell where they were being taken or when the journey might end, though Joe in his mind was venturing a guess.

On occasion, the lid was opened and crumbs of food were handed to their Gray Coat guards for distribution. Then, more nothingness.

At long last, the bumping and sliding in darkness came to a conclusion with a final thud and a sudden burst of light. Joe's sharp senses had, for what felt like forever, compensated for his lack of sight, so the brightness forced his eyes into a pained squint. He realized, though, that the light was moonlight, and the brightness was a sparkling from what appeared to be snow.

Then Joe heard a sound he had at first appreciated but now dreaded. The lid of the jar was squeaking.

The gust of wind that found them, even within the confines of the thick glass, gave a sharp and deadly chill. Joe had no further doubt. Their fairytale journey that had begun in Pyxis was now circling back to the start.

Before long, Joe, Chris, and Cassie were tumbling down the side of the jar. They landed in a Gray Coat's wide palm and were soon feeling the crush of his fat fingers.

The Gray Coat set them down in front of a gate—*the* gate. At the main entrance to the underground city, there were more soldiers than Joe could count. Many were wingless and wore gray, but most were in proud red and blue with the asymmetric star sealed upon their breastplates. And every sharp object known to man and fairy—swords, battle-axes, knives, spears, arrows—were pointed at them, three bound, unarmed fairies. Running was not an option. Even if Joe tripped and fell, he'd likely be impaled in thirty different places.

One word came to his mind—overkill.

With the guidance of many disciplined hands, the gate creaked opened. Then a wave of soldiers descended beneath the snow and rock, and when there was room to move, Joe was tugged forward by the rope tethered to his hands.

Royal Way was a circus, and like tigers, elephants, or bears, the MacRae brothers and Princess Cassiopeia were paraded at the front of the procession like the main attraction. Most of the onlookers were shouting insults—Infidels, Unworthies, Bottom-Dwellers—and were throwing putrid objects at them. But there were also many fairies doing the opposite—mocking, attacking, provoking the soldiers. In a city where the oppressed were nearing desperation, bloodshed on this unprecedented night was a guarantee. And it was happening right before Joe's eyes. The soldiers were clearing the street of opposition with remorseless ease, like bushwhackers through dead reeds.

When they arrived at the Aerial Palace, the soldiers dragged them past the main gate and down a walkway between the palace wall and a graveyard. Behind the angry fairies swarming the curved bars overhead were impressive gargoyle sentinels.

Soon they ducked beneath a gated arch and descended treacherously steep stairs. They plummeted deep into the earth, blazing torches lining the way.

After two turns and more stairs, Joe was pushed into a cell near the end of a dark corridor. Chris was whisked farther on. Just when Joe decided to sit down, find what minimal comfort he could while he still had the chance, he heard the creak of moving metal and then saw Cassie approach. Her wrists bound in front of her, she was no match for the fairy beside her.

He was her antithesis in pride and confidence, and had powerful black wings and a commanding aura. Yet he was undoubtedly her brother. Their hair and eyes were identical in hue and form, and when his black eyes flicked down at Cassie, there was a hint of pity there, for just a moment.

The full power of the black-winged fairy's disdain turned to Joe. "Get up!"

Joe stood as ordered. Once his cage was unlocked, he knew to follow them.

Cassie's brother unlocked the third cell on the left, and there was Chris. As the door opened, Chris sprang to his feet and was beside the entrance, prepped to fight or run. But he wasn't given a chance. A guard pushed him back, and after a chaotic shuffling of feet, hands, wings, and weapons, the cage door creaked closed and slammed shut. Joe, Chris, and Cassie were together again, but behind bars, and they weren't alone. Guards loomed around them on both sides of the bars.

Without hesitation, Joe stumbled toward Chris. "That's her brother," he warned.

"What? Andromeda has a son? How did we miss that little fact?" Chris hissed back.

"Yes, Andromeda has a son, and I am he, Canis Major, heir to the throne of Pyxis!" the prince announced from his front-and-center position on the other side of the bars.

Chris was still staring at Joe with wide, demanding eyes as if to say, *What the hell is going on?*

In response, Joe could only shrug.

"We have still been unable to find your father and your children," the prince said, addressing Chris. "And we need answers."

Joe and Chris exchanged glances, while Cassie retreated into the deepest shadow.

The prince waited a moment, and when no response came, he said, "All right, then. If you are going to test my patience, whom should I kill first? My treasonous half sister? Or perhaps the pitifully inadequate MacRae?" He glanced at Joe with a smug sneer on his face. Then his eyes moved to Chris and lit up with the reflection of fire. "Or better yet, the angry one I've heard so much about. Oh, yes," he said through clenched teeth as he smiled. " 'Christopher the Valiant,' elder son of my mother's most long-standing enemy." His wings flexed, his nose flared, and his voice rose. "You'll *cower* before me and beg for death by the time I am through with you."

He only had eyes for Chris and added the keys to the lock with fiendish commitment.

Suddenly, Cassie emerged from the darkness and threw herself against the door. "Wait! Canis!"

The startled prince dropped the keys.

"Mother would want to make a public spectacle of their deaths. If you let me out of here, I'll tell you everything, I promise," Cassie wheedled. "I know where Scott MacRae is living, and where the children are being hidden. Name what you want, and they will be yours."

Canis raised a curious eyebrow at her. Then his face twisted with doubt and he reached for the keys. His glare and all his fury returned to Chris.

"They're in hotel rooms using false names," she then blurted. "I know because I was there. If you were smart, you'd believe me and then I'll do anything you ask, just—"

Cassie didn't get a chance to finish her plea. After one angry, desperate tug against the rope, Chris freed his hands and lunged at her like a lion toward a gazelle. He pinned her against the wall by her throat before the guards could even ready their swords.

"Don't!" Joe shouted, but his words and his body were pushed aside by all the commotion.

Chris's hand was shaking, his body too, and Cassie closed her eyes. She looked peaceful, as if she were dead already.

She didn't squirm, didn't fight. Chris had the chance to kill her, but he hesitated. Or maybe he just didn't have it in him despite the depth of her betrayal.

"I thought you weren't like her," Chris cried out, as the guards peeled him away from Cassie. "I was wrong!" He freed one hand and swung wildly, threw an elbow into a gut, tried to get in a kick, but once his body hit the ground and the punches started, Chris gave in and lay still.

Meanwhile, Cassie had collapsed to the ground, struggling for breath. The gate opened and Canis crouched beside her. He grabbed her hand and pulled her to her feet. Then he comforted her with an embrace. Afterward, he pushed her away gently by the shoulders and hunched down to look into her face. He cupped her chin and whispered something. She nodded, he nodded back, and then he guided her toward the cell door.

He took a detour though, toward Chris, the bloody mess on the ground. "I'll deal with you later, you poor excuse for a fairy."

Canis kicked Chris with enough force to hear bones crack. And the guards were about to follow his lead.

Joe then found his feet, his voice, his courage—and his magic. "Leave him alone!" He lifted rocks, dirt, debris with his eyes, and flung them at Canis and his guards. The torches on the wall blazed to a roar, their wooden handles splintering and embers raining down. Joe sent Cassie, her brother, and the guards scurrying toward the exit.

The gate slammed and locked behind them with an industrial clank.

Joe dropped his eyes and stumbled toward the bars. He needed to see Cassie one last time. He'd had his qualms about her too, but he wasn't entirely convinced she'd ditch them to make nice with her family. Joe watched and waited for some sign this was all a misunderstanding.

She was securely wrapped in Canis's arm when they approached, her head leaning toward his chest. Then, just before she stepped past him, she gave Joe a subtle wink.

Once they were out of sight, Joe pounded on the bars with both hands and could barely contain his smile.

At least someone has a plan!

Then Joe plopped down next to Chris and gave him a nudge. "Are you completely out of your mind?"

Chris rolled to his hands and knees and crawled over to the wall like a wounded animal. He shrugged, and then he leaned his head against the wall and closed his eyes.

"Play that entire scene back in your head, but give Cassie the benefit of the doubt this time." Joe waited for him to show some sign he was listening. "She was trying to protect you. . . again."

Chris's head jerked forward. "How do you know that?"

Joe shrugged. "She winked at me."

"So what?" Chris leaned his head back against the wall and directed his unfocused eyes at the rocks wedged between the rafters. "What does that mean?"

"Don't you remember? The long walk in the fairy tunnel? The 'Joe, why do you keep doing that with your eye?' conversation?" he said, giving his best impression of Cassie's voice. "You laughed, I got pretty pissed at you, and in the end I tried to explain the wink?"

"Vaguely," Chris stated flatly.

"So the wink means she might be the only hope we have left."

"What does it even matter anymore?"

"C'mon, Chris. Pull it together. This is the championship round, the ninth inning, the last game of the World freakin' Series. We need your A game right now, not whatever *this* is," Joe said, shooing him with his hand, "or we're both gonna die!"

Chris closed his eyes and massaged the bridge of his nose for a long while. Then, finally, his head popped up and eyes opened as if someone had switched on a light inside of him. "You're right."

"Wow, I've never heard those words come out of your mouth before."

"No, seriously, we can do this. We escaped once—why wouldn't we be able to do it again? I've been training hard, and you've got magic. We're the underdogs here, but we can sneak up and bite these bastards in the ass!" Chris began unbinding Joe's hands.

"Now you're talking."

"And, Joe?"

"Yeah?"

"Thanks for having my back before. That was awesome."

Joe couldn't believe his eyes—Chris was actually smiling.

"Did you see their faces? Especially Prince Pompous. I bet he'll never call you 'pitifully inadequate' again."

Joe shrugged nonchalantly but enjoyed the rare compliment. "It was no big deal. You would have done the same for me."

"Well, I appreciate it, and I know I didn't deserve it."

"I haven't exactly been on my best behavior either. So, since we're talking again, are you going to tell me why you've been so sloppy and pathetic around her?" Joe asked, but he immediately cringed. "You know what? On second thought, forget it. I don't want to know."

"Good," Chris said quickly. "I don't want to talk about it. It doesn't matter anyway. If she went to the dark side, we're dead meat. But if she somehow gets us out of this alive . . . ? She'll never speak to me again." His voice, eyes, and posture plummeted back down to hopelessness.

Joe flung a pebble at him with his powers to lighten the mood. "You did kind of level the playing field, didn't you?"

"That would be putting it mildly. Make sure I get an invitation to your wedding!"

"Ha. Good one." *The playing field might be level,* Joe thought, *but the match is still between Mount Everest and Beacon Hill.*

"So what do we do now?" Chris asked.

"We wait for an opportunity to present itself."

"You mean you can't use your powers to bust that lock, mind-erase our babysitters out there, materialize swords—or better yet, miniature assault rifles—and then summon the Kāne Army?"

"I could handle the lock. Everything else you mentioned is probably in book two of *Magical Mechanics*, the master's edition," Joe chuckled.

His laughter was contagious, enough so that Chris was at least sniggering and shaking his head. "I guess we're shit out of luck, then," he replied, throwing his hands in the air.

"We might have to wait and see what Girl Wonder comes up with."

"And then I'll feel like the biggest idiot on the face of the earth."

"Hey, your words," Joe said with his hands up, "not mine,"

"Yeah, but you were thinking it."

Joe paused, put his finger on his chin, and then removed it quickly. "You're right. I totally was."

Chris chuckled once and nodded in acceptance and defeat. "Thanks."

"I'm here for ya, bro."

Joe and Chris sat on the dungeon floor and continued to poke fun at each other's weaknesses. They were on the same team again, and it was about time.

CHAPTER 26
The Fall

Cassie followed Canis Major to her old chamber in the North Tower with her head hanging compliantly low.

She waited silently as he opened the door with the key she recognized. Even though she had never held it, never carried it in her pocket because she was never granted the freedom to come and go as she pleased, she could have drawn it from memory.

She knew it was a bulky, heavy thing from the way her keepers used to handle it. It was iron, with elaborate curves inlaid with rubies. It was morbidly beautiful, befitting its purpose—to entrap a disobedient princess. The key was ancient too, the gems dull with time. Cassie supposed she wasn't the first princess to lead a life at its mercy.

Once inside her chamber, Canis Major stepped across the broken glass as if he didn't notice it was there. He stood beside the only chair in the room and waited there for her, head and chest held high.

Cassie, with one bare foot, had to be more cautious, but managed to lower herself into the seat he intended.

He paced around authoritatively and, without words, demanded she tell him the truth. She cowered before him and then broke down, with tears and over-the-top apologies for her many sins against the city of Pyxis and for being so foolishly seduced by the MacRae brothers.

Then lies spilled from her tongue with more plausibility than the truth—names, directions, landmarks, hotels, and room numbers for the

Jokuras. And then, after a long pause and a gulp for courage, she invented a rhyme—"Protect us from the dead of night, lead us from the dark to light"—as the password for Scott MacRae's tunnels. If Canis believed her, she had just handed over to him the King of the Unworthy and the Kāne Army. And she had some time before he figured out the truth.

As he marched around in deliberation, she leaned toward her knees and shielded her eyes. Then she let her emotions escape in sobs that shook her whole body. It was a catharsis, one that she hoped Canis would accept as regret and remorse rather than for what it actually was.

Every step Canis took—the ones that lifted into a flutter, and the ones that remained grounded—all made her wonder if there was anything left to fight for. Just when Cassie believed she'd be banished to the dungeon again or killed immediately with the sheathed sword bouncing at his leg, Canis set his fingers underneath her chin and lifted her face until their eyes met. "Pack some of your things. I've arranged a new home for you. Your escorts will arrive momentarily."

"A new home?" she murmured. She widened her teary eyes and her chin quiver was hardly by accident.

"Dear sister, you needn't worry," Canis answered in a patronizing tone, as if she were still a child. "The Banker has offered to employ you again. You will be his responsibility from now on. And he'll carry your papers, so you must stay with him this time. It's for your own protection."

"If that's what you feel is best," she replied, and forced a contrite smile.

Canis nodded once with a proud and satisfied expression. Then he left the room.

As soon as the key was removed from the lock, Cassie hopped lightly and soundlessly over the broken glass and grabbed shoes and a cloak from her closet. She fastened the cloak over her bloodstained and mud-caked dress, then skipped over to her old bed.

She crouched beside it and fumbled around underneath until she heard a loose stone rattle. After prying it up, she removed a neat bundle of rope. Then she moved to the only window in the room—tiny, barred, one of the highest in the Aerial Palace. But one of the bars twisted loose, she knew from experience.

Its rusty squeak was louder than it used be. She held her breath, stopped for a second to listen in case there were footsteps coming for her, and then pulled the bar free.

She wasn't as small and wiry as she once was, but there was still enough space for her to squeeze through. With the bar in her hand and the rope around her shoulder, she stepped onto the narrow ledge half a body length below the window. After replacing the bar, she edged her way across the crumbling ledge on her tiptoes while digging her fingertips into the loose spaces between the tower's rocks.

Careful to avoid looking down, she circled around to the opposite side of the tower and knotted the rope around a stone gargoyle. It had its mouth open, tongue out, and she had always tried to imagine that it was smiling. From a sunny perspective, it looked like a wolf with friendly features, so she'd named it Lupus. Though crumbly with age, Lupus still looked as if he would bear her weight.

She carefully stepped off the ledge and eased herself onto the rope. Rubble and dust fell on her head. She cringed, but her knot and the gargoyle held.

When her feet hit the ground, she darted toward the West River, followed it to the bridge, and climbed onto Royal Way. She threw the hood of her cloak over her head and diverted her eyes from onlookers and windows.

Once she turned onto Main Street, the early-morning tavern dwellers helped her whiz south uninterrupted. She wove in and out of alleys, glancing over her shoulder only occasionally, until she arrived at her destination—the Aurora Borealis.

She moved through the hustle and bustle—loud, angry, and opinionated—and made her way to the bar.

Vela was there drying mugs with a white cloth. When Vela saw her, her mouth gaped. Then her wings lifted her over the bar and she took Cassie into an unexpected and powerful embrace. "Thank goodness you're all right!" She pushed Cassie's shoulders away and looked her over with a troubled knot in her brow. "Oh my! What happened? It looks like you've been through the Third Pyxian War and barely lived to tell the tale!"

"It's not important," Cassie answered, cradling her arms over her chest and retreating into her cloak as best she could. "Vela, have you seen Pierre? I need his help, urgently."

Vela's eyes darkened. "Cassiopeia, I hate to be the bearer of bad news, but Pierre is dead."

Cassie swayed and grabbed a table for support. Her thoughts swirled. It wasn't possible to organize a rebellion without Pierre's loyal followers. His charisma and his ability to incite a crowd were crucial to her plan. And aside from all that, he had been her friend.

She could feel the hot tears building in her eyes. But she wouldn't let them fall. There was no time. If she didn't get back to the palace in time, Chris would die thinking she was a traitor and a coward.

She climbed onto a nearby table, one hesitant step at a time. She had spent most of her life cowering in the face of evil. Now was the time for defiance.

Her knees were shaking and her mouth went dry, yet her objective was clear. She had to channel all of her strength into words of persuasion and inspiration. Alone she was powerless, but with enough help there was a chance she could be a threat.

"Could I have your attention please?"

She captured only a few pairs of eyes, but they quickly lost interest. And the noise never dulled. Rather, Cassie's effort had the opposite effect; the blare of impassioned conversation continued to gain momentum.

Then Cassie heard a shrill whistle from behind. "My friend has something to say!" Vela roared. "Please hush or you will have me to answer to!"

The noise in the room tapered off to a purr. "Thank you, Vela, and thanks to all of you for a moment of your time." Cassie's eyes moved from one demanding face to the next. Her thoughts were not initially coalescing into words. Murmurs started to erupt, and her confidence began to drain. *You have a way with words. You can describe a head case like me and make it sound like poetry*, a familiar voice echoed in her mind, and then she was ready to continue. "Listen, please! As you know, Queen Andromeda has long ruled Pyxis with an iron hand of fear. Our lives mean nothing to her, and any among us—Royal or otherwise—who refuse to follow her rules will suffer or even die. So many have already fallen victim to her lust for power. I say we come together and fight for a Pyxis free from tyranny and oppression!"

"I beg your pardon," a scruffy-faced blacksmith interrupted. "I see where this little inspirational sermon is heading. You're here to foment unrest."

A baker sprang from his chair and pointed at the blacksmith. "I knew it! He's loyal to the queen!"

"I agree with the blacksmith," an apothecary's wife stated. "We're not soldiers. What chance do we have against the queen's army? What good will come if we all die?"

"Freedom cannot be achieved without sacrifice, you imbecile!" shouted one of the writers for the *Pyxis Discourse*.

Other fairies rose as well to speak their minds, defend their friends, scorn their adversaries.

In the midst, one voice rose above the others. "Why should we let this impractical child lead us to our deaths? After all, she grew up in the palace. What's she doing here anyway?"

Cassie bristled, and a strength rose up in her that she had never before known she could possess. "Yes, I am the onetime Princess Cassiopeia." Her voice rang clear, silencing the bickering coward. "I share Queen Andromeda's blood, but she stopped being my mother the day I was born. I grew up frightened and alone, a child who could only stand by silently as the queen performed unthinkable atrocities."

Perhaps it was the sight of the dried blood against the paleness of her face, but more likely it was the sureness of her newfound strength that drew all eyes toward her and urged her on.

"I was among the lucky, for I escaped with my life the day I turned sixteen. In the years since then, I endured many hardships to survive. And living among your influence, I not only survived, I flourished. I listened, learned, and found my inspiration from those who challenged authority and fought against injustice. I have now been beyond the walls of the palace, and indeed beyond the confines of our fairy city and into the larger world. I have found friends from beyond who will come to our aid; I have learned that peace and freedom are well within our reach. I have pledged myself to scouring the palace and throwing open its treasures and secrets for the good of all that I hold dear."

Cassie watched in astonishment as the crowd roared in support and clamored to the door. Even the blacksmith tossed the keys for his shop to his idealistic apprentice.

They spread through the streets of Pyxis like wildfire, knocking on doors, banging on windows, waking fairies in the alleys. They regrouped at the blacksmith's shop, where they distributed weapons and armor, and when those ran out, they grabbed anything shiny and pointy.

They were a sizable mob, loud and angry too. There was no way they could hide their intention. The time had come.

***

Chris had run out of things to say to his brother, so they waited without speaking.

While Chris's silence was motionless, Joe's wandered. His footsteps may have been just a soft shuffling over loose grit and bare earth, but Chris could hear every one and wished they would stop.

Joe was pacing just behind the bars, pausing when soldiers would pass, sighing or groaning at ragged intervals, and undoubtedly anticipating every morbid detail of their fated execution.

Chris stopped watching after the longest, broadest, sharpest sword he had ever seen passed by in the hands of a hooded, dark-cloaked figure, no doubt the minister of justice. Chris didn't want to think or move. Why should he waste his remaining energy?

"Well, that doesn't look good," Joe mumbled as if he too had finally accepted that they were about to die. He resumed pacing with one arm across his stomach and the other one propping up his chin.

Chris shrugged when their eyes met and figured it might be time to say good-bye, wish his brother luck in the next life.

But then Joe stopped in the middle of his path and grabbed the bars. He wedged his head between them enough to see along the corridor.

Then Chris heard what Joe must have seen. Metal was striking metal, and metal was piercing flesh.

Chris was quick to his feet. As he reached the bars, Andromeda's Crown Champions were charging past with their weapons drawn, but soon they were at a standstill, their motion hindered by some unseen opposition.

Joe magically jimmied the cell's ancient lock and swung the barred door open. Chris followed Joe into the corridor.

Cassie was repeating her actions from the day they had first escaped from the Aerial Palace, running from cell to cell, freeing the prisoners one by one with subtle strength and epic courage. Even in the bustling hallway, Chris noticed only her until she was wrapped in Joe's embrace.

The hug lifted her off the ground. When he put her back down, Joe grasped her behind the neck and kissed her forehead. Then he kissed her again, this time on her lips. An eternity could have passed between the start of that kiss and its finish.

When they broke apart, they each grinned while words poured out of their mouths. Then Cassie handed Joe a sword. While he stayed behind with a cluster of rebels, she continued along the hallway, moving closer to Chris.

He watched her every step, her subtle change of expression, the way her cloak fluttered as she moved closer and closer to him. She ended up stepping past him without acknowledging him in any way. Then she stopped in her tracks, turned back, and tossed him a sword. It wasn't just any sword. It was his sword or, more appropriately, his father's sword, and she had somehow retrieved it for him. What she tossed to him, though, was more than a sword; it was trust. She never said a word, though, and kept her eyes averted as she walked away.

Chris knew he deserved the chilly reception. He hadn't killed her, but for a moment he had wanted to. What could he possibly do or say to make up for that?

"I'm sorry!" Chris finally shouted, but it was like yelling for help in one of his nightmares. His voice did not pierce the noise or travel the distance. He would have to find another way to prove himself worthy of her forgiveness.

Then Joe urged him forward with a slap on his shoulder. Chris envied his broad grin and wished he too could bring himself to smile.

***

Canis Major checked his reflection in his mirror. He was dressed in his monarch's official uniform—blue cloak, four-squared breastplate alternately red and blue with the Crown Star in the center. Upon his head was his golden crown, rubies glittering at the peak of the arches.

He ran through the highlights of his busy schedule one last time. *Execution of the MacRaes by beheading . . . his first Monarchy Address in Pyxis Square . . . and then . . . if all went well in Hawaii . . . his coronation!*

He tweaked the position of his crown one last time and then spent a few moments taming his closed-lip smile. It had to be proud, dignified, but not too forced, and his satisfaction had to be subtle. In truth, he could hardly contain his elation. He was so close to being crowned king, he could almost taste the power and privilege that would come with it.

Before he left his chamber, he glanced at the grandfather clock with a wince—a quarter past three a.m. His mother had asked to speak to him immediately, and that was fifteen minutes ago.

Oh! And Cassiopeia!

He had forgotten about his half sister. She was locked in her room and wasn't going anywhere, though, so she could wait to be moved until morning. Perhaps she should be present for the MacRae execution. For her crimes, he ought to put her in the front and center. A spray of blood in her face and the stink of her lover's ruin might teach her a valuable lesson about loyalty.

Canis left his room at a confident pace, rounded the corner, and headed down North Hall. It was the most direct passage to the East Wing, and frequently traversed by all palace inhabitants, though at this time of the morning, it was empty, or so he believed. But then he heard a taunting voice.

"Prince Canis Major. Home once again."

He paused and turned, but did little to hide his amusement. "Not now, Ursa." He swept his arms open. "Can't you see I'm busy?"

Ursa stepped into the torchlight. Her lips were full and painted red, her copper-colored hair was wavy and untamed. She was wearing a sheer nightgown, the laced tie falling slack. As if she knew exactly which crevice Canis's desire would stumble into, she pressed her breasts into the thin fabric as she sauntered closer. "You always seem to make time for Lyra."

"Lyra is exactly where she's supposed to be when I require attention," the prince intoned.

Ursa's eyes flared with jealousy, just as he'd anticipated. He didn't see anything wrong with a little friendly competition.

After the lift of one eyebrow, she fluttered off her feet for a second and landed close beside him. Then she toyed with the loose strings at her neckline as if to reel him in by more than just his eye.

He received her kiss with an open mouth. In the battle of tongues, hers was the clear victor. It overtook his mouth as if attempting to slither through his innards and coil knots around his groin.

"Be in my bedchamber when I return," he panted when her tongue withdrew from the depths of his libido.

"I shall, Your Highness." She curtsied slowly, and as she rose, slightly bemused, she looked up at him.

He didn't think she would wait. He wasn't sure he could wait. Together, they rarely ever made it to his bed. She was much more arousing on the spur of the moment in some highly inappropriate locale.

Before he could gather his wits, her tongue was back in his mouth and she was working his belt buckle open with practiced hands. Just as her touch made him gasp, the unmistakable clang of swords drowned out his cry of pleasure.

His head snapped left, his eyes narrowed in on the East Hall. Shadows and torchlight were in an uproar.

A wail of defeat spurred Canis into flight. He latched his belt, straightened his crown, and wiped his mouth while he launched into flight, casting Ursa aside.

He drew his sword when he rounded the corner and couldn't believe his eyes. Swordfights were under way and littering the East Hall were wounded bodies, a few of which wore his regime's proud colors.

Canis was out of breath by the time he reached the balcony overlooking the Hall of Crystal. Andromeda was already there, witnessing the insurgence unfold from floor to high ceiling. She was still as an ice sculpture, though her fury was vivid in her black eyes. She didn't even blink when her son appeared by her side.

Canis performed a quick headcount—rebels versus Crown Champions and Gray Coats—and felt much relief. The crown's numbers were fewer than usual by half, but those that remained appeared to be more than enough. His well-trained soldiers were handily subduing peasants, academics, undernourished children, fem-fairies, and the elderly. His mother had to worry only about bloodstains on her shiny white floors.

"Never turn your back on your enemy, Canis Major," Andromeda droned, eyes still fixed on what appeared to be her most prized possession— the grand ruby rotating in the center of the hall. Its red glow flickered across her black eyes. She flinched when its glass display case shattered.

Then there was a new culprit of Andromeda's fixation. Rather than stare, Canis followed her gaze and clenched the hilt of his sword in his fist. His sword may have been pristine and untainted by blood, but that was about to change. He lifted the blade high into the air and watched it glint in the eyes of the overwhelmed rebels. On this momentous occasion, he was about to release its fury for sport rather than necessity.

He leaped from the balcony and used his black wings to hover to the ground before the object of his mother's pointed reproach. "Cassiopeia, my dear," he said, shame and haughtiness mixed in his tone. "I never expected to be deceived by you after I tried so hard to protect you. You're more like our mother than I originally believed."

"You're wrong." Cassie stepped back with one hand in the air, her other hand clinging loosely to her sword. "I'm nothing like her. And I'm sorry I had to betray you, but I refuse to live under her domain. And if you've chosen to succumb to her power, I can no longer consider you my brother. But, if there's any hope, if it's not too late, you could make a different choice . . . your own choice. You could help us defeat her! You are not like our mother either. I've seen your sympathy, decency, compassion. Please, Canis, you don't want to kill me. I can see it in your eyes."

Canis lunged toward her and swiped at her sword, nearly knocking it from her hands. "You're trying to deceive me again!" Cassie's sword bobbled in her grip, but she was quick to regain composure. Canis's second swing at her only disturbed the air in the room with an angry whoosh. She ducked and stumbled out of range. "You lied so that this traitorous lot would rise up and give you the throne that so rightly belongs to me!" he shouted as she backed away. "I've followed our mother's every command, obeyed her every order, and you think I would walk away after all that I've sacrificed? You will die by my hand and I will be king!"

He backed her against the Grand Staircase, and she fell against the marble, losing her balance and her sword. Then her shaky hands went up by her ears and her eyes pinched shut in anticipation of the strike meant to end her life.

Canis aimed for the side of his half sister's neck, and his blade began its lethal swing. But it met with something hard that sent a shudder from its edge up to his straining shoulder—another sword, wielded by Christopher MacRae.

***

Joe's magic had never been more powerful. Dozens of Gray Coats, one after another, fell dead before they realized why their swords were as disobedient as the rebels they were trying to kill.

All he needed was a little inspiration, and in one perfect kiss he had found it. When Cassie had looked up at him with excitement and hope in her eyes, and as if seeking his approval, he couldn't resist the gravitational pull of the moment. He'd stopped thinking, lost control for once, and went for it. And just when he thought she'd pull away, she rested her hands on his shoulders and kissed him back. That was how he remembered it anyway, and even if it was an exaggeration, the memory of the kiss they shared—better, longer, more satisfying every time he relived it—was making him feel invincible.

Even so, his enemies were strong and relentless. When one of them fell, three more seemed to take their place, and he no longer had his brother's strong sword by his side. He was on his own and surrounded. While he kept

Cassie in his peripheral vision, he remained untouchable, but then she fell from sight.

He pushed toward the last place he'd seen her—the main staircase—and for a second, he was too worried to focus. At one point he didn't see a sword swipe toward his gut until it was about to hit him. He dodged away, but the blade did get close enough to tear his shirt.

The risk was worth it. A few steps later, he spotted Cassie sitting on the stairs. He couldn't see any wounds and she wasn't nursing any sight of injury, yet she was immobilized with what looked like distress.

When a few Gray Coats ebbed away from view, Joe then saw what she was seeing—Chris was fighting her brother. The matchup had to be hard to watch, for anyone, but especially for her. Soon, though, she would have to get up and fight or she would be the next to die.

Joe didn't think he could ever be as outwardly heroic as his brother was, but his smaller, subtler examples or heroism, if well planned and executed, might carry him to victory someday. With that in mind and in heart, he helped Cassie to her feet and magically summoned her sword from where it lay at the edge of the stairs. "It's not a good time to be taking a breather, Princess," Joe said with a wink.

As she pulled the sword from the air, she gave him a slight smile. "Thanks, Joe, for . . ." She paused as a group of Gray Coats closed in around them and she and Joe aligned themselves back to back. "Believing in me," she finally shouted over her shoulder.

Joe smiled a smile he was glad she couldn't see.

***

With one hand clutching the balcony's rail, Andromeda licked her lips. She could practically taste Christopher MacRae's blood. It was oozing from a nick on his left shoulder and was spotting his filthy, tattered tunic. Christopher may have mastered the art of fighting ambidextrously, but he wasn't using his left side effectively due to exertion, injury, or both, and with his right arm, every chance he had, he cradled the rib cage below his left arm.

Canis Major, on the other hand, was not a disappointment. He had a superior weapon, the advantage of flight, and had spent his whole life training for this moment with the best instructors his inheritance could buy. He had yet to make a mistake, and even if he did, at this stage in the battle, her Gray Coats were practically fighting each other for the privilege to kill.

One by one, her soldiers joined the circle surrounding the epic duel, as if to close in on Christopher like a vise.

Andromeda's attention then shifted to Joseph MacRae. He was fighting with strength and valor disproportionate to his size. With closer analysis, she noticed how the subtle flicks of his hands could thwart her soldiers. He wasn't changing the course of the battle decisively in favor of the rebels, but he was getting on her nerves.

She stared at the white orb of her scepter until it turned blood red. After three waves of her hand over it, the orb emitted a thin strand of fire. She moved her hand quicker, and the strand lengthened. Then with her scepter, Andromeda circled the strand into a massive ball of fire and lifted it into the air below the crystal chandelier.

Heads turned, jaws dropped, and rebel faces lit up with both color and fear. Even the corpses seemed more lifelike as the fire flickered in their dead eyes.

When Joe diverted his eyes to the side, Andromeda caught and held his focus. She smiled at him to let him know that she could play mind games too. Before she released the ball of fire into the crowd, she wanted to scorch his morale and watch his mental fortress crumble, piece by piece.

She moved the spinning orb of fire closer to him, slowly, as both a threat and a tease. And his eyes moved wildly, from her, to the fire, to the soldiers lunging at him from every angle. The lapses in his concentration were making holes in his wall. The rebels once inside his protection were dying, and as a final desperate effort, he had to use his body rather than his mind to shield his precious princess.

Joe wasn't a strong enough swordsman for even one of her soldiers, not by half, and his brother wasn't faring much better. The end was near for the MacRaes, and Andromeda threw back her head and laughed.

Then, with a crash, the doors of the main entrance flew open. Before Andromeda realized what was happening, her ball of fire spun out of her control. It hissed into the wall behind her and the life-size painting of her father burst into flames. She turned to watch the only accurate likeness of her one and only king peel and distort, dropping into ash.

The fire spread along the row of paintings and licked into the wall that supported them. Andromeda rotated slowly back toward the fighting rebels and sought his face, gathering her powers to use against him. Only the King of the Unworthy would dare such an assault.

Sure enough, Scott MacRae was charging toward the Grand Staircase with a clan of jungle barbarians at his side. He stopped next to Joseph MacRae, and together they diverted her foulest curses, her most treacherous hexes, her most heinous spells.

And when Andromeda's scepter flew from her hands and shattered against what was left of the wall, she retreated into the smoke and shadows.

***

For the first time, Chris could sense his opponent's fear. Rather than fight fairly, as he had done before, Canis kept lifting into the air, higher and more often. Time and again he plunged toward Chris with deadly momentum, his sword prepped to kill.

Each time, at the penultimate moment, Chris dived, rolled, or jumped out of the way, making sure he never set a pattern. While Canis was in flight, Chris had a chance to take a breath and wipe the sweat and blood from his brow before it trickled into his eyes. And then he took his ready stance and waited for his enemy's next move.

Chris quickly realized that the tactics he knew, meant for a fight in which his opponent stayed on the ground, would not be enough to defeat a Royal. Chris would have to outsmart Canis. It wouldn't be an easy feat, but somehow he had to use his winglessness to his advantage.

As usual, Canis was high out of reach and kept Chris guessing by hovering, faking a descent, and then whizzing to a new location. By now, Chris had learned to fake him out as well. If he appeared distracted—glancing at other fights nearby, rubbing a wound, adjusting his grip, drying his palms on his shirt—Canis swooped down on him.

Unfortunately, Chris didn't have to pretend to be distracted. A barrel-chested Gray Coat, a fairy-world colossus, tried to engage Chris in battle with a spiked war flail. He had already taken three Kāne war arrows in the chest, but he didn't seem to be showing any sign of weakness.

The flail swung toward Chris's head at the same time Canis was coming in from behind. Rather than duck underneath and roll away, Chris leaped into a horizontal dive underneath Canis's feet, twisted in midair to get behind him, and used both of his swords to slice across Canis's open wings.

Chris landed hard on his backside and while Canis floundered back into the air, a piece of his wing sliced off. Canis spiraled, then plummeted down.

This time Chris rolled toward his decent. It was a stretch. It was a reach. His left hand allowed its weapon to drop and met his right hand around the hilt of his father's sword. Both hands squeezed and held the blade upright.

Canis's back landed on its tip. Chris shut his eyes against the blood, but he felt its hot spray and the ooze of it on his hands.

Chris's eyes startled open when he felt another crash beside him. A dozen or so arrows later, the Gray Coat with the war flail had finally fallen too.

Chris rose to a crouch and looked upon the fallen heir to the Pyxian throne. His size, strength, and ferocity seemed to drain from him along with his blood. What remained was deathly pale and childlike. *He has his sister's eyes*, Chris thought while he closed Canis's eyelids.

Chris slowly pulled his sword free. Nearly ready to collapse, he gazed at the ongoing battle around him. Lost in the vision of swords swinging, arrows flying, and blood splattering as if an angry god were pounding the scene with a red paintbrush, a distant, high-pitched scream of warning barely pierced Chris's fading awareness. But then an embrace around his shoulders nearly knocked him from his crouch. A flash of silver pierced the air just above his head and was then obscured by a wave of long dark hair.

Cassie. As he turned to hold the fairy princess, he saw the blade of a dagger jutting out of her left shoulder.

Chris rose to standing with Cassie's body draped over his arms. Trying to answer the questions of how and why, he lifted his head instinctively toward the balcony.

Andromeda, framed by the burning portraits of Pyxian monarchs long dead, was watching, a hooded look of satisfaction on her face.

Then, in a blinding burst of white light that halted the fighting throughout the palace, Andromeda vanished and all at once her soldiers stood down, dropped their arms, and vanished as well.

Chris knew there was no time to waste in wonderment. "Cassie. C'mon. Open your eyes!" he pleaded as he elevated her head with his elbow.

Her eyes lolled open in response to his voice, but then drooped shut. Her head fell back and her body went limp.

"Chris!"

He swung toward his father's voice. Scott and Joe were jogging toward him.

"Bring her up these stairs," Scott said, bobbing his nose toward the second floor. "Bear right, and bedchambers should start at the end of the hall. I'll see if I can find a doctor."

Chris nodded and charged up the stairs with Joe close behind. In the long hall, Joe ran ahead. The first few doors he checked were locked. By the third try, Joe broke the door from its hinges with his mind and led the way inside.

With the torch from the hall, he lit every candle in the room, four total, and brought them over to the small circular table beside the four-poster bed. Chris followed. As Joe tried to maneuver Cassie's cloak out of the way, Andromeda's dagger fell out of her shoulder and clattered to the stone floor. The blood gushed more vigorously in its absence.

"That's not good," Joe said, "but at least we can get a better look."

Joe finished removing Cassie's cloak and Chris eased her onto her side. They propped her up with pillows.

From the floor, Joe retrieved the dagger and used it to slice open her saturated sleeve. Then he moved methodically and without hesitation to the pile of extra sheets at the foot of the bed and began to shred them into strips.

Chris, however, was staring down at his shaking hands. They were covered in her blood—and her brother's. He felt dizzy as he tried to wipe the blood away on his shirt. To his horror, a sticky red residue remained.

"Chris, are you going to help me, or what?"

There was a long pause before Joe's question registered in his mind. "What?" He let his hands fall to his sides, but kept them flexed open and stiff in an unnatural position. "Oh . . . what do you . . . need me to do?

"Are you all right?"

"I'm . . . fine."

Joe pulled over a chair to the side of the bed. "First off, sit down. You look like you're about to pass out."

Chris obeyed without question and watched Joe evaluate Cassie's wound. He dabbed it and watched the blood disappear and reappear. His expression remained, for the most part, calm and expressionless, but his eyes and lips twitched from time to time with grim uncertainty. Then he pressed the shredded sheets against the entry wound on the back of her shoulder and handed a bundle to Chris so he would do the same on the front.

"I don't think it's as bad as it looks," Joe said. "See here?" He lifted the cloth for a second and traced the half-circle gash with his index finger. "The dagger didn't fall out, it tore out. That sounds bad, I know, but it means the wound was fairly external. It missed the artery as far as I can tell."

"Are you sure? Then why does she look so . . . terrible? And why did she go unconscious so fast?" Chris paused and listened to Cassie's quick, shallow breaths. "And she's having trouble breathing."

Joe checked her pulse and his eyes widened as if in fear and disbelief. "She's in shock. It seems a little soon to be caused by the bleeding, though."

"Then what else could be wrong?"

"I don't know, Chris."

Chris pulled in a sigh to calm himself. Then he rubbed Cassie's clammy cheek and tucked her hair behind her ear with his free hand. "You're going to be all right, Cass. The doctor will be here soon. Hang in there."

As he removed his hand from her cheek, his wrist rubbed against the edge of her ripped and soiled sleeve. It rolled open and revealed a bloodstain on her undergarments, black and ominous compared to the bloody messes everywhere else. Peeking out from the top was a scab surrounded by yellowing skin.

Chris sprang to his feet to get a better look. "Where's that dagger?" he shouted, as he leaned his finger on the torn cloth. He still couldn't see the bottom of the wound.

When Joe handed him the beautiful killer—silver, hand-crafted, bejeweled, and razor sharp—Chris sliced open the cloth. He also had to tear down the seam of her dress below her arm to see the rest of the wound. The cut went from the top of her bellybutton to her sternum, and it was deep.

As he tossed the dagger back to the bedside table, Chris recalled the day before, the blood on Cassie's dress, with perfect clarity. "What happened to her?"

He stared at Joe, demanding as ever, and Joe fussed with Cassie's bandages, failing to meet his eye. "I . . . don't really know."

"You said she fell," Chris asserted.

"She did!" he replied quickly, glancing up. "I mean, I thought she did."

"What'd she fall on, someone's knife?"

"I didn't see what happened."

Chris was prepared to press on like an interrogator trying to force a confession out of a suspect. "You said you *saw* her fall. I thought you were with her!"

"I was, but we got separated."

"So who was with her?"

Chris hunched over her and took inventory of the other marks on her body. The light was poor and blood was smeared all over her, but still he spotted a bruise on her cheekbone and thin scratches on her neck. Then he looked up and wondered why Joe wasn't answering.

His brother's uncharacteristic silence could only mean one thing. "You know something else!" Chris accused.

And then Chris spotted a scratch of blood on Cassie's left knee under the hem of her skirt. He cautiously lifted the dress with a shaky hand. The deep diagonal slice that started by her knee went farther up her left thigh than he would permit himself to see. Chris dropped the dress and had to sit back down. He closed his unfocused eyes and shook his head in disbelief, in denial, in absolute horror, in rage. "Joe, if you knew something happened to her and you didn't tell me, I swear to God, I'll—"

"You'll what? Try to strangle me too?" Joe mouthed off defensively.

Joe's posture went rigid as if he were expecting an angry outburst in retaliation. But Chris's head fell into his hands and his whole body shook, not with rage but despair. He had no right to judge or make threats on Cassie's behalf after the mistake he had made, and he had never felt closer to broken.

Soon Joe's fists clenched and unclenched. Then he sighed and started again. "I'm sorry, Chris. That was out of line. I screwed up. I do that too sometimes. Is that what you want to hear?"

"No. Just the truth. All of it."

"All right. I'll tell you." Joe pulled over another chair to the opposite side of the bed. He sat and leaned his elbows on his knees, and finally his expression turned honest and open. "So we ran, like you said. I tried to keep up with her, but she was fast and they were faster. And we lost each other, and I was surrounded soon after that. I put up a fight as best I could without magic, saving it as the last card to play, and I felt better about that decision knowing that Cassie got away. Once I was recaptured, this beast of a fairy—he was huge—dropped down with her. Then he said something along the lines of 'Good thing your brother was there to interrupt, or else I would have—'"

"And you let that butcher get away with that?"

Chris exploded out of his chair, bottled up his breath, and trudged around the room aimlessly with a heavy step.

"I thought he was just trying to get a rise out of me," Joe continued. "And I admit I was also thrown off when I first found out that Cassie had a brother. Then I lied to you because I didn't want you to get yourself killed.

Cassie obviously didn't want you to know either, probably for the same reason."

"Did you catch his name?" Chris grilled further.

"Crux Chevalier. He's the general, or soon to be."

"Did you see him here today?"

"No. He and some of the others are probably still in Hawaii," Joe answered, "looking for our father."

There were many long minutes of silence. Chris continued to prowl around the room while Joe squirmed in his chair.

"If you're going to kick the crap out of me, let's just get it over with," Joe suddenly said. "The anticipation is worse than anything else. Well, maybe that's not true."

"I'm not gonna hurt you!" Chris shot back. "I just wish you had told me. One of the reasons I lunged at her was because she was acting so strange. That, on top of Dad's warning she might be dangerous. I can't believe I did that to her. Especially after . . ." He couldn't say anything further. He covered his face and rubbed the bridge of his nose hard with all of his fingertips.

"Look, Chris, if it's any consolation, Cassie was trying to be deceptive. If she hadn't been convincing, and if you had never brought out her brother's protective side, we might all still be rotting in that cell . . . or dead."

Chris shrugged, dropped his hands from his face, and returned to the chair next to Cassie's bed. He started putting pressure on her shoulder wound again, and with his free hand he covered her chest wound back up. It was too painful to look at. Then he grabbed a clean cloth and started wiping the excess blood off her arm and neck. But then, as if his touch were the trigger, she started convulsing, foaming at the mouth.

Chris retracted his hand and stumbled out of his chair. He nearly tripped over it as he backed away. "What the hell is wrong with her?"

"I don't know!" Joe shouted as he jumped forward to stabilize her.

After the agonizingly long fit, Cassie rolled onto her back and went still. Her eyes were open and directed at the ceiling, but she was clearly not awake.

Chris fell to his knees beside her bed and grabbed her hand. "Breathe, Cassie! Don't give up! Do you hear me?"

Joe reached for her neck. "She has no pulse."

"What?" Chris cried out.

While Joe started chest compressions and rescue breaths, Chris squeezed her hand and refused to breathe unless she did. Joe pressed and breathed for her . . . pressed and breathed . . . pressed and breathed.

Finally, she gasped and started breathing on her own again, and both Chris and Joe gasped for air too.

Joe collapsed back down in his chair. This time, he closed his eyes and rubbed the bridge of his nose, a gesture borrowed from his brother.

And even though Joe had clearly acted with competence ever since they'd brought Cassie into the room, Chris needed to lash out at someone. "Don't you think it would be helpful if you finished medical school, you coward?"

When Joe's hands dropped from his face, his expression was livid. "What difference would it make? Does this look like a hospital? Do we have any medicine or supplies other than bedsheets, a dagger, and our bare hands? And don't call me a coward because you feel guilty."

Their bitter staring standoff ended only when their father came into the room with a doctor. The miraculous arrival of Scott MacRae and the Hawaiian fairies was the reason Chris was still alive, but he couldn't make himself feel grateful. The anger previously directed at Joe found a new scapegoat.

"How's she doing?" Scott asked softly. He glanced at Chris first, realized his error, and looked to Joe instead.

"She's lost a lot of blood," Joe replied, "I thought we brought that under control, though. Then for some reason her heart stopped. It seems like there's something else wrong with her."

"Let me see the blade," Scott muttered knowingly.

Joe gave him a quizzical look and then walked to the bedside table where Chris had tossed Andromeda's dagger.

Just as he was about to grab it, Scott turned vivid with alarm. "Don't touch it with your hand!"

Joe picked it up with a rag and handed both the rag and the dagger to him. Scott let it dangle by the handle from his tentative grip.

The doctor lowered his spectacles and squinted. Joe moved closer and squinted too. Chris glanced at it from a more distant location. He was more concerned with his father's expression. Scott's faced turned grim as he pointed out a spot of faint yellow.

"What? What is it?" Joe looked to him and asked.

"My guess, poison . . . or a curse. Probably both."

The doctor set his hand on Joe's shoulder. "I'll do everything I can for her, but we need to prepare ourselves for the worst."

Joe nodded solemnly as if accepting the inevitable without anger or the need to assign blame.

Chris, however, wasn't nearly as forgiving. "You," he whispered, eyes fixed on his father.

"What, Chris? What are you trying to say?"

There was no sympathy in Scott's face, only impatience and irritation. His arrogance . . . his apparent denial of any culpability made Chris even angrier. "You . . . you put doubt in my mind. And I turned on her. Now look at her!" He gestured to Cassie's pale, fragile form with his bloody palms up.

"Chris, I know how upset you must be."

"You're wrong. Wrong again! You couldn't possibly know what this is like. You didn't have to watch your wife die. I had to in place of you. You didn't have your wife's throat slit while you were drugged and helpless. That was me. And now, the only one who would understand what I'm going through is practically dead too, and if that isn't enough, I should be the one lying there. I'm the one who deserves to be dead. I dare you to guess how that feels!"

Everyone looked down and kept silent as Chris reached his breaking point. In his fragile state, he was a danger to himself and to everyone around him, but no one could come up with any consoling words to relieve his anguish.

Scott's eyes finally filled with remorse and sorrow. "Chris, why don't you get some air? Your anger can't possibly improve this situation."

"Air? Oh, right. I should just walk away—because that's what you would do."

Chris couldn't hold the tears back any longer. He didn't even bother to wipe them away as they fell.

Then all eyes shot to Cassie, who started convulsing again. While Joe and the doctor sprang to her aid, Chris backed all the way to the wall and stood there, stunned and paralyzed.

Then someone grasped his arm—his father—and Chris was moving, somewhere, toward the door. But his leaden feet couldn't hold him upright. He stumbled repeatedly, and Scott supported his weight when Chris failed to support himself.

In the hall outside, Scott eased Chris into a sitting position against the wall, and then he returned to the room, closing the door behind him.

Chris leaned his head against the wall and closed his eyes. He couldn't bear to watch Cassie suffer, but listening to every sound that came from her room was almost as horrendous as witnessing her bleed and convulse. Clanging, rustling, voices, footsteps, the occasional pained whimper. But soon everything went still and silent. He could hear only his own heartbeat and each shaky breath.

Each second dragged on like an hour, each minute like an eternity. At last Scott stepped out. He quietly closed the door and leaned against the opposite wall.

"I'm sorry, Chris. It doesn't look good. The bleeding has finally stopped, but . . . whatever was on that blade—"

"Well, she's hanging on. She's made it this long, right? Maybe—"

"Chris . . ." There was a long pause. "She's probably not going to make it much longer. You might want to . . . say good-bye."

"You're wrong. She's . . . she's . . . a fighter."

"The doctor said there is nothing more he can do for her. Her body is shutting down."

Chris shuddered with denial. He looked off into space and his heart began to pound like a war drum. But he did not cry; the rage inside him held the tears hostage this time. He was nothing more than a ticking bomb. *Tick . . . tick . . . tick . . . tick . . .* One more word and . . . *Five . . . four . . . three . . . two . . .*

"Chris . . . ?"

It was as if he burst into billions of tiny particles. "That's not good enough! If he can't do anything for her, find someone who can!"

Chris pushed himself off the ground. Scott followed him and reached for his shoulder, but Chris swatted it off and blazed down the hall like a ball of fire. Then it was as if that ball of fire collided with a crate of gunpowder. He spotted a decorative suit of armor bearing the Pyxis coat of arms. The blue and red shield with that repulsive star!

It was taller than he was, wider too, but Chris never questioned his own strength. He lifted the armor off the ground and jogged with it to the Grand Staircase. Then he flung it over the railing and watched it writhe through the air like a descending body. It hit with a crash that no one left in the castle could miss, and the metal shards ricocheted in every direction.

Scott joined his side and they both watched as the fragmented pieces of armor found their final resting places among the blood and debris that cluttered the Hall of Crystal.

Chris took one last conscious glance at the destruction below and then turned away. He had seen enough. And his father didn't stop him as he walked into a corridor that held no light.

CHAPTER 27
Purpose

Chris wandered through the Aerial Palace like a ghost of himself. He was lost, his journey aimless. As he ascended and descended the staircases, and ambled down the endless maze of hallways, he barely took notice of anything—the grand paintings, the mosaic walls, the rusty armor, the red-and-blue tapestries, the gilded adornment of every archway and window. And he doubted anyone took notice of him. He felt hollowed out to the point of invisibility.

Then, having passed one dark, narrow entryway to a staircase, he stopped for some reason and returned to it. It could have been the sad, solitary candle flickering in the sconce across the hall or the arch's uncharacteristic simplicity. Whatever it was, he needed to know more. He crossed the hall, reached up and took the candle, and then slipped through the arch.

He spiraled up the uneven stairs one tentative step at a time. There were narrow spots where he had to turn sideways and low places where he needed to duck beneath dusty, splintered rafters. As he climbed, he grew colder. The draft, first a whisper, became a sporadic puff. He took extra care to shelter his flame. Among darkness that could have swallowed him whole, he could not lose his light.

Chris finally arrived at a wooden door, well-aged but heavy and obstructive, like it wasn't meant to be opened. Still, he tried to twist the doorknob. When he met resistance, he fiddled with it, turned it the opposite way, but it didn't open. He had his sword on his belt, and he considered using it to pry apart the hinges of the door or use the point in the keyhole to jimmy open the lock.

He looked around for a place to set his candle and as he felt his way around the walls, a dull red between two stones caught his attention. He stuck his hand inside and pulled out a key.

It reminded him of the poisonous dagger—artful and beautiful, yet heavy from centuries of suffering and despair. Before he used it to open the door, he realized where he was—the notorious North Tower.

What was meant to be a last glance at the key became a stare. The rubies captured in its flank had a pulse, or at least the flame in his other hand made it appear that way. A draft crept across his neck, and whispers began in his head like some dark calling. Unable to resist the pull forward, the key seemed to find its own way to the lock. It turned with no resistance, and the door popped open without a need to push. He pocketed the key and followed the creaking door into the room.

The light from his candle reflected off shattered glass. Most of the pieces were shiny, like broken mirrors, though others had a dull sparkle, like porcelain. There were also remnants of what used to be toys. They looked handmade, or scavenged and reconstructed, no match for Andromeda's destructive fury. She had warped metal, charred wooden objects beyond recognition. The broken dolls were the most haunting. Their bodies had burned to ashes, but their faces, a mix of black and gray-white, had vacant stares that made the room feel like a tomb.

I don't need to see this. . . .

Chris had an urge to run. He almost made it out the door, but his foot nudged a damaged music box. The lid popped open, and an armless, broken-winged ballerina sprang to life with a tiny pirouette while the cracked base played a few notes out of tune. And then he couldn't leave, not with Cassie's childhood room in such tragic disarray.

He found the bed, removed a pillowcase, and started chucking pieces of glass into it. Big pieces. Small pieces. *Smash. Crack. Crash.* The noise was satisfying, but then he heard something unexpected—a loud, shaky sigh.

A winged fairy with long blond hair was standing in the doorway with her arms crossed over her uniformed chest. She had a handkerchief balled in her tight white fist. Her swollen and mournful eyes must have only moments before shed tears; now they were dry and pointed at Chris.

"Hi . . . um . . . I'm sorry. I'm . . . pretty loud. Did I wake you?"

"Why the sudden concern for noise?" the blond fairy scolded, arms still crossed. "It didn't seem to bother you while you were tossing armor from ledges."

"Yeah, sorry, not my finest . . . moment. Chris . . . my name is Chris, by the way." He attempted to sound pleasant. He wasn't sure if the castle staff would see him and his family as liberators or intruders. But he knew his attempt had failed. He was too tired, distracted, and miserable to fool anyone.

"I know who you are. What are you doing here? It's forbidden!"

It was evident in her tone that she despised him, but he didn't get the sense that she wished him harm. Her face, her voice, her sad blue eyes—all had a kindness to them that her anger couldn't overshadow.

"I'm not good at waiting around," he replied sincerely, looking her in the eye, hoping she wouldn't see him as yet another arrogant warrior. "I need to be doing something, and this looks like the right place to be. And if it is Andromeda who forbids anyone from being here, you can guarantee I'll be here anyway."

The fairy nodded somberly. "Lyra," she said, compassion now present in her tone. "My name is Lyra." She curtsied dutifully. "Do you need any assistance, sir?"

He almost smiled. "Please, just call me Chris. And, no thanks. I'm fine."

I deserve to pick up every shard of glass, one by one, all by myself. . . .

"Let me at least get you a broom."

Before he had a chance to say otherwise, she disappeared, and returned a few minutes later.

"Thanks," he said as she handed it to him. He started working immediately but paused to glance at her as she fluttered toward the door. She had beautiful wings, prettier than any others he'd seen, and nothing to fear or resent. They were white and glittered like fresh snow. More than ever, life seemed so fickle and arbitrary in Pyxis. Hatred was resting on such a weak foundation he wondered how it could sustain itself for so many years. Then he understood and he was to blame too. It was a lot easier to hate someone who hated him than to ask questions and challenge what has always been.

"Since you're here," Lyra said, "you must know what occurred in this room four years ago."

"Yes, I do." His eyes darted back to his work to make it seem like he wasn't staring. "What I don't know is how she got out alive."

"Her half brother intervened, just in time."

And I put a sword through his chest . . .

"If you don't mind me asking, Lyra, is this where her brother brought her last night?"

"Yes, I believe so."

"How do you think she escaped?"

"The window." She pointed to it with her eyes. "There's a loose bar, or so I've heard. Is there anything else I can do for you, Chris?"

"No, no thanks. I'm all set. It was nice meeting you, Lyra," he said, and he realized he wasn't the only one grieving in the room, so he added, "And I'm sorry for your loss."

She nodded and her eyes filled with tears. As her handkerchief went to collect them, her candle crashed to the ground. Then, as if she had been stabbed in the stomach, she cried out in pain and fell against the doorframe with her arms cradling her center.

"Are you all right?" he asked as he approached her.

Her eyes filled again, this time with fear. And then, before he could offer his hand to help her up, she was in flight and out the door.

"I'm not gonna . . . ," he called after her. He peeked his head into the dark, twisted maze of a stairwell. It was empty. *Hurt you . . .*

Alone again, Chris was confused for a moment, but his thoughts quickly darted to the window Lyra had mentioned. He went over to it and tried twisting the bars. The one at the edge gave way and pulled free.

He stuck his head out the window, and though he tried to get a shoulder out too, he couldn't. His amazement didn't stop there either. The jagged ledge below was narrower than a hand's width, and the ground was so far down he couldn't see it. How Cassie had managed to avoid plummeting to her death was a mystery. This adventure clearly had a heroine, not a hero. And he couldn't have felt worse for what he had said to her. *I thought you weren't like her. I was wrong.*

His hand rested on the key in his pocket. He pulled it out and wanted to crush it into dust, and when he couldn't, he chucked it out the window and heard a distant splash. He may never be able to make things right with her, but at least that key was where it should be, in the West River, and gone forever.

After that, Chris collapsed against the wall and buried his head in his arms. He wasn't sure if there was a god, but he prayed hard regardless. There were many things he could have asked for—forgiveness, peace of mind, strength, endurance—but he kept it simple. He prayed for her life. And his heavy eyes remained shut. His body and mind shut down before he had a chance to persuade them otherwise.

***

A few hours later, Chris woke up, sore and disoriented with glass pressed into his cheek. He quickly realized the nightmare didn't end when his eyes opened. For some reason, though, he woke up with a clearer head and a cleaner conscience than before. He had made mistakes and behaved regrettably in so many ways, but evil pulled his strings at every crossroad.

Chris sat up, dusted off the shards, and attempted to rub some life into his face. Then he finished cleaning Cassie's room. While doing so, he had a renewed sense of purpose. He knew what he had to do and would do it before anyone had the chance to talk him out of it. After flinging the pillowcase full of broken glass into West River, he left the room, shutting the unlocked door behind him.

With candle in hand, he climbed down stairwell after stairwell until he returned to the spot where he had last seen his father—the balcony overlooking the Hall of Crystal. He was one turn and a hallway away.

He entered Cassie's room, bracing himself for bad news, expecting to see blood everywhere, dirty medical instruments littered about, or an empty bed. But that was not the case. White was the color that captured his eye. Her sheets were new, her bandages looked fresh, and she was no longer wearing the nightmarish gray dress that embodied all of her pain and suffering. In the white nightgown, she glowed with purity, like a sleeping angel. Most important, she was alive.

Then Chris's eyes shifted to his kid brother, asleep in a chair beside her bed with one hand wrapped around hers, his hair hopelessly disoriented, his breathing rhythmic. Chris was reminded of better times—those carefree childhood days when he and Joe had fought over things like a new toy or their mother's attention.

They'd definitely had their differences, both before and after Andromeda had reunited them. And they'd exchanged some hurtful words, but they'd also shared a lot of laughs and they were there for each other when it counted most. Deep down, they loved each other. And Chris hoped it would always be that way.

Chris wanted him to remain at peace, so he walked with a light step to the other side of Cassie's bed and took a seat in the other chair. A few minutes later, Joe's elbow slipped off the bed. He woke up with a jolt, stretched, rubbed his eyes and smiled. "Hey, you're back!" he said while yawning.

"You always were the observant one, weren't you?" Chris replied drily.

Joe chuckled with one eye squinted. "And you seem light years better."

"I am. You?"

"Hanging in. Things got more interesting once you left, but she's hanging in there too."

"Good to hear. And good job last night. Sorry I was in no place to appreciate it."

"Uh, thanks," Joe said, both eyes now squinted in suspicious amusement. He had to be wondering what the catch was, but he never asked. His growling stomach seemed to take priority. "Hey, it feels like eons have passed since I've had a decent meal. If I find something edible in this place, do you want me to bring you back something?"

"No, I'm cool."

Joe shrugged and rose from his chair. "Okay then."

"Good-bye, Joe."

"Good-bye? I'll be back in ten minutes."

Joe disappeared into the hall without looking back. He didn't pick up on Chris's sincerity, and Chris believed that might be for the best.

When Chris touched Cassie's cold, limp hand, his better mood vanished. He tried to rub some warmth into her fingers, and then he attempted to do the same with her pale cheeks. They turned slightly pink, but cooled back to white once he stopped. Then, with a deep shaky sigh, he interlaced her fingers between his. "See? You did make it through the night. That means, surprisingly enough, I wasn't being completely irrational last night. You *are* a fighter. Don't let anybody ever tell you otherwise."

Attempting to keep things light for her sake wasn't easy. He wanted more than anything to hear her laugh again. He spent a few moments staring at her restful face, trying to will her back to consciousness. When nothing changed, he sighed and his body drooped.

"I'm not sure you can even hear me. Can you?"

Silence.

"That's okay. I would be giving me the silent treatment right now if I were you. I definitely deserve it. I'll pretend you're awake anyway, because there's a lot I need to get off my chest before I go. If you don't hear my words, maybe you'll *feel* them like you always could. It's worth a try, right?

"First, I want to thank you. Thanks for taking a chance on two clueless brothers. We owe you our lives, me the most. The final score is four to three, in your favor. Just thought you should know. And I wish I'd gotten a chance to tell you how much the past couple of weeks have meant to me. The truth is, I've learned so much from you. You've lived through a nightmare, yet you show no sign of hate or bitterness. How is that possible? No one ever gave you love, yet for some reason your heart bubbles over with it. I still don't know why you chose to share some of that love with me, but thanks for seeing something in me that was worthy of your affection.

"No, no, don't get up. I'm not finished yet. There's more. I am well aware that I owe you the biggest apology in the history of apologies. Well, here it goes . . ."

Chris kissed her cold fingertips. "I am so sorry for how I treated you. I will never forgive myself if you die in my place. That blade was meant for me, not you. Like me, you are reckless and impulsive, but, unlike me, you are also completely selfless. And you once called *me* brave. Ha! You were wrong. Because you're the brave one, the bravest soul I've ever met, and I hope someday you can find it in your heart to forgive me. And know that I'm out there somewhere doing whatever it takes to make your mother pay for this. And that . . . that . . ." He took in a sigh, pressurized it to the point that it was dangerously explosive. "There aren't words suitable for your ears that could describe the fairy who hurt you or what I would like to do to him. I intend to take care of him. That, I promise.

"Well, Cass, I have to go." The resolve in his voice abandoned him as his whole head seemed to fill with tears. "But I know I'm leaving you in good hands. Wake up soon and get well . . . please," he muttered with a sniffle. "Someone needs to make sure Joe behaves himself. I will never forget you, and I hope you find all the happiness you deserve."

Even as she teetered on the edge of death, her beauty drew him in once again. His lips first touched her pale forehead and then moved along to share with her a good-bye kiss.

Chris released her lips and waited above her. He watched, listened breathlessly for some change in her, and when nothing happened, he stepped away. His head dropped in acceptance and defeat. She didn't love him, couldn't forgive him, or perhaps she was just too far gone. Whatever the reason, in his kiss there was no magic.

***

Cassie lay there in a deep, dark sleep, barely breathing. Her body remained still, yet her mind's eye saw Chris running away. No one tried to stop him. No one even noticed.

He pushed open the palace doors, hurried past the front gate, and charged away from Pyxis without looking back.

It was a bad end to a bad dream, and then her eyes were open. "Chris, are you there?" she moaned, and as she struggled to lift her head for a better look, the pain held her down, and she had never felt more alone. That's how she knew, even though no one was around to tell her, that Chris was gone.

***

When Chris emerged from the caves of Pyxis, he faced the frigid winter wind, yet for some reason, he did not feel cold. And even though it was early morning in the far north, he closed his eyes and felt the sun.

He took a moment to think of his loved ones—those lost and those that remained. They were the reason he still had the will to live on. They were worth fighting for. Worth dying for.

Most of all, he thought of what it would be like if Cassie were standing in his arms, alive and well, the sun lighting up their faces, warming their hearts, bonding their souls. A nagging thought lingered that she would never be able to forgive him even if he begged, groveled on his knees, admitted he was as dense as lead. But then he heard her song in his head and felt that wherever her consciousness resided, she wished him well, sent her love, and blessed him with the courage and strength he would need for his journey.

> *Good-bye until the day*
> *when flesh is warm no longer.*
> *Meet me on the other side,*
> *where love will make us stronger.*

ACKNOWLEDGEMENTS

There are many people I would like to thank. I'll begin with my husband, Greg. In the early days, you raised an eyebrow or two, but you humored me during some tough times. You didn't complain (too much) when I crawled out of bed at obscene hours to engage in fairy frivolity. Then you read *Fairy Tale* and enjoyed it, and that meant a lot to me. You fielded my "man" questions "like a pro," and talked me through the pain of rejection. Andy, Jacob, and Emily Rose (a.k.a. the Bee, the Bear, and the Peach)–thanks for your patience. You occasionally let me get away with the "Mommy is writing" excuse, and for that I am grateful and so are the fairies. Next, I'd like to thank Janet Renard for the copyediting.

Eileen—You've read every project I've dumped upon you. You were thorough and meticulous, and won, hands down, for loyalty and punctuality. So thanks. Carissa—you were tough on my grammar and style. You opened my eyes to a few bad habits that I may not have noticed otherwise. And thank you for admitting to the tears. It was a compliment that had no equal. To Brooke, the same holds true for the tears and thanks for helping me find the confidence for the last and most challenging leg of this journey. And to my father, I would like to say thanks for reading Tolkien to me when I was a kid. Plus, your enthusiasm for astronomy played a key role in story development. And even though I was hesitant to let you read my rough draft, I was glad I did. You ended up being one of my staunchest supporters. To Jeanne and Katie—I had to understand the true definition of "mother" and "maternal" before I could embark on a successful good–versus–evil journey. Special thanks also to Mike and Leo for reading my synopsis (and hopefully, now, my book) and actively participating in *Fairy Tale* Sunday dinner conversations/debates.

I'd also like to thank my Wattpad colleagues, those who took the time to read and comment on *Disgrace*, the series prequel: @Moonvibe, @RDBrooks, @Teresa_Soto, @Wuckster, @KenMagee, @kristebelle, @rsrdiall, @maryltabor, and @JayVictor. Lastly, I'd like to thank the friends, family, noteworthy acquaintances and educators who have made a lasting impression me. Perhaps you may recognize your influence somewhere on these pages. My stories and characters would not be as rich or as colorful without you.

ABOUT THE AUTHOR

Alicia is originally from Albany, New York, and attended The College of Saint Rose in her hometown. She earned a Bachelor of Arts in biology in 2003 and received her Master of Science in developmental biology at Tufts University. Her "Fairy Tale" series came alive in the dark microscopy "caves" of Skidmore College in 2009, and she has been writing ever since. Today, she is an author and poet (www.wattpad.com/user/Fairytale_Fabler) and an active blogger (www.nesmalltownparenting.blogspot.com). Alicia lives in Upstate New York with her husband, three children, and her German Shepherd.

Also by ALICIA J. BRITTON

Disgrace (a *Fairy Tale* prequel), www.wattpad.com/story/11656358-disgrace

Emily Rose: A Pregnancy Story (non-fiction), www.wattpad.com/story/9084309-emily-rose-a-pregnancy-story

Right of Passage (poetry), www.wattpad.com/story/13472933-right-of-passage

Fairy Tale: The Rising Star, Book II, coming soon.

For up-to-date information about the *Fairy Tale* series, please follow **Alicia Britton—Author** on Facebook:

www.facebook.com/pages/Alicia-Britton-Author/351622061645290

Made in the USA
Lexington, KY
24 June 2014